A
FINE
TAPESTRY
OF MURDER

ANN MARTI
FRIEDMAN

Headline's policy is to use papers that are natural, renewable and recyclable products and made from wood grown in well-managed forests and other controlled sources. The logging and manufacturing processes are expected to conform to the environmental regulations of the country of origin.

HEADLINE PUBLISHING GROUP
An Hachette UK Company
Carmelite House
50 Victoria Embankment
London EC4Y 0DZ

www.headline.co.uk
www.hachette.co.uk

ACCENT

First published in 2020 by Headline Accent
An imprint of HEADLINE PUBLISHING GROUP

1

Cataloguing in Publication Data is available from the British Library

ISBN 978 1 7861 5752 2

Typeset in 10.5/13pt Bembo Std by Jouve (UK), Milton Keynes

Printed and bound in Great Britain by Clays Ltd, Elcograf S.p.A.

MIX
Paper from
responsible sources
FSC

Headline's ... ...clable
products a ... ...ther
controlled ... ...ected
to confo... ...in.

American museum educator, grant writer and lecturer, Ann Marti Friedman has published numerous articles on art and artists in various academic journals. Her first novel, *An Artist in her Own Right* was a semi-finalist on the 2008 Amazon.com Breakthrough Novel Contest. She lives in Kansas, in the USA.

Also by Ann Marti Friedman and available from Headline Accent

An Artist in her Own Right

Chapter One

Paris, France: The Gobelins at Dawn, November 1676

The day the body was found floating in the Bièvre, the malodorous stream that flowed by the Gobelins, started out much like any other. It was just before dawn on a cold Friday in November. Already most of the tapestry weavers at the Gobelins Manufactory, a sprawling collection of buildings on the southern outskirts of Paris, were up and about. They took advantage of all the daylight hours they could to earn as much as possible, and their schedule set the standard for the other craftsmen of the Manufactory. Lights shone faintly through the windows of the living quarters as lanterns and fires were lit. A few people came out to the central well for water, carefully picking their way across the frosty cobbles. When the gates opened to admit two coffee sellers into the courtyard, more men began to emerge from the buildings to purchase their morning drink. Coffee was a new habit, quickly gaining popularity: those who had imbibed too much the night before found it helped to clear their heads. Even those who had not, found the energy boost well worth the two sous. Most drank out of the coffee-seller's bowl, but the more fastidious brought their own.

A few bolder men slipped out to the public street where the brandy sellers waited. They tried to do so unobtrusively, as Monsieur Le Brun, the director, disapproved of this habit. Anyone who showed up for work drunk was given a warning. Still, they

1

grumbled to each other, it was so bloody cold that a body needed something stronger than coffee to warm up. The Bièvre, which usually stank with the waste of the tanners, smelters and slaughterhouses upriver, was not so noxious as usual. They wondered if it had frozen over last night.

As the men gathered, one could hear conversations in several languages. Louis XIV's generous patronage attracted the best craftsmen of Europe to the Gobelins. It served as workshop and home to Flemish tapestry weavers, the French dyers who supplied the yarn, English silversmiths, Italian sculptors and craftsmen in marble, and French makers of marquetry furniture of all kinds. Collectively, these talented men produced the tapestries, monumental silver vessels, and elaborately decorated tables and cabinets for the King to use in his palaces or to give away to show off the wealth of France.

Niccolò Bruno, a sculptor in wood, had come to Paris from Rome six months before. Twenty-three years old, tall and robust, with richly curling brown hair, he had an easy smile. He chatted with the Romans and Florentines who worked in *pietra dura*, marble slabs inlaid with colored stones in enchanting scenes and patterns. When, he asked them, did they anticipate finishing the pair of tabletops for which he would be carving the elaborate supports? He gave a huge yawn, to the amusement of the others who teased him about being a newlywed not wanting to leave his soft bed and generously curved Anne-Marie. He blushed and concentrated on drinking his coffee.

When the courtyard clock struck seven, the coffee vendors departed and the brandy drinkers slipped back inside. The apprentices in the silver workshops were already at work, their furnace chimneys sending plumes of black smoke into the lightening sky.

Niccolò called farewells to his friends and flexed and blew on his fingers to warm them. He huddled into his coat, hands in his pockets, and walked rapidly to the sculpture studio in the adjoining courtyard. Once inside, he gave a cheerful greeting to the pair of roughed-out sculptures on the platform and lovingly examined

2

his tools for any needed sharpening or repairs. Carefully, he laid and lit a fire in the stove in the corner of the studio. A large fire was a hazard, but he worked without gloves and a small blaze would enable him to warm his hands from time to time.

His preparations completed, he turned a critical eye on the sculptures of Hercules and an Amazon, one of the warrior women of mythology. Three feet tall, they would serve as supports for a cabinet being made at one of the furniture workshops. The cabinet, with its marquetry picture of the Gallic rooster striding triumphant over the Dutch lion, celebrated France's early success in its current war with the Netherlands. The two sculptures underlined this message of strength and victory, shouldering the weight of the cabinet as they strode forward with confidence. There was some optimism in this because the war, undertaken so cheerfully with initial success four years before, had been at a stalemate now for three. More than one Dutch or Flemish artisan at the Gobelins had lamented to Niccolò the difficulties of getting news of their families or sending money for their support.

Niccolò was proud of the figures. Lovingly he picked up his tools and set to work, breathing deeply the freshly cut wood. Gradually the curly mane of Hercules' lion skin cloak began to emerge under the chisel, then the lion's fearsome eyes and mouth. Under it, the hero's noble brow took shape, his own bushy eyebrows echoing the lion's locks. His fierce eyes directed a look of raw power that seemed destined for greater things than holding the upper half of a cabinet. Niccolò had just begun to work on the nose when a knock on the door startled him and broke his concentration. His chisel slipped and left a gouge in the cheek. It could be repaired and wouldn't be noticeable at all once the figure was covered with gesso and painted, but it annoyed him to do less than perfect work. He put down the chisel and strode to the door.

'What?' he demanded of the boy, one of the weavers' apprentices, who stood outside. The apprentice jumped and gave a nervous glance at the mallet still in Niccolò's left hand. He opened and closed his mouth but no sound came out.

Despite himself, Niccolò laughed. '*Scusi – pardonnez-moi, mon brave.*' He put down the mallet and smiled at the boy. 'What were you in such a hurry to tell me?'

The boy found his voice. 'There's a man's body in the Bièvre,' he said, striving to give the news the solemnity he felt appropriate but not quite able to damp down his excitement and importance at being the first with the news. 'They want to know if any of us recognize who it is.'

Chapter Two

When Niccolò arrived at the Bièvre, a crowd had already formed on its narrow banks, trampling the muddy brown grass. Workers from the barn on the other bank, glad of an excuse to pause in mucking out, shifted from foot to foot and blew on their hands in between snatches of conversation. They would be happy enough to return to work, he thought. Already he regretted leaving his studio. The Gobelins adults were solemn, but the children, who had raced out of their classroom as soon as they heard the news, ran excitedly up and down. Père Ferré, the priest who taught them their letters, tried in vain to gather them together.

Niccolò caught sight of his wife's brown cloak and yellow knitted coif and went to stand by Anne-Marie, drawing her close to him. She smiled as she raised her face for a kiss. A few blond curls had escaped the coif, tempting his fingers. He loved the feeling of them when she let her hair down at night. Her shivering gradually ceased. Her expression, which had relaxed when she smiled up at her husband, grew serious when she looked again at the men pulling the corpse to shore. A sudden gust of wind added the pungent odor of the barn's manure pile to the stink of the Bièvre, but at least that was a smell redolent of life.

Old Jean was a familiar figure to the onlookers. A veteran of the Thirty Years' War, he looked after the barn at night and watched the Bièvre during the day to retrieve whatever he might use or sell. One suspected his odd assortment of mismatched clothing had come from that source. He wore patched pantaloons too big for him, a far from white shirt, and a coat missing all but one of its buttons, fastened with a piece of rope with frayed ends. There were prominent stains around the pockets, where he had put all his smaller finds. He often said that years in the army, on the march and in the melee of battle, had taught him to keep his possessions on him at all times. His hardships had not soured his disposition, however; a genial soul, he knew many of the Gobelins residents by name. They in turn, conscious of the fine wools and silver stored on the premises, appreciated the added measure of security his presence provided, and they often brought him gifts of food. His weather-beaten face was animated and his long white hair flew in wisps about his head as he described his find to an attentive audience.

'I thought it was a coat, see? That's worth something, when it's washed and dried and I can wear it or sell it. So I pulled it over with my pole.' He brandished a long-handled implement with a metal hook on one end as if he were Moses parting the Red Sea. A few at the front of the crowd eyed it nervously and stepped back out of its reach. 'But when I towed it to the bank I realized there was a man still in it. It's fair game, what you take from the river, but I'm not so desperate as to rob the dead!' There was a note of pride in his voice as he stated his code of honor. 'When I hauled him out, his hair was dyed all green and I thought, maybe it's one of the yarn dyers at the tapestry works. So I asked you to come look.'

The master dyer came forward. A solidly built man with an air of authority, he wore the ordinary brown coat of most workmen and a scarf of deep red – his signature color – around his neck. He helped Old Jean to turn the body over but backed away from it with a cry of distress echoed by the crowd. Lying face down for so long, the dead man's features were swollen and distorted from the water and from his blood settling into them, coloring them a dark red. The blue-grey eyes were open and staring. The arms, stiff in the rigor of death, were raised in front of his chest as if to ward off whatever had confronted and killed him.

The master dyer visibly steeled himself to look again more closely. 'He's not one of ours,' he finally announced. The crowd exhaled a collective sigh of relief, but he continued, 'It's hard to tell who he might be in this condition.'

Niccolò felt Anne-Marie shiver as she caught her breath in a sob. 'What's wrong?' he asked. 'Do you know him?'

'No. I was thinking of the night you were attacked and left for dead in the street. Oh, Niccolò, it could so easily have been you!'

He shuddered, feeling again the ruffians' boots and fists. A good thing it had happened at some distance from the Seine. He looked at the unknown dead man now with a sense of fellow feeling: no longer merely a random body in the river, but a glimpse of what he could have become. It gave him an eerie sense of two alternative selves, one living and one dead. Noticing that Charles Le Brun, the director of the Gobelins, had joined the group, Niccolò appealed to him. 'We can't just leave him here. Couldn't we bring him inside?'

Le Brun threw him a sharp, inquiring glance but gave calm orders. 'Yes. Dr Lunague can examine him.' Looking around, 'Is he here?'

'He is attending Mother Abbess,' said one of the weavers, gesturing toward the lands and buildings of the Convent of the Cordelière Nuns on the other side of the Bièvre.

Le Brun nodded. Though employed by the Gobelins to see to the injuries of the workmen, Dr Lunague served as a physician to the residents of the neighborhood when called upon and waived his fee for the poorest patients. 'I will have Père Ferré say mass for the man, God rest his soul.'

'God rest his soul,' murmured the crowd, making the sign of the Cross.

Two porters brought a stretcher and Niccolò stepped forward to help them place the man on it. The subdued but relieved crowd made way and followed them into the Gobelins courtyard. Madame Martine, the doctor's formidable grey-haired housekeeper, grumbled at the intrusion of muddy feet onto the immaculate floor of the examining room. She had the men with the stretcher wait while she took a clean sheet from the linen press and put it on the examining table. They placed the dead man on it. 'It can serve now for examining him and burying him later,' she told them.

'You'll need to clean him up,' someone was bold enough to tell her.

'Not me,' snapped Madame Martine. 'I take care of the doctor. Dealing with corpses has never been part of my duties. Someone else will need to do it.'

At that, the crowd shook off its solemnity and remembered other things to do – the men their studios, the children their lessons, the women their housework. 'Don't know him, not my husband, don't need to,' they muttered to each other.

'I'll do it,' Anne-Marie volunteered, not at all sure she wanted to but not liking to identify with these squeamish women who backed away from the dead man with a flick of skirts.

Niccolò looked at her with concern. 'Will you be all right?'

She gestured with a sweep of her hand at the now empty courtyard. 'No one else is volunteering.'

His voice was gentle. 'You don't need to. That's not me there. Don't take it so to heart.'

She shook her head. 'It's not just him. I can't help thinking, what if he had someone waiting for him to come home last night – as I did that night – wondering this morning what has happened to him? *She* would want him treated with respect.' Her eyes held his, and he nodded.

'You'll need clean water. I'll draw it for you.' He picked up the doctor's water bucket and went out to the well.

Anne-Marie went to their rooms in the attic of one of the Gobelins buildings to exchange her cloak for a warm knitted jacket. She clicked her tongue at the sight of the breakfast dishes not yet washed, the bed unmade, but these things could wait. Taking up a clean apron, basin and rags, she returned to the doctor's examining room.

Madame Martine, hearing the door open and close, brought down water Niccolò had drawn which she had warmed in the fireplace of the upstairs room. 'He won't know the difference, but your hands will,' she said with gruff kindness. Lest Anne-Marie think she was going soft, however, she refused to light a fire in the corner stove, although it was almost as cold indoors as out. 'It's a blessing in disguise, being this cold. I don't want to think what he'll smell like when he thaws out.' She wrinkled her nose in disgust. 'No point in cleaning the floor now — there'll be people tramping in and out all day with *him* here.' She grimaced at the corpse as if she held him responsible. 'There's a fire upstairs,' she told Anne-Marie, 'when you need more water, or to warm up for a bit.'

It was eerily quiet in the examining room. Anne-Marie gently wiped the green dye and river filth from the man's cold face. His flesh felt so different from Niccolò's warm face in her hands, with its animated play of muscles and the blood pulsing beneath her fingers. Her fingers and toes grew numb as she worked, but she remained at her chosen post, singing softly the lullabies she sang to her infant nephew. Methodically, she wrung out her rags again and again. The water in the basin turned a greenish grey. She emptied it outside, surprised to see life continuing as usual and went upstairs for more warm water. Immersed in her task, she did not notice the doctor's return until he stood beside her. Startled, she splashed water on his coat.

'I'm sorry.' A flush of embarrassment rose to her cheeks. 'This is—' She started to explain, but he interrupted her.

'I stopped to see Le Brun on my way in, and he told me about our mystery visitor. I told him I would examine him' — he tipped his head at the corpse — 'myself.'

'Don't clean his hands yet,' he added. 'I'll want to examine them for wounds.' She nodded.

He surprised her again by asking, 'Can you read and write?'

'Yes, I can. I kept the accounts for my father's bakery.'

'Good. It helps to remember details when someone takes notes and I have no assistant at the moment. Would you be willing to assist me this morning? Or would seeing more of the body upset you?'

More of the body? She had never seen a naked man other than her husband. She squared her shoulders and assented. 'I would be happy to help you, doctor.'

He thought for a moment. 'We should have a drawing of his face. He will be more recognizable with the plain lines of it in black and white, than with the swelling and the blood settling. And I have not yet had my breakfast. Could you please fetch one of the painters while I get something to eat?'

She nodded, this time happily. She and Niccolò had lived at the Gobelins for only a few months and she was always glad of an excuse to visit the artists' studios. 'Is there anyone in particular I should ask for?'

'Saint-André would be best. He specializes in faces. But if he is not available, bring whoever you can.'

In the tapestry painters' studio, several men collaborated on the large cartoons that served as patterns for the weavers. Today it was a landscape with one of the King's châteaux in the background. Anne-Marie wished she could linger to look at the details of the cartoon and take away the memory of bright colors to warm her on this cold day. One painter was imparting a lively expression to the face of a royal page in the foreground. Intent upon his task, he confirmed that he was Monsieur Saint-André without looking up. A few more deft strokes; then he put down his brush and turned to look at her.

Reluctantly, she explained her errand. The painter exchanged his smock for a coat, grabbed his pencil – a cylinder of graphite in a reed holder – and sketch portfolio, and accompanied her to the doctor's consulting room.

When they returned, they found Old Jean chatting with Dr Lunague with the easy familiarity of a comrade-in-arms. Anne-Marie had heard that the doctor, too, had taken part in the Thirty Years' War. Seeing the two men side-by-side, however, it was difficult to believe they were a similar age. Life had been kinder to Lunague, with a secure post, the care of Madame Martine, and enough to eat. Unlike Old Jean, he had retained most of his teeth. A few crumbs of his breakfast were caught in his mustache. Anne-Marie had to restrain her impulse to brush them from his face, as she would have done for Niccolò.

While the doctor put on a clean apron and got out his tools for the examination, Saint-André began to sketch. The hair, now drying, revealed itself as blond. The face that emerged on paper, devoid of the green tint the water had given it, was noticeably more human but not tranquil, with a mournful downturn of the mouth.

'How long has he been dead?' asked Saint-André.

'Several hours at least – the rigor is beginning to pass,' the doctor explained, demonstrating how the man's arms could be re-positioned with only a little effort.

'His clothes have been soaking for at least that long,' agreed Old Jean.

The painter looked as if he wished he hadn't asked. He made to hand Anne-Marie the finished sketch, but Dr Lunague asked him to make two copies of it. Saint-André nodded and departed briskly, happy to leave.

The doctor placed several sheets of paper and a writing set with quills, ink and sanding pot on his desk for Anne-Marie, and a piece of velvet to hold the paper in place as she wrote. He pulled back the chair and gestured for her to sit. She wrote 'The Body in the Bièvre' and the date at the top of the page. Anne-Marie had never attended a medical examination, even for her own living body, much less a dead one. She found her fascination overcoming her initial repulsion, sometimes forgetting to write things down until the doctor reminded her. He carried on a dialogue with the dead man as he did the exam, asking him questions while looking for the answers. 'Who are you? What happened that put you in the river? Let's see if we can find out, shall we?'

'Do you expect him to answer you?' she asked.

'Not with his voice, but he will tell me in other ways.' He turned his attention back to the dead man. 'Male, in your thirties, average height, well-fed' – he squeezed the muscles of the man's arm – 'not a laborer by the feel of you. No finger or ligature marks around your throat, no smell of poison in your mouth, though after the river it's hard to tell.' He picked up the hands. 'Wrists intact, no wounds, palms and fingers callused – so you worked with your hands, at least. What's this? A button?'

Lunague carefully unwound the threads and minute fragment of blue cloth that had caught in the man's fingers and beckoned Anne-Marie and Old Jean to look. The metal button, about an inch across, had a raised design on the front, a linked D and L. Anne-Marie made a rubbing of it with a stub of graphite Saint-André had left behind.

'It appears to be from a servant's livery,' she said, but none of them recognized the insignia. She turned it over and frowned. The loop was inexpertly soldered to the disc and the texture of the back was not finished as smoothly as one would expect a fine button to be.

The doctor put it to one side and returned to his examination of the body.

'Looks like someone caught you by surprise.' He asked Old Jean to help him remove the man's coat. There was blood on his shirt.

'Look – he was stabbed, and not with a knife.' Old Jean pointed to the wound.

Once again, he called Anne-Marie over to look, so that she could describe it accurately. She approached the table with trepidation, fearing a great gash, but saw instead a mere hole, perhaps a quarter-inch across.

'What sort of weapon would make a wound like that?'

'A stiletto, perhaps?' suggested the doctor. 'It's shaped like a miniature sword, with a very fine, sharp point.'

'It is hard to believe a man's life could bleed out through that,' she said.

'It could if the weapon was long enough,' the doctor told her. 'Penetrating between the ribs, it could nick a vital organ and kill him outright or incapacitate him and let the river do the rest. We could open him up to find out, I suppose' – he cast a glance at Anne-Marie, who looked unhappy but dared not protest – 'but let us see what else we can learn from him before we resort to that.' Slowly she let out her breath in relief. He gave her an understanding smile.

Old Jean helped him turn the body over. A nasty wound on the back of the head had broken the skin but not, said Lunague, probing it with his fingers, the skull underneath.

He then turned his attention to the man's clothing. The leather shoes did not yield any clues. The wool coat and trousers, of good quality, were worn and repaired in several places. The coat pockets contained only a few sous, a sodden handkerchief and a small half-finished carving of a child's toy. The darning on the linen shirt had been done with an expert needle.

'It seems he had a wife,' Anne-Marie suggested.

'Or a housekeeper. Mine keeps me in good repair.'

Anne-Marie pointed out the series of small hearts in running stitch worked into one of the darns. 'And does she add these to your linens when she mends them?'

He gave a startled bark of laughter. 'I hope not. I've never looked, but I wouldn't think so.' He gave Anne-Marie an admiring glance. 'You have a good eye.' He pointed to the stitched hearts. 'I did not notice that.'

She flushed with pleasure at his praise.

Old Jean had picked up the man's coat and was examining it, out of habit, to see whether something might be tucked away – in a hidden inner pocket, perhaps. Prudent men did not carry valuables where pickpockets could easily find them. His attention drawn to a clumsily stitched place on the hem, his fingers discerned a coin beneath it. He looked for other areas similarly stitched and found them on the cuffs, hem and lapels, six in all. The doctor snipped the thread with his scissors to reveal a *louis d'or* in each one.

'Gold?' exclaimed Anne-Marie. The others were as surprised as she. The doctor placed the coins on the tray, where they contrasted strangely with the humble contents of the pockets.

'It looks like he did his own sewing in those places,' Anne-Marie said, turning her attention back to the coat. 'Why didn't he ask his wife? She is a much better seamstress.'

'Perhaps he didn't want her to know,' the doctor replied. 'Or maybe she's gone, and he was doing his best on his own.'

'But if she is alive,' Anne-Marie countered, 'she will want to know what happened to him – and she will need this money.'

Old Jean cleared his throat. 'Remember it was me that found him.' His eyes flicked from the gleaming coins to the doctor's face. He might not rob a dead man of his coat, but gold was much harder to resist.

The doctor thought briefly and agreed. 'Take this now.' Lunague handed him a *louis d'or*. 'I'll keep the rest in my strongbox in case there is a widow as Madame Bruno believes. If there isn't, you may have them.'

Old Jean grinned at them as he pocketed the coin and stepped back against the wall. Anne-Marie wondered how long it had been since he had had so much money at one time.

There was no puncture in the coat corresponding to the one in the shirt.

'Was he stabbed with his coat off, and someone put the coat on him again afterwards?'

'Not necessarily. Professional killers can get the stiletto in under the coat. If you'll excuse me,' he faced her and in a quick smooth motion tapped her jacket at the side of her rib and drew the hand back, 'that's all it would take.'

She shivered. 'Did he know his attacker, then, facing him like that? Or was he set upon by surprise?'

The doctor shook his head. 'We don't know that – yet.'

Anne-Marie's glance fell on the carving that had been in the man's pocket. 'Shall I ask Niccolò to come look at it?' she asked with shy pride.

The doctor, glad of a reason to smile after this sad examination, consented. 'Yes, bring your husband.'

It was good to be out in the fresh air, however cold. She tapped on the studio door with their special signal, the one they had used when he was a lodger in her father's house.

He was smiling as he opened the door. 'Here? Now?'

'Don't be ridiculous,' she scoffed, but offered her lips for a kiss. When she explained her errand, he gathered up his kit of tools. At the surgery, he examined the small toy, roughed out in the shape of a cat sleeping on her side, her paws tucked neatly under her. He exclaimed with pleasure at the quality of the workmanship of the finished parts.

'Was it a gift for a child? His child? Did he leave behind a family as well as a wife?' Anne-Marie did not realize she had spoken out loud. She was surprised when Niccolò answered, 'Not necessarily. He could have been making it for one of the booths at a Christmas market. I made toys to sell when I was an apprentice in Rome.'

He felt the man's hands and pointed to identical calluses on his own. 'He was a woodcarver by profession.' He looked over the contents of the pockets with a puzzled expression. 'Where did you put his knife?'

'There wasn't one,' Anne-Marie replied.

'Are you sure?'

'I wrote down all the contents myself.' She shuffled through her notes to find the list.

'I believe you,' he hastened to assure her. 'But a woodcarver does not carry unfinished work in his pockets without carrying also the tools he would need to finish it.' He took the appropriate knife from his kit to show them. 'If it is not here, where is it?'

'Perhaps he left it in his killer,' the doctor suggested. 'At least, we can hope he did.' His voice and face displayed a grim satisfaction at the thought.

'Could he have killed the other man with a blade as small as that?' Anne-Marie asked.

15

'Yes, if it cut him here,' the doctor responded pointing to a vein in his own neck.

Niccolò paled at the thought; his hand went instinctively to protect his neck. 'I should return to the studio,' he said as he prepared to take his leave.

As he stepped outside, they could see a man striding purposefully across the courtyard toward the doctor's office. Anne-Marie held the door open for him. 'Gabriel Ferrand, Commissaire of Police,' the visitor introduced himself. 'Monsieur Le Brun sent for me earlier this morning, but I was not able to get away until now.'

'Anne-Marie Bruno,' she replied, making the curtsy a man of his rank would expect. Ferrand was dressed entirely in brown – wig, suit, gloves, and boots – relieved only by the white of his shirt. He was young for such a responsibility, she thought, no more than thirty-five or so, but there was no mistaking the intelligence of the brown eyes that gave her a quick assessing look, as if wondering whether she might be some miscreant he sought.

He greeted the doctor and Old Jean with the familiarity of long acquaintance. Clearly, they had been of help to him on other occasions.

Ferrand crossed the room to look intently at the face of the dead man. 'I don't know him, and he does not fit the description of anyone we've been looking for. He came from the Bièvre, Le Brun said. Another drunk falling into the water, I take it?'

'No,' replied Lunague, and showed him the wounds.

The Commissaire grimaced with a sharp intake of breath. 'Murder.' His glance flicked to the man's face. 'Who did this to you?' His own expression had hardened.

'This was caught in his fingers.' Lunague handed him the button and thread. 'None of us recognize the crest. Do you?' Ferrand shook his head.

'With your permission, I will keep the button a little longer,' the doctor said. 'I'll ask the Gobelins residents to come here to see if any of them can identify him. One of them may recognize the crest as well. I will also have a report for you and a drawing of the face.'

Ferrand gave the first warm, open smile than Anne-Marie had seen him make. 'I wish everyone we dealt with was as cooperative. I appreciate your assistance.'

'And Madame Bruno's – she is my scribe this morning.'

Ferrand inclined his head to her as she held the door open for his departure. She did not curtsy this time.

Dr Lunague resumed his examination, but there was little more the body could tell them. To Anne-Marie's relief he did not open the corpse. She had seen viscera at the butcher's shop often enough, but it was one thing when it was a cow and another when it was a man being rent apart. She shivered.

One shiver set off another, and she realized how cold she was. She was relieved when Madame Martine came down to announce that she had soup and wine upstairs for them. Gratefully they mounted to the warm room, where Old Jean was already seated at the table, joking and flirting with Madame Martine and eliciting the first smile Anne-Marie had seen her give that day. They did not speak of the morning's events but applied themselves to the hot food in silence.

After they had eaten and Madame Martine had cleared the table, the doctor asked Anne-Marie to fetch the writing set and the notes she had taken so that they could go over them together. He corrected her wording from time to time and spelled for her the unfamiliar words she had written phonetically. He asked her to make two copies that he would sign and went downstairs again. It was pleasant working there, with the slow ticking of the mantle clock, the crackle of the logs, and the smooth feel of the piece of velvet under the paper. She took pains to copy slowly and carefully, in her best script, sanding each completed page to dry the ink, making the experience last as long as possible. When she had finished, she returned downstairs, fastening her jacket snugly.

She was surprised to see a line of Gobelins residents walking past the dead man, most of him now decently covered with a sheet, and examining his face briefly. The weavers and dyers, the painters and sculptors, the silversmiths and *pietra dura* craftsmen, the cabinetmakers, the porters and the servants, the wives and children had come singly or in groups, but they had all shaken their heads. One man apologized that his wife refused to come; she was pregnant and afraid that viewing a dead man would cause their child to be born dead.

His companion, a weaver with a thick Flemish accent, looked as if he too would have liked to stay away. He took one quick glance at the dead man and clamped a hand to his mouth, hurrying to the door. They could hear him being sick on the cobblestones. The other man apologized: 'He's had an upset stomach all day.' The weaver did not return.

Most paid scant attention to the button. But Claude de Villiers, head of the silver atelier, picked it up and rubbed it with a polishing cloth he carried out of habit. 'It is silver,' he confirmed. He turned the button over and lifted his eyebrows in surprise. 'But the hallmark which would identify the maker is so faint as to be unreadable.'

A draftsman, his eye caught by the gleaming disc, reached eagerly for it. 'It is the crest of the Duc de Languedoc. I designed a bookplate for him. The L stands for the Duc's family, Languedoc, and the D for Delalande, the Duchess's family.'

'Are you sure?' The doctor was surprised. 'The Duc is an advisor to King Louis XIV and a man of unblemished reputation. He is the last man I would have thought involved in a murder.'

But the draftsman was certain about the crest.

'Commissaire Ferrand will need to look into this,' Lunague told Anne-Marie.

During a lull in the visits, Anne-Marie handed her documents to the doctor, who read them and nodded his approval. She turned to go. 'Wait,' he said. 'I'll get your wages.'

'Oh!' She was surprised.

He counted twelve sous into her hand – a man's wage, twice

what her father had paid her for a long day's work behind the counter of the family bakery. 'It is what I pay my assistant, when I have one,' he said firmly. 'Take it.'

She smiled as she put the coins in her skirt pocket. 'What will happen to him next?' she asked, indicating the dead man.

'That is for Commissaire Ferrand to decide. He will probably be put in a common grave with the rest of the unknowns.'

'But he had money. Surely one of those gold coins could pay for a plain but decent burial.'

Dr Lunague smiled at Anne-Marie. 'So it could. I will speak with Ferrand about it.

'You see how it is with the dead,' he told her, as she turned to go. 'When you get to know them, they come back to life.'

Chapter Three

Anne-Marie climbed the stairs to the attic, as always slightly out of breath at the top. She knew she and Niccolò were lucky to have two small rooms, tucked away under the eaves as they were, with the inconvenience of carrying firewood and water up three flights. In the crowded center of Paris, whole families often had to make do with one room. The apartment was cold. She lit a fire and swung the kettle over it before hurrying into the other room to change her apron. The tiny bedroom, barely large enough for their bed and her hope chest, had a window but no fireplace. A row of pegs held her garments and Niccolò's good suit. A carpet was something only the wealthy could afford, but there was a woven rush mat to stave off the cold underfoot.

She put the doctor's coins away in the chest. She planned to make a new shirt for Niccolò for Christmas and was gratified to see that she now had enough to purchase the material to make one for her father as well. Turning around, she straightened the down bed cover that had been a wedding gift from her parents. Someday when she and Niccolò moved to larger quarters they would have a proper four-poster bed with feather mattresses and curtains she would embroider, one set for summer, one for winter. But for now, it was enough to know that this simple frame bed with its straw mattress was theirs to share.

The fire had taken the edge off the chill of the front room. She washed the breakfast dishes and put them away in the dresser that held their modest supplies of food and utensils. She smiled as she handled the silver forks that Nic's family had sent from Italy, where the new implements were all the rage. Niccolò had made their table and chairs, for which she was embroidering a cloth and matching cushions. He had made the elaborate frame for the mirror, a wedding gift from her sister Toinette and brother-in-law Pierre; it hung over the fireplace and reflected the candlelight in the evenings. The rose he had carved for her during their court-ship held pride of place on the mantelpiece. She felt better when she surveyed the room and saw that everything was again in its proper place. At least in here there could be order and peace, even if the world outside might deliver unpredictable violence and death.

Violent death. Much as she tried to leave the dead man behind at the doctor's, she could not help thinking about him. She shivered and held her hands out to the fire. 'God rest his soul,' she murmured. She wondered again if the woman who stitched the hearts into his shirt was waiting for him, making dinner and hoping he would soon be home to share it . . .

Dinner! Anne-Marie came out of her reverie and shook her head. Nic would be home soon. Usually on Fridays she visited her parents in the Latin Quarter, bringing back bread from their bakery and supplies from the nearby market on Place Maubert, but she would never make it there and back before dark. Her face brightened when she remembered that the *poissonière* making delivery to the Convent of the Cordelières on Friday afternoon brought extra fish to sell to the local housewives. She carefully banked the fire and headed out with her basket and housekeeping money.

As she went through the gateway to the riverbank, her eyes were drawn to the spot where the body had lain after Old Jean pulled it out of the water. The ground around it was trampled but no one had wanted to step on the spot itself – whether out of superstition or respect, she wasn't sure. She hesitated in the middle of the footbridge to look upstream. Where had he gone into the Bièvre? Strange that no one had thought to ask that this morning! The hours he had been in the flowing water suggested it had been at some distance rather than the immediate neighborhood.

She tried to remember what she had heard of the areas upstream. They depended on the same trades as the Gobelins area – the tanners, dyers, butchers, and washerwomen originally drawn to the stream for its clean water – no little irony, considering the filth they contributed to it. She wrinkled her nose. She was no stranger to the strong smells of Paris, but she had grown up in her father's bakery with the delicious fragrance of baking bread. They had their own well and her father was unusually scrupulous in his insistence on cleanliness.

The area upstream was perhaps best known among the Gobelins men for its cheap wine. Located outside Paris, it was not subject to the city's wine tax. Its taverns thrived, drawing large crowds that drank all they could afford, and more. Tavern brawls were legion. (Or so she had heard. Respectable women did not go there, but prostitutes plied a brisk trade.) No wonder the Commissaire had assumed the dead man was yet another drunk falling into the water.

A gust of cold wind jolted her back to the business at hand. Resolving to think no more about the morning's grisly discovery, she hurried across and into the convent grounds. The neat order of its walled gardens, with graveled footpaths between the beds and borders of pear trees, always pleased her. The apple orchard was dormant now in November, but in the spring, it would be fragrant and heavy with blossom and buzzing with bees from the convent hives, now inside the apiary next to the orchard.

The Cordelières might be a part of the order of 'poor' Clares, but they were in fact prosperous, producing most of the fruits and vegetables, milk and cheese eaten by the nuns, with the surplus sold or traded for other foods, or given to the poor. The sun, at last breaking through the cloud cover, gave the last hours of daylight a more cheerful aspect, but it was no warmer.

Fine ladies in fashion plates might pin back their cloaks to show off their silk skirts, but she drew hers close around her, making sure it was well-fastened. As she walked, she planned what to serve with the fish that she could make with supplies on hand, perhaps a lentil soup with onions and carrots, made fragrant with dried herbs. For dessert, she would bake apples in the coals, sweet and comforting. The dead man broke into her thoughts from time to time, but she resolutely returned to the mental picture of dinner with her husband.

'What would you like?' The normally foul-mouthed fishwife was subdued, perhaps out of respect for the nearby nuns.

'Three carp,' replied Anne-Marie, knowing Niccolò would want two.

'Shall I gut them for you?'

'Please.' Anne-Marie smiled and nodded. When the woman was done, she paid for the fish, wrapped them in a cloth and placed them in her basket.

The neighborhood cats gathered in a hopeful cluster around the wagon for the treats afforded by the gutting. She gave an admiring glance to one who made an agile leap to snatch a fish head. Then she noticed, a little way off, a thin young grey, clearly an outsider: every time it dared to dart forward to claim a share of the bounty one cat or another at the forefront would turn and hiss. On impulse, Anne-Marie picked up a piece of offal and tossed it to the grey cat, which caught and quickly swallowed it. Anne-Marie laughed aloud for the first time that day. It was worth handling the awful stuff, with its smell lingering on her fingers. But when she threw a second morsel, another cat snarled at the outsider with a swipe of claws that left a jagged red gash in its side.

'Stop that!' Anne-Marie screamed, to the astonishment of the cats and the crowd, and burst into tears.

One of the nuns approached her. 'Are you all right? What is troubling you?' Her lined face, framed by the white wimple and black veil, radiated compassion, and her voice was gentle.

It was some moments before Anne-Marie could regain her composure to reply, 'I'm sorry, I don't usually . . .' She wiped her eyes with the back of her hand. 'There was a dead man in the Bièvre this morning, next to where I live. It's had me more upset than I thought.' Faces cleared; the women had heard about that. 'Seeing that big cat turn on the little one . . .' More nods of understanding. But she could not stop crying now she had begun.

'Perhaps you would like to sit in the garden to compose yourself?' Anne-Marie nodded gratefully, and the nun led her to a gate in the wall. The little grey cat slipped through the gate after them. 'Oh, look! Your new friend has followed you.' Anne-Marie managed a weak smile in response.

The nun crouched to look more closely at the cat's injuries. The animal, sensing another friend, submitted to be examined.

'It is all right,' the sister announced, stifling a groan as she stood up again. 'It looks worse than it is. She will heal.'

Anne-Marie smiled her thanks.

It was pleasant in this part of the cloister garden, where a niche trapped the weak rays of sun. The cat sat peacefully at her feet, gazing at her steadily with clear green eyes. Bending down to stroke the animal, she could feel its spine and ribs through its gritty fur, but the vibration of its purr was strong. It licked her fingers where she had handled the fish, and the warm rough tongue was a comfort. Anne-Marie drew her cloak around her, making sure it was well-fastened.

Unbidden, the image of the silver button came to mind, with its entwined initials. Languedoc and Delalande – she ran the elegant, musical names over her tongue – so unlike the purely descriptive Boulanger (her maiden name) and Bruno, baker and brown. How did a Duc with so sterling a reputation come to be involved in this sordid business? The way the button threads were wound about the dead man's fingers – had the man himself done that, or had someone else, to call attention to the Duc?

The little grey cat looked up and meowed, breaking her thoughts. It would be dark soon; she must get home to start dinner. The cat nosed her basket and reached in a paw to get at the fish. She laughed as she picked up the basket to get it out of harm's way. 'Come home with me and you may share our dinner.' She beckoned the cat to follow her and strode happily through the gardens, looking forward to Nic and home.

Niccolò, working on the pair of figures for the cabinet, also found himself thinking of the unknown man with the hands of a wood-carver and a half-finished toy cat in his pocket. He wondered if he had come across the man when he was newly arrived and searching for work. He was sure the man had not been one of the *maîtres* he had visited, but perhaps he had worked in a studio? Niccolò tried to visualize the men in the ateliers, but they remained a blur of faces in his memory.

Perhaps he too had been a foreigner drawn to Paris by the prospect of working for Louis XIV and had been attacked in the street? But his body did not bear the evidence of ruffians' fists as Niccolò's had done, just the small neat wound made by a weapon the doctor and Ferrand attributed to a professional killer. What had the man done to meet with such a fate? Did it have something to do with the gold coins secreted in his coat?

Absorbed by his work and his thoughts, Niccolò was startled to realize the light had faded. It was time to put away his tools for the day and go home to Anne-Marie.

Niccolò liked to wash by the hearth when he returned from his studio, coming to the dinner table clean and scrubbed. It was something his mother insisted on after a day of sweaty work on the farm, and the habit had stayed with him despite the ridicule of his less fastidious co-workers. Anne-Marie always had a kettle of warm water ready for him. At first, he did not notice the cat watching from the shadows. Only when he had finished washing and gone into the other room to put on a clean shirt did the animal allow Anne-Marie and the smell of frying fish to coax it back to the hearth.

'When did we get a cat?' He held out his hand, fingers twitching. Warily, it allowed itself to be won over.

'*She* adopted *us*. She followed me home from the fishmonger's wagon at the convent. There was a group of cats that had come for the gutting and she was on the edge of the group trying to get some, and one of them turned on her . . .' A tear ran down her cheek. 'I could not help that poor man from the river, but I had to help someone, even if it's just a skinny grey . . .' She could not go on. He gathered her in his arms until her tears subsided.

'What shall we call her?' he asked.

'How do you say "cat" in Italian?'

'Gatto,' he replied, putting the emphasis on the first syllable.

'Gatto,' she repeated, and smiled. 'Well, as she is French, and I am a baker's daughter, we'll call her Gâteau.' She put the emphasis on the second syllable.

He laughed, and his stomach growled at the thought of cake. 'I'm starved – let us eat.'

He might have known after this upsetting day that the bad dream would return, but it always caught him by surprise, much as his attackers had. The attack had taken place the previous June, when he had been in Paris only a few weeks and had not found permanent employment, but he had picked up a few days' work making *boiseries*, elaborately carved wood paneling for fashionable houses. He was walking cheerfully down the street on a warm spring night, pleased to have coins in his pocket. The *maître* liked his work, and he was hopeful of being taken on at that studio. Three men, seeming to come out of nowhere, confronted him. When he turned to run, two more appeared behind him. High walls enclosed the private *hôtels* on each side of the street; no one was around to help. Startled, he addressed the men in Italian, then repeated himself as well as he could in French. He tried to reach for his knife and swung his rucksack as a weapon, but one of the men caught it while the others pinned his arms. Another rifled his pockets and took his money. He hoped that they would let him go after the robbery, but a short, sandy-haired fellow with a pitted face, evidently the ringleader, went through the rucksack, too, and found his tools.

'What have we here? A foreigner taking jobs and money from us?' He nodded at a squat, dark-haired youth. 'Antoine was an apprentice carpenter until some Flemish fellow showed up and the master decided he liked him better. We're all in the same boat.' His face brightened as an idea came to him. 'Here, Antoine' – tossing him the leather pouch of tools – 'show him you remember how to use them.' Niccolò struggled, shouting as loudly as he could, but no one came to his aid. The others made free with their fists. He watched Antoine come at him with a gouge, closer and closer until it seemed inevitable it would enter his eye.

He woke up screaming in terror. He put his hands to his face and was reassured to discover he still had two good eyes, but his body continued to shudder and protest.

He felt Anne-Marie press him to her soft warmth, heard her assuring him over and over, 'I'm here. You're safe. You're safe.' He took deep breaths, willing himself to relax, murmuring endearments into her hair until she fell back to sleep.

Somehow that day, step by painful step, he had managed to make his way back to his lodgings at the Boulangers', collapsing by the well in the courtyard. It was she who had found him there and washed his bloody face, so that he regained consciousness feeling cool, clean water and the gentle touch of her hands. It was she who called her father to help him upstairs to bed and refused her mother's suggestion that he be sent to hospital, where he would surely have died of infection. It was Anne-Marie whom he saw at his bedside whenever he opened his eyes, those first days of convalescence. And it was she who, when he was only just back on his feet, turned down a marriage proposal from her father's prosperous friend to throw in her lot with a penniless Italian woodcarver.

In gratitude for his recovery, he had borrowed tools from the studio he had worked in and carved an infant Christ as a thank-offering for Anne-Marie's parish church, Saint-Nicolas-du-Chardonnet. This brought him to the attention of Charles Le Brun, who, he discovered, was not only a parishioner there

27

but also in charge of its decoration. Le Brun had then commissioned a large panel of St Peter for one of the chapels. Doubly satisfied with Niccolò's work, he had employed him at the Gobelins. With a steady job, Niccolò could afford to keep a wife and had married Anne-Marie.

Smiling now, he fell back to sleep.

Chapter Four

The funeral of the unknown man, held at the Gobelins Oratory, was a subdued event, attended by only a few: the doctor, Old Jean, Niccolò and Anne-Marie, and the weaver who had become ill when viewing the body. He still looked unwell – the circles under his eyes emphasized the pasty hue of the rest of his face, and he would not look the others in the eye – but he seemed compelled to come despite himself. The dead man was laid to rest in a nearby cemetery. Niccolò made the simple wooden marker: *Inconnu, mort le 27 Novembre 1676*. Unknown man, died 27 November 1676.

The doctor invited them to his house afterward for a glass of wine. The weaver declined, saying he wished to get back to his loom, but the others gathered in the welcome warmth of the upstairs room. They said little – there were no memories to exchange, no explanations for what had happened, no comfort to be had.

'Who is the man who came to the cemetery?' Anne-Marie asked Dr Lunague. 'I saw him here on Friday but I still don't know his name.'

'His name is Willem, a Fleming, though he prefers to go by Guillaume ever since the war shifted to the Spanish Netherlands. Poor soul, his family has suffered a lot in the war.'

She was about to ask more about this Willem when the Gobelins clock struck noon and Niccolò came up to suggest that they should go home for lunch. The question went unasked, but she tucked it away in the back of her mind for future consideration.

★

It was not until Wednesday, 9 December, almost two weeks after the finding of the body, that Commissaire Ferrand returned to the Gobelins to report on the progress of the police investigation. Le Brun summoned Anne-Marie and Niccolò, Dr Lunague and Old Jean to his office at ten in the morning to hear him.

As director of the Gobelins, Charles Le Brun lived with his wife Suzanne in the yellow stone house facing the main court-yard. On the exterior of the house was a series of hooks where recently completed tapestries could be displayed to the King and other important visitors. Anne-Marie remembered the day when a tapestry showing a diplomatic triumph of Louis XIV was hung for viewing by Jean-Baptiste Colbert, the Minister of Finance who oversaw the Gobelins. At the celebration afterward, Anne-Marie, dazzled by the tapestry's rich colors, its gold and silver threads sparkling in the sun, felt so fortunate to be part of this magical world of people who made beautiful things. It was a warming thought on this cold day.

Le Brun's manservant admitted them and showed them into the office. They hesitated to step on the Turkish carpet, but Le Brun beckoned them to enter and not worry about it. The doctor, Old Jean and Commissaire Ferrand were already present. The servant poured bowls of coffee from a pot on the side table and handed them around.

Anne-Marie drank hers eagerly and exclaimed at the lightness of the empty blue and white bowl.

'It is porcelain,' Le Brun told her, 'imported from China by the Dutch. It is much admired in Europe but we have not yet found the secret of making it, although both potters and alche-mists have been hard at work attempting to do so. I would gladly add a porcelain studio to the Gobelins. I know that Monsieur Colbert' – he gestured to the portrait that hung behind his left shoulder – 'would like to keep in France the money that is spent on these imports.'

And you are ambitious that the Gobelins and its director should be well thought of, Anne-Marie thought shrewdly. Le Brun had spent most of his career in service to the King and was now fifty-six. With Colbert's patronage and the King's continued favor, his tenure seemed secure. Yet she sensed, under the self-assurance, a wariness alert to anticipating and preventing the next possible turn of fortune.

When Le Brun turned to speak to the manservant, she examined the richly appointed office, which served as a showroom for the Manufactory. The intricately patterned marquetry desk and tables, the small *torchères* with dangling semi-precious stones, the large cabinet with scenes in *pietra dura*, the table clock with its case veneered in tortoiseshell and brass, and above all the tapestries – the panels of the folding screen that stood by the door to keep out drafts, the chair cushions, and the magnificent scene that hung on the wall – were all examples of the fine wares produced by the Gobelins.

Le Brun, dressed in a suit of a rich golden-brown fabric embroidered with silver thread, looked as though he too were covered in tortoiseshell marquetry. His shoes, for indoor wear, were ornamented by ribbon bows – not so wide and colorful ribbons as the ones worn at court, where Louis XIV encouraged his noblemen into lavish competition – but following the fashion set by them. The quality of his dress proclaimed the status of gentleman that the Royal Academy of Painting and Sculpture had long sought for its members. Half-length portraits of the King and Colbert hung on the wall behind him, displaying his skill as a painter and underscoring the sources of his authority; to question his was to question theirs. On the opposite wall, flanking the fireplace, were a portrait of Madame Le Brun and a Biblical scene. So intent was Anne-Marie on her examination of the room that she started when the table clock struck the hour and Le Brun invited Commissaire Ferrand to speak.

Ferrand began by detailing the visit that he and Gabriel Nicolas de la Reynie, the Lieutenant-General of the police, had paid to the Duc de Languedoc at the Place Royale. The Duc had received them in his cabinet, the warm, comfortable book-lined room in which, clearly, he felt most at ease. Ferrand's voice still held some of the awe he had felt to be permitted into the inner sanctum of a duke.

The Duc answered every question openly and frankly. No, he did not recognize the drawing of the dead man, and he was certain that he had never met him nor seen him at the house. Yes, that was his crest; he had had a set of silver buttons made for the Duchesse on her birthday years ago, and they were transferred from the summer livery to the winter livery and back again every change of season, inventoried each time. The household buttons were made by a reputable silversmith and so were clearly hallmarked. The button in the dead man's hand would seem to have been cast from one of these by a less skillful hand – it bore only traces of the legitimate hallmarks and wasn't finished as well as the household buttons. The household books were brought out; all buttons had been accounted for at the last inventory. A coat was brought out so that he could compare its buttons to the one in the dead man's hand. Seeing the two side by side and feeling the differences in the crispness of detail and the finish on the back, it was clear that the latter was a rather crude copy. Nor did the scrap of cloth to which it was attached match the quality of either the summer or winter liveries, although the color was similar.

The manservants – the Duc's valet, footman, and coachman, a surprisingly small number given the Duc's importance – had then been summoned. None of them recognized the dead man. All could account for the whereabouts of both themselves and their buttons – the suspicion of a smile hovered about Ferrand's face – on the night in question. None had lost one and needed a replacement. The buttons were made by the family jeweler, Monsieur de Lamerie, who kept the mold in his safe and had certainly not been given permission to cast them for anyone else. Yes, the Duc vouched for him; the family had done business with his father before him, and the Duchesse had been godmother to the current jeweler, who was proud of the connection. Yes, the

Duc's privileged position at court aroused a certain amount of envy, and of course there were intrigues at court; but he would not add to them by speculation, nor by pointing a finger at anyone without evidence. Ferrand made clear to the group assembled in Le Brun's office that La Reynie had been persuaded of the Duc's innocence in the matter and wanted to be sure it was made known at the Gobelins. His report concluded, he sat back in his chair.

Anne-Marie was incredulous. The police did not seem to have concerned themselves with the victim at all, only with exonerating the Duc. 'What about the murdered man? Did you find out who he is? Did you find and tell his wife? What are you doing to find his killer, if the Duc and his household are not involved?'

'You seem to know more about him than we do, Madame,' Ferrand replied ironically, with a raised eyebrow.

She reminded him that he had seen the embroidered hearts on the man's shirt.

He was unimpressed. 'His wife – if she exists – has not come to us to report him missing. The money in his coat suggests that he might have been planning to leave her. Perhaps his absence didn't take her by surprise? With everything else for which the police are responsible in a city the size of Paris, we cannot go looking for a hypothetical woman based on a bit of embroidery.' There was more than a hint of condescension in his voice.

Le Brun intervened to thank Ferrand before she could say anything else that might antagonize him. He asked Niccolò and Anne-Marie to stay and then rose to see Ferrand to the gate of the Gobelins. Dr Lunague and Old Jean followed them out.

Niccolò had not spoken up while Ferrand was present, but now he said with some bitterness, 'What did you expect? How much concern did the police show for me when I was attacked?'

She reached out to grasp his hand and squeeze it sympathetically. Fetched by the baker, the Commissaire of the Latin Quarter had visited Niccolò, arriving in his attic room warm and panting after coming up four flights of stairs and happy to accept a drink of water from the jug by the bed. He had listened to Niccolò's story without surprise, having heard too many like it. Reliving its details had been painful for Niccolò, who several times had to stop his narrative to wipe away tears. Anne-Marie had taken his hand to help him regain his composure. At least he could give the man some solid information: the one who had come at him with the knife was Antoine, the journeyman woodworker who had been replaced by a Fleming. Also, Nic had put his initials on his tools, the better to identify them in a busy workshop. Surely, they could trace this Antoine by interviewing carpenters and sculptors, checking Guild records for a journeyman of that name? The man said that they would try but had not been hopeful. Such an investigation would take time and men. The prosecution of the criminals, if they were apprehended, would cost money, and recovering the costs from the rogue journeymen was highly unlikely. He had said then, as Ferrand had said just now, that there was only so much a police force could do in a city the size of Paris. He was sorry, but there it was.

'No wonder the men are bold enough to attack, if this is all they have to fear,' Anne-Marie had said tartly. The Commissaire flushed but had not allowed himself to be drawn into an argument. Later, however, he returned with Niccolò's rucksack, which had been found by the *Guet*, the night watch, in another part of the city. 'The tools are gone, but I thought you would be glad of your leather bag, since you went to the trouble of branding your initials on it,' he told Niccolò. 'I regret that the *Guet* could not help you earlier that night, but I wanted to do for you what I could.'

Le Brun returned from seeing out Commissaire Ferrand. He did not sit behind his desk this time but took a chair facing the couple. He leaned forward earnestly as he spoke, seeking to persuade rather than issue orders.

'Madame Bruno, I applaud your wish to learn more about the dead man and discover whether he had any next of kin. Dr Lunague

34

has told me what a help you were to him during the medical examination.' Anne-Marie smiled at this build-up, bracing for the letdown she knew was coming. 'However, I must now ask you to abstain from taking this matter further.'

'But—' she began. Niccolò placed a hand on her arm to calm or warn her, or perhaps both.

'The dead man is not the Gobelins' business. He was neither an employee nor anyone known to any of us. He was not killed on the premises. He merely came to rest, by chance, on the other side of our wall. The Manufactory has done its duty in providing what assistance it could to the police. Whatever action La Reynie and Ferrand decide to take – or not – is none of our business.'

She would not be put off so easily. 'Yes, but even so, shouldn't his family be found and informed? Shouldn't his killer be brought to justice?'

'There is more at stake than justice for a stranger.' Le Brun sighed. 'You and your husband are newcomers to our community, so you may not be aware of the intrigues that can threaten us. The police have already been here twice. The Marquis de Louvois, the Minister of War and Colbert's rival for pre-eminence among the King's advisors, is known to have spies among them. He would gladly use this occasion to make trouble for the Gobelins as a way of discrediting Colbert. Monsieur Louvois considers the luxury goods we make as a drain of resources better spent on the army, and he would have the Manufactory much reduced in size or even shut down. I am not about to let that happen.

'I say again, it is a shame about the man's family, *if* indeed they exist, and I applaud your impulse to help, but my first duty is to the Manufactory and the people it employs, who, may I remind you' – his voice took on a steely edge – 'include your husband. Do I make myself clear?'

'*Oui*, Monsieur le Directeur,' they replied in tandem.

'Very clear,' added Anne-Marie.

'Then I will bid you good day. I know Niccolò must be eager to return to his studio.' He smiled at the young man. 'I am very pleased with the pair of sculptures for the cabinet. I look forward to seeing what else you can do for us.'

With that, he turned and asked his manservant to show them out.

Niccolò glanced nervously at his wife as they retraced their steps through the courtyard. She said nothing, but her indignation was plain. He sympathized, knowing first-hand her tenacity once she had undertaken a task, but he had come too far to risk losing his position. He did not want to argue with her. 'I'm going to the studio,' he said. There, he would find solace and purpose in his work. He kissed his wife and walked away with a quickening step.

Anne-Marie hesitated. She was in no mood to be alone in their rooms. Le Brun's reproof stung, although she knew he had the interests of the Manufactory – hence of Niccolò – at heart. She decided to visit Dr Lunague.

The doctor was attending to a dyer's wife who had accidentally cut open her finger, but he smiled at Anne-Marie and asked her to be seated. Again, it was almost as cold inside his consulting room as out, even with a fire in the corner stove. When the other woman had left, he poured two glasses of red wine and handed one to Anne-Marie.

'Let me guess,' he said to her, before she could begin. 'Monsieur Le Brun had things to say to you that were not entirely welcome but that you cannot ignore. So, you have come here to make your protest.'

'Am I that transparent?' she asked with the ghost of a smile.

He laughed. 'Out with it. What did he say?'

He listened attentively as she told him. When she had finished, he gave a sigh very like Le Brun's and poured them more wine.

'I know you don't want to hear this—'

'But,' she interjected, with a wry twist of her mouth.

'But he is right. He must look out for the welfare of the Gobelins. I know that you find it frustrating, but it is safest not to

36

pursue the matter further. Would you jeopardize your husband's career to pursue an unknown man's conjectural wife and child?'

'No, of course not,' she muttered. What else could she say?

'I am sorry to be so blunt, but it would be for the best.' He set down his wineglass and stood to indicate the discussion was over.

'Thank you for hearing me out,' she said, and left. She liked Dr Lunague and did not wish to antagonize him as well.

And yet. The doctor considered his responsibility to the dead man to have ended. She remembered his army service: he had seen many more men die in battle, and one lone death was not of great importance to him. But it is to me, she thought.

On impulse, she decided to visit her father. Her mother and sister visited a friend on Wednesdays, so Anne-Marie would be able to see him on his own. She was always more comfortable when it was just the two of them. Her father might agree with the necessity of leaving well enough alone, but he would respect and understand her wish to do more.

As she approached Boulangerie Robert, she looked up fondly at the shop sign, the letters B and R spelled out in intertwined braided loaves of bread that spoke of the skill of the baker and the quality of his goods. Designed and executed by Armand, the young painter who had lodged with them before winning the Prix de Rome, it stood out among the many others on Rue St Victor. 'For those who can read and those who can't,' her father would say with a grin. 'No other shop in this quartier has an Academy painter work for them.'

It was as if the thought brought her father to her side. He greeted her lovingly with kisses on both cheeks. She waved to Thérèse, her colleague behind the counter. She would talk with her later. Now, the long walk in the cold air had given her an appetite.

She followed her father into the cobbled courtyard with its private well, another point of pride for the baker: 'No need to go to the public fountains or the river for our water.' After the disastrous fire in London ten years before, Robert Boulanger had had the house, which included the shop on the ground floor, rebuilt of stone and made the bakehouse separate for safety. He stored the flour and other ingredients in a stone room to one side, to make it more difficult for mice and rats to get at them, as they would otherwise gnaw holes in the wood to squeeze through. One of the bakery cats was washing itself by the door.

An ample lunch awaited them. They ate at a long trestle table in the main room. The wooden chairs had colorful embroidered cushions on the seats made by Anne-Marie and her mother, with matching embroidered curtains at the window. A plaited rush mat covered the wood floor.

'Toinette is expecting again. Your mother is already happily knitting small garments for the new grandchild.' He chuckled. 'You and Niccolò – not expecting yet?'

Anne-Marie was taken aback. 'We've been married only three months, Papa.'

He grunted. 'So – what brings you here midweek? If it were good news you would have told me already. Is something wrong? Is everything all right between you two?'

'Oh yes. No worries there, Papa. Except . . .' She took a deep breath. 'You remember last week I told you about the dead man? The Commissaire visited the Gobelins this morning to report on the progress of the investigation.' She gave him a summary of what Ferrand had said and Le Brun's subsequent warning. 'I wish I could look for his widow myself. I feel so—' She looked for words to describe the kinship she felt for this woman, but her father did not wait for her to find them.

'Anne-Marie, I wish I could tell you to do as you wish, but you are a wife now, and your first duty is what is in the best interests of your husband. He came a long distance and worked hard and endured so much last year, to achieve his goal of working at the Gobelins. You cannot jeopardize that for him.'

'I know, Papa. It is the last thing I would want to do.' She sighed as she rose to clear the table.

Her father spoke again, more gently. 'I know you are worried about the man's family. But you don't even know that they need to be rescued. Friends may be taking care of them.'

'But she would want to know what happened to her husband – it's better to know the truth than always be imagining something worse.'

'You should worry more about your husband's job and heeding his employer.' His voice was flat and brooked no protest. The subject was closed. There was silence between them for several minutes while she finished washing and putting away the dishes.

'Before you go, come into the shop and say hello to Thérèse.'

Thérèse, the plump, cheerful shop assistant who knew all the customers by name, loved to fill in Anne-Marie on the latest events in their lives, but they did not have much time to gossip. The shop was unusually busy for that hour, and Anne-Marie willingly helped out.

A kitchen maid from a grand house in the Place Royale had come all the way across the Seine to buy fine white rolls for a dinner to be given that evening. She had received strict instructions from the *maître d'hotel* as to what kinds she should buy. Anne-Marie happily assembled the order – it was good business for the bakery, as white bread sold for a much higher price than the heavy brown loaves bought by working people, and it could attract other customers of high rank if the dinner guests were pleased. Her calm efficiency put the nervous servant at ease.

'Do you work for the Duc de Languedoc?' she asked casually. 'I heard that he lives on the Place Royale.'

'No, I work in a house on the north side. The Duc and his family live in one of the larger houses, the third from the right on the east side.' Anne-Marie thanked her for her order and gave her an additional roll for herself. The girl accepted it with a big smile. Her employer and his guests might be served fine white bread, but the servants, especially one as lowly in status as she, had to make do with brown.

The chat with the kitchen maid had given Anne-Marie an

idea. Perhaps the Duc de Languedoc would consider becoming a customer – and she could continue her own investigation under that guise. She lined a delivery basket with a snowy white cloth and filled it with an assortment of best breads. She was deliberately vague in telling Thérèse where she was going, not wishing to have it repeated to her father. She strode briskly out the door and down the street in the direction of the Place Royale before she could change her mind or lose her courage.

Chapter Five

Anne-Marie walked down the Rue des Fossés St-Bernard towards the Seine. She loved the bustle of this street leading to the Port St-Bernard and the Port aux Vins, important entry points for boats bringing the food, wine and cloth needed to feed and clothe the inhabitants. As a native Parisienne and a baker's daughter, she took pride in being part of the commercial life of the city. Taverns' drays piled with casks of wine rumbled past, while men who had bought only a cask or two to drink at home were followed by porters bearing their purchases. Anne-Marie had to step lively and watch her feet.

'Anne-Marie! Anne-Marie!'

She heard her name being called with an insistence that suggested repetition. It was her mother's brother, the miller, his cart piled high with sacks of flour for the bakery. She darted across the road to smile up at him and blew him a kiss, though she could barely see him huddled into his coat.

'What are you doing in Paris on a Wednesday? Isn't Thursday your usual day for deliveries?'

'Yes, but tomorrow I have village business to attend to. I was elected mayor,' he reminded her. 'So I came a day early. I'd hoped to join Robert at lunch but there was a long delay at the Port de Blé.' This was the landing site on the Right Bank for merchants bringing grain and flour into the city.

His bay horse, an old friend of Anne-Marie's, whinnied for recognition. She took off her glove to pat his muzzle, loving the feel of the soft skin around his nose. He sniffed hopefully at her hand. She petted him some more as she apologized she had no sugar or apple for him.

'If you wait until I finish my delivery, I can give you a ride to wherever you are going.'

She smiled and shook her head. 'I'm halfway there,' she assured him, though she had just started out. She gave fond greetings for her aunt and cousins and continued on her way.

Being back in the bakery had put her in mind of the time before her marriage, when just getting out for a stroll on her own, even the short distance to the bookseller's, was not easily managed. She was not allowed to go out alone and her mother insisted she take her sister with her, but Toinette was bored by the bookshop and the efforts of the owner to find something she would like to read – until she was old enough to discover the pleasures of flirting with the students who frequented the place. For Anne-Marie, to be able now to wander where she wanted, alone, without being subjected to questioning was one of the joys of married life. Her status of wife gave the always-pleasurable excuse, to anyone who might ask, of doing an errand for her husband.

At the river, she turned left onto the Quai St-Bernard, inhaling deeply the yeasty, satisfying smell of wine-in-wood as she passed the Port aux Vins. She hurried across the open Pont de la Tournelle to the Ile St-Louis and into the comparative shelter of the Rue des Deux Ponts. It seemed only a few steps to the Pont Marie. In the summer this bridge to the Right Bank would be a hub of activity, but on this bitter day, those few who found it necessary to go out were intent on reaching their destinations as rapidly as possible. The houses built up on either side of the bridge sheltered her from the wind off the river but caught and channeled the wind blowing from the Right Bank, and it was cold underfoot as well. A roast chestnut seller huddled over his brazier in a sheltered niche. Anne-Marie bought a small cone of chestnuts in a twist of cheap paper to warm her hands. Doggedly she continued on her way.

A whiff of freshly sawn wood coming out an opened door in the Rue des Nonnains d'Hyères brought her back to the matter at hand, reminding her that the Quartier St Antoine was home to many furniture makers' workshops. Under the jealously guarded privileges of its powerful Abbess, it was exempt from the guild laws of the rest of Paris, allowing foreign craftsmen and others not welcomed into the guilds to thrive there. Niccolò had looked for work in the quartier before being taken on at the Gobelins. Perhaps the dead man had sought work in one of these ateliers? She could ask Niccolò to find out – were it not, she thought uncomfortably, that for him to do so would mean disobeying Le Brun's direct, very specific orders. As indeed she was doing at this very moment.

She pressed on, nonetheless, and turned the corner onto the bustle of the Rue St-Antoine. In the distance she could see the immense grey-brown bulk of the Bastille, a reminder of the penalty for all who disobeyed authority. Legends were told of men and women who had disappeared inside, never to be seen again. It was even said that some well-born parents would send a son or daughter there as a means of punishment or persuasion. She gave an apprehensive shiver.

A shout from an angry coachman as she stepped almost beneath his horses' hooves made her aware of more immediate dangers. She stepped back, only to bump into a woman carrying pails of water from the tower-like Fontaine Sainte-Catherine, one of the city's public fountains. She turned to apologize but the woman did not wait to hear, hurrying to get home with her burden. Anne-Marie flushed uncomfortably at the coachman's mocking laugh. She quickened her steps toward the Rue Royale.

Even while most of her attention focused on getting safely to her destination, a part of her mind turned over what she planned to say when she arrived. She would not try to talk to the Duc de Languedoc or his daughter Mademoiselle de Toulouse. Merely meeting with people of their status, never mind questioning them, was a matter for people like Nicolas de La Reynie or Charles

Le Brun. She would hope to see the *maître d'hôtel*, the head servant of a wealthy household such as this one, who supervised the staff and chose the firms and individuals who supplied the house. Ferrand had no doubt interviewed him – he was thorough in his job – but perhaps there was something he had overlooked or that the staff was reluctant to admit to their employers but could discuss freely amongst themselves. His questions might have started someone's train of thought that would produce a useful theory. Or her visit might come to nothing. But the button with the Duc's crest, however spurious, was the only lead she had.

After the perils of Rue St-Antoine and the narrow Rue Royale, the calm open expanse of Henri IV's Place Royale was a delight. An equestrian statue of his son Louis XIII formed the sole ornament to the grassy square. Around it, the handsome brick residences with stone facings glowed red and yellow in the afternoon sun. The warm colors, in their orderly symmetry, were immensely appealing. The current fashion, Anne-Marie had learned from Le Brun and others at the Gobelins, was for freestanding *hôtels* fronted entirely with stone, more formal and imposing, as befitted the grandeur of the age of Louis XIV. Admiring the handsome façade of the Hôtel de Languedoc, Anne-Marie could understand why the Duc had chosen to remain here.

Anne-Marie asked a woman sweeping outside a neighboring *hôtel* for directions to the servants' entrance at the rear of the building. The area behind the Place Royale was a surprise. While the façades were linked and symmetrical, each house had been built out in the back as a separate building. The Hôtel de Languedoc, four storeys high and of imposing length, was much larger than its front implied, and had, as well, a separate carriage house in the courtyard behind the house. Her knock at the service door was answered by a kitchen maid wiping wet hands on a towel. Anne-Marie asked to speak to the *maître d'hôtel*.

To her surprise, the young woman replied, 'We haven't got one. You'll have to speak to Madame Hugues, the housekeeper. Wait here until she gives me permission to admit you.' She shut the door again. Anne-Marie could appreciate the precaution against thieves and other undesirables, but it was too cold to wait for long. She shifted from foot to foot, trying to keep warm. Finally, the door was unbolted a second time and the maid bade her enter.

The kitchen was deliciously warm, with not one but two great fireplaces, each flanked by two ovens. One oven emitted an enticing scent of onions and herbs. Gleaming copper cooking pots and molds lined with tin hung above the well-scrubbed table in the center of the room. A female cook, not a male chef – another surprise – read aloud from a thick book of recipes, directing the kitchen maid who had answered the door (Rose, the cook called her) to the bowls and utensils to take down from the dressers, the supplies to bring out of the larder, the bottles and packets to remove from the spice cupboard. An adjacent cupboard was padlocked; Anne-Marie guessed that it would contain delicacies restricted to the use of the family – coffee, tea and chocolate. At the far end of the room was a sink with a pump. The Hôtel de Languedoc was evidently one of the few houses in the city with water piped indoors. A door next to it opened to reveal a glimpse of corridor and to admit a woman whose age, dress and air of authority proclaimed her as the Duc's housekeeper. At her waist she wore a ring of keys, her badge of office.

'I am Madame Hugues,' she introduced herself. 'Madame Dupont' – she nodded at the cook – 'and I decide which tradesmen will supply the household.' Her manner implied that she was conferring a favor upon Anne-Marie even to grant her an interview, and her next words confirmed it. 'We are very selective about giving our custom.'

'Of course, Madame,' Anne-Marie replied, bobbing the curtsy the housekeeper clearly expected. 'That is why we are eager to list the Duc among our clients. But I think you will find my father's breads worth your while. If I may . . .?' She held out the basket and made to unfasten her cloak.

'Yes – come here by the fire and sit down.' Madame Hugues picked up a small saucepan simmering on the side of one of the

45

hearths and poured broth into a bowl for her guest. Anne-Marie sipped appreciatively. The housekeeper poured another for herself and sat in another of the chairs drawn up to the fire. 'We always have broth ready in weather like this.'

The cook and Rose had finished their preparations for the moment, and Anne-Marie heard Rose ask for an hour off. 'You want to visit Marc, I'll bet,' smiled the cook. 'Very well – but be back when the bells at St Catherine's ring four o'clock, or I'll come looking for you,' she warned.

'*Oui*, Madame. *Bien sûr*, Madame,' the girl replied happily. She poured broth into a jar to take with her and cast a hopeful look at the basket. The housekeeper had got up to confer with the cook, and Anne-Marie slipped a small round loaf to the girl with a wink. The girl gave her a hurried smile of thanks and scurried out before the others could notice.

With both women now seated before her, sampling what she had brought, Anne-Marie expounded on the quality and cleanliness of her father's bakery and the variety of breads it could provide. Boulangerie Robert supplied other families in the Place Royale, she told them, and wished to supply the Duc, its most important resident.

The women, after eating their fill, regretted to inform Anne-Marie that the household already had a long-standing arrangement with one of the neighborhood bakeries. It was not often that they needed fine breads for the family, however, as the Duc de Languedoc and Mademoiselle de Toulouse spent most of their time at Saint-Germain-en-Laye in attendance upon the King. Rose went to the twice-weekly bread fair to buy the servants' loaves. 'But we are pleased to know of such a fine establishment as Boulangerie Robert, should an occasion ever arise when we would need it. In that event, we would send a message to you at the bakery and expect our order to be delivered.'

'It would be best to send it to my father, Robert Boulanger, as I am not there regularly. I married earlier this year to a sculptor at the Gobelins and we live there.'

This revived their fading interest in her. 'The Gobelins! Were you there the day that man's body found in the Bièvre?'

'Yes, it was dreadful.' Anne-Marie shuddered delicately, in good taste in keeping with her surroundings. 'The Gobelins doctor said the man had been stabbed. The police don't seem to have made any progress in finding out who he was or why he was killed.' She assumed a puzzled expression. 'Why such a lively interest all the way over here in the Place Royale?'

'Did the doctor tell you the man had something in his hand?' the housekeeper asked.

Anne-Marie furrowed her brow as if trying to remember. 'A button, was it? The Commissaire took it with him.'

'It was a button that supposedly came from the livery worn by the Duc's manservants. The police came here and questioned us about it. I could tell from the outset that it was counterfeit, but would they take my word for it? No, they had to bother the Duc and all the other servants as well.'

'How could you tell that it was counterfeit?'

'The original set was made as a gift for the Duchesse. There was a nouveau-riche family of financiers whose servants wore silver buttons, and it incensed the Duchesse that her servants had to make do with pewter. The Duc ordered a set in silver to placate her. She died two years ago, poor lady, but the Duc continues to have the servants wear them in her memory. They are always carefully inventoried as they are transferred from summer to winter livery and back again. The family silversmith keeps the mold for them – it is simply unthinkable he would make them for anyone else. If one of the buttons is scratched or dented, he melts it down and remakes it. I keep excellent records of each instance in my book and Monsieur de Lamerie's books will confirm it. I have kept house for the Duc for twelve years and am proud to say that my records are immaculate.'

Anne-Marie nodded her appreciation.

'That Commissaire had me summon all the servants and asked them himself as if he doubted my word. The cheek of it! And the

47

scrap of cloth he showed us that the button was sewn onto – anyone who knew the first thing about fabric, which clearly, he didn't, could see it was the wrong color and quality. As if the Duc would ever dress his footmen in something as shoddy as that!' Madame Hugues's cheeks were flushed, and she fanned herself with her hand.

Anne-Marie, who did not need to dissemble the appearance of hanging on her every word, shook her head slowly in amazement. 'I had no idea.' She hesitated. 'I wish – do you suppose – I could see one of those buttons? The real ones, I mean.' She gave the two women a wide-eyed, imploring look, hoping that she wasn't overdoing it, but Madame Hugues rose to fetch one. She returned with a box in hand.

'I keep a set in a locked drawer,' she explained, 'in case a replacement is needed.'

Anne-Marie peered closely at the button the housekeeper handed to her. The design was the same, its details crisper than on the dead man's button. Its back surface was smooth to the touch, well finished, not rough as the other had been. She could not help turning it over and looking as closely at the back with its crisp, legible hallmark.

The housekeeper joked, 'You must be nearsighted. That's the wrong side of the button – there is nothing to see on the back.' Anne-Marie laughed at herself, sharing the joke.

'Did one of the men ever lose a button?'

'His wages would be docked if he did! Young Marc, he was careless enough to lose one last summer and he was in a terrible state about it because of the lost wages, with him and Rose saving up to be married. But it turned up again two days later in the carriage house, the next time the Duc took out the carriage. Marc swore he'd searched it thoroughly but he must have overlooked it.'

Anne-Marie felt a warm spark of satisfaction inside her. This was what she had hoped to find out. One of the buttons had been missing long enough for someone to have taken an impression of it. There were other jewelers and silversmiths not so scrupulous as Monsieur de Lamerie – and other trades involved in the casting of metal. Gunsmiths, for example, or the cannon foundry at the Arsenal, the Marquis de Louvois's territory.

Or, her conscience pricked her, sculptors. Could it have been made in the silver workshops at the Gobelins? What if it was not a coincidence after all that the body had turned up just outside the walls of the Manufactory? What if an enemy lurked within? She shivered at the thought. In that case, wouldn't Monsieur Le Brun want to know about it? Wouldn't her investigating be in *his* interest?

All she said aloud was, 'But who would want to cast suspicion on the Duc? Everyone speaks so well of him.'

'Oh, any man as important as the Duc has enemies! He has the ear of the King, and there's always someone who would prefer the King listen to him instead.' They looked very knowing, as if fully conversant with the ways of the world and the intrigues of the court but couldn't be more specific than that.

The bells of St Catherine's struck the hour. Anne-Marie stood to go, saying she must return to the bakery. The outside door opened to admit Rose, brushing fragments of hay from her skirt after her rendezvous which Anne-Marie deduced had taken place in the carriage house. She stopped abruptly to stare at the door leading from the corridor. The trio at the fireplace turned to see what had caught her attention.

Anne-Marie caught her breath in wonder at the beautiful young woman who stood framed by the doorway. Her gown of pale green silk shot with silver, its cuffs trimmed with foamy lace, was beyond anything Anne-Marie could ever hope to own. The toes of soft leather slippers peeped out from beneath the hem. Her brown hair, arranged in rows of artful ringlets by a skillful maid, glinted red as the swinging curls caught the firelight. Her smooth complexion was pale but needed no help from rouge or kohl, and her blue eyes—

Anne-Marie quailed. Never had she seen such fury in a woman's face. Hastily she followed the example of the other women and sank into a deep curtsy, dropping her eyes as well.

'Mademoiselle de Toulouse!' exclaimed Madame Hugues. 'Was there something you wanted? How long – we didn't notice you standing there, or we would have—'

'I've been standing here long enough,' the young woman told them in a voice as flinty as her expression. 'You were warned not to gossip about the dead man. If I hear you spreading that story again, I'll see to it that you're dismissed, no matter how long you have served this family.'

'*Oui*, Mademoiselle,' they chorused in subdued voices with red, downcast faces. 'Our apologies, Mademoiselle.'

'*You*,' she said curtly, turning her wrath upon Anne-Marie, 'come with me.'

Chapter Six

While Anne-Marie was hurrying across Paris, Elisabeth-Suzanne-Cécile Sainterre de Languedoc, Mademoiselle de Toulouse—Elisabeth to her late mother, Suzanne to her father and her friends, Zanbé-cile to her older brother Geoffroi who loved to tease her — sat at the harpsichord, practicing a difficult passage from a d'Anglebert sonata. The instrument, made by Jean-Antoine Vaudry, was her pride and joy. She had paid frequent visits to his nearby workshop while it was being built and then chosen, as the decoration for the inside of the lid, a scene of Apollo and the Muses in a verdant landscape. Her music master had given the sonata to her to learn this week. Usually she enjoyed the challenges he set for her, but today mastery proved elusive. She muttered to herself when her fingering refused to right itself. 'DUM – da – DAH, DUM – da – DAH. No, it's too regular, too singsong. Dum-da-DAH – dum – DAH – DAH – dum – da.'

She looked around the room and frowned. The matched set of hangings on the tall, four-poster bed, windows and dressing table had not yet been changed from the pale green of summer to the deep green of winter. It was true she had impulsively decided to come home this morning with no prior warning, but surely by mid-December it was high time? Was Madame Hugues waiting until the last minute before the Duc returned home for Christmas? Her father had come to Paris to answer the questions put to him by La Reynie, but he would have had no reason to come up to her bedroom. She must speak to the woman about it.

Then she regretted her spurt of ill-temper. It was not the housekeeper's fault that she was forced to manage with a much smaller staff than before. The Duchesse had loved to entertain, giving elaborate dinner parties for twenty or thirty guests every month. The house had been kept in readiness by a staff of a size befitting a ducal household. The *maître d'hôtel* and chef gladly took on the challenge of producing two dozen dishes for each dinner. On the night, a dozen footmen were in attendance in their blue livery with brightly polished silver buttons, while half a dozen sous-chefs and kitchen maids scurried about, putting the finishing touches on each dish.

These were served at tables covered with fine damask cloths woven in the Netherlands with fruit and floral motifs and napkins, into which were woven the D&L armorial device. The Duchesse presided over her dinner table like Louis XIV over his meals at court – except that the guests at her meals ate with her, not merely observed her eating. At his end of the table, the Duc said and ate little but seemed content with his wife's enjoyment.

Suzanne had absented herself from these events as much as possible, although she did enjoy the snowy whiteness of the linens, smooth to the touch, revealing their patterns in the play of light. Like her father, she preferred solitude, he with his books, she with her music. The Duchesse considered this unnatural behavior and complained about it loud and long. Of course, this only drove them to further solitude to escape her laments. When the Duchesse died, Suzanne resisted all urging to fill her mother's shoes as a hostess, and the Duc, with a sigh of relief, respected her wishes. The disgruntled *maître d'hôtel* and the chef, seeking more scope for their skills than the simple family dinners that were all father and daughter asked of them, went to work for the Duchesse's sister, and many of the staff followed. The Duc watched them go with equanimity and, determining that the kitchen maid was well capable of producing the simple dishes he preferred, took the unprecedented step of promoting her to cook with the honorary title of Madame. The household functioned well with the reduced staff – footman, coachman, and valet; housekeeper, cook, kitchen maid, housemaid, and Suzanne's personal maid – except when major tasks such as the summer and winter changeovers took place. Then, they would employ everyone, even the coachman, to shift the heavy furniture and textiles, and even hire outside help.

Suzanne smiled when her eyes rested on the little carriage desk on the dressing table. It and a ream of fine paper had been Geoffroi's parting gifts to her before he left for New France. She always kept it with her, whether in her apartment at court or her room at home. 'Write to me often,' he had told her.

She got up to run her hand lovingly over the half-finished letter that lay on its lid, awaiting completion, and glanced out the window. A movement on the grassy square below caught her eye. A woman in a blue cloak with a basket of bread on her arm was surveying the houses, clearly looking for an address. Did she not know that deliveries came to the back of the house? Then the woman paused and looked up and down the full height of the façade of the Hôtel de Languedoc. Instinctively Suzanne pulled back, out of sight. Ever since that wretched man had been found dead with one of their supposed livery buttons between his fingers, gawkers had made their way to the Place Royale to stare and point.

It was even worse at Saint-Germain-en-Laye, where Louis XIV's court was in residence. There, one lived out in the open among one's fellow courtiers, and there was no place to hide from the scornful gaze of others. Music provided a much-needed escape and solace, in which she could lose herself and get far away from the intrigue and backbiting at court. Until now she had managed to avoid being the subject of gossip. Her fluent Spanish and skill at cards made her a favorite of Queen Marie-Thérèse, who occupied a position of honor rather than influence. Suzanne was serious about her music, devoted to her father and absent brother, and had no interest in catching the wandering eye of the King, nor indeed of any other man. Young ladies and their hopeful mothers who inquired eagerly after her brother were answered with animated descriptions of his most recent observations of the flora and fauna of New France and the customs of *les sauvages*, as its natives were referred to, until their eyes glazed over and they made their escape. Now it was impossible to ignore the whispers and innuendos, the sly asides spoken behind fan or hand. She had fled back to Paris for a respite from it.

She turned back to her music and made another half-hearted attempt at the passage – 'DUM – da – DAH, DUM – da – DAH' – her fingers would not work as they should – before abandoning the harpsichord for the day. She lowered the keyboard lid with more force than necessary, startling the aged mastiff that lay sprawled on the hearth. 'Sorry, Carlo,' she told him. He raised his white muzzle briefly at the sound of his name, then settled back to sleep with a contented grunt. She smiled at him and put away her music in a better frame of mind.

The Duchesse had never liked having Carlo in the house. 'The kennel is where a dog like that belongs! Or the stable,' she would add, before Suzanne could remind her that there was no kennel at the Place Royale. Carlo was her brother's dog. She had promised to look after him for Geoffroi. This room had been her brother's, too. Although it had been redecorated in a manner the Duchesse felt more fitting for feminine tastes and interests, replacing the dark green hunting tapestries with lighter ones of children at play, Carlo still thought it was his.

'Why you want *him* in your room instead of Belle, I have yet to understand.' Belle was a brown-and-white King Charles spaniel, the expensive and highly fashionable pet that the Duchesse had given her four years ago for her sixteenth birthday, ignoring her request for a flute. Once, the Queen had petted the dog and praised it in Spanish. 'After all, she *is* a Spaniel!' she had said afterward in French, in a rare show of wit. No higher accolade existed for the Duchesse, who was beside herself at this mark of favor.

'Because Belle whines and howls when I play the harpsichord, Maman, and Carlo does not. Why don't *you* carry Belle around if you're so fond of her?' After her mother's death, Suzanne gave the lapdog to a delighted lady-in-waiting so that the Queen could pet her as often as she liked.

She stretched and yawned. She had sent her maid out in search of a new unguent for the hands, much recommended by the ladies of the court who paid attention to such things, and given her the rest of the afternoon off. She would ring for coffee to help get her through this endless afternoon. No, she would go down to the kitchen to chat with Madame Dupont, an old friend, while it was being prepared. As children, Suzanne and Geoffroi had enjoyed escaping from their tutors to watch her, then a mere kitchen maid called Marie, help prepare the meals. Since the Duchesse rarely descended to the nether regions of the kitchen, it had been a safe place to hide from her as well. They had not been allowed to do any of the actual cooking over the fire, of course, but if Madame Dupont was making a *tarte tatin*, she might let them very carefully cut up the apples and roll out the crust. Geoffroi, even then a keen observer of activities and customs, wrote in one of his letters that he had absorbed much knowledge that stood him in good stead when he had to fend for himself in the forests of New France.

Suzanne smiled at the memories. It was always warm in the kitchen, and the chef had kept a special crock of *sablés* for the children. Her mouth watered for the buttery taste of them. She wondered if Madame Dupont still kept them in supply; if not, she would ask her to make some. She was looking forward to the treat as she went down the stairs. She could hear voices in animated discussion behind the kitchen door.

Suzanne walked rapidly up the two flights of stairs, anger fueling her steps. She could hear the stout blonde woman puffing and wheezing behind her, struggling to keep up, but she was in no mood to slow her pace to accommodate her visitor. Only at the door of her room did she pause to turn and glare again at the woman.

'In here,' she ordered, in the tone the Governor of the Bastille might have used to usher a prisoner into his cell.

The woman sidled in, still incongruously clutching her basket, trepidation written on her face. Suzanne pulled forward a *tabouret*, a backless, armless stool reserved for visitors of lower rank. 'Sit,' she told the woman.

The mastiff struggled to get to his feet.

'Not you, Carlo,' she told the dog in a much gentler voice, with amusement in it. 'Go back to sleep, *mon brave*.' She turned to the blonde woman and said, in a less peremptory tone, gesturing to the *tabouret*, 'Please – sit.'

Perhaps she should have kept the woman standing while she interrogated her from her chair – that is what etiquette would have prescribed and doing so would have established firmly their relative rank. But she was reluctant to let this taller, larger person loom over her. She wanted her where she could keep an eye on her.

The woman placed her basket on the floor and her hands in her lap. She braced her shoulders and sat up straight. Suzanne, placing herself opposite, sat in an armchair, occupying its space like the Queen on her throne. She was glad of the extra height afforded her by the seat pillow. Her pulse and breathing had returned to normal, but her mind raced.

This woman was asking entirely too many pointed questions, more than could be excused by mere gossip. Was she spying on the family? If so, who was she working for? The Marquis de Louvois, with his well-known malice toward the Duc, was the most obvious possibility. He usually employed men, though his network might encompass so unlikely a creature as this. But if she were Louvois's spy, what to do with or about her, without creating still more trouble?

If she wasn't a spy for Louvois, what was her game? Was she an affiliate of the dead man's, spying on the household because she thought it was privy to his secrets? Or did she believe someone here was responsible for the man's death and wish to seek retribution?

The Duc had told his daughter to ignore the scandal; it would blow over as all scandals did; but Suzanne could not regard it with the same sang-froid. She wished, not for the first time, that Geoffroi were here to help her decide what to do. There was no one else in the family to turn to for help. Her Aunt Delalande had never liked her brother-in-law very much. Her response to the current situation was to try to separate father and daughter – 'for your mother's sake' – reminding Suzanne that she was as much a Delalande as a Sainterre of Languedoc. Suzanne had never been very fond of this aunt, who had taken it upon herself to fill in for her dead sister in providing unsolicited advice – including offering to replace the Spaniel with – Suzanne shuddered – a pug.

'Now – who are you? What is your interest in this matter?'

'My name is Anne-Marie Bruno, Mademoiselle. My husband Niccolò is a sculptor at the Gobelins, and we live there. I was there the day the man was found. I took notes for Dr Lunague when he performed the autopsy. I cleaned the man's face and unwound the loose threads with the button from around his fingers. One of the artists recognized the Languedoc crest.'

'So, you decided we must be guilty and came here to prove it? Who are you working for?'

'No, of course not! I am working for no one, Mademoiselle. My husband works for Monsieur Le Brun at the Gobelins. We received a visit from Commissaire Ferrand this morning notifying us that the police had established your innocence. Of course, I accept that.'

In the circumstances, she could hardly say otherwise, thought Suzanne cynically. 'Then I repeat: what is your interest in this matter?'

'A tear in the man's shirt was expertly repaired, with hearts embroidered on it next to the darning. In his coat pocket there was a half-finished child's toy he was making. I feel strongly that he had a sweetheart or wife, perhaps also a child, who may be wondering what became of him. I told the Commissaire about it during his first visit, but he is not interested in finding them.

I am. The button was the only clue I had, so I came here in case there was something the police had overlooked that would lead me to the man's family.'

This Madame Bruno – if that was her real name – might be sincerely concerned for them, or she might be a confederate of the murderer, seeking to find out from the widow something the dead man refused to give or tell, or to eliminate an inconvenient witness.

'And this masquerade as a baker's daughter?'

'It is not a masquerade, Mademoiselle! My father is Robert Boulanger, and our family have been bakers for generations. The Boulangerie Robert has been on Rue St-Victor for more than thirty years. We make some of the finest breads in the city.' Spirited in defense of her father, she spoke forcefully and proudly. Only when she had finished did she belatedly remember to whom she spoke and clapped her hand over her mouth in embarrassment. 'I apologize, Mademoiselle,' she said hastily. 'I got carried away . . .' Her voice faltered.

Suzanne smiled faintly. 'I feel much the same about my own father,' she said. 'That is why this attempt to implicate him in this man's murder distresses me so deeply.'

'But it *wasn't* one of your livery buttons!' the woman protested.

Suzanne leaned forward intently. 'Why are you so sure of that? How do you know? Tell me!'

'I handled the button the dead man had. The back was rough, not finished as well as you would expect something of that quality to be. And the hallmarks were indistinct. Just now I handled the one your housekeeper showed me. The back was smoothly finished, the hallmarks clear. And the details of the crest on the front were much crisper.'

Mademoiselle nodded with growing excitement at each point she made.

'I just learned that your footman Marc lost a button last summer. It was found again after two days, so nothing more was thought of it, and his wages were not docked.'

'This is very interesting. I had not realized it had gone missing.' The small mantel clock in its Boulle case of tortoiseshell and brass chimed five times. 'He will be here any minute – it is his job to take Carlo out. We can ask him about it.'

There was a discreet knock on the bedroom door. Marc entered with the dog's collar and leash in hand. Tall and dark-haired with boyish good looks, he walked with a spring in his step. Carlo greeted his arrival by lumbering to his feet and wagging his tail.

'Marc,' Mademoiselle de Toulouse addressed him, 'I just heard about your livery button that was missing for two days.'

Marc reddened and dropped his gaze in embarrassment.

'I am not angry with you – you have served this family well since you were a boy. Ordinarily I would not have thought any more about it. But this wretched business of the dead man makes me wonder how his killer could have obtained one of our buttons to copy.' She hesitated, not sure what to say next.

It was her visitor who stepped in to ask (cheerfully but with diffidence, as if knowing she had no authority here) if there was anyone unknown or suspicious around the stable the days it was lost and found. Had he noticed any new beggars, vagrants, or drunks? Were the sellers of coffee and eau-de-vie the usual ones who served the neighborhood, or was there one he had not seen before?

Marc tried to think back to the summer, but he was clearly perplexed, and upset he'd been found out, and could not remember anyone suspicious. His accent showed he had come from the Duc's estates in Languedoc not long before. He was still a bit in awe of being in Paris, and it was easy to see how he could have been fooled by street-wise natives.

Carlo was whining to go out and he obviously was glad to have this excuse to escape. They let him go.

Suzanne turned to Anne-Marie, excited, all animosity forgotten. 'I knew it. I *knew* it. As if our family could be involved in this despicable crime!'

'The police do not believe you are. Commissaire Ferrand was very clear on that point.'

'It is not the opinion of the police I am worried about – it is the opinion of the court, and ultimately of the King. It is the gossip and rumors that are spread about my father and me, the Duc des Langoustines and Mademoiselle Toute-ours.' She pronounced these mocking nicknames, the Duc of Lobsters and Mademoiselle All-bear, with great bitterness.

Anne-Marie stared at her in amazement. 'Who would dare to say such things?'

The Duc's daughter gave a harsh unladylike bark of laughter that made her visitor wince. 'I can see you do not know the court. No one would dare to repeat these rumors to our faces, where they could be roundly challenged and refuted. They whisper it to each other behind our backs. They watch eagerly to see if the King has heard and changed his behavior toward my father. All the while these hypocrites smile at us as if they bear us no ill will. Not everyone, of course – we still have some loyal friends. But it is suffocating to live in such an atmosphere of suspicion. I came home to Paris to be able to breathe.'

'And then you walked into the kitchen to find the same rumor and innuendo had come here. I am truly sorry to have distressed you, Mademoiselle.'

The Duc's daughter acknowledged her apology with a graceful inclination of her head. There was a thoughtful silence, and Anne-Marie spoke again. 'Why did the assailant choose *your* family's crest for his costume? Was it done intentionally or at random?'

'At random?'

'Someone needed a crest to make their imitation livery believable. Did they just happen to select yours when they found the button, or did they go in search of one of your buttons?'

Mademoiselle shook her head. 'There are simpler ones to imitate. I believe ours was chosen on purpose.'

'Is there someone you suspect?'

The Duc's daughter grimaced. 'I don't need to suspect. I am

certain it is the work of the Marquis de Louvois or one of his creatures.' She gave Anne-Marie an enquiring glance to see if her visitor recognized the name. At the same time, she lowered her voice out of habit, as if afraid of being overheard by a member of court only too eager to carry tales.

'I know who he is.' Anne-Marie repeated what Le Brun had told her, including the presence of his spies among the police. 'Why? What would he gain by disgracing you?'

'My father spoke up in favor of the policies of Colbert and made mild criticism of a comment made by Louvois, who is notorious at never forgetting what he perceives as an insult. He fears and dislikes those who have more influence with the King than he does. And he does not need to gain anything from my father's disgrace. The knowledge that he has the power to destroy someone is reward enough for him.'

'Can't anything be done to limit his abuse?'

'Only the King has that power, and it is unlikely he would restrain him over so trivial a matter as our family's honor when the honor of France itself is at stake in our war with the Netherlands.'

After a brief mournful silence, Mademoiselle de Toulouse stirred and shook herself lightly, as if to shake off oppressive thoughts.

'Tell me more about the dead man. The police did not say very much – I suppose they wanted to see how much we knew, in case we were guilty after all.'

'He was stabbed in the side with a stiletto. Dr Lunague – the doctor at the Gobelins – and Commissaire Ferrand said it was an assassin's way of killing, not the sort of knifing one would get in an ordinary tavern fight. Now I think about it, the way the button threads were wrapped around his fingers was also deliberate. We don't know why he should have been singled out by a professional killer. It wasn't robbery – no one took his good coat to sell it. If they had, they would have discovered several *louis d'or* stitched into the collar and hem.'

Suzanne's eyebrows shot up.

'It puzzled us too, Mademoiselle.'

'What else can you tell me?'

'The man had the hands of a woodcarver, my Niccolò said, pointing out similar calluses on his own fingers. He had a partially carved toy shaped like a cat in his pocket, but no knife. As I told you, his linen shirt was expertly darned and the repair embellished by a row of little hearts embroidered in running stitch. I could not help thinking, what if he was married and had a family somewhere that has been wondering what happened to him? I have been married only a short time myself, but I know how I would feel if Niccolò were missing this many days. I worry and worry about this woman and what she must be feeling. I told the police about it but they are not interested in finding her; they don't even believe she exists.' A note of bitterness had crept into her tone. 'I know you are not married, Mademoiselle, but if you can imagine—'

Mademoiselle de Toulouse stirred in her chair and looked towards the window, tears shining in her eyes. 'I do not need to imagine how she would feel. My brother Geoffroi – Monsieur de Roussillon – has been in New France these last four years, and sometimes we don't hear from him for months at a time.' Her hand went up to the gold cross at her throat, another of his gifts. Each day she prayed for his safety, and her hand would go to it whenever she thought or spoke of him. It was a comfort and gave her a sense of connection she needed now more than ever.

'What does he do there? Is he with the army?'

'No, he is a naturalist. He studies the plants and animals and sends back examples for the King's gardens and the Menagerie. He has made friends with the native people as well and sends us curious things they have made.' Her voice grew steadier as she spoke, and she dabbed at her eyes with a scented handkerchief as she turned to face her guest. 'We last heard from him in September, and he was well then. But yes, I know what it is like to worry.'

Impulsively Madame Bruno reached out to her in sympathy.

'May God keep him in good health, Mademoiselle, and bring him safely home.' Suzanne leaned forward to grip the proffered hand. Its skin was dry and rough and had clearly never made acquaintance with the creams and oils used by the ladies of the court. Geoffroi's hands must feel like this now, she thought.

A discreet knock at the door made them draw apart, embarrassed. It was Marc, bringing Carlo back. The old dog returned to his place by the hearth with a contented sigh. Mademoiselle de Toulouse asked Marc to have hot chocolate and biscuits sent up to them.

'So, you see, Mademoiselle, why I must look for the man's family. I am not sure how to go about it, only that I must.'

'Yes, of course you must.' The interview was drawing to a close, but Suzanne was reluctant to let her visitor go. Here, she sensed against all odds, was an ally. She cast about for a way of meeting her again.

'I regret that I did not have an opportunity to sample your father's bread – I am sure it must be excellent. Perhaps I could send a message the next time I am in Paris, and you would bring me an assortment? You could tell me how you are faring in your search.'

Madame Bruno smiled. 'Of course, Mademoiselle, I would be happy to do that.'

There were the sounds of loud voices and running feet on the stairs, and the bedroom door was flung open with a force that sent it crashing against the wall.

Chapter Seven

Niccolò climbed the stairs to their rooms hoping that Anne-Marie was not as upset as she had been earlier. He was torn between his sympathy for her feelings, his respect for Le Brun, and his own desire to keep his position. He could not go against Le Brun's orders. His stomach growled; he was looking forward to his dinner.

But there was no kettle warming for him on the hearth, no fragrant smell of cooking – no Anne-Marie, in fact. The embers they had carefully banked after breakfast had been allowed to go out. As he rebuilt the fire and put water on to heat, he wondered what could have kept her away for so long. Gâteau, the grey cat, emerged from the corner she had curled up in, to bask in the fire's warmth and exchange greetings with Niccolò. She rubbed her head against his hand and licked his fingers. He fed her a dish of meat scraps that had been put to one side in the cupboard, hoping Anne-Marie had not been saving them for another purpose. Gâteau had no such qualms, accepting them as her right, loudly purring her thanks as she ate. When she finished, she stretched out before the fire to take full advantage of it, obliging Niccolò, chuckling, to move back his chair to accommodate her.

The courtyard clock struck six. It was full dark outside. Still Anne-Marie did not return. Why hadn't she left a note saying where she had gone? It was unlike her to simply vanish. She loved to be here to greet him at the end of the day. Where could she be? Perhaps Dr Lunague would know. He was the most likely person with whom she might talk over this morning's events.

'Yes, she came to see me,' the doctor told him. 'She was not happy with the Commissaire, nor with Monsieur Le Brun, as I'm sure you know. I did my best to persuade her to accept his orders, but she was no happier with my advice.' He smiled ruefully. 'She is young and passionate. I envy her indignation – it hasn't been smoothed away into a world-weary acceptance yet.'

That's all very well, thought Niccolò, *but where could she have gone?*

'Is there someone in her family she would turn to for advice?' the doctor asked.

'Of course – her father – she would go to him. I should have thought of that. If she stayed to help out in the shop for the dinner hour, she will still be there.' He thanked Lunague and returned to their rooms for his coat and the stout walking staff he always took with him now when venturing out after dark. He knew the route Anne-Marie preferred to take; perhaps he would meet her returning. But he arrived at Boulangerie Robert without encountering her.

His father-in-law had just finished hoisting the street lantern on the Rue d'Arras side of the bakery. Niccolò helped him lift the lantern on the Rue St Victor side. The baker greeted him with a floury embrace and hearty kisses on both cheeks. 'She came here. She was upset about this morning and asked my advice. I reminded her that her first loyalty is to her husband, now, and that she must not do anything to jeopardize your position.' He said this proudly, man-to-man. 'But she left hours ago. She went to say hello to Thérèse, and then she was gone. I assumed she went to Place Maubert to shop, and then home.'

Thérèse was still in the shop, wiping down the shelves and counter after selling the last of the loaves. It had been a busy afternoon and evening, and she had to think for a moment. 'She was serving a customer from one of the houses on the Place Royale. The next thing I knew, she was filling a basket and talking about getting a Duc's household as a customer for us. Then she scurried out as if afraid someone would stop her.'

'The Duc de Languedoc?'

'Yes, that was the name. I told her they never shopped here, but—'

He was gone before she had finished speaking.

Hurrying down the Rue des Fossés Saint-Bernard, it occurred to Niccolò that perhaps he should have let the baker know where he had gone in case he too disappeared, but there was no time to be lost by turning back.

Of all the places for her to have gone! The house of one of the foremost noblemen in France, who had the power to have her arrested simply for annoying him. What if the police were wrong, and the Duc and his household were guilty of a man's murder? Would they stop at just one?

He had been walking quickly, but this new fear made him hasten his steps even more. Other pedestrians stepped out of his way. Nearing the Place Royale, however, he forced himself to slow down and ask directions in a gentle tone of voice, so as not to alarm others and perhaps bring the night watch scurrying to find him. At last he was at the kitchen door of the Hôtel de Languedoc. It took all his self-control not to pound upon the door in a panic.

His knock was answered by a tall, dark-haired young man hastily buttoning a blue coat. Niccolò forced a smile. 'Excuse me, but I am looking for my wife. I understand she came here earlier today with a basket of bread, and she has not yet come home.'

'Who is it, Marc?' called a woman's voice from inside the kitchen.

'He says he's the husband of the woman from the bakery.'

'Well, let him in and close the door. If you let a draft hit my oven . . .'

Marc stepped aside to let him in. Reluctantly Niccolò surrendered his cloak and staff.

'Pour our visitor a cup of broth – he looks as if he could use it.'

66

She spoke calmly, matter-of-factly while putting the finishing touches on a meat pie. A pot of stew was simmering on the hearth. Niccolò's stomach growled. *Stop it*, he admonished himself. *Anne-Marie is in danger; eating can wait.*

Marc handed him a steaming bowl and went out.

The soup smelled good but Niccolò did not drink it, lest this Marc had slipped something into it. 'My wife – where is she?'

'Mademoiselle de Toulouse took her up to her room more than an hour ago, and she hasn't come down yet, so they must still be talking. Mademoiselle requested hot chocolate and biscuits, and all was calm when I took them in.' She put the pie into the oven at the side of the fireplace and shut the oven door. When she turned to face him again, her visitor was gone.

Niccolò ran down the corridor in search of the back stairs. The cook might think a pot of chocolate was harmless, but its flavor could mask poison. He could imagine the Duc's daughter smiling and offering to enhance the drink with a special flavoring, pouring it with a judicious hand, while his unsuspecting Anne-Marie eagerly took the proffered cup . . . He raced up the back stairs, ignoring the protesting cries of the cook behind him. He knew he could outrun the stout old woman.

Without knowing the precise location of Mademoiselle's suite of rooms, he could make a shrewd guess based on other *hôtels* his fellow artisans had told him about. The ground floor was for utilitarian rooms like the kitchen; the first floor for the public reception rooms; the second floor for the family bedrooms; the top floors for the nursery and the servants' sleeping quarters. Mademoiselle's room would be two flights up. It was dark in the stairwell, and he almost tripped on the first landing, but he made it up the rest of the way without mishap. He could hear the cook's labored breathing as she lumbered after him, her gasps of 'No – wait!' growing faint.

He came out of the stairwell into a dark corridor with a crack of light around a door at one end. He ran toward the light and flung the door open.

The two women, who had been leaning toward each other in calm conversation, turned to him, startled, and leapt to their feet. The old dog dozing at the fireplace lumbered to his feet and gave a series of deep barks – whether in defense of its mistress or in protest at the interruption of its nap was not clear. Niccolò was too well prepared to rescue an endangered Anne-Marie to think what to do in this situation. He came to a sudden halt and stared back at them, just as the cook finally caught up with him, armed with the wooden rolling pin she had been using to make the pie-crust. She brandished it ready to use at her mistress's command. 'Don't worry, Mademoiselle, I've got him!' she panted.

Mademoiselle de Toulouse stared at the two intruders in amazement.

Now I've done it, Niccolò thought. *She'll send for the watch and have me thrown in prison. Anne-Marie is not the only one whose impetuosity leads to trouble.* He braced for Mademoiselle's fury.

To his amazement, she burst into peal after peal of laughter until tears ran down her cheeks and she had to hold her sides. She dabbed at her eyes with a lace-edged handkerchief and regained her composure. Anne-Marie tried to hold back her mirth but soon joined her.

'Madame Dupont, put that down before someone is hurt.' Slowly the cook lowered her rolling pin, still breathing hard. 'Carlo, be quiet.' The barking ceased. Mademoiselle turned to Niccolò. 'You must be Monsieur Bruno,' she said with the courtesy and aplomb born of court life. 'I have just been talking with your charming wife.'

To Niccolò's embarrassment, his stomach growled loudly in response. It seemed as if Mademoiselle would collapse in laughter again, but with some effort she regained control of herself. 'Madame Dupont, please send up three bowls of stew. Make one of them a large bowl.'

'But, Mademoiselle, that's no fit dinner for you! I was planning an omelet, your favorite kind with shavings of ham and cheese.'

'Then you may bring the omelet afterward. Make a large one

that all three of us can share. And a bottle of *vin rouge* as well.'
The cook curtsied and left.

'Monsieur Bruno, please take a seat next to your wife.' She gestured to a second *tabouret* and sat down again in her armchair. 'I would like to hear what you can tell me.'

Thus it was that they found themselves, three nights later, following Marc, the footman, through the frosty streets on their way to meet the Duc de Languedoc. As the invited guests of Mademoiselle de Toulouse, no longer suppliants at the tradesman's entrance, they were admitted through the front door, relieved of their cloaks (and Niccolò of his staff) and taken up the ceremonial stair that doubled back to reach the first floor. Marc had traded his outdoor lantern for a silver candelabrum, but its three candles did little to dispel the general gloom. Anne-Marie looked in eagerly as they walked through the great public rooms, but it was difficult to make out any details of the décor with the rooms in such darkness, their furniture shrouded in sheets. An occasional reflection from the gilding on the elaborately carved paneling and picture frames, a gleam of bright color here and there from the paintings and ceiling decoration whetted her appetite for more. She must not linger, however, and quickened her steps to keep up with the men. She slipped her hand into Nic's and was comforted.

Only when they had entered the fourth room, in which numerous candles shed a brighter light, did Marc pause to let them take in their surroundings. To Anne-Marie's surprise, it was a bedroom – evidently the Duc's, as a manservant was taking a nightshirt and nightcap out of a chest, prior to laying them out on the bed. It was the same kind of bed she had seen in the room of Mademoiselle de Toulouse, a four-poster made even taller by high ostrich plumes on each post, and entirely enclosed by curtains. But while the daughter's bed curtains were plain green velvet, these were composed of panels of deep red velvet framed by wide bands of ribbon worked in gold and silver threads – a bed fit for a Duc or a King. On either side of the bed hung portraits of Louis XIII, who had once spent the night, and of the young Louis XIV in coronation robes. (Anne-Marie wondered whether he had accepted an invitation. He was known to be uneasy at the thought of spending the night in his capital city, with however loyal a subject.) The tapestries on side walls continued the royal theme with triumphal scenes of what appeared to be Roman emperors. Across from the bed two windows were hung with curtains matching the bed hangings; between them, a dressing table with a deep red velvet covering held stands with wigs and caps. A carpet in a scrolling floral pattern with a dark blue background lay underfoot.

In this room at last they could see the scene on the ceiling. In the center, the ancient gods gathered peacefully in a sunlit blue sky, lolling on beds of fat white clouds. In the compartments of the eaves, fat putti played with the attributes of the gods. Anne-Marie was able to make out Jupiter's eagle, Juno's peacock, and Mars' shield and helmet, before Marc admitted them into the Duc's cabinet.

After the dark chilly rooms, the bright light inside the Duc's cabinet was almost painful to their eyes. A cheerful fire burned in the grate and sweet-smelling beeswax candles were scattered throughout the room. Their light glinted off the polished parquet floor, the gilt bronze mounts on the tall bookshelves that lined three walls of the room and the gilt lettering on the spines of the books. A large mirror over the fireplace in the fourth wall seemed to expand both the light and the space. The mantelpiece displayed a pair of Japanese porcelain bowls mounted in silver and several curious wooden objects. Niccolò's eye was drawn to these immediately; it was only with an effort that he restrained himself from crossing the room to examine them before making a proper greeting to their host. Dominating the center of the room was the Duc's armchair with a reclining mechanism, an unusual item of furniture he had ordered from England. A *torchère* to one side of the chair supported a silver candelabrum to provide plentiful light for reading; on the other side a small folding table held a glass carafe of wine and four goblets. Three chairs had been brought in; Anne-Marie noted with amusement that she and Nic had risen in status from being seated on *tabourets* to being offered chairs with a back.

Mademoiselle de Toulouse rose to welcome them. 'Madame Bruno, Monsieur Bruno, welcome. Come meet my father – and see what my brother sent us!'

Anne-Marie had never before met a Duc; she had imagined him as very like the provost of the Bakers' Guild, a tall imposing man with a booming voice who strutted rather than walked and left one in no doubt of his position of authority. Henri Armand François Sainterre, Duc de Languedoc, carried instead an air of quiet self-confidence. He was small and fine-boned like his daughter. In his presence Anne-Marie again felt awkward about her size. His eyes were the same blue as his daughter's, his glance shrewd; even when his face was in shadow Anne-Marie could see that flash of color and feel them on her. His hands were well cared for. He was clean-shaven and appeared to have only sparse grey hair under his cap; his dressing gown and cap of gold silk brocade were edged with fur. His shoes, however, were of a kind she had never seen before, made of supple, unpolished animal skin, fringed in the same material, with curious embroidery on the tops in a material she did not recognize. The shoes were so much at odds with the rest of his appearance that she could not help staring; only a sharp nudge from Nic recalled her to good manners. To her embarrassment, the Duc laughed, but it was a good-natured rather than derisive sound.

'You are looking at a pair of moccassins. Monsieur de Roussillon – my son – sent them to me from New France,' he told her. 'The *sauvages* make them out of deerskin for their own use and decorate them with the quills of an animal we don't have in Europe, *un porc-épic*. They are surprisingly comfortable. My son wrote that he owns several pairs.'

The Duc was far from being intimidated by men of lesser rank who towered over him, but he had found it wise, as a rule, to defuse any potentially awkward situation through courtesy. He chattered on, seeking to put this big woman and her even taller husband at ease. Too, it gave him the opportunity to examine and assess these visitors whom his daughter had insisted that he meet.

Although he had told his daughter that the scandal would pass, he was less nonchalant than he liked to appear. He had worked hard all his life to retain the King's trust and did not wish to lose it now. During the Fronde, the civil war of his youth, when the nobles of Paris took up arms against Anne of Austria and Cardinal Mazarin, the boy King's Spanish mother and his Italian chief minister, the Duc de Languedoc declined to join his friends, spending most of those years at his estates far from Paris and writing to Louis to pledge his support. He had been shrewd enough, even then, to see beyond the current situation to the memories the adult King would carry. He had seen, too, how quickly and mercilessly the King could act to punish those whose loyalty he doubted. It was one thing to retire at will to one's estates in Languedoc; it was quite another to be banished to them in disgrace.

When Suzanne told him delightedly about her new allies, an Italian sculptor and a baker's daughter, who had no experience in matters of this sort, and who seemed to have stumbled across evidence by accident, he was skeptical. He did not see how they could help. But Suzanne wanted so desperately to help and pleaded her case – citing Geoffroi's experience of mixing with all classes of people in Quebec, finding that they often possessed experience and skills that he did not, and was grateful for – that he had agreed to meet the couple. It was always a relief to get away from the inadequacies of his small rooms at Saint-Germain-en-Laye and return to the house he had lived in all his life, where Madame Dupont knew how to cook a dinner precisely to his taste and he could dip again into favorite natural history and travel books in his extensive library.

Today there had been the added pleasure of a package and long letters from Geoffroi. Suzanne had opened hers right away, but the Duc deliberately delayed reading his letter until he was comfortably seated in his cabinet in dressing gown and cap, with moccasins on his feet. He always wore them when reading letters from his son or writing to him. The package contained a large wooden bowl of smooth burled elm with a rudimentary bird's head rising above the rim. The letter included a long description of the making of the bowl, the copy of one he had admired on a visit to the Algonquin tribe, and of the ceremonial uses sacred to their religion to which it would be put. Tactfully, Geoffroi's letter had refrained from comment on the Jesuits who were there to convert the tribes. He wrote little about himself except to reassure his father that he was in good health and good spirits. To Suzanne he had sent a letter illustrated with pen sketches and observations of the Native women, comparing them with their European counterparts.

While Geoffroi's letters were a welcome distraction from the Duc's present worries, they brought up others. He had always assumed that his son would come home but it was now four years that he had been away, and he showed no sign of wanting to do so. Instead Geoffroi always looked forward to the exploring he would do the next summer, the notes he would compile over the winter, the book he would eventually write to take its place in his father's library among the others that had whetted his curiosity about New France. At times the Duc worried, with a painful squeeze of the heart, whether he would ever see his son again. He was finding it more and more difficult to imagine Geoffroi taking his rightful place at court as one of the always-loyal Sainterres of Languedoc.

'What a handsome bowl,' his visitor said, interrupting his thoughts. 'May I see it?'

The Duc watched Niccolò's hands run over its smooth surface with an almost voluptuous caress. He could see, in his mind's eye, Geoffroi doing the same, and felt a fresh surge of longing for his son; but he pushed the thought away to focus on their guests and the matter at hand. The two men talked about the bowl, Niccolò making observations from his experience that, the Duc was interested to note, agreed with what Geoffroi had described. His respect for the young man rose.

The Duc directed Niccolò in placing the bowl among the other native artifacts on the library shelves.

When Niccolò was again seated, the Duc poured wine for each of them and turned the conversation to the unpleasant issue of the dead man and the counterfeit button. 'My daughter has told me something of how you became involved and what you found out, but I should like to hear all of it from yourselves.' He looked inquiringly at Anne-Marie, inviting her to speak. He paid close attention to her account of the doctor's examination, Commissaire Ferrand's report, Le Brun's warning, and the conversation in his own kitchen. Niccolò added his observations. When they had done, he refilled their glasses and sat back, thinking.

Niccolò broke into his thoughts. 'We regret your good name should have come to be mixed up in this. Who would want to slander you in this way?'

'There are many at court who are jealous that I have the ear of the King and who wish to put themselves in my place. I always have to be on my guard against slander and gossip. Fortunately, the King does not listen to them as my enemies do and knows my true worth.'

'But this is far worse than a war of words or a matter of honor,' Anne-Marie said. 'This is murder. Which of your enemies would have the means and the will to cause murder to be done?'

'It is not difficult to hire someone to do murder – so I have been told, you understand – not from personal experience! And anyone may order a suit of clothes from a tailor, saying he admired someone else's suit. But silver buttons require an investment.' He shook his head. 'Most of the men who mutter against me do no more than that – mutter. Few have the energy and ability to hatch a plot such as this. Monsieur Colbert could do so, and as the minister in charge of manufactures and trade, he would certainly have access to silversmiths only too willing to do him a favor, but he prefers to use his energy for the benefit of the realm. The Marquis de Louvois, on the other hand . . .'

'Papa, I told her it must be he! He has resented you for years, and he is the sort of man who would not think twice about ordering murder to be done.'

'I suppose I must be thankful that it was not *my* murder that he ordered,' replied the Duc drily. 'But I am sorry for the man who got caught up in this. Do we know anything about him that would tell us how he came to be involved?'

'We know only that he was a woodworker by trade,' replied Niccolò. 'There was a half-finished toy cat in his pocket and his hands were callused where mine are.' He pointed out the areas on his own hands. 'His clothes were those of an ordinary workman. He was not killed for a robbery. His coat was not taken, and several gold coins hidden in the collar and hem were still there. Anne-Marie believes he was married, perhaps with a young child, but we do not know that for certain.'

'I would like to know if he was killed simply to have my name involved in a murder or if there was some other reason, and the person behind it took that as an opportunity to add slander to murder.'

'Does it matter, Papa? The use of the livery and buttons shows premeditation either way.'

'I would feel better if I did not think an innocent man had died simply to have me slandered.' His voice was calm, but there was reproof in the look he gave his daughter.

Mademoiselle de Toulouse blushed and hung her head. 'I am sorry, Papa. I was thinking of him only as he related to you, not as an individual in his own right.' She crossed herself and shivered, as if only now waking up to the fact of a man's death.

They were all quiet for a moment, listening to the crackle of the logs in the fireplace.

'How do we go about finding the jeweler or silversmith who made the buttons?' Anne-Marie asked.

'What do you mean?' Niccolò replied. 'We can ask them. Surely there aren't so many, even in Paris.'

'Yes, of course, but – I would not want the fact that someone was asking questions to get back to whoever is behind this. Especially a person like me, who would have no other business at a jeweler's. I want to find out who killed the man in the Bièvre, not share his fate.'

'I think,' said Mademoiselle de Toulouse slowly, 'that it is not too early for me to start buying gifts for Noël. They will not be surprised to see me in their shops, and it will seem very natural if I inquire after the buttons.' She smiled a little. 'And I do not think the Marquis de Louvois would try to kill *me*.'

'Suzanne?'

'I want to *do* something, Papa. We cannot leave all the effort to our friends here. Don't worry; I can sound as silly and empty-headed as you like, to throw off suspicion. I've had a lifetime's practice at court,' she finished tartly.

'You could send a servant to inquire,' Anne-Marie pointed out.

'I don't want servants gossiping about the reaction of the household and putting words in our mouths. I want to control the conversation.'

The Duc held up his hand and the others fell silent, turning to him expectantly. He took another sip of wine while he thought over what he wanted to say. He liked the young couple and could understand what had attracted his daughter's attention to them. There would be advantages to employing them: they could go places and ask questions that he and Suzanne could not. But could he, in good conscience, encourage them to go forward with the investigation?

Finally, he spoke, looking directly at his visitors. 'I would welcome your help, but you must weigh carefully the very real risks involved. You have seen the dead man and know what the result could be. We have no clear idea of whether the murder was committed in order to slander the Languedoc family, or whether the slander was merely an additional bonus for whoever planned this. I would like to have our name cleared,' he said, with a glance at his daughter, 'but not at the cost of your lives.'

He paused. In the silence they could hear the hiss of a guttering candle. Even Suzanne was silent, as if realizing for the first time the enormity of what she would ask of them.

'I will not ask you for an answer tonight,' he told Niccolò and Anne-Marie. 'You must talk it over between you. I will talk with Suzanne. If you have decided to go ahead, perhaps next week Anne-Marie could bring another basket from the excellent Boulangerie Robert. Your husband would naturally wish to accompany you at this hour to make sure you come to no harm. Agreed?' They all nodded. 'Then I will thank you for a very agreeable, informative visit, and wish you good night.'

Marc led Anne-Marie and Niccolò to a waiting fiacre. He paid the driver generously, to judge by the man's thanks.

Anne-Marie was eager to talk, but Niccolò put his finger to his lips. As the small vehicle began to move, he cautioned her to be alert and ready to get out at a moment's notice should he give her a signal. He looked out the window the whole journey to make sure that they really were being taken home. The Duc's friendly demeanor could have been a ruse, he thought, and this journey a convenient way of being rid of them. He felt faintly foolish when they arrived home at the Gobelins without incident, to be admitted by the yawning porter.

It had been an exciting evening, but as they climbed the stairs to their rooms they were overcome with weariness and were soon fast asleep with Gâteau purring on the covers between them.

Chapter Eight

They overslept the next morning, waking only as the Gobelins clock was striking eight. They had arranged to attend St Nicolas-du-Chardonnet instead of the Gobelins Oratory, and to have Sunday dinner with Anne-Marie's family. There was no time now to discuss the decisions to be made, if they were to arrive in time for the ten o'clock Mass preferred by the Boulangers. The ringing of church bells en route hurried their steps. They arrived as St Nicolas' final peal was dying in the frosty air and took their seats next to Anne-Marie's father and mother. The service began, soothing in its familiar ritual; but today they responded by rote rather than in their usual heartfelt way, each occupied with other thoughts.

Help me to find the right thing to do. Anne-Marie addressed her prayer to her patron saints, Anne and the Virgin Mary. *There are many good reasons to go no further with this matter: my father and Monsieur Le Brun and Dr Lunague and the Duc de Languedoc have enumerated them. Niccolò, too, would be more than willing to let the matter drop. I wish with all my heart that I could do so and not feel uneasy about it. But what if there is a loving widow, possibly a child as well, who are missing the man from the Bièvre, wondering what became of him. Are they all right? Are they safe? Do they have the money, with him gone, for food and fires and warm clothing, now winter is closing in? Do they have friends who can help? I need to know if they exist, that they are safe, even if none of the others concerned in this seem to care. Holy Virgin and Saint Anne, you were wives and mothers. You knew what it was like to have a loving husband, raise a family, have tragedy strike.*

I too love my husband and long for his welfare with all my heart. And yet. And yet. She gazed earnestly at the painted faces that looked adoringly at the sleeping Christ Child and composed her mind to receive their reply.

Is it for the widow's sake you want to continue, a woman's voice gently rebuked her, *or for your own? You enjoyed helping the doctor and being paid a man's wages for it. You have met Mademoiselle de Toulouse and her father the Duc and been encouraged eagerly by one and cautioned by the other. Your path and theirs would never have crossed but for this enquiry – and if you give it up, you will give up the acquaintance with them, as it is the only thing you have in common. Are you sure,* the voice asked again, *that it is not pleasure and pride that drive you forward?*

Anne-Marie blushed, glad that her face was bent in prayer so that none would see it. It was true, she had been enjoying the pursuit of the enquiry, a continuation of the way in which her life had opened up, these past several months. No longer was she the fat, unmarriageable daughter trapped forever between the counter and the accounts. Niccolò had given her the respected status of a married woman and brought her to live in a wonderful place dedicated to the making of beautiful things.

Then she sobered. As her father had reminded her, she was a wife now and must always keep her husband's best interests at heart. She did not think Niccolò would outright forbid her to go forward, though as her husband he had every right to do so. But if he told her with sad finality that he did not wish her to do this, then she would not.

She thought again of the dead man and said a small prayer to him asking his forgiveness for enjoying the benefits bestowed by his arrival. She should not be enjoying this quite so much. *If I can,* she promised him, *I will make amends by finding your family, making sure they are safe, and doing what I can to bring your killer to justice.*

Niccolò, kneeling beside his wife, addressed his prayers to St Nicolas, his patron saint as well as patron of this church. *I am happy at the Gobelins, finding fulfillment in what I do, and I have no wish to lose my position. I respect Monsieur Le Brun and owe him a good deal for the personal interest he has taken in me. I don't yearn to break out of a mold as Anne-Marie does. I worked hard to get where I am, learning my skills and then walking all the way from Italy in the hope of working for Louis XIV.*

But I love Anne-Marie. When I was attacked, she took care of me. No one else in Paris cared about me. I could so easily have ended up like the poor wretch in the Bièvre. Her mother would have been just as happy to send me to the impersonal care of the crowded city hospital. It was in thanks for my recovery under Anne-Marie's care that I carved, as an offering to this church, the Christ Child that caught the attention of Monsieur Le Brun. She has brought me both health and luck.

And she is more – she is my wife, my home. Without her, what sort of second-rate lodgings would I be living in? What sort of women would I be forced to consort with? Anne-Marie owes me obedience as her husband, but I owe her something as well: we have pledged our lives to each other. I have always admired the courage and determination she showed in facing down her mother's objections. Her determination now reminds me of how she was then, and I cannot but admire her for it, even if in this instance it may be to my disadvantage. I wish to support her. But Monsieur Le Brun has forbidden us to take any such step. Dare I disobey him?

When Mass ended, the rest of the family returned immediately to the Boulanger house, but Niccolò and Anne-Marie, as was their custom, took a stroll through the unfinished church interior, noting what progress in its decoration had been made since their last visit. Anne-Marie had watched the church being built and decorated, and its dedication had coincided with her first communion. She and it had grown up together, and she felt a proprietary interest in it, looking to see all that was new. Coming around the apse, with its series of chapels devoted to individual saints, they were surprised to come face to face with Monsieur and Madame Le Brun. He had been so much in their thoughts that they started guiltily at the sight of him, only belatedly recovering their wits to make the proper bow and curtsy due him.

He regarded them with an eye at once benign and wary. 'I was visiting my mother's tomb in the Chapel of St Charles.'

'I remember when it was put in place last year,' Anne-Marie told him, thinking back to that day when the dray and horses had delivered the elaborate black sarcophagus and white marble figures. The men grunted as they slowly moved it into the church from the door on the Rue des Bernardins, the tomb's sculptor Jean-Baptiste Tuby exhorting them in Italian and Le Brun in French, to be careful with the precious cargo.

Le Brun now took Niccolò into the chapel to show him the details of the carving, and how the placement of the tomb in relation to the window put his mother's figure in the light and consigned Death to the shadows.

The chapel's small space did not allow for many visitors, so Anne-Marie remained in the nave to exchange a few words with Madame Le Brun. Ordinarily she would have excused herself to help her mother finish preparing the dinner, but today she felt the need to stay close to Niccolò. She knew he was less than happy about the course of action she wanted to take, and she was afraid lest he make a clean breast of the matter to Le Brun, earning them another injunction that she would not be able to rationalize and find a way around. She kept one ear cocked to the men's conversation as she and Madame Le Brun talked about their plans for Noël. But the two artists seemed absorbed in the fall of light from the chapel window and Le Brun's further plans for the space.

The church bell struck the noon hour.

'We must go, Charles,' said Madame Le Brun. 'Remember we are dining at the Testelins. We must not keep them waiting.'

'I beg your pardon for keeping you from your dinner,' said Niccolò. 'Anne-Marie and I must be going as well.'

He chatted about the church and the tomb all the way down the street, and Anne-Marie's heart sank. What had he decided?

★

Like her new allies, Mademoiselle de Toulouse prepared for church. When at Saint-Germain-en-Laye she would attend Mass with the King and Queen, but this morning she would go instead to the nearby convent church of St Catherine. Like many of the well-born young women of the Place Royale, she had been a pupil of its school. The nuns had encouraged her quick intelligence and she had fond memories of her days there. She dressed more soberly than usual. Even after several years, it was hard to deviate from the schoolgirl custom of wearing a plain grey dress (even if those particular dresses had been given to her maid long since) – and went with the women of the household to the mid-morning Mass at which the public was welcome. They parted at the door, she to sit at the front of the nave in a seat for worshippers of high rank, while her servants sat in back. To sit together in public would smack of Protestantism and radical thinking and upset the order of things. She was a Duc's daughter, was known to the neighborhood as a Duc's daughter, and must therefore be seen to act like one.

Her offering for the collection plate this morning was a *louis d' or* – an unusually generous amount, offered up not in ostentation but in wholehearted gratitude. Her first prayers of thanksgiving, as always, were for her father and brother: Geoffroi was in good health and good spirits and undaunted by the prospect of another North American winter. Today these were followed by expressions of gratitude for bringing Anne-Marie and Niccolò into her life: with all that had gone wrong since the discovery of the body, all the snide asides and suspicious looks and false smiles at court, it was heartening to meet people who believed in her family's innocence and were willing to help. People who, though unrelated to the family and not of their class, neither looked the other way nor calculated what there might be to gain from the situation.

After the couple had gone home the night before, Mademoiselle de Toulouse had tried to talk with her father about whether to go ahead with her plan to visit jewelers and silversmiths, but he had told her that he would not make up her mind for her: she would need to come to her own decision about it. He had given her fair warning about the dangers involved: she would need to look to her own conscience and courage.

She prayed for guidance, and to find some of that courage: to St Elisabeth, her patron saint, and to St Catherine, patron saint of the convent, who had given herself as the bride of Christ and endured horrible tortures on the wheel in consequence. *Would I have had that sort of courage?* she asked herself. *I would not* – her whole body shuddered in revulsion – *the saints were, after all, exceptional individuals.* There were no answers there.

But then she thought again of her brother, the boy with the pampered upbringing who had voluntarily undertaken a dangerous, strenuous life in search of knowledge that was dearer to him than safety. Geoffroi was not a saint, far from it – she earned reproving looks from those around her in the middle of their prayers by laughing out loud at a sudden memory of his youthful mischief – but he showed the kind of human courage she could emulate: the courage of a Sainterre de Languedoc. She had her answer.

She finished her prayers, as always, with one for her brother's continued safety. Afterwards she sat up a little straighter, if possible given the amount of boning in her stays. With jubilant steps she walked down the nave of the church after the service to rejoin the household servants. Her father, returning from Mass at the Church of St Paul on the Rue St Antoine, was waiting for her at the door. Her heart brimmed over with love for him and gladness at the task she had undertaken. She would do her part to clear their name and bring the perpetrators to justice.

Dinner with the family was an unusually tense affair for Anne-Marie. She enjoyed being with her niece and nephews, but today they were fretful, jangling her already raw nerves. While Niccolò was in conversation with Toinette's husband and Madame Boulanger was busy with Toinette and the grandchildren, Robert took the opportunity to re-open the conversation from Wednesday's lunch, repeating much of what he said then and elaborating upon it. He told her how worried he had been when Niccolò had come looking for her that evening! Not until he had got word the next day that she was safe, could he breathe easily again. He had not said anything to his wife, 'not wanting to worry your mother'.

More likely, Anne-Marie thought cynically, *not wanting to hear her laments and complaints about me, her worries that whatever I might be involved in, I would prove yet again to be the fat ungainly daughter whose competencies she ignored and awkwardness enlarged upon.* Anne-Marie found she was grinding her teeth and forced herself to stop. She had hoped to leave this sort of resentment behind when she married, but its tug seemed irresistible whenever she returned to her parents' house.

She longed to tell her father that the Duc de Languedoc and his daughter had given their approval and asked her to continue investigating, but she knew better than to say so. Alarmed rather than reassured, he would warn her that mixing with the Duc's family was not for the likes of them, that they could be using her and might not lift a finger to help if she got into trouble – especially if what she did got *them* into trouble.

Her mother would have loved this glimpse into a world she had always longed for, the description of Mademoiselle de Toulouse and her father, of their fine clothes and jewelry and elegant home. Silver buttons! Lace cuffs! A chiming Boulle clock on the mantelpiece! Hot chocolate to drink every day, not only special occasions! Her mother would be purring like Gâteau at the thought of all this, reveling in their family's association with the noble house. Alas, it was all too likely she would make a bragging point of it among her acquaintances. The news was bound to spread and could reach the wrong ears. Four lives depended on Anne-Marie's discretion.

There was also a note of sadness in her thoughts. *Suzanne has met me only twice and liked and accepted me for who I am, while my mother has known me my whole life and can only perceive my shortcomings. And Maman will never change.*

As if summoned by her daughter's thoughts, Marguerite Boulanger appeared in the doorway, an annoyed look on her face. 'Anne-Marie, come help with the children! Your sister and I have our hands full enough.'

'*Oui*, Maman,' she sighed, and followed her out.

When the Languedoc household returned to the Place Royale, Madame Dupont told them dinner would be ready in about an hour. Suzanne was surprised to hear the Duc request that it be served in her room. His custom was to eat in his cabinet; she had expected that he would do so today so that he could reread and ponder Geoffroi's letter. He liked to read the letters aloud, interspersing commentary as though he were carrying on a conversation with his son. Once, when she had teased him about it, she was astounded to see tears glittering in his eyes. One had escaped to roll down his cheek. Through the surface of the urbane courtier had emerged an old man in grief and pain, missing his son. Embarrassed at having intruded upon such private feelings, she had darted forward to kiss his cheek before retreating, but he had caught her hand and held it firm while he regained control of himself. It was not a memory she liked to recall, catching her father at that vulnerable moment, but it came to mind now when he asked to dine in her room and gave her an intuitive leap of understanding: he had lost one child for far too long to the North American wilderness, and he was frightened of losing the other to foolhardiness and intrigue. He was storing up memories of her in case his worst fears came to pass. It must be costing him a good deal to not outright forbid her further involvement, and her purpose, so pure and intent this morning at church, wavered for a long moment. *I will be careful,* she promised him silently, *I will make you as proud of my courage as you are of Geoffroi's.*

'I requested your room, my dear, because I was hoping you would play for me. Your teacher goes into raptures about the difficult pieces you have mastered. I would like to hear for myself. I have been too long remiss . . .'

She placed a hand on his arm and the flow of words came to a halt.

'You owe me no apologies, Papa. Of course, I will play for you. We so rarely have a day to ourselves,' she added wistfully.

He nodded and smiled. 'I will go to my room to change. I'll come to yours when dinner is ready.' He raised her hand to his lips and was gone.

Suzanne climbed the stairs slowly, more wearily than a morning in church would warrant. Carlo, from his usual position on the hearth, greeted her with a happy bark and several thumps of his tail. She smiled and crossed the room to rub his belly and pat his white muzzle. While they were all out, the fire had died down to a few coals glowing in the ashes. Just then the housemaid, who had changed from her church dress back into the one she wore for her domestic tasks, came in with a bundle of wood to clear the fireplace and start a new fire. Startled by the sight of Suzanne kneeling on the cold hearth, she broke into apologies.

'Nonsense,' Suzanne waved them away. 'It's in the nature of fires to burn out. You are here now.' Then, impulsively, 'Show me how to build a fire.'

'You, Mademoiselle? But that's my job!'

'Yes, and you are an expert at it.' She smiled at the startled girl. 'Monsieur de Roussillon – my brother – he left before you came to us – writes in his letters that he often needs to build his own fires on his travels in New France. He had to learn how when he first went there. I want to learn too. Show me.'

No less startled, but trained to obey, the girl knelt next to her mistress and showed her how to pick up the live coals carefully with the fire shovel, how to sweep up the ashes, build a nest of kindling with the larger pieces on top, and when to reintroduce the coals. Suzanne watched intently. It was the first time she had heard the young woman say more than, 'Oui, Mademoiselle' or 'Non, Mademoiselle.'

She thanked the girl when she was done and went to her dressing room, where her maid helped her to remove her now dusty dress and put on a dressing gown. She emerged and sat down at her keyboard to practice.

Just before they parted for the night, Suzanne told her father of her decision. He sighed deeply but smiled at her. 'You have as much courage as your brother.'

She glowed at his praise. 'I know you wish he were here.'

'I do and I do not. It is just as well that one of us is out of it.'

'I will get to the bottom of this, Papa, so that we can all be out of it.'

The Duc sighed again, smiled briefly, and wished her good night.

That night, when they were sitting in their chairs in front of the fireplace, Niccolò said to Anne-Marie: 'I must obey M. Le Brun. I cannot lose the job that is our livelihood, and that I worked so long to get. But I will not stop you from doing what you need to do. Should you ever need my assistance, I will of course give it.' Anne-Marie let out the breath she felt she been holding all day and took his hand. No words were needed.

Chapter Nine

For her day of visits to the jewelers' shops of the Place Dauphine and the arcades of the Palais de Justice, Suzanne hired Marc's brothers to transport her in their *vinaigrette*, a small enclosed two-wheeled coach that one pulled and the other pushed. The Languedoc coach, more suited for travel on the large boulevards and the roads between Paris and Saint-Germain, would not have fitted into the small congested streets of the Ile de la Cité. She told her maid not to come with her, to the girl's disappointment; the vicarious purchasing of jewels and silks was one of the perks of her job. Suzanne began with a visit to Monsieur de Lamerie, the silversmith who had made the original buttons, and from whom she now bought two silver pendants as gifts for her friends. She wanted to reassure him that, although she would be asking questions of other jewelers that would make it seem as if she were looking for a new supplier, this was merely part of her inquiries. He could not offer any suggestions as to who might have made the forgeries, but he wished her luck in her search.

From his shop, she proceeded to several others that made wares for members of the court, choosing other pendants and brooches with care, asking how they were made, casually mentioning buttons to see if anyone had an uneasy reaction. But no one did. It was time-consuming and rather discouraging, all this discussion and semblance of good will, when she just wanted to get on with the matter. Suzanne tried to quell her impatience for results and took an hour's respite at a mercer to buy ribbons to give with the silver trinkets.

Having exhausted the possibilities of the Ile de la Cité, she made her way to the Rue Saint-Honoré, where new shops of luxury goods had opened in recent years. She had the men go slowly as she scanned store windows and made them stop in front of one with a particularly appealing array. Getting out of the small coach, she glanced up at the sign over the door: Le Bouton. She laughed ruefully to herself. Despite its name however, the shop apparently sold few types of buttons, and those made elsewhere.

The next shop seemed promising. The jeweler purred that, the previous week, the Marquis de Louvois had ordered a gift from him for the Marquise. How roundly and proudly those titles rolled off his tongue! The gift, however, turned out to be a necklace and earrings of rare and costly black pearls. Perhaps she would like to see some? She shook her head. Nothing that appealed to Louvois would have any attraction for her. Aloud, she said only that she preferred white pearls. He offered to show her several strands, but she declined and escaped the shop without making any purchases.

She was able to spend two days in this manner before returning to Saint-Germain-en-Laye, where Louis XIV, ever averse to living in Paris, held court during the winter months. Twelve leagues to the northwest of the city, it was near enough to visit Paris when he needed to, but close to the forests for the hunting that was his preferred sport. Suzanne's heart sank as the great bulk of the Old Château came into view and she mentally turned her thoughts from Paris to life at court. Tonight was the birthday celebration for her best friend Laure. *I can tell her and anyone else who asks that I went from shop to shop looking for just the right thing.*

Laure was delighted with her gift, a silver laurel leaf, a play on her name, and several ribbons to wear with it. Which was all very well, but Suzanne had not succeeded in her goal of discovering the button's maker. Still, it felt good to have a purpose and play an active role in clearing her family's name. Too much of her life at court was spent filling empty hours with amusements that had grown stale, hiding her intelligence in order to fit in, to not be mocked. Yet, as she looked about her at the other guests at the birthday celebration, she also felt a sense of belonging. It was her milieu; as the daughter of a Duc, it was her right to belong. She knew its inhabitants and its rules of etiquette based on everyone's relative rank – who was allowed to sit down, on what sort of seat, in the presence of whom. She knew the strengths of this one, the weaknesses of that one, who was in love with whom, and who had met with success or disappointment – and most important of all, who was in or out of favor with the King. She still felt a thrill in the presence of Louis XIV, the anointed ruler of France. She flushed with pleasure when he spoke to her that evening, reassured that her family remained in his favor.

Afterward, she returned, drooping with fatigue, to the rooms she and her father occupied. Because of their rank, they were able to live in the Old Château instead of renting rooms in the town. She found him enjoying a glass of wine by candlelight. Sipping the wine that he poured for her, she told him apologetically of her futile search.

'It was still useful,' he assured her. 'The process of elimination is as important as discovery. I am very proud of you.'

His words brought tears to her eyes.

'The Marquis de Louvois may not be able to afford such extravagant gifts for his Marquise for much longer,' the Duc remarked conversationally. 'Nothing has been said publicly, but I understand from hints in two or three conversations that the King is displeased over the most recent developments in the war in the Netherlands. Apparently, there was to have been a big surprise assault last month, but it was called off in embarrassing circumstances. A small reconnaissance force was ambushed and most of them killed. Only one man survived to make it back to the main camp. It seems Louvois's spies were sold false information. The whole army could have walked into the trap.'

'Are these rumors true?'

'It would seem so. Louvois's staff is sworn to secrecy, but Colbert was heard to complain about the cost of feeding and paying the army while it sits idle until the spring offensive can begin. It is a costly embarrassment for France in both money and prestige. The King does not easily forgive such things.'

'Then I would pray for Louvois's continued lack of success – if only it did not involve so much loss of life and France's lack of success as well.' Her shoulders sagged as her weariness returned. 'It is difficult to know what to hope for, Papa.'

'A good night's sleep,' he replied. 'We need to dance attendance upon them again in the morning. *Bonne nuit,* Suzanne.'

'*Dors bien,* Papa.'

Niccolò had intended merely to give Anne-Marie consent to pursue her search, not to be involved himself. He knew that she was visiting the fairs and markets where toy-sellers could be found, hoping to find a duplicate of the little wooden cat, but she had not yet succeeded. His heart ached for her disappointment. He longed to help her, but he reminded himself sternly that Monsieur Le Brun had made clear his displeasure and that the consequences of ignoring his employer's command could be dire. Yet his mind could not help speculating, while his hands worked diligently on a pair of figures for another cabinet, where the dead man might have been employed. If what Anne-Marie supposed was true, and the man had a wife, he could not have supported her on the sale of a few toys. Had the man trudged the same path from workshop to workshop that Niccolò had? Had he applied not only to furniture workshops but also to the makers of elaborate picture frames, clock cases, wooden paneling, doors, and architectural ornaments? Had he too faced rejection after rejection? Had the man been a member of the guild of *menuisiers-ébénistes*, carpenters and makers of fine furniture, or had he found himself, like Niccolò, an outsider against whom the guild closed its ranks? Perhaps he had found refuge in one of the guild-exempt workshops of the Quartier Saint-Antoine? Then, what about the gold coins sewn into the man's coat? The source of those was still a mystery. No workman, even the highly skilled, earned enough to warrant being paid in gold.

Well, finding out that answer would have to wait. Perhaps once he had found where the man had worked, he could trace the rest of his steps.

Stop it! You cannot take any further action in this matter. He shook his head to clear it of such thoughts.

Monsieur Le Brun need never know, whispered a treacherous voice in his head. *When does he ever visit the Quartier Saint-Antoine? He's always at the Gobelins or at court. He's at Saint-Germain-en-Laye today, in fact. You could go now, this afternoon.*

Even as part of his mind continued to protest that this undertaking was a folly, Niccolò had stopped working and begun to clean his tools to put away. Mentally he followed the route he would take in and out of the workshops he knew of on the Right Bank.

Coming home for his heavy coat, still struggling with his conscience, he found the copy of Saint-André's portrait drawing of the dead man on their dining table. Anne-Marie had carried it everywhere she went the last few days, but today she had left it behind, almost as if she knew he would want to use it. He snatched it up with a groan and folded it away in his pocket.

At the first three shops, no one recognized the man in the drawing. Niccolò began to relax, half-hoping nothing would come of this mad questioning. But in the fourth, they said the man had applied for work there. Niccolò felt a leap of excitement. His instincts had been right. They remembered he was not a Frenchman. He spoke the language well enough, but with an accent.

Encouraged, Niccolò pressed on, although he drew a blank at the next three workshops. He decided to try the workshop of André-Charles Boulle in the Louvre Palace. When Louis XIV decided against living in this traditional Paris residence of the

Kings of France, he ordered it to be made available to artists and craftsmen for studios and workshops, demonstrating his support of the arts. Boulle was the foremost maker of furniture in Paris. If one couldn't work for the King at the Gobelins, one wanted to work for Boulle. His tables, desks, chests of drawers, clocks and cabinets with their signature marquetry of tortoiseshell, brass, pewter, and exotic woods were very much in demand. He had been appointed *ébéniste du roi*, furniture maker to the King, when he was only thirty.

Unfortunately, Boulle's irascible nature was as well known as his work. There was a constant turnover of personnel in his workshop, and he was always looking for new men. Niccolò, who had applied to Boulle earlier that year and been turned down, thought it a miracle that the quality of his furniture remained as high as it did.

With some trepidation, he pushed open the door. The front room had just two pieces on display, a pair of cabinets-on-stands, rectangular chests of drawers set on tables with double legs in the front, one leg slightly in front of the other. One cabinet had the veneer called *première partie*, principally in tortoiseshell, the other the veneer called *contrepartie*, principally in brass and pewter. Their craftsmanship was superb, but before Niccolò could look at them more closely, the ding of the bell over the door brought one of the apprentices out of the back. Niccolò inhaled the odor of freshly sawn wood, which always filled him with happiness.

The boy took him to the Master. Boulle was tall, with brown hair clipped short and a long dour face. His plain brown suit, stockings and shoes were in marked contrast to the elaborate works of marquetry around him. He wore an apron to protect his clothing as he demonstrated to a group of young apprentices the cutting of pieces for marquetry veneers – how to put together the stack of thinly sliced wood with rabbit glue, a little pot of which was cooking over a brazier set safely on the hearth, and how to cut the stacked sheets into petals, leaves, and other pieces of a floral pattern. Sheets of sea-turtle shell, brass and pewter were

93

stored nearby. Two bulbous jewel cabinets stood on one side of the room with sandbags clamped to them to make sure the veneers would remain firmly glued to their undulating surfaces.

Although a comparatively young man in his mid-thirties, Boulle had already developed the mannerisms of a much older man. He recognized Niccolò only to dismiss him a second time: 'No, Italian, I have nothing for you.'

Niccolò was happy to be able to tell him he was no longer in search of work. 'I am at the Gobelins now,' he said with pride.

For the benefit of the apprentices, Boulle dismissed the Gobelins with a flick of his fingers. 'Their *ébénistes* merely imitate me! And I am not restricted by the whims of Monsieur Le Brun. Perhaps they have sent you here to steal my designs, eh?' The apprentices laughed dutifully.

Patiently, Niccolò showed him the portrait drawing.

'Oh, yes, the Dutchman. He worked for me for a time but I had to let him go. We quarreled.'

This was hardly surprising. Boulle managed to quarrel with everyone sooner or later. Nonetheless, Niccolò pressed for more information. 'Is there anything else you can tell me about him – where he came from? Whether he had a family? Where he went after he left here?'

'Evidently he went into the Bièvre.' Boulle gave a mirthless laugh. 'Where he was between my atelier and the river is no business of mine.' He shrugged and made ready to return to the marquetry lesson.

Niccolò gave silent thanks that he had not been taken on here, despite the shop's prestige. Gravely he thanked the master and turned to go. One of the older apprentices showed him out, saying in a quiet undertone, 'His name was Hendrik. He had a wife but I don't remember her name. He was good, too good – the old man doesn't like being shown up.'

'Aren't you done saying goodbye?' came a bellow from the workshop. 'You're not delivering a long speech on the stage – you're supposed to be working for me!'

'I'm coming, *maître*,' replied the apprentice in an impossibly angelic voice, and vanished inside before Niccolò could thank him.

Niccolò had told Anne-Marie that the half-finished wooden cat found in the dead man's coat pocket might have been made to sell at a market. But where should she even begin to look? With Christmas approaching, vendors had set up booths not only at the daily markets at Les Halles, the Place Maubert, and the Saint-Jean Cemetery and the smaller neighborhood markets held on Wednesdays and Saturdays, but also at the holiday fairs that sprang up at this time of year. She spent several days visiting as many as she could, marveling at the bounty of things to be had, but it was not until the Friday before Christmas that she found what she had been looking for.

This market had been set up in the Parvis Notre-Dame, the open space in front of the cathedral. The wall of the hospital called the Hôtel-Dieu, God's house, located on the other side of the Parvis, gave a little shelter from the wind, and the abundant sunshine this day made it a pleasant one to be out despite the cold. Sellers had set up tables and makeshift booths with all manner of toys. Excited children, their mothers and fathers in tow, looked over the assortment and asked for first one thing, then another. Three vendors offered carved wooden objects, from jointed dolls waiting to be dressed in the latest fashion to pull-along animals on wheels to small indestructible solid toys for very young children. It was among the latter that Anne-Marie at last found the sleeping cat she sought. She pounced on it, cat-like, before someone else could claim it, and paid the vendor what he asked without engaging in the usual ritual of bargaining. He pocketed her coins equally quickly as if afraid she might change her mind.

'It's beautiful,' she told the man, 'very skilled work. Who made it?'

The vendor shrugged. He was tall and thin with sunken cheeks and sparse, greying brown hair. 'I never knew his name. He didn't volunteer it. He spoke French well enough but with an accent, and he had blond hair. I just called him the Dutchman. This is the third year I've bought toys from him, and they always sell well. This is the last one I have. He was supposed to bring me more last Saturday but he never came.'

'You did business with him for years and never knew his name?' She was incredulous.

He shrugged again. 'It's not unusual. Many carvers do this in addition to their regular jobs and may not want their employers or the guild to know. It might be against the rules, or they might be expected to share the few sous they get, or they might have used bits of wood that belong to the employer. I never ask questions. If I don't know, I can't be asked to inform on them, can I?' He cocked his head and, with a skeptical raised eyebrow, gave her a searching glance as if he suspected her of being a spy for the forces of order his suppliers sought to circumvent.

Anne-Marie decided honesty was best. 'The reason he has not brought more toys to you is that he is dead. His body was found in the Bièvre almost three weeks ago. I am trying to find his wife and child and make sure they are all right. If you know anything at all that could help me . . .'

'Dead?' The vendor's mouth dropped open. Hastily, he crossed himself.

'Yes. He was working on another of these cats just before he was –' she bit back *stabbed* just in time – 'just before he died,' she amended. 'It was found in his coat pocket.'

The man's shoulders sagged. 'I am sorry to hear it. His things sold well. I was counting on a brisk business in them.'

It was Anne-Marie's turn to be shocked. 'A man is dead, a man you've dealt with for three years, and that is all you can say?' she blurted out.

She wanted to take the words back when she saw the alarm in his eyes, but before she could apologize he replied in a voice sharpened by his fear, 'If he's dead, I can't help him, can I? I've got my own family to feed, don't I? Why do you want to come around asking questions and upsetting people? I can't help you, I tell you. Take your bad news and go.' He meant the last word to come out as a strong directive but could not prevent a rising note of panic from coming into his voice. People were starting to look at them, and one of the other vendors called over, 'Having trouble with a customer, Claude? Do you need help?'

'Not at all,' Anne-Marie answered him. 'I was just going.' To the toy vendor, she said, 'My apologies, Monsieur.' She turned to go.

As she was making her way through the crowd, she felt a hand on her arm. Startled, she looked up. An old woman, her face crisscrossed by wrinkles and framed with curling white hair, regarded her with concern. 'Did Claude say something to upset you?'

'No, I'm afraid it was I who upset him. I was asking about the maker of this.' She produced the toy cat from her dress pocket.

'Oh, Hendrik!' The old woman smiled happily, revealing tooth-less gums. 'He gave me one of those for my granddaughter's girl.'

'You knew him?'

'Yes, of course. I help my granddaughter with her stall, look-ing after her baby while she sells her things.' She waved a hand to indicate a booth at which a young woman was tidying a display of rag dolls. The young woman waved happily back. 'He said the little girl reminded him of his own daughter.'

Anne-Marie's heart seemed to leap in her chest. *I was right!* Aloud, she said, 'Is there somewhere that we could go to talk, where I could buy us something warm to drink? It's too long a story to tell while standing out in the cold.'

The old woman's eyes brightened. She went over to tell the young woman, who nodded and kissed her. Anne-Marie glanced back to the first vendor's booth. He had packed his wares and gone.

The old woman led Anne-Marie past the market tavern, which gave forth sounds of a raucous crowd intent on fortifying itself from the cold, to a quiet tavern in the next street. The land-lord's wife greeted her cheerfully. 'The usual?' she asked.

'Yes, and the same for my young friend.' She led Anne-Marie to an empty table. No sooner were they seated than two enormous bowls of aromatic onion soup and thick slices of bread were placed in front of them. Glasses of hot spiced wine followed shortly.

They applied themselves to the food; Anne-Marie was surprised at how hungry she was. Only when the bowls were emptied and removed, and the old woman had taken a good sip of her wine, did she ask, 'What do you want to know? And if I may be so bold, why are you asking?'

'I am sorry to tell you that Hendrik is dead, Madame. His body was found in the Bièvre three weeks ago.' She paused to give the old woman time to absorb the news.

The grandmother sighed deeply but did not cry. 'And I am sorry to hear it. He was a good man.' She sighed again and raised sad eyes to gaze into Anne-Marie's.

'His body came to rest just outside the Gobelins, where my husband and I live, and was brought into the doctor's surgery there to be examined. I helped to wash it for burial.' She told the old woman about the embroidered hearts, the lack of police interest in finding the widow, her own quest to find the man's family and make sure they were all right. 'You are the first person I have met to know anything about them.'

'I am afraid I don't know very much, not even their names – or Hendrik's last name, for that matter. There was always something closed and guarded about him. He relaxed completely only when talking to my granddaughter's little girl. Then you saw his features open and happiness come into them. But as soon as a man or woman spoke to him, the caution came back.'

Anne-Marie ordered more wine for both of them and thought what to ask next.

'Did he talk with anyone regularly? Was there someone he used to meet at the market? Did someone ask for him? Aside from me,' she finished with a smile.

The old woman shook her head. 'Not that I noticed. We could ask my granddaughter. She might have seen something.' She hesitated. 'I take it, from the manner of your questions, that his death in the river may not have been an accident?'

It was Anne-Marie's turn to sigh. 'He was stabbed. I would rather know whom to avoid. I don't wish to share his fate, and I don't want you and your family to come to any harm either.'

The old woman glanced around uneasily. 'We should return to the market.' Anne-Marie paid for their meal and purchased soup and bread to carry out to the young woman.

The granddaughter did not know the name of Hendrik's wife, but 'His little girl's name was Marie, or something like it. He would call my Rose by that name.'

'Did he ever give you any idea of where they lived?'

The girl thought. 'It was over a boutique that sold luxury goods. He said once, when his baby was fretful because her first teeth were starting to come in, how he wished he could buy a teething coral for her. He had seen one in this shop window, a smooth piece of rich red coral with a silver handle. He had made the baby's cradle himself, and he said his wife had embroidered the curtains and the coverlet so finely that you would never guess they had not come from that shop' – her eyes grew wistful – 'but a coral like that was beyond his means.'

'A fortunate baby indeed who can afford such luxuries,' Anne-Marie said drily, thinking of the gold coins the man had not spent. 'Did he tell you the name of this boutique?'

'No, but the other day I saw a coral such as the one he described, and I wondered if it could be the same one.'

'What was it called?' Anne-Marie could not keep the excitement out of her voice.

'The boutique? Le Bouton. Just off the Rue St Honoré, I think.'

Anne-Marie laughed aloud, to the astonishment of the two women. Little Rose laughed too. Anne-Marie smiled at the baby and tried to think of a way to thank her mother. She looked again at the dolls spread out for sale. 'Did you make all these yourself?'

'I make the dolls, and Grandmère knits their chemises,' she replied proudly.

'I will take one of each size.' The four dolls would take the rest of the money she had brought with her, leaving nothing for the dinner purchases she had planned, but she gave it gladly. She left them after many professions of mutual thanks, eager to be home before dark. Tomorrow she and Niccolò would find Le Bouton and Hendrik's family.

Niccolò paced the floor of their front room, too excited to sit still, idly teasing Gâteau with his waggling fingers, impatient to share his discovery with Anne-Marie. Where was she? It couldn't take her all afternoon to shop for dinner. Was she visiting the Place Royale again? He hadn't thought to go there but had hurried straight home. He wouldn't go rushing to the Duc's house on a fool's errand a second time. *Anne-Marie won't know you've been out asking questions. She'll think you're still working in your studio.* It was illogical to be disappointed she couldn't anticipate his every act, but he wished she could be there.

Make yourself useful, Niccolò, his mother's voice sounded in his ear. He built a fire and started reheating the broth from the night before, chopping carrots, onions and herbs very fine to put in it, sniffing appreciatively the aromatic bouillon. He set the table and was just contemplating adding a couple of eggs to the pot when he heard footsteps on the stairs. He opened the door, all smiles, as she reached the top step, her face alight with excitement.

Chapter Ten

'I have news!' Anne-Marie announced, out of breath.

'So do I!' Niccolò replied, smugly.

'You first!'

'No, you!' He was feeling magnanimous

'His name was . . .'

'Hendrik!' They shouted together, and broke into laughter. 'He was Dutch! He *did* have a wife!'

They set out at first light to find Le Bouton, starting at the western end of the Rue St Honoré and working their way east. Niccolò looked to shops on the left, Anne-Marie to those on the right; and they peered down side streets as well. It was not easy to spot one sign among so many projecting into the street, clamoring to catch their attention. Some were so large that Niccolò, who was taller than most Frenchmen, had to duck his head to avoid being hit. Looking up all the time, they could not watch where they put their feet in the smelly mud. More than once one of them had to pause to scrape something particularly foul-smelling off a shoe. Even at this hour, Rue St Honoré was busy.

'Look out!' bellowed a man's voice. They jumped to one side to let pass two men carrying a heavily laden basket.

'Ouch!' A woman's disgusted voice. In her haste, Anne-Marie had trod on her foot. 'Watch where you're going, why don't you?'

'I'm sorry,' she called out as the woman retreated in a huff. *The problem is, I* am *watching where I'm going — it's just that I need to keep looking overhead.*

They asked some of the shopkeepers preparing to open their doors if they knew where to find Le Bouton but got only shrugs and headshakes in reply. At Église St Roch, they gave a few deniers to the beggars on the church steps, men who were diseased or missing limbs. The latter, wounded soldiers reduced to begging, were yet another unpleasant reminder of the war with the Netherlands.

One of the beggars at St Roch started to grind out a tune on a hurdy-gurdy. A breeze picked up, making the signs swing and creak — even these relatively new signs sounded like the older ones elsewhere in the city. A roast chestnut vendor set up his stand, adding its pungent smell to the street, as did a coffee house that emitted enticing aromas when the door was opened. Sunshine broke through the clouds to add to the festive air of the street. Anne-Marie and Niccolò pressed on.

It was Niccolò who spotted the sign for Le Bouton: round, in the shape of a coat button, with holes punched in the metal where thread-holes would be, and a painted crisscross of thread. It was, they discovered, a shop for millinery and accessories. In its window were hats, ribbons, gloves, scarves of wonderful multi-colored silks, fur muffs, and other items that might appeal to a wealthy young woman or her gift-minded friends. Among these was a baby's coral set in silver. The pale green paint on the wood shop front provided a welcome touch of spring; the name was painted over the door in bold black, with the o's painted as buttons. At any other time, Anne-Marie might have paused to appreciate its cleverness, but now all her attention was on the residential doors between the shops, wondering which one to try. Niccolò boldly put out his hand, pulled one open, and beckoned her inside.

They walked down a short passage to the open courtyard that was common to apartment buildings of this type. The elderly concierge, a grey wisp of a woman who regarded them with

suspicion, had just finished sweeping the frost from the cobblestones and was glad of a chance to go inside for a chat and a
rest. Her name, ironically, was Madame Bonnefoi.

'The Dutchman? Yes, Monsieur Vlieger lived here, until he
got behind on his rent and I had to kick his family out. He had
assured me that he was meeting a client who was going to pay
him for a carved table for some fancy marble top—'

'*Pietra dura*,' Niccolò murmured automatically.

'Yes, that was what he called it. I thought he was making it up,
because he never came back. I assumed he'd done a flit. Even in
this neighborhood you get those. Though I was surprised he'd
run out on his family, his adored Rachel and his precious Mariët.'
She said it sarcastically but without rancor. 'I gave him a week to
return and pay the rent, then told the wife and daughter they had
to leave and that I would keep their things in lieu of rent owing.
I told them to go to one of the charities – that's what they're for.
But Madame Vlieger insisted that her husband must be able to
find her when he returned, so I sent them around the corner to
another house owned by this landlord, where they could stay in
one of the garrets at a much lower rent. I don't know if they're
still there – I thought that when the woman got cold and hungry
enough she'd go to one of the charities.'

Niccolò and Anne-Marie were appalled at this indifference to
the plight of Hendrik's family. It must have shown in their faces,
because the woman said defensively, 'I'm the concierge, not the
owner. My job is to collect rent, not hand out charity. This is a
respectable house in a good neighborhood. I was able to rent out
their apartment to a paying tenant almost immediately.

'Besides,' she added righteously, 'they're Dutch. Aren't we at
war with the Dutch?'

'The reason Monsieur Vlieger did not return, Madame,' said
Anne-Marie with exaggerated courtesy, 'is that he was robbed
and stabbed that night and put into the river. There were no
papers on him to say where he lived. I am sure he would otherwise have returned.'

The concierge bridled. 'Well, how was I to know that?' She told them the address to which she had sent the wife and daughter. Niccolò summoned his most charming manner in which to thank her – Anne-Marie seemed incapable of polite speech – and they took their leave.

'If Hendrik owed money when he disappeared, where did the gold coins come from?' he inquired of Anne-Marie in a soft voice, when they had returned to the anonymity of the street. 'Why didn't he use one to settle his debts? Why did he leave the wife and daughter he adored in such dire need?'

She couldn't understand it either.

The building to which Madame Bonnefoi had directed them was only one street over from the Rue St Honoré, but a world apart from it, reminiscent of the poverty-stricken area surrounding the Gobelins. Anne-Marie's heart constricted with fear when she saw the dilapidated façade of the old building. Smoke rising from the chimneys indicated light and warmth inside but added to the gloomy impression. A dank smell came up from its gratings. The concierge, who did not bother to give them her name, was as gloomy as the rest of the building and indifferent to the plight of her tenants.

'I've heard all the excuses in the book,' she told them, 'and I've stopped believing any of them. That woman has not paid her rent for a month, and I'm tossing her and the girl out after Christmas. I'm not a charity. If the Dutch can't pay their bills, let them clear out and leave room for Frenchmen who can,' she exclaimed in a righteous voice that echoed Madame Bonnefoi. 'Meanwhile, they are still in residence. If you are friends of theirs, perhaps you could pay what's owing?'

While Niccolò paid, Anne-Marie was already racing up the stairs. He followed. At the top, she knocked softly on the door, then with more force.

There was no response.

Anne-Marie knocked more urgently on the door.

'Madame Vlieger!' Niccolò called out. Still no sounds within.

Anne-Marie's hand lifted to rap again when a voice croaked, 'Hendrik? Is that you? Thank God!' They waited, but no one came to the door. Niccolò forced it open.

In the bare, freezing room, mother and daughter were huddled for warmth on a straw pallet under an inadequate cover. Only the woman's face was visible, as white – or grey and unwashed – as her coif. A thin wail came from under the cover, where she had clasped the baby to her. There was no fire, no food, no hope. What little sunshine came through the dirty window served only to illumine the squalor within. As the final indignity for a clean Dutch house-wife, Rachel hadn't had the strength to carry out and wash the chamber pot.

Anne-Marie handed her blue cloak to Niccolò. 'Wrap them in this and bring them down. I'll find a fiacre to take us back.'

Outside, the wind was biting. There were no cabs on the mean little street and she had to run to the Rue St Honoré with only her shawl against the chill. A fiacre was just pulling up to Le Bouton when Anne-Marie hailed it. Two women stepped out. She looked enviously at their fur wraps and bonnets trimmed with expensive feathers and ribbons, their fur muffs. The ladies gave Anne-Marie an indifferent glance; their faces become ani-mated only when they viewed the shop window.

'That's pretty! I don't have one of those yet.'

'Remember, we're here to buy gifts, not things for ourselves.'

'What a pity,' sighed her friend.

The proprietor opened the door for the women, beaming and calling out a welcome. The shop emitted rich scents of perfumes, spices and hot chocolate. Such wealth, in contrast to the bleak poverty nearby. Did none of these people know what was going on four storeys over their heads? Did they not care?

The driver was not pleased at being asked to go all the way out to the Gobelins; it was unlikely he would find a return fare, he said. He was about to refuse her when Niccolò came into sight carrying the woman and child. 'They are the widow and daughter of an old workmate,' Niccolò told him. 'We just found out they are ill.' The driver's sympathies aroused, he helped Niccolò to lift them inside.

Anne-Marie settled onto the seat with relief. It was cold in the cab but at least it was out of the wind. Niccolò did what he could to keep her warm, wrapping his arm around her to keep her close and settling their guests across their laps, but she continued to shiver. The driver made good time, stopping midway at a dairy, suggesting they get milk for the child.

They paid off the fiacre at the gate of the Gobelins, tipping the driver generously, and carried the two inside. A woman drawing water at the well called out a greeting.

'Who have you got there?'

'The wife and child of an old workmate of Niccolò's,' Anne-Marie replied. 'We just found out they've been ill. Could you see if Dr Lunague is at home and ask him to come to see them?' The woman nodded and went toward the doctor's surgery.

Niccolò carried the woman upstairs, Anne-Marie the child. The little girl whimpered at being removed from her mother's arms. In their apartment, Anne-Marie put their guests into their bed while Niccolò built a fire in the front room. Gâteau sniffed at the visitors, then lay down in front of the fireplace. They left the door between the rooms open so that heat could percolate through to the other room. A little later, they took cups of milk to their guests and helped them to drink it. The woman didn't ask who they were, didn't protest being handled by them, but obediently took small sips. A little color started to come into her cheeks, and she fell more happily back to sleep.

The woman they had seen at the well came to their rooms to tell them the doctor was not in at the moment, but she had left a message for him. She brought garments with her for Rachel to borrow – 'She's more my size than yours, Madame Bruno.' Ruefully, Anne-Marie agreed, and thanked her. She hung the clothing where Rachel would see it when she awoke.

The doctor came in the early evening. His face was grim

when he first saw Rachel and Mariët but relieved after he examined them. 'They are weak from too much cold and too little food, but you found them in time. They do not need any medicines; warmth and sleep and good food will do the trick. The child must have fresh milk and the mother should take a little brandy to warm her, but none for the child; it's too power-ful for a little one.'

He smiled at Anne-Marie and raised the glass of wine she had poured for him in a salute. 'So, you were right, Madame.' He eyed her appraisingly. 'Does Monsieur Le Brun know they are here?'

'He is at court – an invitation from the King – I have not had an opportunity to tell him. Surely he would not have me put them out in their condition?'

'Perhaps not. But the fact that you have found them shows that you ignored his express orders to leave the investigation alone.'

'I assure you, it was by pure chance I found them. I was at the toy fair buying gifts for my niece and nephew . . .'

'Oh, yes. It was pure chance that you, the wife of a gifted sculptor in wood, should be looking over a selection of crude wooden toys to purchase. Looking for another sleeping cat, I suppose?'

She blushed; she hadn't known she was that transparent.

'And a good thing you were – they'd have died in a few days if you had not rescued them. I will tell Monsieur Le Brun the same and advise that they not be moved. But you must speak to him first.' Another thought came to him. 'Does she know about her husband?'

'Not yet. When she heard Niccolò's voice at the door, she thought it was her husband – his name is Hendrik. If she asks about him – is she strong enough to be told?'

He shook his head. 'Not yet, I think. Say we're still looking for him. I don't want her giving up in despair. The little girl will need her.' He looked around the small room and a thought struck him. 'Where will you sleep tonight?'

They looked surprised and realized they hadn't yet given it any thought.

'I can lend you straw pallets. They are clean,' he hastened to reassure them as he saw them hesitate. 'I thought it would be better than sleeping on the floor.'

The next day the woman and child were still very weak but by feeding them nutritious food a little at a time – broth, milk, an egg, and soft bread from Boulangerie Robert – they began to recover. Rachel was blonde and petite, with blue eyes; she was very thin, with the promise of being pretty when she felt better. The infant Mariët had her father's coloring with brown hair and blue-grey eyes. She, too, was very weak, her wail more like a kitten's.

Word had spread in the Gobelins community that the Brunos had taken in a woman and child in need. Anne-Marie and Niccolò agreed that it was safest not to reveal that she was the dead man's widow, lest his killer hear about it and think she might know something that would compromise him. To anyone who asked, they said merely that Rachel was the widow of one of Niccolò's workmates elsewhere. Anne-Marie had called on her with a Christmas basket but found them in conditions so poor that she felt it was better to bring them home. Knowing how thin the edge of survival could be, people were sympathetic. Someone brought a warm shawl, another woman a pair of old shoes, yet another, a dress her own infant daughter had outgrown.

By Monday afternoon, Rachel and Mariët were already doing better, sitting up and eating. During the previous two days, Rachel had called Anne-Marie 'Soeur', thinking her a nursing sister in a hospital, an impression reinforced by the doctor's visits. Now she was awake and clear-minded enough to realize she was not in hospital. 'Where are we? Who are you?'

'I am Anne-Marie Bruno, and this is my husband, Niccolò. You have been guests in our home at the Gobelins since Saturday.

We found you in your room near Le Bouton and brought you here to get well again.'

'Are you friends of my Hendrik? Did he send you to me?'

'No, Madame,' Anne-Marie told her very gently. 'I am sorry to have to tell you that Hendrik is dead.'

'I was afraid that was so, but I hoped against hope . . .' Rachel closed her eyes; tears brimmed under the lids. Her whole body sagged in disappointment. 'How? When?'

'He was stabbed and put into the Bièvre the night of November twenty-seventh. He was found in the river the next morning, just outside the walls of the Gobelins.'

Rachel nodded and turned her head to one side as she wept into the pillow without making a sound. Anne-Marie tried to comfort her, to hold her hand or stroke her hair, but Rachel waved her away, wanting to be alone with her sorrow. Anne-Marie left the room and closed the door to give their guest privacy in her grief.

Dr Lunague came up with the last of the daylight to check on his patients. While he was there, Rachel asked him, 'Doctor, what Madame Bruno has told me – is it true?'

He went into the other room and came back with the portrait drawing of the man who was found. 'Is this your husband?'

She nodded, her eyes filling with tears again. 'I wish I were dead, too.'

He took out a handkerchief and dabbed her eyes. 'Madame,' he said firmly, 'you must get well again, for the sake of your daughter. Hendrik is gone and you are far from your family in Holland, but you have friends here' – he waved his arm to encompass Anne-Marie, Niccolò and himself – 'who will help you. Promise us that you will do your utmost to get better. Do you understand?'

'I understand what you say, Doctor. I will get better, I promise. Thank you, all of you, for your kindness to my Mariët and me.'

She started to ask more questions but he told her, 'That can wait until you are stronger. Rest now. You are warm; you are safe; there is enough food; you have friends. Rest now,' he repeated. He had brought a sleeping draught in a vial; he now poured it into a glass and added a little water. 'Drink this; it will help you sleep.' She took it gratefully, and her breathing was soon deep and regular.

The doctor came into the front room and accepted the glass of wine Anne-Marie held out to him. Mariët sat in Niccolò's lap, playing with one of the rag dolls Anne-Marie had bought. He sang to her in Italian while she babbled at him in Dutch, content to be in his arms.

'We are going to my parents tomorrow for Christmas Eve and staying over through Christmas Day. Will it be all right to leave them?' It was the first Noël she would have brought home her new husband and she had been looking forward to it, but she was reluctant to leave these two strangers behind. They felt like family, too – one she had searched for and found. She couldn't disappoint her father, however; he was so proud of her and would be crushed if she and Niccolò didn't come. 'You won't think yourself above us now that you've married someone who works for the King?' he had asked wistfully on her wedding day. 'Papa, I will always be proud to be your daughter,' she had assured him.

'I will look in on them,' Dr Lunague said. 'I'll have my house-keeper prepare meals for them. I do not think they will try to run away, now that she knows there is no Hendrik to return to. Enjoy the holiday with your family.'

They set out after breakfast to the Boulangerie, carrying gifts. She helped her mother and sister prepare the feasts for that night and the next and served at the bakery counter for an hour so Thé-rèse could have a break.

Robert Boulanger had invited his friend Matthieu to spend Christmas Eve and day with them. The old baker was in low spirits. He had been lonely since his Madeleine died, and his nephew Pierre, Toinette's husband, had little time for him between the demands of the bakery and a growing family. With a sudden inspiration Niccolò, who had been worrying about what would become of Rachel and Mariët after their recovery, told him about the plight of the mother and daughter. Could Matthieu give them a home – employ her as his housekeeper, perhaps? The old man was delighted to be asked. 'Bring them to me as soon as you can.' He gave his first wholehearted smile of the day.

In the afternoon, Anne-Marie brought a basket of breads to the house on the Place Royale as a gift. A Christmas feast was being prepared in the kitchen for the staff; both fireplaces were lit with good things roasting and baking. She declined Madame Dupont's invitation to join them but accepted a steaming glass of mulled wine in celebration of the season. The Duc de Languedoc had not yet returned from Saint-Germain-en-Laye, but Marc took her upstairs to see Mademoiselle de Toulouse. Anne-Marie told her about the toy fair, the search for Le Bouton, and finally finding the woman and child she had sought for so long, and the miserable conditions in which she had found them.

Suzanne's look of smiling congratulations was replaced by an appalled expression, her face pinched and white. 'Is there anything I can give to help – food, money, blankets? Can I reimburse you for the money for the fiacre and the landlord and the milk and . . .?' She reached for her purse.

Anne-Marie smiled at her enthusiasm. 'That's all right – we are managing – and they are not without resources – remember the gold coins in the coat.' Suzanne looked so unhappy at being balked in her generosity, however, that Anne-Marie quickly said, 'They will need warm clothes when they venture outside again – and good cloaks and shoes are expensive.'

'I will see to it, and send them over,' Suzanne promised. 'I'm sorry to ask this now, but – have you been able to ask her what her husband was doing and how our family's name came to be involved?'

'Not yet. We will need to wait until she is better before we can ask her.' The clock on the mantelpiece chimed four times. 'I must

111

go now, to get home before dark. *Joyeux Noël* to you and your father.'

'And to you and Niccolò,' the Duc's daughter replied warmly. 'Congratulations on your success!' She held out a small box to Anne-Marie. 'I found this when I was doing my research among the jewelers and thought of you.'

Inside the box was a delicate silver flower suspended from a thin dark blue ribbon. Anne-Marie drew in her breath in delight and slipped it over her head. 'But I have nothing to give you!'

'Your loyalty, your energies, your efforts on our behalf – you have already given more than you know.'

When the Duc returned in the early evening, Suzanne told him Anne-Marie's news. 'Papa, I would like to reward her – reward them – in some way but don't want to insult them by seeming to offer charity. She would not take my money to replace what they had spent in the search, but they cannot have very much to spare. What can I – can we – do?'

The Duc thought for a few minutes and then smiled. 'I will give Niccolò a commission for a portable altar and crucifix to send to Geoffroi in the spring. I would be willing to pay hand-somely for it.'

Father and daughter smiled fondly at one another.

St-Nicolas-du-Chardonnet was full for the late Mass on Christmas Eve. The Boulanger family had arrived early to be sure to find seats together. The infant Christ Niccolò had carved for the crèche on the altar smiled sweetly at all who came to look at Him, and Anne-Marie's heart glowed with pride in her husband. She gave heartfelt thanks to God for finding Rachel and Mariët in time, and prayers for their complete recovery. She felt both elated and let down. She had found Hendrik's family, and was gratified to find out her instincts had been correct, when all the men around her had been saying no. She had enjoyed the search. She would happily continue searching – for what?

I could find the murder site, came the treacherous thought.

No, don't even think about it. Finding the man's family is enough. Looking into the murder means running the risk of being killed. Leave that to the police, she argued with herself.

Oh, yes? And what more will they do now that they didn't before?

Stop it. Your place is with Niccolò, caring for him. She turned to smile up at her husband.

Niccolò, too, gave thanks for the rescue of the mother and daughter, and added a prayer for Anne-Marie. *I hope this will be enough for her, and that she will not want to pursue the matter further. I hope she can again find the satisfaction in her days as she did before Hendrik's body was found. I want peace of mind for both of us.*

Monsieur and Madame Le Brun were also in the church and greeted the couple cheerfully. As Le Brun had been at court, it was the first time she had seen them since bringing Rachel and Mariët to the Gobelins. *They must not have heard about our visitors yet.* It was difficult to look them in the eye as he wished them *Joyeux Noël.*

Midnight supper at the Boulangers was happy but subdued – it was not just the children who were tired out after a long day. The next day's dinner, with everyone well-rested, would be boisterous.

'*Joyeux Noël,*' Anne-Marie and Niccolò wished each other drowsily as they settled into bed.

Chapter Eleven

They returned to their rooms on Christmas night to find Dr Lunague waiting by the fire. Rachel had felt well enough to sit up in bed and eat a modest dinner, he told them, sounding pleased about the return of her appetite. Afterward she had asked about Hendrik. He had told her as gently as possible about the finding of the body and his examination of it, about the shirt with the embroidery that had led Anne-Marie to surmise her existence and look for her, about the little wooden cat in the coat pocket and the silver button. He had touched briefly on the indifference of the police, he said, and dwelt more happily on the efforts of Anne-Marie and Niccolò to find her. She was able to take it calmly, if sadly. 'She started to tell me her story but I told her to wait until you were here as well.'

The next day, they crowded chairs into the tiny bedroom to make an attentive audience.

'My name is Rachel Vlieger. My husband is – was – Hendrik, and as you know my daughter is Mariët. We are from Amsterdam, and we are Catholics. We were always regarded with suspicion at home. Five years ago, we decided to leave Amsterdam to live in a city where those of our faith were welcome. My husband was a wonderful carver in wood. We knew that many Dutch craftsmen and artists had come to Paris to work for King Louis, and that we would find compatriots here. Hendrik applied here – at the Gobelins – but was told there was no need for a woodcarver at that time. He found work at the atelier of André-Charles Boulle' – she said the name proudly, aware of the man's prestige – 'as a joiner, making chair frames and furniture carcasses. Then one day there was an argument, and he was told to leave. After that, things never seemed to go right.

'I did my best to be happy in this country, to learn the language, to rejoice in worshiping freely instead of in secret. But the war started the year after we came and made things difficult for us. In Amsterdam, we were Catholics, as good – or bad – as heretics. In Paris, we were Dutch and therefore the enemy. Hendrik was accused of taking work from Frenchmen. Despite his skills, he was refused work, or if he found it, he would quickly be dismissed.'

Niccolò nodded sympathetically.

'Finally, he stopped looking for work at the furniture makers. I do not know what he was doing, but he continued to bring money home. When Hendrik was working at his profession, he shared everything with me. But then when he started his new work, he would not tell me about it, saying it was safer for me not to know. "Safer? What sort of danger are you in?" I asked him. He refused to say, but he moved us from our old home to the Rue St Honoré at about that time. I was worried because the rent was more expensive than our old room, but he laughed and gave me a handful of silver coins, saying we need not worry about that.

'He seemed to have a lot of meetings at all hours, coming and going at odd times. Sometimes he would be gone for a week at a time, but he always returned. That is why I did not worry at first when he did not come home. I did not want to move; I was so sure he would come back to us . . .' She closed her eyes in pain. Anne-Marie shook open a handkerchief, lest she cry again, but she recovered herself.

'Did Hendrik ever mention the Duc de Languedoc, or meeting with one of his servants?' Anne-Marie asked.

Rachel shook her head. 'I told you, he would not tell me anything about what he was up to.'

'He told Madame Bonnefoi he was going to collect money for a commission, a big table support for a marble top.'

Rachel shook her head. 'He hadn't done any work like that in months. His tools hadn't been taken out of their pouch except to make toys. He did that mostly to amuse himself; he sold them but acted like we didn't need the money.'

'Apparently he did not,' the doctor told her. 'These were sewn into the hem of his coat.' He put the gold coins into her hand.

She stared at the coins in bewilderment that turned to anger. She hurled them across the room with a howl of rage and burst into tears. 'My Hendrik had gold? How could he leave us in such want? Just one of these coins could have kept us going!' She began to hurl accusations at her dead husband in a flow of Dutch words that needed no interpretation. Anne-Marie rose to go to her but the doctor shook his head. *Let her cry it out*, he mouthed. She subsided into her chair. The storm passed, and she again spoke to them in French.

'How could he not tell someone where to find us, to be sure to look after us? There must have been someone he trusted!'

'Perhaps, in his new line of work, that person did not live up to his trust,' the doctor replied drily.

She lay back and closed her eyes. They left her to sleep.

When Le Brun returned to the Gobelins, Niccolò and Anne-Marie went to his office to tell him about their guests. They added hastily that they had found another home for them, as soon as they were well enough to move there.

Le Brun sighed. 'I have just received two important commissions for carved figures, royal gifts for the Heidelberg relatives of the King's sister-in-law, Elisabeth-Charlotte of Bavaria. I need you, Niccolò, to make them. I cannot let you go, even though you have gone against my orders. And from your description of the plight of the dead man's family, it is clear that they could not have been left as they had been living. Still, I don't like having them housed at the Gobelins.' He frowned. 'I would like to talk to Madame Vlieger. Is she well enough to come to this office?'

116

'Yes, I think she is, now – and the fresh air and a little sun will do her good.'

'Then bring her to me this afternoon. I will be free after two o'clock.' He knew that the chime of the courtyard clock could be heard throughout the Manufactory.

'Of course, Monsieur Le Brun.' Anne-Marie happily replied.

But as she turned to go Le Brun said, with a bite in his voice: 'Do not think that you can contravene all my orders in similar fashion.'

'Of course not, Monsieur.' She fled before he could say more.

'Your husband, may he rest in peace, came to us in such mysterious circumstances, Madame Vlieger, that I wanted to talk with you to see if you could shed any light on them.' Le Brun's voice was gentle.

Rachel was exasperated. 'The doctor and Monsieur and Madame Bruno have been asking the same thing, and I been asking it of myself. I just don't *know*. My husband never told me what he was up to, and I can tell you that if he were here before me at this moment, I would not stop questioning until I got the whole story out of him. But I honestly tell you, I just don't *know*.'

Mariët began to cry at the anger in her mother's voice. Rachel looked down at the little girl and stroked her and whispered lovingly until the cries turned to whimpers and finally ceased. The action seemed to calm the mother as well. Her breathing returned to normal. Le Brun poured her a glass of wine to sip while she recovered. She began to make an apology for her outburst, but he waved that away – none was needed. More calmly, she thanked him for all that the Gobelins had done so that Hendrik could be buried with dignity.

No, she had not visited his grave yet, but she would as soon as she was better.

'Have you thought about the future? Will you need to earn your living? I understand that you can embroider,' he said, with

117

an ironical look at Anne-Marie. 'We do not employ needle-women at the Gobelins, but I can make inquiries to find you work.'

'That is kind of you, Monsieur, but my friends have already found a place for me.'

'My father's old friend has offered her a position as his house-keeper. He too is recently widowed, and he is lonely. He needs someone to take care of him, and to care about,' Anne-Marie explained.

Le Brun looked relieved.

After the interview with Le Brun, the women went to the doctor's office so that he could examine mother and daughter. He was pleased with their progress. Rest and good food had done much to improve their condition. Rachel offered money to him and to Anne-Marie for the trouble she had put them to, but they both refused. Seeing her get better was a reward in itself, they told her.

She had a favor to ask of the doctor. 'The concierge took away our things when we could not pay our rent. I would like to pay what we owe to Madame Bonnefoi so that we can get back our clothes and the things that Hendrik made, if she has not already sold them, but I do not want to face that woman again. Would you do this for me, Dr Lunague? Her sort,' she continued with a wry twist of her mouth, 'will be much more amenable to a request made by a Frenchman.' The doctor was happy to consent.

Coming out of his office, Anne-Marie was surprised to hear Rachel call out a greeting in Dutch to a figure crossing the court-yard. It was the weaver Willem who had come to Hendrik's funeral. He whirled around in fright, dropping the box of bob-bins he was carrying. He bent quickly to gather up its contents before the yarn could be soiled. Far from being as happy as Rachel to see a familiar face, he looked stricken and guilty, and opened and shut his mouth several times before a sound finally came out. He had lost weight and shrank into his too-large coat as though

118

trying to disappear within it. 'Madame Vlieger! What are you doing here?'

'I have been ill. Monsieur and Madame Bruno have been taking care of me.'

'That is indeed good of them. Excuse me – I must get these to the atelier – I will come see you later if I may . . .' He fled.

Rachel stared after him, perplexed. 'He did not even ask after Hendrik!'

'Oh, he knows Hendrik is dead. He was one of the few here who came to the funeral . . .' Anne-Marie's voice trailed away. 'The day the body was found, the doctor asked all residents if anyone recognized the man. Willem was sick to his stomach when he saw the body but he didn't admit to knowing him, or we might have found you sooner.'

Rachel began to shiver under the warm cloak Mademoiselle de Toulouse had sent. Anne-Marie hurried her to their rooms and a seat in front of the fire.

They decided Niccolò should be the one to speak to the weaver. He tried to pull the man aside for a private talk but the Fleming proved elusive. Finally, Niccolò ran him to ground in the weaving atelier. The hum of other conversations would provide cover for theirs; and it was unlikely, he thought, that Willem would do violence there, with other people about.

The atelier directed by master weaver Jean Jans was a long narrow room the length of the building, flooded with light by the series of wide floor-to-ceiling windows overlooking the courtyard. Facing the windows was a row of a dozen tapestry looms of varying lengths. Three or four men sat behind the high vertical warps, reaching up to pull at the *hautes lisses*, the loops of strong woolen yarn overhead that opened and closed the warp threads to receive bobbins of colored yarn. The cartoon, the pattern to be followed, was tacked onto the rear wall of the loom, so that the weavers sat with their backs to it. From time to time a weaver would leave his seat and walk around to the front of the loom to compare the completed section of the tapestry to the cartoon. Each man had a specialty. Masters took on the most challenging parts, the heads, hands and feet. Journeymen did landscapes, animals and textiles. Apprentices wove the simple parts, the dark blue borders and the straight lines of the architecture. At one loom, a journeyman was demonstrating to an apprentice how to mark the next section of warp threads with the pattern.

It was said that in Persia, the weaving and knotting of carpets was carried out by young children whose hands fit more easily between the warp threads, but at the Gobelins weaving large tapestries such as these was man's work. Reaching up to pull on the *lisses* required a man's strength, they assured each other, and the weavers were proud of their prowess. The Flemings among them kept up their strength with flagons of beer from the Gobelins brewery. Niccolò wrinkled his nose at the thought of quaffing the disgusting stuff in preference to wine. The air was lively with a low hum of conversation as the men worked companionably side by side, punctuated by the sound of wire combs tamping down the weft yarns to lie tight and flat on the warps.

At an empty loom, the master and his assistants were unrolling and putting in place the thick undyed yarn of the warp. Intent though he was on his purpose, Nic paused for a few moments to watch them toss the large coil of yarn back and forth, over and under the upper and lower parts of the loom, a game of catch as graceful as a ballet. Perhaps, he thought, smiling, one day Monsieur Lully would compose a ballet on the legend of Arachne, the talented weaver of mythology whom a jealous Athena had transformed into a spider, and these weavers would take part. A group of English tourists, one carrying Germain Brice's indispensable Paris guidebook, appeared equally fascinated, chattering in their strange language and applauding each catch of the yarn as though they were at a tennis match.

Reluctantly, Niccolò moved away to continue toward Willem, keeping a wary eye on him, lest he try to evade questioning.

The weaver, his head bent to his task, was working alone on a *portière*, a tapestry that could be pulled across a closed door, or *porte*, to shut out drafts and smells and discourage eavesdroppers. The bright, colorful design of the royal coat of arms surmounting a triumphal chariot dazzled the eye.

'Go away,' Willem said without looking up. 'I do not want to talk to you.'

'Then perhaps you would like me to visit you at home this evening? Does your wife know what you have been involved in? Or perhaps you would like me to inform Monsieur Le Brun and Commissaire Ferrand? I am sure they, too, would be interested in what you might know.' Niccolò disliked making threats, but there seemed to be no other way of getting the man to open up.

'They have sent you to take care of me,' Willem, terrified, shrank from Niccolò's strength and bulk.

'No, they haven't,' Niccolò replied in his most reasonable voice. 'I don't even know who *they* are.'

Willem, now completely miserable, turned his head this way and that, searching for a way out but finding none. Niccolò pressed his advantage. 'If you tell me now, I can decide to keep it between us, or I could pass on the information without mentioning your name.' He dangled these possibilities in front of Willem.

The weaver was pitifully grateful. 'You would do that for me? Leave my name out of it?'

'I said I *might*.' He fixed the man with a hard stare. 'Do not try my patience any further.' What little sympathy Niccolò had for the man was fast fading. Clearly Willem had been involved in something he knew was wrong, but he was hoping, in the most cowardly way, to evade the consequences. If he had so little stomach for it, why had he got involved in the first place? Niccolò wanted to yell at him, 'Act like a man, with courage!' But raising his voice would only frighten the man further and attract unwelcome attention from the others. Niccolò waited, while Willem steadied his nerves and moved from the pictorial part of the tapestry pattern that necessitated manipulating several bobbins of

121

colored yarn to a section of plain dark blue border he could weave without thinking about it, the sort of work ordinarily assigned to an apprentice.

'Why didn't you identify Hendrik right away? It wasn't you who did the murder, was it?'

'No, no, nothing like that!'

'Then what is this all about?'

Willem began to tell him in a dull voice, not meeting his eyes, looking only at the dark wool warps and weft as he pulled the *lisses* and pushed his bobbin of dark blue yarn in and out. Because it was the border rather than part of the pattern, he did not need to check his work in the small mirror turned to the front of the tapestry, but he did so anyway out of habit, and to avoid looking at his questioner.

'Hendrik and I were part of a group of friends, all craftsmen from the Netherlands who came to Paris to ply our skills in the luxury trades. We would meet each week in a tavern. I married a Frenchwoman and spoke French all day in the atelier, so it felt good to speak Dutch. Then the war started and we were cut off from contact with our families and our homeland, tolerated rather than welcomed in Paris, even though some of us, like me, had lived here for years and married into French families.' He sighed. 'It was not so bad during the first year of the war, 1672, when the French won a decisive victory. It was only after the so-called peace negotiations of 1673, when the conflict settled into a long stalemate, that things became difficult for us. Our French neighbors blamed us as Dutchmen for the privations brought about by the war, forgetting that we personally had been in Paris since before it started, and that it was the French king's unprovoked act of aggression that started the war in the first place.'

He said this last in an angry voice; then immediately dared a quick look at Niccolò's face to see the effect of his treasonous utterance. Niccolò only nodded, and Willem continued his story. 'Under such treatment, our attitude changed from one of careful neutrality to pride in being Dutch. We wanted to do something to help bring about an end to the war. But what could we, a mere group of artisans, possibly do?

'Then one day we were approached by a man who said he was the representative of a Dutch agent in Paris. He would not give us his surname, only said to call him Salomon. We could help by passing along information to certain French contacts of his. He said his appearance and name were too well known for the contacts to entirely trust his information if he were to hand it over directly. But a Dutch craftsman, with the credentials he would supply, would be trusted. His information would bring about a decisive Dutch victory and a rapid conclusion to the war. It would teach the aggressive Louis XIV an object lesson, and Louis's subjects would be grateful for the peace. Their sons could come home and the money now spent on the war could be spent on improvements in France.'

Niccolò was incredulous. 'And you believed him? It's hard to think that anyone, let alone a group of grown men, could believe such a far-fetched proposition.'

Willem, at last meeting his eyes, was embarrassed to admit that they did. 'But you must understand – we had prayed for a solution. We thought he had come in answer to our prayers.'

Niccolò again shook his head. 'So, you were approached by this so-called agent's representative. What did he look like, this Salomon?'

'Of medium height, with blond hair worn down to his shoulders and a blond mustache and goatee. He dressed all in black, aside from his white linen shirt, in the Dutch fashion. He said anyone so openly Dutch in appearance would never be suspected of anything clandestine.'

'How was Hendrik chosen to be the one to meet with the French contact?'

'He volunteered. We admired his daring. He was coached by Salomon and the man Salomon worked for – and no, I never met the other one, only heard about him – and the meeting went smoothly. Hendrik told us he was paid handsomely for his role.

He was able to move to a new apartment in the Saint-Honoré district, and he didn't need to look for work anymore.'

'So, Hendrik must have met with this French contact several times. Did Hendrik ever tell you the man's name, or what he did as a cover for his spying? Did he give you a description of him?'

Willem thought for a moment but shook his head. 'No. He said once that the man had remarkably bright blue eyes, and the color of the livery coat he wore made you notice them even more. But he never described him more than that.'

'Where did he meet the Frenchman to whom he passed the information?'

'Various places, mostly taverns, around the city or on the outskirts. Never anywhere that they would be conspicuous. Hendrik never told us a specific location.'

'He was found in the Bièvre, so his final meeting must have been somewhere upstream from the Gobelins. Do you have any idea of where?'

The weaver shuddered. 'No. That area is unpleasant enough in broad daylight. I cannot imagine where they might have met after dark.'

'After Hendrik was killed, did any of you hear from this Salomon?'

'No. We left messages for him, but he never responded. When we asked after him, they claimed not to know who we were talking about, said they'd never heard of him.' He sounded both surprised and put out.

Niccolò sighed in exasperation. '*Where* did you leave messages? Whom did you ask? Who are "they"?'

Willem was reluctant to name the place. 'If the agent finds out I was the one who did so, my family could be in danger.'

'I will not name you as the source.' Niccolò tried to reassure him.

'But if they find out you're at the Gobelins, he'll put two and two together, and know it was me who told you.'

Niccolò's patience was wearing thin. 'Where was it?' he asked again in a flinty voice he barely recognized as his own.

Willem sputtered, looking right and left as if for help, pushed the bobbin in and out of the warp threads, finally made up his mind. 'La Bleue et la Blanche,' Willem replied, giving in. 'The Blue and the White. It is a shop on Rue St Honoré that specializes in Chinese porcelain.' He did not have to state what everyone knew, that the Dutch were the principal importers of the fashionable Chinese blue-and-white porcelain that graced the tables, sideboards, and mantelpieces of many European homes. 'The owner manages to ship goods between France and Holland, even with the war.'

'And sending information to and from Holland with them, it would seem.' Niccolò tried to remember if he had passed by the shop on the day they found Rachel and Mariët, but they had looked at so many shops and signs, that it had faded into a blur. He thought for a moment. 'Is the merchant in fact the agent, or is he merely providing cover for this man?'

Willem shook his head – he did not know.

'Have you been there yourself? Were you the one who went to inquire?'

'No, two of the others went. I didn't – I couldn't . . .' He let his voice tail off, not wishing to put his fright into words.

'Then how do you know where the shop is?'

'I passed by it one day. My – my wife wanted to see what the shops of the famous Rue St Honoré offered for Christmas, so we went on Saturday, two weeks ago.'

'Did you pass the one called Le Bouton?'

'Yes, my wife admired the hats in the window. She went in to inquire the price of her favorite, but it was far above our means.'

'Didn't you think to look in on Rachel while you were there? You did know it was where Hendrik moved his family, didn't you?'

Willem nodded miserably. He had no words to excuse himself.

'They were nearly dead when Anne-Marie and I found them. You could have spared them that.'

'I was afraid for my own wife and child.'

And for your own skin. So, you tried to push away all thought of it, all memory, as though it never happened.

'I felt like St Peter denying acquaintance with Christ on the night He died. I made confession and received absolution – but even though God may have forgiven me, I will never forgive myself.'

When Niccolò repeated their conversation that evening, Rachel said bitterly, 'Hendrik gave his life for the cause Willem professed to believe in. We thought of him as a friend and ally.' She sighed wearily. 'Oh, what is the point of being angry with him? It won't bring Hendrik back.'

Niccolò took her and Mariët to Matthieu's house the next day. He did not think Willem would betray them, but it seemed prudent to move them. The doctor had retrieved her possessions from Madame Bonnefoi – by some miracle she had not yet sold them – and taken them there. The old man was genuinely happy to greet his guests. He had prepared his home as best he could, but Anne-Marie could see that Rachel was already mentally rolling up her sleeves to give the house a thorough cleaning. She would be all right.

And Anne-Marie and Niccolò would have their rooms to themselves again. She thought longingly of sleeping together again in their own bed, after two weeks of straw pallets laid out on the floor. She looked at Niccolò and knew he was thinking the same thing.

Chapter Twelve

Niccolò was once more on the Rue St Honoré, scanning the signs overhead for the one advertising the porcelain shop. It was distinctive and easy to spot – made of metal cut out in the round in the shape of a Chinese vase, painted white with a pair of blue dragons circling it. Unlike the flat signs hanging from hooks, it did not swing in the wind, but was fixed. The wood frame of the shop front was painted black, with 'La Bleue' spelled out in white and 'La Blanche' in blue. When they had passed this shop on the Saturday before Christmas, its wooden shutters had been closed, with an arrangement of blue-and-white jars painted on them. Now they were open and a crowd was gathered in front of the shop window, gawking and pointing. He hurried forward with a sinking heart.

Because of his height Niccolò could see, over their heads, the interior of the shop. It had been ransacked, its contents destroyed. A man's body lay among the shards of porcelain littering the shop floor. His bright golden hair stood out against his black garments. The female shop assistant was in tears and her male counterpart looked not far from it as they spoke to representatives of the police force. The lively, chattering crowd outside simultaneously deplored the event and enjoyed it as a relief from the tedium of everyday life. He listened to their talk but it was all conjecture. He was about to leave when a hand on his arm made him whirl around in fright to see Commissaire Ferrand standing beside him.

'What are you doing here, Monsieur Bruno?'

Niccolò recovered his wits. 'I made a wooden wall bracket of the kind used to display porcelain jars and figures. I hoped the merchant might recommend me to the customers of the shop.' He began to take it out of his rucksack to show to Ferrand, but the Commissaire waved his hand dismissively.

'Put it away – I believe you. But it is entirely too much of a coincidence that you should appear here, at this shop, at just this moment. I need to talk with you. Wait here.' He went inside the shop once again to give instructions to his men.

When he emerged, he said only, 'Come with me. There is a wine shop nearby where we can have a private talk.'

Ferrand walked briskly, a man intent on important business. Men and women scurried to get out of his path, and Niccolò followed in his wake. They passed a new coffee house he had been longing to try, Le Sultan, where women in a theatrical version of harem costume served the coffee. It was said to handle a brisk trade from husbands waiting for their wives to finish shopping at the many boutiques on either side of it. Niccolò, who loved coffee, would have enjoyed experiencing it when Anne-Marie was not with him. He did not think she would be offended by the 'harem women'. Quite the opposite – she would start giggling at the pretense of it all and spoil the illusion and his fantasies that went with it. But Ferrand only looked at the coffee house in passing, with a grimace of disgust.

With a sigh, Niccolò followed the Commissaire into a wine shop and through a doorway into a small private room. Any lingering regrets he might have had were dispelled by the first sip of the full-bodied red wine that the proprietor, knowing Ferrand's preference, put in front of them without asking. He waited until they had nodded their appreciation of his choice – as he clearly knew they would – and returned to his counter with a satisfied look. Ferrand closed the door after him.

'The dead man at the shop was killed in the same manner as the one Old Jean fished out of the Bièvre. It appears that I was wrong to dismiss that one as of no importance. Tell me all you know. What really brings you here?'

Niccolò told him about the finding of Rachel and Mariët and the belated confession of the weaver, without giving him the man's name. Ferrand shook his head, as Niccolò had done, at how gullible the Dutch craftsmen had been to fall in with such a scheme.

'The dead man must be the mysterious Salomon who recruits spies. But I will need the weaver who told you about him to identify him, to be sure. What is this man's name?'

Niccolò hesitated, wanting to honor the assurance he had given Willem, but yielded before Ferrand's intense gaze. He remembered uneasily that he too was a foreigner whose hardwon presence in Paris could be cut short, should he fall afoul of the Commissaire.

'Willem,' he finally said. 'I don't know his surname. He is in Jean Jans's atelier at the Gobelins.'

Ferrand made a note of it and his expression eased. Niccolò felt encouraged to ask another question. 'The merchant who owns the porcelain shop – where is he?'

'He left some weeks ago, the young lady shop assistant said, to spend Christmas with his family. He departed rather quickly after your Dutchman was killed. I doubt we will be seeing him again in Paris. It seems probable that the dead man is the mysterious Salomon who recruited Hendrik. I am sure your friend Willem could confirm that.'

Niccolò asked, hesitantly, 'Will he be punished? Willem is not an evil man, just weak, and easily led.'

'I think that one has learned his lesson. If I arrested every man in Paris who acted foolishly at one time or another, there would be few left to stroll in the streets. The fact that I now have my eye on him will be enough to keep him honest – that, and the punishment for treason is death. I would not hesitate to let him suffer the consequences the next time.'

Niccolò gave an inward shiver. Whichever way he turned in this matter, it seemed to lead to death.

'Is there anything else you wish to tell me about Hendrik's murder, since you and your wife seem to have taken it on yourselves to investigate, despite the warnings I am sure Monsieur Le Brun gave you?' Niccolò blushed. He was surprised when Ferrand continued, in an amused tone of voice, 'Your Anne-Marie has that stubborn look in her eye that I know only too well in my own wife. They always have their way in the end.'

Niccolò told him what Anne-Marie had found out from the Duc de Languedoc's cook and housekeeper about the missing livery button. 'That is a detail they neglected to tell me,' murmured the Commissaire.

He did not mention their meetings with the Duc and his daughter, however. What Ferrand did not know, he could not forbid them to do.

As they were about to depart, Ferrand thanked Niccolò and said, 'Your wife is a woman of enterprise and spirit. I am happy that she met with success in finding the man's wife and child. But you see the sort of man we are dealing with. He is an expert at killing. Two people are already dead in this matter, and he will not hesitate to kill again. Do not let your wife – or you – be another of his victims.' He smiled briefly, humorlessly. 'I have enough murders to investigate.' He nodded to Niccolò and departed.

As Niccolò retraced his steps past the porcelain shop, the police were bringing out Salomon's body. He quickly crossed himself and walked home to the Gobelins with Ferrand's warning ringing in his ears.

Chapter Thirteen

Life seemed to settle back into its normal course in January. Niccolò finished the Hercules and Amazon figures for the pair of cabinets. The new assignment from Le Brun, an altar group of the Holy Family for the family chapel of the King's relatives in Heidelberg, was a satisfying challenge.

Commissaire Ferrand spoke to Willem, who confirmed that the dead man in the porcelain shop was the mysterious Salomon who had recruited Hendrik to sell information on his behalf. The weaver's air of cringing guilt was replaced by indignation with Niccolò for bringing his name to the attention of the police. 'But you gave me your word that you wouldn't!'

Niccolò had little patience with him. 'I would have kept your name out of it if I could, but with another man killed, and one whose activities you could shed light on, I had no choice.'

The weaver, however, continued to look resentful, as though it were Niccolò who had dragged him into this business and not the other way around.

Anne-Marie, celebrating the happy outcome of her search for the dead man's family, tried to put the events of the past two months behind her. She was relieved that Rachel and Mariët continued their recovery under the care of Matthieu, who urged the little girl to call him Grandpère and was delighted when she did. Anne-Marie went with Rachel to the convent cemetery to visit Hendrik's grave and dedicate the marker, a simple Cross with his name that Niccolò had made.

She tried to return to those pursuits she had found so satisfying before but found, to her dismay, that keeping house for Niccolò, shopping for food and cooking dinner, in general basking in her newlywed state, were no longer enough. She had been part of something important that had widened her acquaintance, opened new vistas, challenged her mind, and made her stand her ground against those older and supposedly wiser than she. Now she longed for the excitement of discovery, even the element of danger lurking a comfortable distance in the background that gave it an added piquancy. Too, she missed her visits to the Place Royale. She had no occasion to go there now. The Duc de Languedoc and Mademoiselle de Toulouse had returned to Saint-Germain-en-Laye for the festivities of the pre-Lenten season. She hoped that the Duc's daughter missed her as well.

It was in one of these restless moods that she decided to find out what she could about the making of silver buttons.

Although Anne-Marie had lived at the Gobelins for several months, this was her first visit to the silver studio. It was reputed to be the most lavish in Europe, producing massive objects known for their bold daring in size and complexity: ornate planters for the King's orange trees, immense urns and table fountains – even the tables on which these stood. Claude de Villiers, the English director of the studio, greeted her cheerfully. He and Niccolò, sculptors in different media and admirers of each other's work, had become friends. He beckoned her to examine the piece he was chasing and smoothing. From a distance it appeared to be a small sculpture lying on its side, but as Anne-Marie approached the worktable she realized it was in fact the leg of a table in the shape of a half-length figure on a slender pedestal. It was the goddess Ceres, de Villiers told her, with a sheaf of wheat in one arm, a sickle in her hand, and a coronet of ripe wheat in her hair. 'She embodies the abundant harvests of the summer, and the table will be placed against the wall in the Salon of Abundance. The back legs will be plain but the front legs will be in the form of the classical deities of the four seasons – Flora, Ceres, Bacchus, and Saturn. The table borders will show the fruits, vegetables and flowers grown in France,' he said, sounding as proud of his adopted country as he was of his creation. Anne-Marie praised it wholeheartedly.

In other parts of the studio apprentices were employed in simple tasks. One pulled silver wire through a narrowing series of holes in wooden blocks to create the thin wire that would be wrapped around thread and woven into tapestries. Another counted out and weighed the silver ingots that would be melted down to make the next leg of the table. Every marc, the measure of silver weight, needed to be accounted for.

When she marveled that the King could afford so much silver, de Villiers told her, 'This *is* the treasury of France! Louis XIV can afford to put the wealth of France on display in the open.'

'Won't someone try to steal it?'

He laughed and invited her to try to lift just the one table leg. She could barely do it. Clearly the table was immune to casual theft.

'And now – what brings you to the workshop today?' He gestured to her to take a chair and sat across from her. 'You have the air of a woman who wishes to ask a question but hesitates at how to go about it.'

She smiled. 'You're right, and I am feeling rather foolish in asking about something so simple after seeing the intricacies of your work.' She took a deep breath. 'I wanted to ask about the button in the dead man's hand. How was it made? Could such a thing be made here?'

'Make buttons?' His voice had risen in mock indignation. The apprentice gave a start and dropped an ingot that landed at Anne-Marie's feet, incurring a scolding of 'Be careful, Luc!' from de Villiers.

'Yes, *maître*,' the boy muttered unhappily.

Anne-Marie bent down to pick it up. As she handed it to Luc, she noticed his hands were shaking. He mumbled embarrassed thanks and returned to his task. De Villiers gave a boisterous laugh. 'The buttons could have been cast here, but the craft of it is too simple for me to bother with. As you can see' – he gestured at the table leg – 'the work we do is much more complex, demanding real skill.' He spoke with no false pride. 'The silver we receive from the King's treasury is weighed carefully, and Luc and I can assure you that none has gone missing. Our work schedules are already full. Such a job would be more trouble than it is worth.'

'I did not mean to imply that *you* would make something so simple,' she said in a soothing tone, 'I simply want to know how someone would do it.'

Mollified, he described the molding process to her, from the creation of a wax model, making the mold, pouring the molten silver into the mold, and chasing and smoothing the finished button so that the edges were smooth and the monogram stood out. Finally, small loops of silver would be soldered to the back of the disks, creating buttons that could be attached to a garment.

'But before you sew them on, one would need to take the buttons to the guild hall to be assayed and to pay the tax on them. The guild will strike the marks – for the maker, the city, and the year. The marks confirm the quality of the piece. And the guild collects the tax on the piece and pays it to the authorities.'

She digested this information, comparing it to what she remembered about the button in Hendrik's hand. 'What if there aren't any marks?'

'Then the buttons have been made and sold illegally – outside the guild rules and defrauding the city and the King of their taxes. If the maker is caught, he will face a stiff penalty.' The severity of his expression as he laid down the law was in marked contrast to the friendly demeanor of the first part of the visit.

Anne-Marie observed Luc, who was carefully keeping out of his master's line of sight, give a cough that was halfway to a sob. Hastily he wiped away with his sleeve a tear that rolled down his cheek. The silversmith, intent on his explanation, did not notice, but his glance went to the table leg, clearly eager to get back to it.

Anne-Marie realized it was time for her to go. She stood and thanked de Villiers for taking the time to talk with her. She did not return home immediately, however, but lingered outside the studio door, sensing that Luc had something to say to her.

Sure enough, he came out of the studio and spoke with her quietly. 'That button was cast here – I made it as a favor to my brother. I have been so worried about him. I need to talk to someone.'

She was intrigued. Niccolò, she knew, would be meeting with the other Italians at the Gobelins for an evening of rapid-fire conversations in their native dialects. She arranged to meet Luc at the studio that evening, after his day's work was done and they could speak privately.

It was warm and quiet in the silver workshop. Luc answered the door with broom in hand and invited her to sit near the fire while he put it away. It was his turn to sweep and tidy the studio, he explained, one of the jobs he took in rotation with the other apprentices, and he would remain there overnight to tend the fire and make sure it did not go out.

'I like spending the night here,' he confided, sitting on a stool across from her, and lifting a small pot that had been warming on the edge of the coals. He poured the warm cider into pottery cups and handed one to her. She sipped, smiling at him. She hadn't really taken notice of his appearance during her earlier visit, when her attention was focused on de Villiers, but now she took note of a tall, lanky body, giving promise of developing the strength needed to lift and carry the massive vessels he would one day make. The light brown hair he had tied back during the workday now fell softly on either side of a clean-shaven face. Sad brown eyes looked shyly at her as if not quite daring to believe she could help. 'It's warmer than the attic and there's no one to make fun of me when – I mean if – I cry.'

'Tell me about making the button,' she said.

'I have been apprentice to Monsieur de Villiers these last two years, since I was fifteen. My name is Luc Notaire – my father is

135

a notary. We are a respectable family, but my brother Jacques, who is three years older than I, fell in with bad companions. My father threw him out of the house a year ago. However, our mother always had a soft spot for Jacques, and he would visit her when Papa was not at home. Last summer Maman became ill and needed good food and medicines that our family could not afford. I helped as much as I could but I earn so very little. My brother provided most of the extra money that was needed, and our father tolerated this for our mother's sake.

'One day Jacques came to me to ask a favor. He said a friend of his was going to a costume ball dressed as a Duc and asked if I could make a set of silver buttons for the costume. Jacques provided both the model button and spoons to melt down for the silver. I didn't ask where he had got them, but he knew I would not steal from Monsieur de Villiers – which is after all stealing from the King. I was happy to make them; I am still learning, and this seemed to me something I could do. I am always glad to have a chance to practice. So, I came in on a Sunday when I knew Monsieur de Villiers and the others would be out and made twelve buttons for the coat front and cuffs. A real Duc would wear more, of course, but this was just a costume. They weren't the best quality – the crest on the front was clear enough, but I didn't finish them as smooth as they should be. I told my brother that I needed to take them to the guild hall to be stamped, but Jacques insisted on taking them with him, then and there. He thanked me heartily, and the money he received for them paid for more medicines and delicacies for Maman.

'Then the dead man turned up and I found out that it was one of my buttons he had in his hand.'

'Why didn't you come forward the day the man's body was found? Dr Lunague asked everyone at the Gobelins if they recognized him or the silver button.'

'It was the day of Maman's funeral. My father collapsed afterward and I had to take care of him for a week. Monsieur de Villiers was very understanding and let me stay away that long. I did not return to the Gobelins until after the button had already been turned over to the Commissaire.'

'Did Jacques ever tell you the name of the friend who asked for them?'

Luc shook his head. 'Our family has not seen or heard from him since the end of September, not even a message to say he was all right, or to send our mother his love. Maman's worrying made her condition even worse. He didn't even come to the funeral!' he burst out indignantly.

Anne-Marie said, as gently as she could, 'The buttons you made were used as part of a murderer's disguise, passing himself off as a Duc's servant. If Jacques could link the killer and the disguise, he might be a threat to the man. Perhaps he has left Paris for his own safety.'

Luc went very white.

'Did your brother say anything at all about the man he was doing the favor for?'

'No, he said it was better for me not to know.'

'That's why he didn't want the buttons hallmarked – so they couldn't be traced back to this workshop, and to you. Do you think his associates know you are at the Gobelins?'

'He said he just told them I was an apprentice silversmith. He wanted to protect me, he said. He even called himself by another name when among them so no one would connect us.'

She thought for a moment. 'Has anyone ever contacted you to ask for information about the Gobelins, or to ask you to keep them informed, or threatened to get you dismissed if you didn't?' He shook his head.

She smiled. 'Then your brother's discretion has been effective.' Luc gave a sigh of relief.

'Did your brother say how he came by the button you copied?'

'I asked him that. He laughed and said he'd borrowed it from a friend who worked for a noble family. I raised an eyebrow at "borrowed". He saw my look and said, "Don't worry, I'll return it."'

137

'He did,' Anne-Marie assured him. 'The Duc's footman found it again in the carriage house.' The boy's eyebrows jumped. Anne-Marie smiled slightly. 'I would like to describe him to the footman and see if he remembers meeting him. What did your brother look like?'

'I can do better than describe him. Monsieur de Saint-André made a portrait drawing of him – he is very good-looking. Saint-André collects faces, he told us, to use in his tapestry cartoons. I asked him for a copy of the drawing for our mother, and he was kind enough to make one for me as well. It is in my box in my master's house. Wait here and I will bring it.'

Anne-Marie wondered whether Hendrik's face would one day find its way into a tapestry, and in what context? A Biblical series including the Flood, perhaps, or a historical scene of Alexander crossing the Granicus?

Luc returned cradling the precious piece of paper to his heart. Reluctantly, he handed it to Anne-Marie.

'But I know him!' Anne-Marie exclaimed. She frowned, trying to remember where she had seen that face, and laughed with pleasure when she placed it. 'He is one of the pages holding up a red and blue tapestry in the cartoon for one of the Months.' She thought a bit more. 'It was the month of December, showing the château of Monceaux in the background. Saint-André was just putting the finishing touches on his expression when I came to fetch him to draw the dead man. The figure in the cartoon is wearing the royal livery and his hair is curling much more elegantly than here,' she tapped the drawing lightly, 'but the face is the same.' She smiled warmly at the boy. 'Your brother may not have kept the best company while he was in Paris, but in tapestry form he will hobnob with princes and kings.'

The apprentice looked at her in amazement and burst into tears. Instinctively she embraced him, feeling his grief and worry trickle through the fabric of her shawl and blouse. Had he been younger she would have stroked his hair and whispered endearments as one does to a child in distress, but he was near enough

138

to a young man and she close enough to his age to hold back from either action. She did, however, extract a clean handkerchief from her skirt pocket and hand it to him.

'May I borrow this drawing to show to the footman? Perhaps he will remember Jacques. I promise I will return it to you.' The apprentice nodded.

When he could speak again, he walked her to the door and said, 'Thank you. I will' – his voice was shaky, and he took a gulp of air before continuing – 'visit the tapestry painters' studio tomorrow.' He made her a slight bow as she left.

The following afternoon, after dining with her father, Anne-Marie took the drawing to the Hôtel de Languedoc. She had not been there since Christmas, she realized with a pang, and could not help hoping that the Duc or Mademoiselle might be there. To her disappointment, they were not, but Madame Dupont greeted her with pleasure. Marc came in while they were chatting.

He recognized the man in the portrait right away. 'We got into conversation at the tavern on Rue St Antoine and he walked me back to the coach house, where he made a nuisance of himself to Rose.'

Rose peered over his shoulder at the drawing and confirmed it. 'It was just a mild flirtation, harmless fun, but Marc got all jealous and they came to blows.' Her voice held amused tolerance for the foibles of jealous men.

'Was this about the time you lost the livery button?'

'Yes. I did wonder at first, but when I found the button again, I thought it had merely come loose in the scuffle and fallen off.'

'Did you ever see this man again?' Marc and Rose shook their heads.

He was very discreet in returning it, Anne-Marie thought. *He would not want his presence at the Hôtel de Languedoc noted a second time. A strange one, this Jacques, to pick a fight to get hold of the button, but then have the honesty to return it. Perhaps there was hope for him.*

Anne-Marie asked Madame Dupont about the family. Would

Mademoiselle de Toulouse be returning to Paris anytime soon? The old woman's face brightened at the thought of her darling, but she sighed and replied sadly that she did not know when she or her father would return. She packed fresh *sablés* for Anne-Marie to take home 'to that strapping husband of yours'. Anne-Marie laughed and kissed her cheek.

Commissaire Ferrand's office was on the ground floor of his house, located on the square in front of the Church of Saint-Médard. A weekly market held on the square attracted large crowds, so that it was an ideal spot to make public the notices posted on the exterior of the house. Anne-Marie read about new laws being introduced to the public and old ones worth repeating, such as those pertaining to the marketplace. She read public reports of the latest triumphs of the French army in the Netherlands and elsewhere, private denunciations for non-payment of debt, and a father's demand that N★★★★e G★★★★d, a forward hussy, keep away from his son. Two neighborhood women cackled after Anne-Marie read it out to them and engaged in a lively debate about the identity of the young woman.

To her relief, Commissaire Ferrand was there. In marked contrast to Le Brun's office, Ferrand's contained only plain solid furnishings, no comforts or luxury goods – a reflection of the character of the man, she thought. He listened attentively while she repeated what Luc and Marc had told her. He did not recognize the portrait drawing, but one of his men did.

'Jacques Notaire, called himself André Lespineur. Isn't very particular about the company he keeps, mostly cheats and pickpockets. We see them about at the markets and make it obvious we're keeping an eye on them. We haven't arrested him yet, but it's only a matter of time, the way he's headed.'

She told the men about Luc's worries. 'Do you know what happened to him?'

'We can tell you he hasn't been arrested or imprisoned in Paris. We have our hands full as it is and are glad to hear he's someone else's problem now. But if he got mixed up with the professional who killed the Dutchman, it's just as well he has gone. There's only one way a man like that deals with associates for whom he has no further use.'

Anne-Marie nodded soberly and prepared to take her leave. It had grown dark by then, so Ferrand asked the man who recognized Jacques to escort her to the Gobelins.

'If Jacques's associates wanted to put a man into the Bièvre upstream from the Gobelins, where would they likely do it?'

'There's a tavern we like to keep an eye on. That's all we *can* do, it being outside the city limits. The landlord knows how to keep his mouth shut.'

'Where . . .?'

'I'm not going to tell you – it's no place a respectable woman should go,' he declared stoutly. 'I wouldn't want to go there myself unless I were well-armed and had two soldiers with me. It's best to leave the place well alone.'

'But if the Paris police have no authority there, isn't there someone else who does?'

'Of course, but they've found it best to turn a blind eye. It's rumored the landlord is part of Louvois's network.'

'Ah, Monsieur le Marquis de Louvois! Why am I not surprised?'

'You can be as sarcastic as you like, Madame, but he is truly a man to be feared. Stay well out of his path and beneath his notice. I do not wish to be dragging *your* body out of the Bièvre.'

Chapter Fourteen

Anne-Marie found her curiosity piqued by this place about which she had received so many warnings, about which men like Ferrand's burly second-in-command spoke of with fear. Where, precisely, had Hendrik been killed – and if not by the shadowy, mysterious Salomon, then by whom?

She wanted to find out. She *needed* to find out, to see it in her mind's eye, even if she could not personally visit the site. Who could she turn to for information, who knew the Bièvre and its habits? She thought of Old Jean spending his days on the riverbank salvaging items from the water. Dr Lunague and Commissaire Ferrand respected him as an honest old soldier; his employment by the convent argued for both his trustworthiness and his patience with women. Perhaps he would be willing to answer her questions.

After Niccolò had gone to his studio the next morning, she packed a basket with food and wine and went in search of the old man. The Gobelins clock was striking ten as she crossed the main courtyard. It was an overcast day but not so cold as it had been, the mid-January thaw that holds the promise of spring to come. Rain began to fall, washing clean the muddy cobbles. She drew the hood of her cloak over her head and slipped through the back gate. To her disappointment, Old Jean was not at his usual post on the opposite riverbank. He might be in the barn, however. She glanced nervously at the stream as she crossed the footbridge, as if afraid of finding another body; but there was nothing floating in it except the Bièvre's usual load of refuse turned strange colors by runoff from the Gobelins dye vats. She wrinkled her nose at its stench, made more pungent by the thaw.

Safely on the other bank, she hurried around the corner of the building to the entrance facing the garden. It was raining in earnest now, as she sprinted the last few steps through the large open doors into the gloom of the interior. She put down her basket and shook the rain out of her cloak.

'Watch out!'

Hurriedly she stepped back as a young man passed her carrying a fully laden pitchfork. When he returned from the manure pile with the emptied implement held upright, he greeted her politely and asked if he could help.

'I would like to speak with Old Jean,' she told him. 'Is he here?'

'Yes, I'll call him.' He turned and whistled shrilly to the far end of the space. 'Old Jean!' There was no answer except the nickering of the horses. 'Old Jean!' He called again.

'*Oui*,' came a querulous response out of the distant gloom.

'You have a visitor. She's brought food and drink.' The young man smiled at Anne-Marie. 'That will bring him.' She laughed and offered him one of the cakes. He happily accepted and ate it as he returned to his chores.

The barn housed not only the convent's horses that she had seen being led in and out but also dairy cows and the tools and equipment needed for the care of the convent's extensive gardens and orchards. A dozen large crocks of seeds, neatly labeled and tightly sealed against vermin, stood in a tidy row against the wall. A staircase at one end, and footsteps overhead, indicated that the gardener, his family and apprentices lived on the floor above. Old Jean lived there as well, to judge by the sound of purposeful footsteps that made their way across the loft and down the ladder.

Old Jean appeared, brushing bits of hay from his clothes and greeting her like an old friend. 'Madame Bruno! What brings you here?'

She smiled at him. 'I wanted to draw upon your expertise. I've brought wine and cakes to tempt your palate.'

'And loosen my tongue, no doubt.' He winked at her and indicated the row of hay bales used as seats by the workers. They were placed where sweet fresh air from the garden dispelled the animal scents. He fetched cups for the wine and she handed him the cakes. He munched appreciatively. 'So – what portion of my so-called expertise do you wish to consult?'

'I wanted to ask you about the Bièvre.'

'The Bièvre?' He gestured in its direction and shrugged. 'It's there. It flows to the Seine. What is there to know about it?'

'It carries things as it flows that sometimes come to rest at the Gobelins.'

'Ah – still looking into the matter of the dead man?'

'His widow had no idea what her husband was doing upstream. With your knowledge of the flow of the river in all weathers, could you guess from looking at him where he went into the water? Could the flotsam surrounding the body be a clue? Or is the stream so filthy in general that you can't?'

He shook his head at all her questions. 'I just know that it sometimes brings, amidst all the refuse, things I can use or sell. I never thought to question the source of these finds.'

Anne-Marie's disappointment showed in the sag of her shoulders; her brows scrunched together in frustration; she drummed her heels impatiently.

He looked at her intently for a long moment. 'You've found the woman and child no one else believed in. Dr Lunague told me you saved their lives and found them a place to live where they will be safe and looked after. Isn't that enough?'

'I thought it would be. But now that we know why and when and how he was killed, I want to know more. I want to find where, and above all who killed him.' *There*, she thought. *I've said it out loud, admitted it.*

'Are you mad? Do you want to share his fate? I was a soldier. I was paid to kill or be killed. You're a respectable young woman with a husband who loves you. Why risk it all – for no pay, for nothing?'

'But it's not for nothing!' she burst out. 'Ever since Hendrik's body was found, men have been warning me not to get involved, to look away, to play it safe and mind my own business. If I had done that, Rachel and Mariët would be dead now. The police would have had no idea of Hendrik's identity, or why he was killed, or how the Duc's livery came to be involved. I found that out when all these men couldn't. No, it's not for nothing.'

'Hmph.' He grunted and took another cake, eating it slowly as he thought over what she had said. Encouraged, she continued her argument.

'I know I am just a baker's daughter and a sculptor's wife, an ordinary Parisienne. But don't you see? That's what enables me to find things out. Ordinary people talk to me when they would hesitate to say something to Ferrand and his men, for fear of bringing trouble upon themselves or their friends. I'm the baker's daughter bringing bread, another housewife buying provisions or Christmas gifts. I've spent years behind the bakery counter listening to gossip and making the expected responses, and now I can put that skill to some use.'

Old Jean gave a grudging half-smile and she plunged on. 'And I'm fat, which you think would make me stand out, but it's just the opposite. People don't look at you when you're fat – their eyes slide right over and past you as if you're a painful sight, and they avert their gaze to linger on the thin pretty ones. "Oh, I didn't see you there," ' she said in sarcastic mimicry. 'Why not put their blindness to good use as well? All these things I've thought of as disadvantages all my life are now of use. No – it's not for nothing.'

She had finally run out of breath. He picked up the bottle of wine and poured more into her cup. The rain continued to lash down. At the other end of the building, someone started to play a popular song on a flute. She could hear the other men's voices belting out the bawdy words.

Old Jean suddenly chuckled. 'No, you're not going to leave well enough alone, I can see that. And my telling you about it is going to get the better of you, and you're going to have to see for yourself. But up the Bièvre isn't a neighborhood where the baker's daughter would find high-class customers. Nor would a Parisian housewife venture there for her shopping. You'd stick out like a sore thumb even before you started asking questions.

'One of my army mates likes to do his drinking at the Bièvre taverns. He would be your best guide to the neighborhood. I will send word to him and let you know when to meet us here.' He continued in a sharp voice, 'Until then, you are *not* to visit that area on your own – do you understand?'

She nodded.

'Madame Bruno,' he said sternly, fixing her with his gaze, 'this is important. Do I have your word that you will not go there until my friend is able to go with you?'

She stood to attention. '*Oui, mon capitaine*! You have my word.'

'Good,' he grunted. 'I'll send word to him at the Arsenal.'

The Arsenal, the complex housing soldiers as well as munitions, was near the Hôtel de Languedoc. 'He goes from the Arsenal to the Bièvre to drink? That's a long walk, isn't it?'

'Oh, he drinks enough to make it worthwhile. His name is Paul Vincent, but everyone calls him Pot-de-vin – wine pot.'

Anne-Marie spent an impatient three days before Old Jean sent word that Paul Vincent would be spending the night with him after an evening's drinking. Following his instructions, she brought coffee purchased from the early morning vendor and a large loaf of bread.

Pot-de-vin – Paul Vincent – was seated comfortably on one of the hay bales at the entrance, looking surprisingly clear-eyed and neatly dressed for a man who had imbibed heavily the night before. She had visualized someone as old as Old Jean and large, shaggy and unkempt, and similarly invalided out of the army. She was surprised to find instead a man in his forties only a little taller

146

than she, clean-shaven and clean-smelling, with weather-beaten skin and greying blond hair, mild blue-grey eyes, some facial scars but still in possession of all his limbs and retaining most of his teeth. He wore sturdy boots, rough woolen trousers, and a leather jerkin over a stained but clean white linen shirt. A wide cuff of stout leather circled each wrist. Despite the lingering chill indoors, he had taken off his coat and hung it on a nail by the door. He was clearly at home here.

She wondered, given his state of health, why such an experienced soldier was not in the Netherlands. In its effort to break the stalemate of the war, the French army was fully engaged in laying siege to several cities. The King himself had left the comforts of the court at Saint-Germain-en-Laye to personally supervise the progress of the siege at Valenciennes and had invited Le Brun to accompany him.

Paul Vincent did not make a formal bow but inclined his head and greeted her with a brief 'Madame'. His voice was low-pitched and surprisingly gentle. Without preamble, he came to the point. 'Why would a law-abiding woman like you want to know about the disreputable taverns along the Bièvre?'

He listened attentively as she summed up for him what she had learned, and the warnings she had received from Ferrand, his second-in-command, and Old Jean. To her surprise, he did not add to them but asked simply, 'What would you like me to tell you? What do you want to know?'

'The tavern that Ferrand's man spoke of – do you know it?'

'There are two or three like that. But I think I know the one you mean – Le Renard. I cannot vouch for the absolute honesty of the landlord. There's an air of wariness when soldiers walk in. Even off-duty we represent the forces of order, the King's forces.'

'Did you ever see this man there, or do you recognize him from other taverns?' She showed him Saint-André's portrait of Hendrik.

'This is the man who was killed?' She nodded. He studied the drawing with care before shaking his head and handing it back.

147

'I'll anticipate your next question. I was not in the vicinity the night of the murder. I was confined to barracks at the Arsenal.'

She thought for a moment. 'You said the patrons are an unfriendly bunch. Have any of them ever threatened you?'

'They know better. I can take care of myself, and the landlord doesn't want the attention an assault would bring about. Besides,' he continued with a grin, 'not everyone is unwelcoming. The girls are always eager to see a soldier.'

'The girls? Oh – those girls, the ones men are shocked at the thought of my encountering.'

'They know us to be good business, at least early in the evening, when we're still able to—' Old Jean gave him a sharp dig in the ribs and his words tailed off.

Anne-Marie laughed. 'I'm a married woman – no need to be embarrassed.' She thought over what he had said. 'Do these women stake out a particular territory in a tavern – do the same ones show up each time, or are there different ones?'

'Depends. There's Lisette at Le Renard, Angèle at Le Bon Vivant, Babette at La Belle Madeleine . . .'

She laughed again. 'I can see this is an area in which you take pride in your expertise.'

Paul was happy enough to preen himself on this, but Old Jean realized this was not merely idle questioning. 'You're not thinking of visiting these places – or even sending Niccolò? It's no fit place for an honest woman to go, only whores and beggars.'

'He's right.' Paul nodded his agreement.

'I have been told again and again,' with a nod to Old Jean, 'that it is not a place to which a respectable woman would go for even the most innocent of reasons. Moreover, the killer has already had two victims, and I have no desire to be the third. But I want – I *need* – to understand, to know what happened.'

'That knowledge is what could get you killed.'

'And not finding and identifying the killer and bringing him to justice will get other people killed.' She blew out her breath in frustration. 'No one wants to look this in the face. Everyone glances at it sideways for a moment or two and then looks away. "The victim was a man of no importance, no connections." "As long as we can prove the Duc de Languedoc is innocent, that's enough." "The man's family – if indeed they exist – is no concern of ours. It has nothing to do with the Gobelins and would give the Marquis de Louvois an excuse to interfere here." "It's not our jurisdiction." "It's a place no respectable woman should go."' She gave savage imitations of her naysayers, scowling at the thought of them and their cautious, self-interested advice.

'Well, the victim turns out to have been a member of a spy ring – of which the police are now aware. His wife and daughter would be dead by now had Niccolò and I not gone in search of them. At least two people at the Gobelins played a role in this matter. Louvois may wish to threaten the Gobelins but if we can prove that the killer was one of his minions, the Duc de Languedoc can take steps to counter him. I've pushed ahead and found all this out without the encouragement of the police or Monsieur Le Brun – because I am willing to look at what *is*, whether or not danger is involved.'

Old Jean was shaking his head but Paul regarded her with undisguised admiration. 'If we had had more like you in the Netherlands, the war would have been over a year ago.'

A corner of her mouth flicked up. 'I appreciate the compliment, but will you help me?'

'Yes. I'll take you there if you like.' He turned to Old Jean, who was spluttering with indignation. 'Courage deserves to be given its opportunity to succeed.' He shook his head, bemused. 'I've introduced my comrades to the pleasures to be found along the Bièvre but I never thought I would be taking a woman there – a respectable married woman, at that.'

'You're as mad as she is!'

'It won't be the first time,' Pot-de-vin replied calmly.

The Gobelins clock struck half-past eleven, reminding her that she must start preparing food for Niccolò, who liked a hearty midday meal. As she rose to go, Old Jean asked, 'And what will your husband think of his wife going to a disreputable tavern in the company of a soldier?'

It brought her up short. 'We have not discussed it,' she admitted, red-faced. She thanked the men again and hurried back to the Gobelins.

How am I going to broach the subject with Niccolò? What arguments could I marshal to overcome his objections? What if he flat-out forbade me to go? Would I defy him? Could I defy him? Would Pot-de-vin, for all he admired my courage, side with my husband and refuse to take me?

She mulled over these questions as she stirred the stew that had been simmering on the coals, adding water and checking the tenderness of the meat, laying the table and slicing the bread. Usually Niccolò was home immediately after noon, but today she did not hear his step bounding up the stairs until half-past. He burst into the room in high spirits, picking her up and whirling her around until they were both out of breath.

'I have been summoned to Saint-Germain-en-Laye to repair the Angel of the Annunciation in the Chapel. One of Gabriel's wings broke off because of woodworm and a new one needs to be carved and fitted to the sculpture. They want me to come immediately so that I can begin work at first light tomorrow. I will be out there at least a week. I'll be paid well and the King will see, perhaps even say his prayers before, my handiwork. It's the opportunity I've been waiting for since I came to Paris. And I will see the palace for myself!'

He paused for breath.

While he ate, Anne-Marie assembled the clothing he would take. 'I wish I could come with you,' she told him with what she hoped was a convincing wistfulness, with her relief decently hidden. She need not tell him about her plans to visit the Bièvre; and he need not forbid her to go. Remembering his reaction to her impromptu visit to the Hotel de Languedoc, she felt uneasy at keeping this second foray from him. *But I will be perfectly safe with Pot-de-vin,* she assured her guilty conscience. She sent Niccolò off with a hearty kiss and a whispered, 'Hurry back!'

It was the first night she had spent alone since their wedding. She could keep herself busy while Niccolò was in the studio all day, with the pleasant undercurrent of anticipating his return to spend the evening together chatting and the night lying in his arms. His absence made her unexpectedly uneasy, listening for a familiar footstep that wouldn't come, missing his reassuring presence beside her in bed. Gâteau, taking advantage of his absence, was purring at her side, but it was scant comfort. More forcefully than his presence, his absence brought home how much he was part of the fabric of her life, warp and weft. She thought of the tapestry weavers moving their colorful shuttles back and forth, using stout combs to tamp down the rows for durability as well as design.

She regretted now the cowardice that had prevented her from telling him about Saturday's planned visit to the murder site. He might not approve, might argue, might even forbid her, and she might argue with him or desist – but he deserved to know. *I'll tell him as soon as he returns*, she promised as she finally fell asleep.

Chapter Fifteen

With Niccolò in Saint-Germain-en-Laye, she could turn her mind to the visit to the Bièvre, planning the disguise she would assume to blend into the neighborhood, and assembling her arguments to persuade Pot-de-vin that she could pull it off.

Old Jean sent word three days later that Paul would be scouting the terrain that night, and that she should meet them the following morning. She hurried across the footbridge with coffee and bread. 'Le Renard – the Fox – is the tavern we want to visit,' Paul Vincent told them. 'As a regular there, I can come and go as myself, but I haven't decided yet how you should appear.'

'I've been giving that some thought,' she said. Old Jean looked up with apprehension clearly written in every wrinkle, but Pot-de-vin regarded her with simple curiosity. 'I'm told it's mostly beggars and whores one encounters there. I'm clearly too fat to make a convincing beggar,' she grimaced, 'so – she took a deep breath – 'I thought I would masquerade as a prostitute – providing you'll come along as my protector, of course.'

There was silence as her words sank in.

Old Jean choked on the mouthful of wine he was attempting to swallow and pitched forward in a cough that sprayed red wine at her feet, a few drops spattering the hem of her gown. Paul Vincent let out a great bellow of laughter that rang through the space, causing a cow to moo loudly in protest and startling the pigeons from their perches in the rafters. He wiped his eyes as he leaned forward to pound Old Jean on the back.

The cow mooed again. 'Quiet!' he ordered. 'Who asked for your opinion?' This set off a fresh round of laughter, Old Jean joining him.

Anne-Marie forced herself to sit still and regard them with what she hoped was the calm gaze of rational intent. At last the men calmed down. The pigeons fluttered again to their roost.

'Say that again,' Paul demanded. 'I want to be sure I heard you correctly.' Old Jean seemed beyond words.

'As you wish,' replied Anne-Marie evenly. 'I repeat: As it is not a place where respectable women are likely to venture, and as I am too fat to make a convincing beggar, I thought that it would be most plausible if I posed as a prostitute. With you at my back, of course, to see that I come to no harm.'

'That's what I thought you said.' He drained his cup and opened a second bottle. He gave her another of his assessing looks. Like a soldier, she thought, scanning unfamiliar terrain for places where the enemy might lie in ambush.

As she watched, his face lost its genial cast and became older, harder, shut-down, the face of a man who brooked no opposition to getting what he wanted. He leered knowingly at her and slurred to Old Jean with a dig in the ribs, 'Now that's a well-built lass – it'd be like settling into a feather bed, it would, with pillows all over.' He turned to Anne-Marie. 'Stand up, lass. Let's see what you've got.'

She stared at him.

'Well, come on, girl, you want my business, you've got to show me the goods for sale. Stand up!'

She continued to stare at him as she rose to her feet, uncertain what to do next.

'Put your hands on your hips. Throw your head back and your chest out,' he ordered. 'Now turn around for me nice and slow, so I can see what I'm going to get my hands on.' He leered at her and licked his lips suggestively.

Her face flaming, she began to turn slowly, swaying her hips like the women she had seen in the Latin Quarter. As she turned her backside to him, she smiled over her shoulder and winked. When she had completed her turn, she stood again with hands on hips, giving him a bold look with eyebrows raised in inquiry or invitation.

'That's better,' Paul said in his normal voice. His face had dropped its harsh mask and resumed its genial cast. 'With a little practice, you'll do nicely.'

They arranged to meet on Saturday afternoon. 'Wear something bright and low-cut,' he ordered. 'You want to attract men's attention. See if you can get something from a *revendeuse*.' She wrinkled her nose at him. The sellers of used clothing were not particular about the cleanliness of their wares, which often gave off a ripe smell.

He only grinned at her discomfiture. *Get used to it,* his expression seemed to say. 'And it wouldn't hurt for you to observe a few, see how they act with a man.'

Anne-Marie gave an unexpected snort of laughter. 'This is a strange conversation to be having at a convent.'

Old Jean tsk'd and tch'd, but Paul Vincent gave another of his bellowing laughs. 'Keep that sense of humor, Madame: you are going to need it.'

She spent the days doing diligent research on the dress and manners of prostitutes – strolling, observing their behavior. She did not stay in one place for long, not wishing to be observed at observing. In the evening she practiced the women's speech and movements. She altered an old blouse that had grown too tight, compressing and displaying her breasts over its low-cut neckline. On Paul Vincent's instructions, she left off the bodice she usually wore underneath it. 'You don't want a man to fight his way through a cage,' he told her, 'you want to give him easy access to the tempting goods on offer.' From a *revendeuse* she was able to purchase a yellow skirt and bright red shawl, each ragged at the edges. Pot-de-vin had been right in his advice; she looked as though she had been on the streets for years. It was hard to wear with ease, however; even in the privacy of her apartment, with only an indifferent Gâteau to take notice, she had to fight a strong desire to cover herself. She began to wonder if she fully realized what taking on this persona would mean. She hoped she could go through with the masquerade on Saturday night.

Nonetheless, when she dressed to meet Pot-de-vin on Saturday evening, the costume was beginning to feel less alien, her actions while wearing it more natural. It was another frosty night, so she wore her bright blue cloak over it – Niccolò's wedding gift, she thought with a pang. But her only other cloak was brown and drab. She would wash it well afterward. She wrapped it tightly about her as she hurried across the courtyard, praying she would not encounter anyone. She let herself out the back gate with a sigh of relief, but a sudden gust of wind blew open the cloak as she crossed the footbridge. She fastened it again, looking around in embarrassment. She was glad Nic could not see her now.

Neither Paul nor Old Jean was in sight when she entered the building. Glad to be out of the wind, she hung up her cloak and adjusted her red shawl. She looked forward to the expression on their faces when they saw her dressed for the part.

They still had not appeared when the clock struck half-past. Had Paul been confined to barracks, tonight of all nights?

She was startled to hear a woman singing. She hadn't realized anyone else was there. Perhaps it was the gardener's wife, and she would know when the men would return. Anne-Marie followed the sound to one of the stalls, where a young woman with a postulant's wimple was sitting on a three-legged stool, milking a red-and-white cow. The skirts of her habit were tucked up to avoid the muck on the floor. She leaned her cheek against the cow's flank, her eyes closed, singing to the animal as her practiced hands squeezed the milk from the teats in a regular rhythm. Anne-Marie, who had never milked a cow, looked on in some amazement.

The song finished, the young woman opened her eyes. She

looked embarrassed at being observed, and Anne-Marie realized she had intruded upon a private moment. She began to apologize but the young woman shook her head and smiled again.

'Blanche-rouge was my dowry when I entered the convent. I come to milk her sometimes when I'm homesick.' Her face took on a wistful expression. 'When I close my eyes and sing to her, I'm back on our farm again, at least for a little while.'

'Are you allowed to go back for a visit?'

The young woman shrugged. 'There is nothing to visit. My parents died two years ago; the creditors took the farm, but Blanche-rouge belonged to me. My brother and I came here because our aunt is one of the Cordelières. She arranged for him to be apprenticed to the gardener and for me to enter the convent. It is what I have always wanted.'

'When will you take your vows?'

'On the first of May, the day of Our Lady. Then I shall truly belong.'

Anne-Marie listened with some amazement. She had always felt restricted by her life behind the bakery counter, so relieved to break out into the open by marrying Niccolò. The inclination to spend one's life in such a restricted existence was beyond her understanding. But happiness shone in the young woman's face, in contrast to her own restless wanting more and more. That one could be content within restrictions was a new idea for her. Most people probably were. *And where would Rachel and Mariët be now, if you had been? Where would you be now if Niccolò had been?* Gently she asked the young woman to say a prayer that all people should be as content with their lives as she was with hers.

The girl nodded happily. 'I already do.'

Footsteps at the stable door caused Anne-Marie to turn her head. As she did, she remembered belatedly that she was dressed as a prostitute. She blushed to think of how she must appear to the young nun.

'Listen,' she said urgently, 'these clothes – I'm not really a—'

'There is no need to explain or excuse,' the young woman

156

replied with equanimity. 'God accepts us all as His creatures, if we have faith in Him.'

Tears sprang to Anne-Marie's eyes. She felt humbled in the presence of so much love and acceptance. 'Thank you, Sister,' she said quietly, and turned to go.

It was indeed Paul Vincent she had heard. He sat on one of the hay bales, peering anxiously into the garden as though afraid she had backed out after all.

'I'm here, Paul,' she said quietly.

He turned to look at her, and his jaw dropped.

She laughed delightedly, her self-confidence returning. 'I take it I look the part?'

'I'm going to have more trouble than I thought, keeping men off you,' he said seriously.

She gave him one of the saucy looks she had so diligently practiced. 'Are you sure you are' – slight pause – 'up to it?'

He chuckled. 'I think we had better get this visit over with before you get in any more practice.' He rose. 'Shall we go?'

Paul led her through the convent gardens and orchard and out by a side gate, using a key he had borrowed from Old Jean. Going from the sweet-smelling, calmly ordered world of vegetable beds and trees laid out in neat rows to the smells and chaos of the streets took her aback. The businesses were no different from those in the Quartier Latin, but everything seemed smaller, meaner, with a layer of grime. It struck her forcefully that the expedition she had undertaken so lightheartedly was one that the residents must undergo every day in earnest. She wondered whether the rogue journeymen who had attacked Niccolò had ended up in a place such as this.

Paul Vincent took the place and its denizens in his stride, not stopping to exclaim in pity as Anne-Marie did. When she commented on this, he said shortly, 'I've seen worse.'

She turned to look at him, but he would not meet her gaze. A spasm of pain crossed his face. 'The army was quartered on a town after we had laid siege to it and we ate up what little food was left. I remember the day we left, people and dogs were fighting over scraps of food in the gutters, snarling at each other. And then they – the people and the dogs – each realized that the other was food.' His voice was rough and choked with unshed tears. 'They turned on each other.' He shuddered and swallowed with difficulty. 'I have seen many gruesome sights on the battlefield, but none so bad as that.'

After that he was not disposed to talk; his eyes moved back and forth, scanning the crowds and the dark recesses of the buildings for malefactors and other unwelcome surprises. He had decorously taken her arm when they first set out, but now his arm was around her waist, proclaiming her his woman and guarding against anyone cold and desperate who might tear the cloak off her back. She was grateful to have him there and told him so.

He turned to face her then. 'You can still go back. I won't think the less of you for it.'

She hesitated, but only for a moment. 'I've come this far – let's go on.'

They picked their way carefully. Only a sliver of moon shed a gleam of light on their surroundings. In Paris the street lamps would be lit, but here there were none. After a half-hour's walk, they came to Le Renard, a rough squat building set about thirty paces back from the river's edge. A slaughterhouse stood next to it. They could hear a calf bawling for its mother which had probably been butchered that afternoon, its plaintive calls heart-wrenching. Anne-Marie did not enter the tavern immediately but went first to the riverbank, to get an idea of how easy it would be to put a body into the water there. Paul remained watchful in the shadows.

She stepped carefully to the edge and peered over. The water was moving more swiftly since the thaw. She picked up a stone and threw it into the stream to hear its splash and imagine what sort of sound Hendrik's body might have made when it was put over the bank.

'Are you looking for customers? You won't find any out here.'

She stifled a scream. Intent on her thoughts, she had not heard anyone come up to her. She whirled around to face the speaker, a stocky boy of no more than ten years old.

'You have to go into the tavern to get them, and the landlord will want a cut.'

She stared at him. Surely he was too young to be conversant with the customs of prostitutes? 'Who are you?'

'My father owns the slaughterhouse.' He nodded to the building next to them. Clearly, he dined well, thanks to his father's job. His face and hands were filthy, and he was eating something – a blood sausage, she realized with a lurch of her stomach.

'*What* did you say?'

'I said you have to go into the tavern to get customers. But that's Lisette's territory. She does okay even if she's got just half an arm on the left side.' He spoke, matter-of-factly, as if such things were common knowledge. She couldn't think how to answer him. He pressed on, undaunted by her silence. 'Well maybe you could go in, come to think of it – I haven't seen her since the day that man was killed and put in the river.'

Anne-Marie found her voice. 'You heard about that?'

'I saw it! The man in the blue suit came out of the tavern holding up the other man like he was drunk, and dragged him to the riverbank and put him in. Then he went back into the tavern.'

'I hope he didn't see you.'

'Of course not,' the boy said scornfully. 'I know how to stay out of sight. But you can see everything that happens on the river from my window.'

'Can you tell me more about the man in the blue suit – so I can be sure to avoid him?'

'It was a servant's suit, light blue – stupid sort of color, it'd catch all the dirt – with silver braid on the cuffs and hem and shiny buttons. I saw them glint in the lights from the tavern as he came out the door.'

'Has he come back since then?'

He thought. 'Yes, but in other clothes.'

This was the sort of information she had come here to find,

159

and her excitement overcame her repulsion for its source. She was about to ask him more about the killer's appearance when a man emerged from the slaughterhouse wearing a bloody apron, with great splashes of blood on his hands and arms. He looked as if he could well be a murderer. Instinctively she stepped back.

'Get away from here,' he said roughly. 'I've warned your sort to stay off my property and away from my son.'

The little boy who had initiated the conversation looked immensely pleased to have got her into trouble.

Anne-Marie was not used to being spoken to like dirt. It bothered her, much as she tried to carry it off with an air of indifference. Their jeering laughter followed her to the door of the tavern.

Chapter Sixteen

The interior of the tavern seemed even darker than outside, despite the large log ablaze in the fireplace and several lanterns hanging from the ceiling. Anne-Marie stood for a moment at the door, letting her eyes adjust to the dim light. Men in dark clothes were huddled in groups of three or four around tables just large enough to hold several beakers of wine. Some looked up at her entrance but turned back to the conversations, uninterested. No one looked particularly villainous. Did she think there would be a character sneering as he cleaned his nails with the point of his stiletto? She was relieved to see Paul Vincent sitting alone at a corner table, almost lost in the shadows.

The landlord regarded her stolidly from behind his counter. She took off her cloak and threaded her way through to him. As she reached into her pocket to pay for her wine, he caught her hand and said roughly in a low voice, 'You solicit in here, I'll expect thirty per cent.' He gave a grimace which might have passed for hospitality. 'Your wine is on the house.'

She nodded as though this were commonplace to her and picked up her drink, turning to find a table. A man was at her elbow. 'Come. Sit at my table. Please.' He gestured at one close to the fireplace. She smiled her thanks and followed him.

It was warmer than she expected in that spot, and after a few minutes she let the red shawl fall open. The man eyed her appreciatively but made no move to solicit her favors, to her surprise.

'I'm looking for my friend Lisette,' she said, 'a pretty girl, but with a short arm. She told me she does good business here. Have you seen her?'

The man shook his head. 'Not for weeks.'

That confirmed what the boy had told her. She tried not to let her excitement show and made her body sag with disappointment. Her companion continued to stare at her breasts, his breath coming more rapidly now. His right hand was still curled around his beaker in a show of innocence, but his left hand, she came to realize, was under the table, working himself into a state of excitement. The virtuous wife in her was relieved but the prostitute she was playing was indignant that he saw fit to use her in such a manner without paying.

Another customer thought so, too. A man, whose blue eyes had been steadily boring into her from a table against the wall, came over to them. 'Here, you,' he said roughly to the man she had been sitting with, 'the lady has to earn her living. She can't do that with you goggling at her while you get your jollies.' He clouted the man on the back. The left hand rose again above the table to the amusement of those who overheard him. 'If you've got to entertain yourself, do it in the corner, while I show the lady what a *real* man is about.'

The new arrival roughly hauled the would-be client to his feet with his right hand, while his left hand lifted the man's coat, revealing his flies undone and his private parts spilling out of them. When the man tried to protest, the other responded by lifting him higher and letting the rest of him dangle as well. 'Let the woman have a good look at what she inspired,' the taunting voice continued. 'After all, it's only fair.' His voice had risen so that a number of customers were watching them, laughing at the first man's predicament. His tormentor finally let go of his coat and dropped him back to earth. The man stumbled but managed to right himself and, propelled by a none-too-gentle shove, slunk to the table the other had vacated.

Her new acquaintance seated himself at her table and smiled at her, a movement of the lips that never reached his eyes. Of a pale blue that seemed to shine with their own internal light, they stared at her with an intensity that made it difficult to look away. She had an impression of pitted skin framed by dark blond hair.

'You're new here,' he said. 'What's your name?'

'Anne-Marie,' she said without thinking, and inwardly berated herself. 'But the boys like to call me Pomme.'

'Ah. And what brings you out here, Anne-Marie-called-Pomme?'

'I'm looking for my friend Lisette. She told me she does good trade here, and she owes me ten sous. Have you seen her?'

'No, not for some weeks – but if you need those ten sous, I would be happy to help you earn them.' He smiled again. 'Unlike that pathetic fellow' – he jerked his head in the direction of the table whose occupant stared fixedly at them while both his hands were busy out of sight – 'I'm willing to pay generously for my pleasures. I'd like to feast on these apples tonight.' His right hand reached out, his forefinger tracing the neckline of her blouse, his smile broadening as he watched her nipples stiffen beneath the thin fabric.

This is what you get for parading around like this. Keep calm. Keep calm. She forced herself not to pull away from his touch and was annoyed to find she was roused by it. She thought of Niccolò and wished it was his hand caressing her. She made no reply to her companion. He did not seem to need one and took her silence as assent.

'You're an accommodating lass,' he said approvingly. She arched her eyebrows at him. 'We can go out back for a few minutes for four sous, or you can come up to my room for the night and earn those ten sous Lisette seems to have made off with. I'm an exacting taskmaster – you won't have the energy for anyone else tonight – but I pay well.'

She was completely out of her depth. She gave a nervous glance at Pot-de-vin's table, but he was no longer there. Adding to her discomfort was the man's evident enjoyment of her unease. She had seen how he dealt with the other man; he might well treat

163

her in similar fashion if she crossed him. *I must keep stalling,* she thought frantically. *What can I do?* Her legs were like jelly; she couldn't get up even if she had wanted to.

The tavern door opened with a crash, and Pot-de-vin came in. He gave the room a sweeping glance and strode to her, his face the picture of outraged propriety. 'I thought you'd given all that up when you became my woman!' He glared at her companion. 'Any man here who touches her will have *me* to answer to.'

She gaped at him before she recovered herself.

'I thought you were at the barracks tonight,' she replied sulkily. 'That's where you said you'd be. I got lonely and wanted company. Not much to do in a room by myself.'

'Oh, I'll give you plenty of company. But first I've a mind to—' And to her amazement he sat down, pulled her roughly over his knee, and administered a sound spanking, to the delight of the other customers. She did not have to pretend to protest loudly. When she tried to twist around to tell him to stop, her breasts fell out of her low-cut blouse, to the men's further delight. Finally, he let go of her and growled, 'Cover yourself, woman! I'm not sharing *them* with everyone!'

She wrapped her shawl around her and picked up her cloak. She was in tears, unable to think what her next line should be.

He looked her up and down with satisfaction. 'I think that's enough for one night. Let's get you home so you can apologize proper-like.' Grunting with the effort, he hoisted her over his shoulder and carried her out the door of Le Renard.

Chapter Seventeen

Michel Glacis sat at the table near the tavern fireplace, nursing his second beaker of wine. He didn't want to get too drunk tonight, not after the woman had put him in the mood for a vigorous romp in bed. It was a pity that oaf had shown up to claim her just as the evening looked particularly promising. The regular girls bored him, but this buxom newcomer was amusing.

He was in the mood for a little fun tonight. He had just been paid for his last job, the spy Salomon. It had felt good to plunge his stiletto into this one, who recruited others to do his dirty work. Ransacking the porcelain shop afterward had been a risk – it was safest to quit the scene as soon as possible – but his enjoyment made it worthwhile. All those vases and bowls meant for ornament – stupid, useless things – with their uselessness displayed now for all to see. They would be swept up and thrown away like the trash they were.

From Salomon his thoughts turned to the Dutchman. A stupid man trying to sell him false information about terrain and forces in Holland. As if he or anyone else in the Marquis de Louvois's network would take someone's word without first checking it! That supposed shortcut had been a trap that would have put a large part of the French army in peril. Michel had wanted to kill the Dutchman then and there, but Louvois's man ordered him to wait until they had used him to convey equally damaging messages to his cohorts in Holland.

Finally, permission had come. There would be a bonus, he was told, if he could do so in such a way that the Duc de Languedoc – whose livery Michel had borrowed for his negotiations with the spies – could be discredited by it. He had been pleased by this assignment, no commonplace knifing.

He had cleaned his ducal livery for the occasion, sponging off the dirt from the pale blue fabric, giving a polish to the silver buttons that Jacques had got for him, polishing his shoes and buckles, careful to look the image of a servant of that oh-so-upright nobleman. He had carried out all these preparations in the room he rented upstairs, to which only he had the key.

He had come down the stairs and surveyed the room, a cautious habit he had long adopted. As usual few men were inside at this hour, and Lisette, sitting alone at a table, was the only woman. Each time a man entered, she loosened her shawl to show off her bosom, then wrapped up warmly again. He purchased a beaker of wine and sat down at another table, to wait.

The door opened; his quarry had arrived. The landlord greeted him easily, 'Hello, Dutchman! Beer for you tonight?' The other customers snickered. Even someone as stupid as this foreigner knew better than to say yes; the beer served here was of such poor quality that it was rumored the landlord mixed it with dog's piss. The Dutchman ordered red wine instead, coarse but at least drinkable. He greeted Michel with a nod and sat down at the table. Automatically he took out his knife and the piece of wood he was carving into the curled form of a sleeping cat. 'A toy for the Christmas market,' he explained to Michel, who gave a perfunctory smile in reply, his wary eyes following the movements of the knife.

'So, friend, you have information for me?' Michel put a small leather pouch on the table. Lisette, hearing the clink of coins, looked up eagerly. Michel listened intently as the Dutchman gave him information on troop positions and strengths, planned movements. 'Ah, this will indeed be of use – unless it's as worthless and misleading as the last shit you fed us.' The man's eyes opened wide in alarm – Michel's favorite moment in a killing, when the victim's fear began to mount to panic. 'You didn't think we'd check? I was a soldier in the last war in the Netherlands. I know what it is like to be ambushed by the enemy. As you, too, are about to discover.' He gave a genuine laugh as he pulled out his stiletto and, in a deft movement, pushed the Dutchman's coat aside to insert and withdraw the knife, covering the wound again with the coat.

With his last strength, the Dutchman grabbed at Michel, who stepped back quickly, but not before the man fastened on one of his coat buttons with a convulsive grip, tearing it off as he slumped forward. The knife and toy clattered onto the floor.

When the other tavern occupants looked up, Michel laughed easily and said jokingly to the dying man, 'I thought you had a better head for wine than this, my friend. Let's get you out into the fresh air.' He put the pouch of coins and the knife into his pocket and the toy into the Dutchman's. He lifted the Dutchman up as if he were a drunk he was helping out. Carrying out the Dutchman would have meant enlisting an accomplice; it was always safest to work alone. The others drinkers shrugged and went back to their conversations.

Out the front door of the tavern to the riverbank: the water would finish the job. He paused for a moment to wrap the button threads securely around the Dutchman's fingers. Afterward he stood the man upright and gave him a shove so that he fell face down into the water. The Dutchman made a few weak movements to lift up his head, but Michel stood on the bank with a long pole from the slaughterhouse and hit him none too gently on the back of the head, holding it firmly in the water until all struggles ceased. He used the pole to push the body out into the current and watched it begin to make its way downstream. With luck, it would be in the Seine by mid-morning. As an afterthought, he threw the woodcarver's knife in after him.

Michel had re-entered the tavern by the front door, calling out a good night to a supposedly recovered Hendrik. Then he had gone up to his room to change into his own clothes and come back down for a celebratory drink.

He was quite pleased with how quickly, quietly and professionally he had handled the killing and the disposal of the body. The body had been found, as he knew it would be, and the Duc's involvement had been made too obvious to ignore. His Noble Uprightness had been inconvenienced by the police. He had earned his bonus. Instead of being paid off in a tavern as usual, he was summoned to the office of Louvois's agent, Leclerc, whom Michel privately called the Paymaster. He strode confidently into the Arsenal and was escorted to the appropriate door. He entered after a perfunctory knock.

The Paymaster, a thin wraith of a man, sat behind his desk in the center of the windowless room, wheezing noisily. Despite the weather, only a meager fire burned in the grate. Shelves crammed with dossiers lined the walls, but the desk held only writing materials, a carafe of water, a large bell, and a single dossier. There were no chairs for visitors, who were not encouraged to linger.

'Monsieur Mendiant.' He greeted Michel with a perfunctory grimace perhaps meant to pass for a welcoming smile.

Michel ground his teeth at the use of his real name, Mendiant – beggar. He had not used it in years. How had this man, who insisted on being called *Monsieur* Leclerc, found it out? He hated all that it implied. He had always liked the name Michel, the powerful Archangel depicted so often with sword in hand. It was as if the human Michel's profession had been decided at birth. He had chosen his last name, Glacis, suggesting ice and glaciers. He liked the idea that people would shiver at the mere mention of it.

'Monsieur Louvois commends your work. We are able to go ahead with the siege of Valenciennes as planned.'

Michel nodded curtly at the praise, accepting it as his due. It would, he knew, be followed by criticism calculated to prevent him from getting above himself.

'However, suspicion has not centered on the Duc as Monsieur Louvois intended it to. People have been asking awkward questions. You've always done your job well for us, so we can forgive this mistake. But I would not want to make the Minister angry a second time.' The Paymaster rubbed the back of his neck uneasily. 'Got a tongue like the lash of a whip, he has.'

Really? Have you *ever been whipped?* Michel gave a skeptical glance at the man's plain but expensive suit of brown wool. *To you it's just a figure of speech.*

The Paymaster intercepted the glance; he and Michel glared at each other for a long minute. He opened the dossier on his desk, drew in a wheezing breath, and began to read aloud.

'Michel Mendiant, calls himself Glacis. Age approximately thirty. Grandfather, also Michel Mendiant, is fined for begging in six towns between Nantes and Paris. Father, André Mendiant, also a professional beggar, is first fined in Paris in 1648. Excuses himself by saying he needs to support wife and infant son. Is arrested five more times and dies in Hôpital Saint Louis in 1653. After his death his wife works as a domestic in a series of taverns until her death from convulsions in 1661.

'Son Michel is left to fend for himself on the streets but is clever enough to stay ahead of the law. Enlists in the army in 1664, calling himself Michel Glacis. Serves for five years, the last two in the first war with the Dutch. Wounded 1669 and discharged, but his facility with a knife and the enjoyment with which he kills is noted by his commanding officer.

'First assignment from this office, November 1670, successfully carried out, as have been all subsequent assignments. Works alone. Keeps a room in Le Renard tavern.' He looked up at Michel for the first time since he had started reading. 'With your help, France is no longer troubled by sixteen enemies of the State.' It was said in a flat voice with neither gratitude nor respect; it might have been just another figure to tabulate in a ledger.

'We will pay you for the Dutchman – but your secondary objective was not achieved. We wanted the Duc disgraced so that anything he has said, or will say, will lose its credibility. Unfortunately, he is still in favor.'

'What is it that you would like me to do? Kill the Duc de

Languedoc?' His tone was thoughtful, measured, considering options.

'No, the King is fond of him and trusts him. To kill him while he is in favor would only increase the influence of those ideas he has inculcated in the King and cause His Majesty to want his murderer found and punished. Monsieur Louvois might find himself forced to have you killed. You have been of such use to us that it would be a shame to do so.'

Had Michel imagined it, or was there a trace of regret in that expressionless voice?

He opened a desk drawer and brought out a small leather bag. 'Here is your pay.'

Michel accepted it as it was given, without thanks. 'My next assignment?' he asked.

The Paymaster gave a dismissive flick of his fingers. 'There is none at present. We will contact you when we have need of you.' He rang the bell upon his desk; it made a discordant, tinny sound. The office door opened and the guard came in, his hand on his sword hilt. 'Show this man out,' the Paymaster said to him. He pulled out another dossier and did not look up as Michel was led from the room.

Michel had not been unduly worried. They would need him again. He spat and shrugged. The number of men he had killed would barely equal the deaths from one skirmish in this endless war in the Netherlands that Louvois was so badly mismanaging. They were in the same line of work, he and the mighty Marquis. Louvois merely carried it out on a grand scale, hundreds of lives at once.

Sure enough, a month later Salomon had been assigned to him. Once again, he had chosen a busy locale, the popular Rue St Honoré. This time the Paymaster had actually sounded pleased by both the killing and the destruction of the shop, the owner of which had decided to return to Amsterdam for good. Michel's pay had made a satisfying *clink* in his pocket.

Yet, despite these successes, he was restless. He had been delighted

170

to join Louvois's organization at first. He liked the aura of power that surrounded the Marquis, the way men leapt to do his bidding. But he had not risen in the ranks; he was merely useful to them, and when he had finished being useful – had either lost his knack or decided to retire – he would be disposed of, unless he managed to disappear before another of Louvois's paid assassins could get to him.

His thoughts turned to how he might bring about that disappearance. He was already experienced in reinventing himself – first as a soldier, and then as a killer for hire – and in adopting disguises and personae to carry out those killings. He might not be a gentleman, but this last assignment had demonstrated that he was adept in the role of a gentleman's gentleman.

Moreover, he had accumulated a tidy sum to aid him in this next transition. It was his habit to put to one side one-half of his fee as well as any bonuses, living upon only the other half and spending it prudently. He had become, by his standards, a man of substance; no one would ever be able to call him a beggar. But he would need to find another place to store his hoard of gold and silver coins. If the Paymaster knew about his room at Le Renard, it was no longer safe to keep it there.

How had Leclerc known about it? Who could have told him? Was the landlord, though well-paid for his silence, part of Louvois's network? Who else might have known? Lisette? She had been a regular at Le Renard for months. Had she seen him go up to his room while he had thought her too occupied with a man to take notice? He did not think she was an employee of Louvois, but she might have been paid to be an informant.

When had he last seen Lisette here, and why had she stayed away?

Now he thought about it, he had not seen her since the night he had killed the Dutchman – since before the Dutchman came, in fact. She had been outside when he had put the Dutchman in the Bièvre. Had she witnessed what he had done? She knew to keep her mouth shut, but it was always safer not to leave witnesses.

He would need to make sure she had no opportunity to tell anyone what she had seen, even if it had been nothing at all. He couldn't take that chance.

She would not have gone very far; most likely she had gone into Paris, hoping to disappear in the vastness of the city. He knew where the prostitutes were usually to be found. While he was looking for her, he could also look for the one who had been in earlier tonight. The bright blue cloak she had worn over her dress should be easy to spot. He smiled. He would have another go at her when the soldier wasn't around.

Chapter Eighteen

Niccolò was well satisfied with his week at Saint-Germain-en-Laye. The angel's worm-eaten wing was damaged beyond repair, but his design for a new wing was approved, one that flared out at a slight angle to suggest Gabriel had just alighted and was in the act of folding his wings. He was assigned a quiet studio next to the château stables and given several pieces of well-seasoned wood to work with. It was arranged that he should lodge in a nearby hostel that catered to the steady stream of craftsmen who kept the château in good repair; Niccolò took his meals with painters, carpenters, gilders and workers in stucco from all over Europe.

On the third day, after he had glued the pieces of wood and left them to set, he decided to explore the château and its park. The King was not in residence. Niccolò was disappointed – he had been looking forward to getting at least a glimpse of the monarch he had come to France to serve – but he could observe the glitter of the court. He changed into his wedding suit, which he had brought with him for just this purpose and rented a hat and sword so that he would not appear to disadvantage among the members of the court. Niccolò felt a bit foolish in these trappings of a gentleman. He knew it was the ambition of many painters and sculptors to be considered as such, rather than 'mere' artisans, but he had never minded the latter designation for himself. He was a woodcarver and proud of the fact.

He intended to begin by viewing the splendidly decorated

rooms of the château, but the heat and smell of all those bodies pressed together drove him back into the fresh air before he had progressed very far. The garden parterre was not nearly so crowded. A gust of wind sent his rented hat down the lawn. Cursing in Italian, he ran after it. He had just fitted it more securely on his head when he heard laughter. He looked up to see three young women – two ladies in fur cloaks and muffs and a maid in a wool cloak – not so beautiful as the one he had given Anne-Marie, he thought proudly – approach him, giggling in amusement.

Hastily he snatched his hat off again and made an awkward bow.

'You are new to the court,' one of the young ladies said, regarding him with frank interest in her blue eyes. She had full red lips parted in a smile and a clear complexion that owed little to artifice. Her abundantly curling blonde hair, threaded with blue-green ribbons, escaped from the hood of her cloak to cascade artfully over one shoulder. 'Perhaps we can show you our favorite secluded spot in the garden?' she added with a wink.

'It's a cold day for a walk,' the other chimed in. She looked very like the first – they must be sisters – except that her hair was a rich brown, in which she wore dark red ribbons. 'I'm sure you'd welcome the chance to warm up.' She said the last two words roguishly. The maid said nothing, but she too looked at him hungrily.

Niccolò hesitated to accompany this trio anywhere, but he knew that to demur would be to invite more laughter, so he replied with every appearance of delight, 'I would be so grateful if you would, so that I can share them with my wife.'

It was comical how quickly the young ladies' faces fell; only the maid's eyes, glancing quickly from his face to theirs, held a gleam of amusement.

'*Désolée*,' responded the first lady, 'but we need to return to the château for the . . .' She hesitated.

'. . .viola da gamba concert in the Queen's apartment,' finished the other smoothly.

'Oh, yes,' added the maid, 'they'd be disappointed to miss it.'

Niccolò made another bow to the trio and continued on his way. He was delighted to encounter the Duc de Languedoc a few minutes later. In this sea of unfamiliar faces, the Duc felt like an old friend. Niccolò explained his presence at the château; inquired after Mademoiselle de Toulouse; and accepted with alacrity the Duc's offer to show him around the park. They began the long walk down the Grande Terrasse overlooking the Seine.

Before Niccolò could discuss the progress of the investigation, however, they were joined by the trio of young women, who had not gone indoors after all. Observing Niccolò's relaxed presence in the company of an older man, one of them remarked, 'Oh, I understand – he prefers men.'

Niccolò did his best to ignore the remark but he felt himself blush with embarrassment.

The Duc nodded to the young women but, as they were of lesser rank, did not remove his hat. 'Allow me to present to you Marie-France and her sister Marie-Ange, daughters of the Comte et Comtesse de Kéroualle, and' – he hesitated, not recognizing the third. 'Mesdemoiselles, Signor Niccolò Bruno, late of Rome, now resident in Paris.'

Niccolò made another bow, snatching off his hat yet again. 'Mesdemoiselles, er' – he hesitated at their difficult Breton name – 'Kerallo.'

The young women giggled, made their curtsies to the Duc, and left them.

'Don't take it personally,' the Duc said ruefully. 'Nothing will tame that one's tongue. They are often called l'Ange et la Diable. The family is from Brittany. One of their older cousins, Louise, is the mistress of King Charles of England, a favorite cousin of our King.'

They walked on but before Niccolò could return to the investigation, the Duc took up a new subject. 'I am glad to have met up with you. I have an idea in mind for a commission. Monsieur de Roussillon has written of small towns in New France in which the churches have only rudimentary altars. I would like to send an altarpiece to him to make a gift to one of these. Would this be of interest to you?' His eyes were twinkling.

'*Would* it!' Niccolò's eyes were shining as he stared intently ahead as if trying to see all the way to Canada. 'I have tried to imagine from your tales of your son's letters what it looks like, as if I were standing with him to survey the forests. To have my work known even in that far corner of France . . .' He bowed to his companion. 'It would be an honor, Monsieur le Duc.'

'I thought you would be pleased. Will you be in Paris again next week?'

'Yes, I hope to be.'

'Then come to see me after you have given it some thought, and we will discuss terms.'

Niccolò nodded happily.

'Good! I must leave you now, but I look forward to seeing you at the Place Royale.' He smiled, turned, and was gone.

Niccolò continued to the end of the Grande Terrasse. He needed to stretch his legs and think about this new commission. When he arrived at the basin at its end, he paused to look toward Paris. On still days a pall of smoke would hang over the city, but today the wind had cleared it away. The bulk of the Bastille and of Notre-Dame stood out, as did, farther away, the new church of the Invalides, with its Dome only partly finished. The rest of the city appeared as a forest of church spires. Chimneys sent out wood smoke, ethereal spires that quickly vanished.

It was the first time Niccolò had been away from Paris since arriving two years ago with his tightly cherished dream of working for Louis XIV. He had been astonished at its size, dwarfing even Papal Rome. He had known no one, only the name of a bakery where he might find a bed. Now Paris was his home. Anne-Marie was there awaiting his return – a warming thought. And a killer was there as well, a shadowy figure he could not put a face to, only visualize as a hand thrusting a long thin knife.

He shivered again and began the long walk back to the château and his lodgings. Resolutely he turned his thoughts away from murder to the altarpiece he would make for the Duc, imagining how he could make the forests and animals of New France a part of it.

Mademoiselle de Toulouse stood with her friend Laure de Segonzac in a window niche of the Salle des Comédies, the ball-room of the Old Château that Louis XIV had transformed into one of the finest theaters in France. She ignored the actors and dancers in rehearsal, preferring to look out into the central court-yard. Though the King was not in residence, he would still expect his court to carry on as usual. Courtiers strolled, laughed, gos-siped, and flirted to the fluttering of fans, the rustle of skirts and petticoats, the soft steps of the women, the sharper tread of the men. Despite the cold, she opened the window a fraction of an inch for a thread of fresh air.

Laure, beside her, preferred to stand with her back to the view, surveying the activity in the room. She kept up a steady stream of chatter. 'I thought the silver ribbon would be the best to wear with the flower pendant you gave me for Christmas. But then it was hard to distinguish between the pendant and the ribbon. I chose a pale green instead, suggesting its stem. Clever, don't you think? And it will stand out against the pink dress I'm planning to wear tonight, and I hope distract attention from the fact that it's the second year I've worn it. But the Comte de Chamilly admired it last year. Perhaps he'll see me in that dress and remem-ber . . .' She cast an envious glance at Suzanne's dark blue gown in the latest fashion, with triple tiers of foamy white lace at the sleeves. It was ironic – almost unfair – that someone who cared as little for fashion as Suzanne should be able to afford the latest styles without thinking twice about the cost.

Suzanne gave a sudden exclamation as she saw Niccolò come out of the chapel. At least, she thought it was he; she had never seen him dressed like that. What was he doing here? Had he come with a message from Anne-Marie? Had they discovered something new? But he had not sent her or her father a message, and he didn't appear to be looking for her. She was seized with a longing to talk to him. Anything had to be better than listening to Laure chatter about ribbons and clothes. She loved her like the sister she had never had, but today her patience was wearing thin. She did not want to do or say anything that would hurt her friend's feelings.

'You're not listening,' Laure said accusingly. Suzanne did not respond, did not even seem to hear her. Her friend's annoyance turned to worry. 'Suzanne, is everything all right?'

'What?' Suzanne came out of her reverie at the sound of her name.

'I asked, are you all right? You haven't been listening.'

Matters of life and death and family honor are at stake, and instead of finding out useful information I'm listening to your chatter. But Laure had been a dear friend since they were both at the convent school, so she said only, 'I know, I'm not myself today.'

'Is it this business of the silver button that has you worried?'

'Where did you hear about that?' Her tone was sharp. Neither she nor her father had spoken of it at court; it was a matter they wished to remain in Paris. The bustling activity of the room halted as people paused to listen in the hope of hearing a quarrel. It would be something new to talk about, and there was the delicious prospect of taking the side of one or the other, even if they barely knew either woman.

Laure, startled by her friend's tone of voice, drew back defensively but lowered her voice to scarcely above a whisper. Disappointed, the crowd moved on. 'At cards last night, when you were at the Queen's table. The three others at my table seemed to know all about it and were surprised I didn't, since they know we're friends. When I said you had never mentioned it, they couldn't wait to tell me, and put the worst possible interpretation on your silence on the subject. I spoke up in your defense, but it would have been easier if I had known about it before.' She could not help the note of accusation that came into her voice.

Suzanne barely heard it. If the story was spreading through the château – no doubt through Louvois and his supporters – it would soon reach the King's ears; it might have done so already. She felt choked for air, smothered by suspicion; she had to get outside into the fresh air of the park, even if it was too cold to stay out for long. She rose abruptly.

'I'm sorry, Laure – I need to go out for some air – alone – I will tell you the story later, I promise.'

She went briskly to her apartment for her fur cape, pausing to curtsy to the King's vast silver throne – even in his absence, everyone was required to do this – before threading her way back through the public rooms and down the *escalier d'honneur*. It seemed to her that she could hear 'button' being repeated on all sides.

She set out to find Niccolò. Before she had got very far, however, she encountered the Kéroualle sisters, who were eager to tell her about seeing her father in the gardens with a strapping young Italian. She recognized Niccolò from their description, looking so pleased that they teased her. 'The virtuous Suzanne has a lover at last!' exclaimed Marie-Ange.

'I wouldn't be too sure of that – he seems to prefer her father!' retorted Marie-France. As always, her comment had to top her sister's.

'Don't be ridiculous,' Suzanne snapped. 'He's the husband of a friend of mine in Paris.' Yes, despite the difference in their social position, she could easily call Anne-Marie a friend as well as an ally. These women were neither. 'Monsieur Bruno is a sculptor at the Gobelins.'

'A woodcarver trying to pass himself off as a gentleman?' The sisters let out a peal of laughter. Under its cover the third woman, their maid, whispered, 'We saw them on the Grande Terrasse and came directly back from there – they are still probably at that end of the park.'

Before Suzanne could go very far in that direction, however, a biting gust of wind made her seek shelter under one of the arcades of the long wing of the Château Neuf, the 'new château'. Though built only a few decades before, it now leaked so badly that it was uninhabitable. As she paused to wrap her cloak more tightly around her, she heard men's voices echoing in the empty stone space. She didn't recognize one of the speakers, but the other was certainly the Marquis de Louvois. She stood still, almost forgetting to breathe, mindless of the cold, listening with all her might.

'His Majesty reports that the business at Valenciennes is going well,' Louvois said in a satisfied tone. 'The Spanish defenders of the city have been worn down by the long siege and our troops have systematically overcome the outer defenses. It is only a matter of days, perhaps hours, before the city falls into our hands. I wish I could be there to see it. The King invited André Le Nôtre and Charles Le Brun – a landscape architect and an artist – to be at his side observing the siege, but you and I, who have been much more essential to the war effort, are left behind.' Then he chuckled, making Suzanne's skin crawl. Louvois's amusements always involved another's humiliation. 'Once our forces are in control of the city, we will levy a substantial contribution from the good citizens that will help to recoup the costs of the siege. No doubt they will be relieved to be rid of their Spanish overlords and their gratitude will give an added impulse to the generosity.'

His companion laughed appreciatively. Reparations were one of the rewards of war. 'Monsieur Vauban has once again shown his mastery in the field.' The man's voice was warm with approval.

'Indeed.' Louvois's reply was terse and grudging. How like him, Suzanne thought, to begrudge the success of others. Sebastien Le Prestre de Vauban, Louis XIV's chief military architect, was unrivaled in Europe for his expertise in mounting and defending sieges. While he was nominally under Louvois's direction, his genius – no other word for it – at what he did meant that in the field he reported directly to the King. He collaborated with the Minister of War – his plans, however brilliant, needed the army's manpower to implement them – but he did not need

Louvois's patronage in order to succeed. The thought of how galling it must be for Louvois to publicly celebrate Vauban's victories was immensely satisfying. Suzanne smiled. It was comforting to know that there was one area of his life that was as uncomfortable for him as he made life for others.

'I wish you would find out something I could hold over him.' Now Louvois's voice had returned to its usual gruff, demanding tone, exacting obedience, reminding his subordinate that he was the master. 'He does not fear me as he should. But the man seems as impregnable as one of his fortresses.'

The other man said nothing.

Louvois went on to air another grievance. 'The Duc de Languedoc remains in the King's favor . . .'

Just then a group of lapdogs erupted into the open space next to the arcade, yapping their joy at being free of the restraints of good behavior and drowning out his next words. Suzanne ground her teeth.

'. . .silver button . . . Glacis . . .' Suzanne heard, and then a fresh outburst of barking again prevented her from overhearing. She looked with loathing at the dogs and the pages attempting to catch them. Belle, the spaniel she had given to the Queen, was among them. Trust her to make noise when it was least wanted!

At last the dogs were caught and taken back inside, but the men's conversation had again turned to the course of the war, the second man soothing and praising. 'The tide is turning with our recent victories – no doubt the war would soon come to a successful conclusion. You will be celebrated, Monsieur le Marquis, for your adroit handling of manpower and resources.'

'It is not the current war I am worried about, so much as the years of peace that will follow. I fear we will not be able to maintain the army in its optimum state of readiness and be at a disadvantage when war inevitably comes around again. I look forward to victory, but I tell you frankly that I fear peace.' His voice was low and intense; there could be no doubt of his sincerity.

181

'WITHOUT WAR, WHAT IS LOUVOIS? SOME-
ONE OF NO IMPORTANCE.'

Suzanne said it boldly, a verbal gauntlet thrown down, the empty stone arcade magnifying her voice as it had theirs. She heard them gasp in surprise as she approached them with a deliberate tread, like a man's sure footsteps. But when she reached the spot where they had stood, Louvois was alone, his companion nowhere in sight.

'What is Louvois without a war to fight?' she asked again. 'A person of no importance.' She flicked her fingers as she said it, as if he were merely dust to be brushed off her sleeve. She halted several feet away from him, meeting his eyes. His expression changed from one of surprise to indignation, then anger, then hate. His face was red and his eyes seemed to bore holes into hers. His hand was on his sword hilt as if ready for a physical as well as verbal duel, although they both knew that to attack an unarmed woman would put him beyond the pale of the court – or indeed of any polite society. The hairs rose on the back of her neck and she felt cold all over despite her fur cloak. It took all her courage not to turn and run but to stand her ground, willing her fear not to show. She waited for the bow he owed her as a hereditary duc's daughter, his superior in noble rank. His family had earned their titles only after arduous work on behalf of the State.

He finally gave a deep bow that appeared appropriately deferential but was in fact just exaggerated enough to be sarcastic. As usual, his smile never reached his eyes, which regarded her with cold, calculated insult.

She nodded equally coldly and left with the same deliberate tread, forcing herself not to run. Her heart was beating wildly, and she took great gulps of the cold air. She was too agitated to return immediately to the château and set out for the Grande Terrasse again despite the cold wind coming off the river. She was just as glad not to encounter her father and Niccolò. She needed to calm her emotions and gather her thoughts.

I stood up for myself and my family. I stood my ground, alone and unarmed, in the face of the physical threat he presented with his anger, his hand on his sword, the sheer bulk of him. I didn't know I had the courage to do that. Geoffroi would be so proud! She threw her head back and shouted a celebratory 'Ha!' that drew odd looks from others on the path. Then caution returned. She had brought the enmity between them into the open, never a safe thing to do, especially in the case of a man like Louvois. The Duc's principal defense had always been the quiet rectitude with which he behaved. His daughter had broken that code of behavior to challenge Louvois – like taunting a caged bear, she thought, recalling a traveling show of her youth that had brought one down from the Pyrenees. She remembered the beast's impressive display of fearsome teeth and claws when prodded by its handlers and barked at by snarling dogs. But Louvois was not caged, and the weapons at his disposal were numerous and subtler.

Suzanne returned to the château to soothe an indignant Laure and explain the situation to her. They sat on one of the silver benches in the Salle des Comédies. Daylight was fast fading and footmen were filling the silver chandeliers, wall lights, and candelabra with sweet-smelling beeswax candles. Few courtiers were about; she had chosen a quiet moment when most were at dinner. She herself had lost her appetite. Suzanne was careful not to name the Marquis de Louvois. Nor did she mention Niccolò and Anne-Marie and their role in investigating the matter, concerned for their safety lest word get back to him.

Laure listened open-mouthed to this tale of murder and intrigue. So, the rumors she had heard were not idle ones. It was common knowledge that, ever since the civil war of his youth, the King employed a network of domestic spies both inside and outside the court, to forestall any treacherous behavior on the part of his subjects. But as the daughter of a minor nobleman with a small estate, a smaller income, and little or no influence, she counted herself lucky to be at court at all. She was careful to obey the rules of behavior and etiquette and to gossip no more than was necessary to pass the time. She envied Suzanne's wealth and the standing her father's rank and importance gave her. It would be lovely to not have to think twice about buying a new gown or silver pendants and silk ribbons for a dozen friends, and to know that you would be financially secure whether or not you made an advantageous match. Laure's father had hinted that if he could not arrange a suitable husband for her within the next year, she should give serious consideration to taking the veil. She had no vocation, and the thought of convent life filled her with dread. Or she could return to the Segonzac estate and carry out the thankless role of the unmarried daughter living at home, an object of usefulness to her parents, condescension from her wealthy brother-in-law, and pity from everyone else. Suzanne would never be faced with so humiliating a choice. But now, Laure felt frightened for her friend. Suzanne had not mentioned Louvois by name, but Louvois's enmity toward the Duc was well-known and it was no great leap of the imagination to believe he was behind this. Impulsively she reached out to squeeze her friend's hand, and Suzanne responded in kind.

'Does Geoffroi know about this? Will he be coming home to help you and your father deal with it?' She had asked out of concern for her friend but could not keep the hope out of her voice. Geoffroi, four years their senior, had been like the older brother she had never had. She had still been young and gawky when he left for New France; upon his return he would see her full-grown, polished, sophisticated, wise in the ways of court life, an asset to a noble husband . . .

'I pray the matter will be dealt with long before a letter would reach him.' Suzanne's reply cut into her thoughts. 'But I would be happy to have him back here,' she smiled mischievously at her friend, 'especially now that Maman is no longer here to raise objections.'

Laure blushed that her thoughts were so transparent. The Duch-esse de Languedoc, acutely aware of everyone's relative rank, had accepted the girls' friendship but drew the line at the thought of her son paying court to Laure. Of course, she hadn't been pleased at the thought of his mixing with the riffraff in Québec, either.

A nearby clock chimed the hour. It was time to make their way to the Queen's apartment for the concert. Once there, Suzanne would be allowed to sit upon a *tabouret* or even a chair with a back because of her rank and the Queen's fondness for her. Laure would need to stand at the back of the salon. To stand or sit side-by-side would give rise to censure and gossip.

Marie-France and Marie-Ange de Kéroualle were there as well, standing at the back. The sisters tittered and winked at Suzanne; she acknowledged them with what she hoped was a gracious nod, while mentally rolling her eyes in exasperation at the empty-headed pair. Eagerly she turned to face forward again. Tonight's performer was a twenty-year-old prodigy with the amusing name of Marin Marais – the sailor in the swamp – and a growing reputation in musical circles. Her harpsichord master had praised him. She rose and curtsied as the Queen and her ladies entered the salon but was dismayed to see that one of the ladies carried Belle. *I hope she doesn't whine at Monsieur Marais's playing as she did at mine.* At the Queen's gesture the lady-in-waiting seated herself next to Suzanne so she and her former pet could be re-acquainted. Belle, cat-like, ignored her completely, with an air of having moved on to better things. Worn out by the afternoon's exercise at the Château Neuf, she settled down for a nap and slept quietly through the concert. To Suzanne's relief, she could ignore the dog and devote her attention to Monsieur Marais's engaging performance.

All pleasure from the concert was forgotten, however, when the Queen asked to see her afterward. A most distressing story had reached her about the involvement of Suzanne's family in a man's murder. Someone had made it their business to inform her, hoping to drive a wedge between them. She practically begged for reassurance, in so far as a Queen could do so. When Suzanne told her it was an error, she was relieved.

★

185

The Duc, waiting up for her after the concert, was looking forward to telling her about meeting Niccolò and the commission he had offered the young man. The minuscule apartment they shared in the Old Château – two bedrooms and a sitting room, with even smaller attic spaces for the maid and valet – was no worse than the living spaces of many members of the court. It was a measure of the Duc's influence that he had been able to obtain separate rooms for their servants. At least he and Suzanne could easily return to the spacious Hôtel de Languedoc, unlike those provincial nobles who could undertake the arduous journey home only once a year.

Usually after a concert Suzanne would be eager to tell him about the performers and the music, but tonight she sank into her armchair with a sigh and drank deeply from the goblet he offered her.

'What is troubling you?' he asked as he refilled the glass.

She sighed again, shaking her head. 'Oh, Papa, where shall I begin?' As she told him of the day's events – sighting Niccolò from the château window, Laure's questions, the encounter with the Kéroualle sisters, overhearing Louvois's conversation with his subordinate, the disturbing interview with the Queen – the Duc made soothing responses, patting her hand reassuringly from time to time.

Her account of the meeting with Louvois gave rise to a new worry he tried to hide from her: would *she* become the object of the minister's wrath? The Duc wished she had never put herself in his path. A man like Louvois did not stop because people were aware of his activities; it just made him more vicious. He was afraid that this new attack would come from a direction he could not anticipate and build defenses against.

'Is there nothing we can do about him, Papa?'

'The King trusts me, but he needs Louvois's genius for organizing the military to ensure his victories. His Majesty is not going to dismiss him for slander.'

'So, he is just going to get away with it?'

'Rest assured, God sees all and knows what he has been doing. His reckoning will come, but in God's time.'

'Well, I wish God would hurry up,' she replied.

At breakfast Wednesday morning, the Duc told Suzanne that Niccolò was working in a studio adjacent to the château stables, where the Languedoc horses were quartered while father and daughter were at court. Although there was the risk of one of the grooms seeing her and gossiping about it, Suzanne could not resist seeing Niccolò again. He was a reminder of a time when she was doing something useful and purposeful. Her existence at court was neither.

On a cold morning such as this, most women of the court and older men like her father hired sedan chairs or carriages to travel from their lodgings to the château. Younger men with too little to expend their energies on at court welcomed the chance to walk – careful, however, to make sure no slush or mud splashed on their clothing. To attend court in less than pristine condition was to invite censure from the King. Even though he was in Valenciennes, with far more important things on his mind, one never knew when he might hear of one's lapses and make comment.

Suzanne wore sturdy boots for her walk, as though she were planning to ride her black gelding, César. She approached the studio by a circuitous route that avoided the stables' front entrance where the grooms liked to gather. The delicious odor of freshly cut wood wafting out the open door of the studio beckoned her. Niccolò had placed his worktable and the rough planks of the angel's wing where he could take advantage of the morning light shining through the doorway. She stood there for a moment watching him as he was absorbed in his task. He wore his coat and wool scarf but was bare-headed. The sunlight playing over his brown curls revealed hints of red, even gold. Then something made him look up. He frowned at first, not seeing her clearly against the light, but when he recognized her, his smile of welcome was dazzling. Her heart leapt in her chest even as she chastised herself for feeling this attraction to another woman's husband. *Anne-Marie is lucky,* she thought.

'Mademoiselle de Toulouse!' He put down his tools and came to the door to invite her inside. 'It is a pleasure to see you again. What brings you to the studio?'

'My father told me he asked you to carve an altarpiece for my brother to present as a gift, and I wanted to hear your ideas and tell you some of my own.'

His smile broadened. 'I began making sketches last night.' He dusted the seat of a chair and bade her sit down while he fetched the drawings from across the room. Unrolled, they revealed a three-part folding altar carved in low relief, pictorial in its effect. He explained that he had decided upon the low relief because of the distance and difficulty of travel to reach its destination and the lack of skilled artisans to carry out any needed repairs on the more delicate three-dimensional figures carved in high relief. The central scene was a traditional one of Jesus's birth, but the wings showed the native people and animals of the New World – bear, deer, beavers, turkeys – coming to adore the baby, with a background of thick forest. Suzanne laughed out loud in delight.

Just then a groom gave a perfunctory knock on the doorframe and poked his head inside the studio without waiting for a reply. 'Niccolò, have your heard? Our troops have begun the assault on Valenciennes in broad daylight. That will take the Spanish by surprise – nobody would suspect—' He broke off in embarrassment when he noticed a woman sitting there. 'I'm sorry, I did not realize you had a visitor.'

'Hello, Étienne,' Suzanne said calmly. 'How is my César this morning?'

'Mademoiselle de Toulouse!' Hastily the groom took off his cap and bowed. If he was astonished to see her conversing in familiar terms with a woodcarver who had been in residence only a few days, he was too well trained to show it. 'Eating well, Mademoiselle, and longing for a run. Will you be taking him out today?'

'No, I won't be able to get away from court, but you may take him for a ride if you like.'

The boy's face lit up. A mount of César's quality was a rare treat. He made a hasty bow and dashed back to the stables, giving a whoop of delight.

To Niccolò, Suzanne said loudly, 'I must get to the château. I look forward to seeing more drawings as you develop your ideas further.' Once she could be sure the groom was out of earshot, she spoke in a low urgent voice, telling him what she had heard Louvois discuss with the agent and warning him to be careful. 'My father and I appreciate what you and Anne-Marie have done for us. Tell her that I am looking forward to seeing her the next time I am in Paris.'

When she arrived back at the château the court was abuzz with news from Valenciennes, punctuated by prayers for the success of the siege and the safety of the King. There was little chance to speak to Laure, as the Queen sought Suzanne out to play music to soothe her nerves. Mercifully, she did not see Louvois. She hoped he was too occupied with dispatches from the front to think of further ways of discrediting her father.

Te Deum laudamus: te Dominum confitemur. We praise thee, O God: we acknowledge thee to be the Lord.

The Te Deum giving thanks for the victory at Valenciennes took place in the château chapel on Saturday, 20 March. Jean-Baptiste Lully, who seemed to have a new composition in his pocket for every occasion, had outdone himself in the magnificence of brass, drums and soaring voices. Suzanne gave herself wholeheartedly to the service, happy to sit still and be able to think for the first time since Wednesday morning. Not only had Valenciennes fallen but St Omer was also expected to fall in a matter of days. The long stalemate of the war in the Netherlands seemed at last to be turning in favor of France.

Louvois appeared to be taking compensation for not being present at the siege in soaking up the congratulations that came to him from all sides. He seemed to swell with pride as he made his way through the château with his proud father at his side, beaming at the accolades bestowed upon his son. It was as though Vauban's role in the victory could be ignored in his absence. Louvois was only too happy to take credit — except, of course, for giving the King his due. It made Suzanne ill to watch people fawn over him. Her father had to remind her to keep a glad face. He was his usual gracious self, saying the requisite polite words. Louvois gave them a triumphant glare and then ignored them as if they didn't exist.

In contrast to the celebration in the King's apartment, the atmosphere in the Queen's private apartments was one of mourning, as the city had been a Spanish possession. Suzanne could smell hot chocolate being made, a sure sign of the Queen's need for solace. Louis had married Marie-Thérèse supposedly for an alliance and peace but had then used her as a pretext for acts of aggression against Spain, with excuses invented by his lawyers. She lamented that she was like the queen of a chess set, moved around by other hands and always checked by the king. 'I have been Queen of France for sixteen years but the court will always be suspicious of me as a Spaniard.'

She had cheered up slightly when one of her ladies entered with the chocolate pot and Chinese porcelain bowls and invited Suzanne to partake with her. The drink was rich, intoxicating, a sensual pleasure that Suzanne enjoyed despite the conflicting emotions stirred by the day's events.

Suzanne curtsied and reassured Marie-Thérèse that she would always be proud to serve her. 'I know,' said the Queen sadly, and leaned forward to give her an uncharacteristic kiss on the cheek. Then she straightened, shook her head as if to rid it of sadness, and assumed an expression of happiness. 'Let us go and celebrate His Majesty's victory.' She walked out with Suzanne and her ladies-in-waiting with her head held high.

Pleni sunt caeli et terra maiestatis gloriae tuae. Heaven and earth are full of the Majesty of thy glory.

Suzanne's thoughts returned to the present, watching the fifteen-year-old Dauphin, son of Louis XIV and Marie-Thérèse and heir to the throne. He, like Louvois, had complained of being left behind. He would have been so proud to accompany the King, to see more of the country his father was intent upon expanding, and that he would one day inherit. He would have liked to observe Vauban's military tactics instead of being left home like a child. He was proudly self-conscious about standing in for his father at this important thanksgiving.

Aeterna fac cum sanctis tuis in gloria numerari. Make them to be numbered with the saints in glory everlasting.

'Amen.'

Niccolò did not attend the Te Deum. He was finishing the carving of the intricate details of the feathers on the angel's wing, eager to be on his way home. By Saturday midday he was done: the wing could now be turned over to those who would apply gesso, paint and gilding to it. He happily packed his clothes and tools, bade farewell to the others at his lodgings, and took the public coach to Paris. He looked forward to sharing the events of this momentous week with Anne-Marie.

Chapter Nineteen

Niccolò walked through the Gobelins gate with a happy greeting to the porter and ran up the stairs to their rooms, imagining the feel of Anne-Marie in his arms as he swept her into an embrace and gave her a smacking kiss. But there was only Gâteau to greet him. She had grown and filled out in the last few months and had a shining coat. She submitted to being picked up and kissed, but it wasn't the same.

The fire was out, the water bucket empty. Where was Anne-Marie? He thought of the last time she had disappeared, when he had run to the Duc's house in a panic. He would not make a fool of himself again. She was probably getting food for their supper. He would have his usual wash, and then she should be home.

Niccolò was surprised when Willem came up to him at the well. Usually the weaver avoided him, but now he was smiling.

'Are you looking for Madame Bruno? I saw her cross the footbridge two hours ago and enter the convent barn.'

A frown creased Niccolò's forehead. What was she doing there?

'It's not the first time I've seen her go there,' Willem continued, unable to keep the glee out of his voice. 'Dressed most beguilingly, too.' His smile broadened – if that was possible – and he gave Niccolò a friendly clout on the shoulder. 'It's generous of you to share so much of her.' He stepped back hastily to avoid being hit by the swinging bucket but gave a startled yelp as the icy water drenched his shoes. His smile returned at the sight of

Niccolò's face, in which disbelief and fury competed for dominance. 'I just thought you should know.'

Niccolò finally found his voice. 'Liar,' he hissed. 'Why would I believe the lies of a coward like you? Get out of my sight!'

'Most gladly,' Willem replied. 'Good evening.' When he was safely out of reach of the bucket and its contents he added, 'Give my regards to your lovely wife.'

Niccolò turned with a snarl of rage but the man had disappeared inside the weavers' building.

He tried to put aside his disquiet as he washed and changed clothes. Anne-Marie was a true and loyal wife. An hour passed, and still she did not appear. Chewing on a crust of bread that was all he could find in the cupboard, he began to worry. Of course, the weaver's assertions were ridiculous, a pure fabrication! But he was drawn to the convent stables despite himself.

Old Jean greeted him amiably. 'Are you looking for your wife? She and Pot-de-vin have gone up the Bièvre to the tavern. They should be back in a couple of hours. You're welcome to wait here.'

Niccolò's heart sank. What Willem had said was true, then. 'Who the hell is Pot-de-vin? *What* tavern?'

Old Jean was surprised. 'Didn't Anne-Marie tell you?'

'Told me what? One of the weavers tells me my wife has come here more than once while I've been away, dressed for an assignation. He's just being spiteful to pay me back, I think. Then I come here and find she's gone to the worst possible place with some man I've never heard of, and you know all about it.' He gave a short harsh bark of laughter. 'I suppose the husband is always the last to know.'

'It's not what you think,' Old Jean said hastily. He sighed. 'I can see I had better tell you.'

When Old Jean had finished, however, Niccolò said only, 'Are you sure she is safe? I do not need to go look for them?'

'Yes,' Old Jean replied firmly. 'She has nothing to fear from him, and nothing to fear from anyone else while she is with him.'

'Good. Then I will wait here for them. I want to meet this Pot-de-vin for myself.' He would not say anything more but sat where he could keep watch on the entrance. He sat rigid with anger at first but gradually his posture – hunched over, head sunk between his shoulders, large hands opening and closing in agitation and finally dangling between his knees, too dispirited to take out his knife to make even the most rudimentary of carvings – reflected the misery of his thoughts.

After all Le Brun's orders not to pursue this matter, and Ferrand's warning, she had gone with a man he had never met – never even heard of – without telling her husband. It was his right to know what his wife was doing – the more so as her actions might threaten his hard-won position at the Gobelins by going in direct disobedience to Le Brun. If he were to be dismissed because of it, while not even aware of what his wife was up to, he would be a laughing stock. Perhaps he already was, as a reputed cuckold. Perhaps she hadn't told him because, whatever Old Jean claimed, there was something going on with this fellow? The mere thought of it made the sour contents of his stomach rise, and he rushed out the door to empty them on the dung heap. Sitting down again, he reviewed her behavior of the last weeks to see if there was any indication of an affair. He had always taken pride in her friendly nature and her ability to put others at ease. Now these traits took on a sinister aspect, hinting at secret liaisons. He thought again of every smile, every laugh, every friendly greeting to the other men who worked there. He had just come to the conclusion that there was no indication of a liaison, when his wife and a man, presumably this Pot-de-vin, strolled in laughing, arm-in-arm.

The man wore the buff coat of a soldier. He was only a little taller than Anne-Marie but solidly built. His face lost its genial expression when it caught sight of Niccolò, sizing him up as a potential enemy. His body tensed and his right hand went to the hilt of his sword, ready to use it. As for Anne-Marie, he scarcely recognized her. Her face was rouged and raddled and she wore a tattered, gaudy blouse and skirt he had never seen before. The lovely breasts that had been his private delight were exposed down to the nipples for all to see. Adding insult to injury, she wore the blue cloak that had been his gift to her – his *wedding* gift. Anger clouded his vision.

Her face lit up when she saw him. 'Niccolò, you're back!' She ran forward to kiss him. He stood rigid and neither returned her kiss nor put his arms around her. She stepped back, surprised. Suddenly his arm lashed out.

Pot-de-vin caught his wrist in an iron grip. 'Your wife is a courageous young woman and completely faithful to you. My job was to make sure she came to no harm. Neither her life nor her virtue was at risk so long as I was with her. I have no quarrel with you, but I will continue to protect her if you lift your hand to her again.' He did not raise his voice, but the intensity of his words left Niccolò with little doubt that he would carry out his threat.

Niccolò, cursing fluidly in Italian, tried to free his hand. The other man only smiled and tightened his grip. Niccolò could not strike back at him; his walking staff leaned against the wall at the entrance.

'Enough, you two!' bellowed Old Jean, who could sound like a parade-ground sergeant when he wanted to. Even Niccolò, a civilian, instinctively obeyed.

The two men drew apart, glaring at each other.

'Niccolò, take care of your wife.'

Anne-Marie, who had instinctively turned away from him when he raised his arm, had stumbled and fallen, emitting a scream as her cheek hit something sharp. She was crumpled on the ground, sobbing, holding her hand to the profusely bleeding cut in her cheek. Niccolò, though still angry at her behavior, was contrite for his own. Without being asked, Pot-de-vin handed him a cloth and cold water. Niccolò nodded his thanks even while continuing to glare at him.

Once the bleeding had stopped, Anne-Marie and Niccolò were

both exhausted. 'Let us go home,' he said, wrapping her in the cloak.

Back in their rooms, she realized he had not had dinner and went to prepare it, but he told her, 'I'm not hungry. Go to bed.'

'Niccolò?' she pleaded.

'How *could* you?'

He was furious enough to shout it at the top of his lungs, but if he did that the rest of the Gobelins would hear, living as close to one another as they did – precisely what he wanted to avoid. The words came out in a low hiss that sounded menacing even to his own ears and caused Anne-Marie to shrink back, round-eyed, starting at him as though he were a complete stranger. Had she stared like this at other men tonight? Or had she put on that bold smiling face he'd seen when she strolled in with that soldier? The thought of it fueled his anger even further. It poured out of him.

'You go off without telling me – your husband, might I remind you – with a man I've never met, dressed like that – and not on impulse. You planned it for days behind my back, Old Jean tells me.'

'But it wasn't for—'

'And you can't even do it discreetly,' he hissed, cutting her off. 'You were seen and recognized on your way to meet him by Willem, of all people. Willem, who hates the two of us for bringing him to the attention of the police, who would do anything he could to make life miserable for us. And you give him the perfect opportunity! He doesn't have to concoct some lie to make me look like a *cornuto,* a cuckold – you've given him all the evidence he needs. Do you suppose I'm the only one to whom he'll repeat this delicious piece of gossip? Or will it be all over the Manufactory by Monday morning, with everyone winking and smirking as they say *Bonjour?*'

'But Niccolò, I was only trying—'

'And then there are the repeated warnings we've received from Monsieur Le Brun,' he continued, unrelenting. 'How much further do you want to try his good will, before he decides he's had enough and throws us out? Just because he's let you get away with disobeying his orders so far doesn't mean you can continue to try his patience further. Everything I've worked for to come to France, to work for Louis XIV, will be for nothing. Did you think of that when you hatched your merry little plan?'

He glared at her expectantly, but she had no answer for him.

'And if I'm dismissed from the Gobelins, and the story gets around it's because I can't control my wife – she put my place of employment at risk of retaliation – do you think I'll find another position in Paris? Eh? You know what I went through before I got this one. Remember? Do you want us to go back to living with your parents? You know what they're going to say about this business.

'And that's just your family. If mine were to learn of it, I would be the butt of endless jokes and more ridicule. In my village a man who cannot control is wife is spoken of as a *cornuto* whether she's slept with another man or not. And you would be ostracized by all respectable men and women, though the less reputable men might come sniffing around. What kind of life would that be for us?'

The flow of words finally came to a halt. His mouth and throat were parched. He started to go to the water bucket but it brought to mind Willem at the well, and he recoiled from it. He found a bottle of red wine and opened it, drinking two tumblers in rapid succession. He did not offer any to his wife, nor look at her while he did this. Finally, he said, his face still averted, 'Get out of those ridiculous clothes and go to bed.'

She went into the other room and sat down heavily. The tears welled up again. She began to remove the rouge on her lips and cheeks. Hiding her face in the washcloth so her sobs could not be heard, she cried, her whole body shaking. First, the fright of being with that insistent stranger, then the humiliation of being spanked – she had told Paul firmly that he was never to do that again – and now Niccolò's tirade. It was too much to bear. The

197

cat came over to comfort her, and she transferred her face from the cloth to its furry neck. Gâteau's steady purring had a soothing effect. Gradually she stopped weeping and put on her nightgown. She hung the gaudy clothes on one of the hooks on the bedroom wall. *I'll take them somewhere tomorrow to burn them,* she promised herself. Drained of energy and emotion, she was just falling asleep when she heard Niccolò enter the room. *He's coming to bed*, she thought drowsily.

When she awoke the next morning, he was rolled in a blanket on top of the bed, not touching her. Normally she would have woken him with a kiss, but today she needed time alone to think how to repair the situation. She went into the other room and gasped. He had shredded the blouse and skirt. The cat was batting colorful scraps of fabric all over the floor. She crossed the room to light the fire and caught sight of her face in the mantelpiece mirror, drawing a sharp breath at the jagged cut on her cheek. She had forgotten this physical wound in the much larger hurt of the angry words he had poured over her last night. How was she going to explain it in the small, enclosed world of the Gobelins? Would people think she had been attacked, or that Niccolò had beaten her? She would need to find something to cover the wound.

It was the first serious rift in their partnership. He had not even listened when she tried to tell him her reasons for what she had done nor the important information she had found out. She was belatedly afraid – not for her life, she never really believed it could be in danger – but for her marriage. She had never seen or heard him this angry before. Would he start to put restrictions on her movements, like the horrible man down the street from the bakery who barely let his wife out of the house? Had her impulsiveness irreparably damaged the trust of their marriage? She shivered, longing for his arms about her as she never had before.

She wished there were another woman in whom she could confide. Her mother and sister she discounted; Madame Le Brun was too remote and did not invite confidences from her husband's employees; Mademoiselle de Toulouse was unmarried and not a confidante for personal matters such as these; and she had not yet formed deep friendships with the other Gobelins wives. Rachel Vlieger, now happily caring for Matthieu, would understand the consequences of keeping secrets from one's spouse, and the dangers this could lead to; but Anne-Marie's tale of foolishness would re-open old wounds for her. The only one in whom she could confide, in fact, was Niccolò.

Niccolò groaned when he awoke and memory flooded in. Last night, he had been angry at Anne-Marie. This morning, he was even more appalled at himself. In his village, there was a farmer notorious for ill-treating his wife, and he had sworn he would never be like that man. It did not matter how angry he had been in the heat of the moment. Thank God the soldier had stopped him before he lost all self-control!

He came out into the other room, where scraps of fabric eddied around his feet. She had made no attempt to gather them up or to light the fire but was sunk in misery in her armchair staring at the ashes. She raised her eyes to his. Each wanted to apologize but was reluctant to make the first move.

In the light of the candle she had placed on the chair-side table, Niccolò saw the nasty wound on her cheek clearly for the first time. He reached out to feel it, give her cheek a caress that would bring a smile to her face, but she flinched from his touch. His hand fell to his side.

'Dr Lunague should look at that.'

'You'll have to bring him here. I'm not going to show myself looking like this.'

He bit back the retort that she had shown a good deal more of herself the night before and went to fetch Lunague. While he was gone, perhaps she would pick up the remains of her costume and put them in a cloth bag, so that the doctor at least would not see it.

*

The doctor, accustomed to being summoned at all hours, arrived looking only a little disheveled. He carefully cleaned and salved her cheek and sent Niccolò back to his surgery for more ointment so that he could talk with Anne-Marie in private. The doctor asked her quietly if the wound was caused by a blow from her husband. She was happy to be able to reply truthfully that it was not. She did not tell him that she had incurred it while avoiding Niccolò's fist but asked him to remain while she talked with Nic.

When the latter returned Anne-Marie, bolstered by the doctor's presence, was able to tell them both of the events of the previous week. She emphasized that Pot-de-vin had kept her safe at the tavern the night before. The masquerade had been worth it, she said proudly, as she had been able to learn of two witnesses to Hendrik's killing, the butcher's son and the prostitute Lisette. Ferrand should be told about them without delay. She would happily leave to him the butcher and his repulsive child. Perhaps he would also know where to find Lisette.

'If he does not,' said Niccolò firmly, 'then I will look for her. It will seem more natural if I do. You are not to go out dressed like that again.'

She gestured at the sack containing the scraps of her dress. 'I can't very well, can I?' She tried to smile to bring them back into their old accustomed playful relationship, but her eyes were full of doubt and mute appeal.

The doctor tiptoed quietly out as Niccolò took his wife in his arms.

There was no question of going to Mass with Anne-Marie's family today. Niccolò wrote a note to her parents and gave it to one of the urchins outside the gate who often ran errands for the people of the Gobelins. He had the boy carry another message to Ferrand at his house, telling him Anne-Marie had new information to share, and invited him to come to the Gobelins to hear it, as she had been injured and could not leave home. Then, feeling in need of confession and absolution, he went to the church of

Saint-Médard – it was nearby, but he was not known there. He felt better after he had prayed his penance.

To his surprise, Ferrand was waiting for him in the Gobelins courtyard when he returned. As they walked toward Niccolò's building, Ferrand called out a cheerful greeting to Willem, who had just emerged from the weavers' building with a water bucket in hand. 'You're keeping up all honest activity, I hope?' He grinned broadly when Willem cringed, nodded, and beat a hasty retreat.

Another surprise awaited him in their rooms: dinner was on the table, a gift from the doctor and his housekeeper. Anne-Marie put out an extra plate so that Ferrand could join them. After they had eaten, she told him of her visit to Le Renard the previous evening. He raised his eyebrows when she described her disguise and her companion but did not otherwise comment. He paid eager attention to her account of the boy's evidence and the possibility that Lisette had been a second witness to the crime. Anne-Marie flushed with pleasure at his praise.

Niccolò asked if he knew Lisette, but she had not come to the attention of the police before this. Ferrand hesitated to ask his constables, he told them, because he knew there were Louvois's spies among them, and he did not want the assassin to reach her before she could be questioned.

Niccolò nodded. 'Mademoiselle de Toulouse overheard the Marquis talking with one of his employees about this matter at Saint-Germain-en-Laye.' He repeated the gist of what she had told him.

Ferrand turned to Anne-Marie again. 'Go on,' he urged her. 'What went on inside the tavern?'

She had not gone into detail with Niccolò and the doctor, but she told Ferrand, keeping her eyes fixed on him and not looking at Niccolò as she talked about her would-be customer who turned the question about Lisette in a whole new direction.

'Is he the one who cut your cheek?'

'No, I fell on the way home.' She didn't look at Niccolò as she said it. She returned to the events in the tavern. 'Fortunately,

Pot-de-vin was on hand to rescue me. I felt I was under the spell of those intense blue eyes staring at me.'

Ferrand started and leaned forward eagerly. 'Blue eyes, pitted face, blond hair, middle height?'

'Yes.' She was surprised he could describe the man so accurately. 'Why?'

'A man of that description has been implicated in two other killings we know about. He was dressed differently each time, and one time he had a beard that covered much of his face, but he couldn't disguise his eyes and skin.'

Anne-Marie stared at Ferrand, appalled. 'You mean he was – I actually met with the – the –' She grabbed a bowl and vomited into it.

'You are fortunate indeed that he did not realize what you were up to,' Ferrand replied drily. He waited while Niccolò poured her a cup of water and she composed herself.

'He said he would take you up to his room? There in the tavern?'

She nodded.

He gave a small gesture of triumph and sat back with a satisfied look on his face. 'Then we know where to find him.'

'You can arrest him?' Niccolò asked eagerly.

'It is outside the jurisdiction of the Paris police, as you know, but because he is wanted for murders in Paris, I believe Monsieur de La Reynie can exercise authority in this case.'

'Providing one of Louvois's spies among the police doesn't warn him,' Anne-Marie added. 'And you would need to send someone he didn't recognize as police.'

'Don't teach me my job, Madame,' Ferrand replied crisply. 'Just because you were able to get close to him once does not mean that I would recommend you going to him a second time.' She blushed and looked down. 'You may feel that you are safe because he has only known you in your role of prostitute but remember that he himself is an expert at disguise and may well discern your identity in other circumstances.'

Niccolò said suddenly, 'You wore your cloak last night. It is a distinctive shade of blue – there are so few in that color. He could identify the cloak if he saw you wearing it.'

'Then I would recommend you wear a drab one until this business is resolved,' Ferrand said firmly. 'Be prudent, Madame, and on your guard.' There was tenderness in his tone as well as exasperation. Anne-Marie looked up in surprise, but he had turned to Niccolò and was taking leave of him in a hearty, man-to-man voice.

Alone once more, the young couple looked at each other. Anne-Marie said suddenly, 'We need to warn Paul.'

'Paul?'

'Pot-de-vin. His real name is Paul Vincent. When he took me out of the inn and out of the reach of the' – she swallowed hard – 'killer, the man cannot have been pleased. He may do Paul harm if they meet again.'

'Surely this Paul Vincent can take care of himself?' Niccolò replied grudgingly. He was not going to confront the soldier again if he could help it.

'He can,' Anne-Marie confirmed, 'but he should be told.'

His innate sense of fairness overcoming his reluctance, Niccolò sighed and got up to put on his coat. 'Where can one find him when he's not escorting young women to taverns?'

'He is quartered at the Arsenal. Old Jean would know which section.'

Niccolò shook his head. He was ashamed of his behavior the night before and didn't want to see the old man again so soon.

'Then you'll need to go to the Arsenal and ask for him. Tell him what Ferrand told us. We owe him that much.'

'We?' inquired Niccolò with a raised eyebrow. Then he was gone.

The Arsenal, a bustling complex of buildings on the eastern edge of Paris, housed more than two thousand troops and the various craftsmen who served them – cooks, bakers, brewers, tailors, cobblers, armorers, gunsmiths, surgeons, and the horde of clerks who kept accounts, wrote memoranda, and chronicled the exploits of the men in a manner calculated to please the Minister and the King. A platoon of inventory clerks kept track of the vast amounts of foodstuffs, fuel, fabric, leather, iron, weapons, ammunition and other supplies that came to the Arsenal each day by boats that docked at its quays on the Seine. As Niccolò approached the site, it seemed to him that the buildings were like a vast human bee-hive humming with voices and purposeful activity.

A man came out, throwing a friendly farewell over his shoulder at one of the guards. When the man faced front, revealing blue eyes and pitted skin, Niccolò went cold all over. The man passed by him without a glance, however, and Niccolò shook his head to clear it. *I'm seeing assassins everywhere. There must be thousands of blue-eyed men in Paris.*

After inquiring at the gate, he was taken to Paul Vincent, who was chatting with several others. Observing Paul's wary greeting to the stranger, they instinctively closed ranks behind their colleague. 'What you have to say to me you can say to my friends.'

Choosing his words carefully, to persuade them he was not a threat, Niccolò began, 'Last night you were kind enough to rescue my wife from her would-be seducer.'

'That's a change,' said one of the soldiers. 'Usually he's the one doing the seducing.'

The others laughed, but Niccolò ignored the interruption and continued, 'The police believe he may well have been the assassin they have been seeking, and your confrontation may have put you in danger. My wife and' – he hesitated a fraction – 'I thought you should know this so that you could be on your guard.'

The other soldiers, surprised into silence, looked to Paul, expecting him to laugh it off. But he regarded Niccolò soberly and thoughtfully, saying only, 'Thank you.' He gestured to his friends to go about their business. To Niccolò he said, 'We need to talk. Come with me.'

Niccolò expected that they would visit a tavern, but to his

surprise Paul Vincent led him out of the Arsenal into a tangle of nearby streets, and through a courtyard to a residence several storeys high. On the top floor he took out a key and opened the door to a room furnished only with a bed, a cupboard, and a rough table with two three-legged stools. He took wine and cups from the cupboard and gestured to his guest to sit. 'I like my mates at the Arsenal,' he explained, 'but sometimes I need to get away by myself. And I like my women in bed, not up against the wall in an alley.'

Niccolò repeated what Ferrand had told them about the blue-eyed man. 'Would you recognize him, if you saw him again?'

Paul shrugged. 'I might. I wasn't paying particular attention to him – I thought he was just another "client". I was watching her, seeing how she handled it, ready to step in when she needed me. She's a brave one, but I could see he was making her uncomfortable, so I got her out of there. We were putting on an act, and I was concentrating more on my role than on his reaction.'

'Thank you,' Niccolò replied fervently.

'No hard feelings?'

Niccolò shook his head. 'In fact,' he said hesitantly, 'I wanted to ask your advice. I promised Anne-Marie I would look for the prostitute Lisette who witnessed the murder. How would I go about finding her?'

Paul Vincent looked at him in amazement. 'Don't you know where to find women of that trade?'

'No – not in Paris. There has always been Anne-Marie and no one else.'

'And you want to find one particular woman among what must be thousands in the city, without rousing the suspicion of anyone who may also be looking for her?'

Niccolò nodded.

Paul sighed in mock exasperation and burst into laughter. 'You and your wife are a right pair of innocents, aren't you? I should start charging a fee for my services.'

Niccolò said nothing, waiting for him to make up his mind.

'I'll help you,' Paul said suddenly. 'Not out of any fondness for you, mind. But if *we* don't find her, Anne-Marie may take it into her head to do so, and she has put herself in enough peril already. Also, for Lisette's sake – I would see her at Le Renard and admire her for making the best of her life despite her arm. I once heard her speak of a baby girl she was supporting somewhere. She wasn't my type, so I never went into the alley with her, but I gave her a few sous for the girl.

'I am on duty the next two nights but come back on Wednesday after supper and I will take you around.'

Niccolò thanked him. When they went out into the street again, it had grown dark and the houses seemed to lean into each other in a menacing fashion. It was a good thing he had Paul to lead him through the narrow twisting streets. He would never have found his way out on his own. To his surprise, they emerged into the broad, familiar Rue St Antoine, not far from the Place Royale and the Hôtel de Languedoc. Was it only a few days since he had walked in the gardens of Saint-Germain-en-Laye and received a commission from the Duc? It seemed much longer than that. Thinking of the beauty he could create for the Duc was a respite from the ugly matters of prostitutes and assassins.

Chapter Twenty

Niccolò had promised Anne-Marie in the contrition of the moment that he would look for Lisette. Thankfully Le Brun was still at Valenciennes with the King and did not yet know of this latest contravention of his orders. Niccolò sighed. Whichever course of action he took, he would break a promise. He felt a spurt of irritation with Anne-Marie for putting him in this position, but he shook that off. Paul Vincent was right. If he did not go out to look for this wretched Lisette, sooner or later Anne-Marie was bound to do so, whatever assurances she had given.

Even with Paul's help, where would he find one particular prostitute amongst the many that patrolled the city of Paris? He remembered that there had been a gaggle of them at the location where the public coach had discharged its passengers. After parting from Paul, he returned to the place. A row of revealingly dressed young women waited there to welcome visitors to Paris. He thought of Anne-Marie dressed like that and distaste rose in his throat, but at the same time he found he was looking closely at them and wondering if one was the missing Lisette who had been a potential witness to the killing. One of the women mistook his scrutiny for interest and approached him. He shook his head. Her shoulders sagged and he could see how thin and tired she was under the bright paint. He pressed a few sous into her hand. 'Get yourself something to eat.' Thrusting the money into the pocket of her dress, she turned to accost another man before he could ask if she knew Lisette.

★

On the Wednesday, as arranged, he met Paul Vincent at the Arsenal. The soldier led him to the Rue de Glatigny, a notoriously active area of the Ile de la Cité in Medieval times that was making a regrettable comeback. It was only a few streets from the Parvis Notre-Dame where Anne-Marie had visited the Christmas market. He draped his arm around Niccolò's shoulder and told the girls and the innkeeper expansively, 'My Italian friend has just come to Paris – I'm showing him around.'

Business was slow, so they sat at a table with four of the women. Niccolò paid for the wine but did not drink his share. Paul Vincent – called Pot-de-vin in these surroundings – was evidently a great favorite with the women and the landlord. The woman on Niccolò's right snuggled against him suggestively. 'You'll find we're even better than the women of Rome in giving a man what he wants.'

Niccolò nodded politely. He had visited his share of brothels in the company of other apprentices but had found them depressing. Much better to flirt with a maidservant or a friend's sister. He was accustomed to being called to in the street but not to the bold actions of these women, one of whom thrust an exploratory hand between his legs, laughing delightedly when he nearly leapt out of his seat. Pot-de-vin picked up her hand, kissed it, and kept it firmly clasped in his.

'Have you seen Lisette?' he asked her.

'Which Lisette? I know several.'

'The one with the short arm.' He touched hers lightly where Lisette's ended.

'Oh – *her*.' She shrugged. 'Not for months.'

'Do you know where we might find her?'

'Why is she suddenly so popular? What has she got to give a man that I haven't?'

He winked at her and lowered his voice confidentially. 'My friend' – he slid his eyes towards Niccolò – 'has very particular tastes.'

The women gave Niccolò a look of distaste and edged primly

away from him. He could not decide whether to give a splutter of indignation or a sigh of relief.

'Ladies, we'll be saying good night now.' Pot-de-vin led Niccolò out.

They tried two other taverns in different parts of the Ile de la Cité without finding a trace of Lisette. Pot-de-vin was teased for being unusually prone to talk rather than action, but he took it with rough good humor, giving as good as he got. Niccolò retreated behind a nearly impenetrable Italian accent, pretending to understand little of what was said. He was very glad to have the soldier with him.

Finally, after crossing the Seine and venturing into a tavern in the Latin Quarter, they met a young woman who could tell them that Lisette had boarded her baby at the Hôpital Sainte-Marthe, a maternity hospital run by nuns. She described its location. To Niccolò's surprise, it was not far from the Gobelins and its grounds bordered on the Bièvre. The young woman had boarded her child there as well, but her little girl had died. Her mouth quivered as she told them this, but she did not give way to tears. She said flatly, 'It's better for her to have died – what sort of life would she have to look forward to?'

'Come, Signorina, you must have hope.' Niccolò was repelled by her person – he could not imagine going to bed with her – but touched by her grief, wanting to comfort and cheer her. He was about to reach into his pocket for a coin when Paul placed a hand on his arm and, shaking his head, led Niccolò outside.

'It won't help her,' he explained. 'It will just go to her pimp. If she tries to keep it as a gift, not part of her earnings, he'll beat her for withholding it.'

Niccolò scowled but before he could suggest looking for this pimp to teach him a lesson, Paul said bluntly, 'It's the way things are. There is nothing you can do.' His voice held a suppressed fury as if he, too, were sickened by the thought.

'We've found out what we came for. Lisette is keeping the child at Hôpital Sainte-Marthe, not far from the Gobelins. She

209

might even be hiding there herself, exchanging work for room and board for her and the child.'

'Shall we go there? Not now, it's too late, but tomorrow?'

A look of pure horror crossed Paul's face. 'A maternity hospital? No, thank you, I'd rather face the Spanish and the Dutch. That's women's business. Send Anne-Marie. I think it will be a safe enough place for her to ask questions.'

A nearby church clock struck ten.

'It's time I was getting home,' Niccolò said. 'Thank you for your help. If I can ever return the favor . . .'

Paul Vincent grinned. 'I'll hold you to it.'

Earlier that day, after Niccolò had gone to his studio, Marc, the Duc's footman, had delivered a note from Mademoiselle de Toulouse inviting Anne-Marie to visit the Hôtel de Languedoc that day. Delighted, she told him she would come in the afternoon after dining with her father at the bakery. Preparing to go out, she looked with distaste at the drab brown cloak that Ferrand had recommended. It was suitable for errands but simply wasn't good enough for a visit to the Place Royale. Besides, it might cause her father – who knew nothing of her visit to the insalubrious reaches of the Bièvre – to ask awkward questions. Uttering a brief prayer to St Anne for protection, she put on the blue cloak and went out.

Michel Glacis wandered moodily through the streets of the Latin Quarter. Dressed in a sober black suit, white shirt, and broad-brimmed black hat, carrying a book, he had the appearance of a tutor or trustworthy manservant that an anxious father might send to keep an eye on his son. Indeed, he observed the young men shrewdly, and their bawdy companions even more closely. But neither Lisette nor the woman from Le Renard was among them.

Glacis had ordered his new clothes as part of laying the groundwork for his eventual escape from Louvois's service, presenting himself to the tailor as a bourgeois from the provinces who came to Paris from time to time on business and needed a city suit so that he would not be perceived as a country bumpkin. Along with his suit, he purchased an extra shirt, new underclothes, and a nightshirt. The tailor agreed to keep the ensemble for him in between visits. Dressed in his new clothes, he found a room in a respectable quarter, in one of the houses owned by the Abbot of Saint-Germain-des-Prés, a cleric who, it was said, prized highly his independent control of the district and resented any intrusion of La Reynie's police. Glacis transferred his hoarded coins there. He took the precaution of never visiting his room in any but these clothes, so that no one who saw him could connect his new and old selves.

A flash of blue caught his eye. It was a cloak of the color worn by the woman at the tavern, the one that had got away from him. Was she plying her trade here? No, it was just another housewife or servant coming out of a bakery with a basket of bread on her arm. He looked more sharply at her face and abundant yellow hair. It *was* the same woman, but she was clearly no prostitute. No wonder she had been so ill at ease in her chosen role. But why play that role? What was her game?

She set off down the street at a purposeful pace. He followed at a distance, his hat low on his forehead so she would not recognize him should she turn around. But she never looked back. She made her way down to the Seine, across the Ile Saint-Louis and into the Quartier Saint-Antoine. It seemed she was heading to the Arsenal to see that soldier of hers. Maybe the tavern outing was one of those games that some couples played to arouse each other? He had heard of such things. And arousing *him* was part of the fun? He would teach her what that could lead to!

To his surprise, she turned down the Rue Royale instead of continuing to the Arsenal. Now what was she up to? Was she a servant in one of the houses of the Place Royale? Yes, she had turned left to enter the mews behind the square where the kitchens and stables were located. She knocked confidently at one of the doors. He could not see who answered – he was keeping safely

211

out of sight around a corner – but he could hear a cheerful woman's voice welcoming her. 'Ah, Madame – come in! Mademoiselle is expecting you!' He heard the door shut again.

A manservant came out of a neighboring *hôtel* to dispose of some refuse. 'Whose residence is that?' Glacis asked him idly.

The man eyed him suspiciously but decided there was no harm in answering.

'It belongs to the Duc de Languedoc.'

Glacis nodded his thanks to the man as though it were no more than a matter of idle curiosity, but his thoughts were a whirl of unanswered questions. A comment of the Paymaster's came to his mind. 'People have been asking questions.' Which people? Was this woman – whoever she was – one of them? He remembered how she had asked about Lisette, who supposedly owed her ten sous – Lisette, who had gone missing the night he had killed the Dutchman. Had Lisette seen something she shouldn't have? 'Don't worry,' the landlord of Le Renard had told Michel when he first took the room at the tavern. 'She knows when to turn a blind eye and keep her mouth shut.' But what if someone were to persuade her to talk? He must prevent that. Where had she gone to ground? Had the woman in the blue cloak discovered her whereabouts? Could she lead him to her?

Who *was* the woman in the blue cloak? A servant of the Duc? An agent employed by him? An agent employed by an ally of the Duc – Nicolas de La Reynie, perhaps? Clever of them to hire a woman to ask questions – the sex as a whole were incurably nosy and gossipy. He thought over the greeting given her just now. She had gone to the kitchen entrance, as befitted a delivery from the bakery, but the woman answering the door had said, 'Mademoiselle is expecting you.' That formality could only mean Mademoiselle de Toulouse, the Duc's daughter. Another indication that the woman in the blue cloak was not a common prostitute: when did a woman like that have an appointment with a Duc's daughter? Unless she was a go-between for a lover – but no breath of scandal attached itself to Mademoiselle de Toulouse, who was reported to be more interested in her music than in romantic dalliance, and who was unfathomably dedicated to Louis's dreary Spanish queen.

Glacis settled down to wait for Anne-Marie to emerge, opening the book he had brought to appear as a man of letters. It was literally a book of letters, recommended by the tutor he had hired, for practicing the alphabet and the signature of his new name. He silently repeated the lessons to himself. He was proud of his appearance of learning and secretly of the learning itself.

But the tutor's disguise that had blended into the crowds of the Latin Quarter stood out in the mews of the Place Royale. Marc remarked upon it to Rose (they had made up their quarrel); she told Madame Dupont, who in turn informed Mademoiselle de Toulouse and Anne-Marie. The three women left Suzanne's apartment and crossed the hall to look out the window of the Duc's dressing room. They did not recognize him at this distance but his presence made them uneasy. 'I will have Marc summon and pay a fiacre to take you home,' Suzanne reassured her friend.

Unaware that his presence had been noted, Glacis stayed at his post for hours after Anne-Marie had left by the front door, until accosted by the night watch demanding to know his business in the mews. He tried to explain that he was a tutor and had followed his charge here, where the young man was dallying with a maidservant. He was waiting for the young man to emerge, to give him a piece of his mind.

'You will have to give it to him tomorrow. You can't wait here.'

'*Mea culpa*,' replied Glacis, trotting out his one phrase of Latin he had picked up somewhere, and departed. There was no point in antagonizing the watch unnecessarily. She had slipped through his fingers once again, but tomorrow he would go back to the bakery where he had first seen her and trace her from there.

He decided to stay at a lodging house on the Rue Victor that night, taking a room with a view not only of Boulangerie Robert but also of its courtyard and bake house. He was able to observe the comings and goings of the baker and his journeyman, the baker's wife and the shop assistant, and the customers. Finally, there was a lull in the mid-morning. Still wearing his tutor's garb of the day before, he slipped out of his lodgings and crossed the street to the bakery. No one gave him a second glance.

The shop assistant looked up happily when he entered the shop. Glacis gave her his most charming smile and requested a white loaf, biting into it appreciatively when she handed it over. Adopting a Breton accent, he explained that he had recently arrived in Paris as chaperon to a young man from the country who was attending the Sorbonne, and that he didn't yet know many people in Paris. He took advantage of the time his charge spent with his tutors to explore the neighborhood and find the best bakeries and patisseries, and the prettiest women. He winked at her and she laughed hopefully.

'In fact,' he said confidingly, 'I was hoping you could help me. I saw a handsome woman come out of here yesterday, blonde, generously formed, in a bright blue cloak . . .'

Her face had fallen at his first words, but now she looked cheerful again. 'That was the baker's daughter, but she has been married these last six months. Monsieur Bruno, her husband, is a wood carver from Italy – so clever at what he does that he was hired by the Gobelins. Anne-Marie – Madame Bruno – she'd never look at another man. You'd be wasting your time,' she concluded with a sympathetic grimace. She bent down to pick up a cloth she had dropped, and Glacis took the opportunity to leave.

A baker's fat daughter, an artisan's wife, a supposedly devoted newlywed who paraded as a prostitute in the taverns of the Bièvre in the company of a soldier and had appointments with Mademoiselle de Toulouse: he had found out who she was but was no wiser about her reasons for her actions. She was not a foreign spy; she had expressed little interest in the progress and outcome of the war. Her only inquiries had been about Lisette – who clearly would not have borrowed money from her. What was her business with Lisette?

Perhaps it is the same as my own – to find the witness to a murder.
Perhaps, ultimately, she is looking for me.

He felt a chill run through him and then laughed out loud as the ridiculous side of it struck him. A man of his experience being stalked by someone like that – he would be a laughing-stock. He would go to the Gobelins to take care of the problem.

Chapter Twenty-one

After witnessing the Dutchman's murder and the disposal of his body in the Bièvre, Lisette had not gone back to Le Renard but had taken refuge in the Church of the Madeleine in Paris. The nuns there promised a new life and redemption for prostitutes who wanted to reform. But she did not wish to become a nun; she wanted to take care of her baby daughter and make sure the little girl had a better life. She wanted to leave her old life, but she did not repent it; she found herself annoyed at the do-gooders who would rescue fallen women but not prevent them from the necessity of taking up that life. She had left the Madeleine and come to the Hôpital Sainte-Marthe, where she helped out in the nursery in exchange for room and board for herself and the child, whom she had named Marthe. She wore the plain grey habit of the lay worker as proudly as she had once worn the gaudy garb of the streetwalker. The sisters were understanding, too, about her short arm. One of them, with some ingenuity, fashioned a sling for her to wear to enable her to hold two children in her arms. She wore it now as she rocked Marthe and another child after their morning feeding. She felt safe in this world of women and infants and new life. She closed her eyes as she sang to them and imagined herself doing this in a real home, *her* home, with a husband who loved her and provided for her and their children.

To have a real home had been her dream ever since her childhood in the Grand Huleu, the sprawling slum on the northern edge of the city that was a breeding ground for villains and

216

beggars – not far, ironically, from the Cathedral of Saint Denis, the burial place of the Kings of France. She and her mother had shared a hovel of a room with two other women and their children. The mothers had earned their living on the streets and left their children to fend for themselves most of the time. Her mother had died of a fever when Lisette was ten.

It hurt too much to think of her, she missed her so acutely. But as she held and rocked her baby, the memories came despite her efforts to keep them at bay. She could not give way to sobs or Marthe would cry, in turn causing all the other babies to wail. Nor could Lisette cry at night in the dormitory, as she would wake the other women. Solitude was a precious commodity – and as afraid for her life as she was, an uncomfortable one. She felt safer when others were around. Not that that had helped the poor Dutchman . . .

After her mother died, she had been approached by a man who employed a ring of young beggars and who offered to take care of her in exchange for what she brought in. But she hated putting the short arm she has been born with on public display, hated the looks of mingled pity and disgust from those who dropped coins in her hand, hated the praise she received from her employer for work she so despised. After working for him for two years, she ran away with her day's takings and presented herself at an orphanage. The other children there made fun of her arm, but one of the wealthy benefactors who periodically toured the premises saw other potential in her. Her seducer grumbled at having to pay but conceded she was worth it and recommended her to other men. She was gratified to find something she was good at, where her handicap did not matter. She left the orphanage and began to earn her living on the streets.

René, the landlord of Le Renard, had always liked her and treated her well. Once he had intervened on her behalf with a customer whose idea of a good time was slapping her around, sending him on his way with some black and blue marks of his own. Afterwards, René had offered her marriage, or as good as.

'Bring your little girl here,' he'd told her, 'I'll look after both of you. You won't have to look for customers anymore.' He'd even shown her the room, tidied in the rough way of bachelors, and hadn't suggested she share his bed then and there. His offer was so tempting; she knew he meant to be true to his word. But he was also a confederate of Michel's, whom she had often seen in the tavern downstairs. She could never be sure, if she and Michel were to come into conflict, whose side he would be obliged to take.

She looked down at Marthe and said softly, 'You're perfectly formed, with two hands. You can do something else with your life. When you're old enough, I'll see that you go to school. You'll learn to read and write and embroider and knit and play music . . .' Her eyes were shining as she imagined a bright future for her daughter.

'Lisette?'

She looked up and smiled at Sister Berthe.

'You have a visitor.'

Her heart constricted with fear. 'Who is it?'

'A woman – very respectable,' the nun said reassuringly.

She meant to be reassuring but Lisette worried nonetheless. What did the woman want? Was she a wife coming to scold the woman her husband had lain with?

A plump woman with curling blonde hair stood waiting in one of the rooms for visitors. Lisette inspected the woman's appearance, fearing a trap, but her solid person, removing and folding a greyish brown cloak that did nothing for her looks, and her pleasant, neutral expression did not seem to indicate she was bent on mischief or righteous anger. Lisette decided she was probably one of the do-gooders who sought to reform women of the streets. If so, Lisette would give her short shrift.

'I don't know you,' she said flatly. 'If you've come to complain your husband caught the pox, it wasn't from me. I'm clean! And if you're looking to reform women like me, I've left that life and am working here now.'

218

The blonde woman was literally taken aback. She retreated a pace and blinked in surprise. 'No, that's not it at all. I – I came to ask about something else.' She gestured at the chairs. 'Shall we sit down?'

'I'm perfectly comfortable on my feet, thank you.' Lisette had had a lot of practice in standing and waiting. Perhaps this other woman hadn't. To sit down was to invite a long conversation she wasn't sure she wanted. If only the blonde woman would come to the point!

Again, the woman seemed taken aback. Good. Perhaps she'd give up on Lisette and pick on some other fallen woman.

'My name is Anne-Marie Bruno,' the woman began. 'My husband and I live at the Gobelins.' She gestured in its direction. 'In November, a man's body floating in the Bièvre came to rest just outside our walls. I have been looking into his death. I know that he was stabbed and put into the river just outside Le Renard. One of the witnesses to this was the son of the butcher next door to the tavern. The boy told me you, too, witnessed it. I've come to ask you about it.'

Lisette had not expected that. Feeling sick, she stumbled to a chair and sat down. The blonde woman sat as well.

'The boy is mistaken. I have nothing to tell you.' She meant to sound defiant but could not keep the fear out of her voice. She should have been cool, puzzled, disinterested and indifferent, but the upward squeak of her voice gave her away. Marthe whimpered at the sound and Lisette held her tightly, as if to keep her from being snatched out of her arms.

'I would be willing to pay you for the information,' the woman from the Gobelins said gently. 'Surely there are things you would like to buy for your little one?'

The memory of an idle conversation with Hendrik flashed into Lisette's mind – a red teething coral mounted in silver that he wished he could buy for his infant daughter. She had no such ambition for Marthe. Soft clothes and blankets instead of the rough basic materials provided by the hospital, fresh milk to supplement the portions allowed her here – she would dearly love to supply her with those things. But she had learned some hard lessons on the streets. A paid informant was soon dead. Hendrik, whatever his business had been with Michel, was evidence of that. No amount of money was worth the risk.

She shook her head. 'Of course, there are things I would like her to have, but first and foremost is a mother who will live to see her grow up.' She glared at the woman. 'Don't you realize what you're asking of me? Who the hell are you to ask it? Who are you working for – the police?'

'No! The police had no interest in pursuing Hendrik's murder. He wasn't anyone important enough. They didn't want to look for Hendrik's family, either, to make sure they were all right.' Her voice was indignant. '*I* found his wife and daughter – just in time. The police just wanted to exonerate the Duc de Languedoc. That's whose livery the assassin was borrowing when Hendrik was killed.

'No one has been paying me,' the woman concluded proudly. 'I'm doing this because I need to know what happened, and why, and who is trying to place blame on the Duc. I want to see justice done.'

Lisette exploded.

'You *need* to find out? The Duc *needs* to have his name cleared? You're asking questions that could get me killed because you *need* to know.' Her tone was venomous. 'You'll go home to your husband and your comfortable life and worrying about the Duc's reputation. I'm just a means to an end for you. Well, this may not look like much of a life, but I did an honest night's work and gave good value for the money I was paid. Now I'm starting a new life for my daughter's sake. Michel will kill me if I talk to you. So clear out! Take your *needs* to someone else.' She drew a ragged breath.

'Michel who? Is he the man with the blue eyes?'

Lisette was furious. 'You don't even know who you're dealing with? Naming him could get me killed.'

The woman from the Gobelins opened and closed her mouth but she had no counter-arguments to give her. Tears came to her eyes and she seemed to shrivel into herself. She got up, weary and defeated, and went out without saying anything more.

Seeing the blonde woman's vulnerability, Lisette wavered, but for no more than a moment. She could not afford to feel sorry for the woman, not if it would put her own life and her daughter's in danger.

She remained seated in the visiting room after the woman from the Gobelins had left. She struggled to regain her composure, knowing that if she returned to the nursery in this state, the babies would sense her agitated mood and all begin to cry at once. Marthe was wailing even now. Lisette took deep calming breaths and talked cheerful nonsense to the child until the crying subsided and the little girl fell back to sleep.

Hendrik's death. She had done her best to forget it or at least not think of it. If that woman from the Gobelins knew what was good for her, she would forget about it, too.

Poor Hendrik – a nice man – he had picked up her shawl, once, off the filthy tavern floor and brushed off the worst of the filth before giving it back to her with a flourish and a small bow, oblivious to the sniggers of the tavern regulars. Another night, he had spoken of his little girl as he was fashioning a wooden toy, and in an unguarded moment she had told him about Marthe. It was dangerous to be close to anyone who had business with Michel and she had taken care that their conversation could be overheard by others who would attest to its innocence. She had moved away from the table as Michel came down from his room upstairs. She went outside with a customer shortly afterward, re-entering the tavern just in time to see Michel help the slumping Dutchman out of his chair and through the front door.

Curious, she slipped outside by a side door to follow the men in case Hendrik needed help – or to help herself to the contents of his pockets in case he was beyond it. She would be sorry to do it but she had to live, after all. She saw Michel tip him into the river and bit back a protest. She tried to step silently back into the shadows but knocked over a wooden bucket someone had carelessly left out. Michel looked sharply around and muttered something under his breath. She stood very still, scarcely daring to breathe. Then a rat scuttled out of its hiding place with a cat in pursuit and he shrugged, turning his attention to finishing the task at hand.

She waited until he had gone back into the tavern before she dared to move out of the shadows and away from the Bièvre. She couldn't go to René with what she had seen; such knowledge could get him killed as well as her. It was easier to just fade from sight. She'd sent an urchin with a message that she was all right but was going to try for a better life. Perhaps one day when it was safe, she would contact him again. But she did not want Marthe to grow up in the insalubrious atmosphere of Le Renard, with companions like that nasty-minded child at the slaughterhouse – better a start in life here with the gentle nuns.

She was so absorbed in her memories that she did not notice a new visitor standing in the doorway until he said, like a bad echo of that night, 'Hello, Lisette.'

She looked up and gasped. Michel Glacis stood in the doorway.

As Michel Glacis approached the entrance to the Gobelins, he wondered what excuse he could give to the porter to gain entrance to the complex. He knew very little about what was made there, beyond a certainty that they were, like the blue-and-white vases of the Rue St Honoré boutique, elaborate, repulsive objects for people who had nothing better to spend their money on. That it was the King's Manufactory employing men to create objects for his palaces, made no difference to him. It was not an aspect of the monarch he valued.

The Gobelins gate opened and the blonde woman came out. She was wearing a dark cloak this morning instead of her all-too-recognizable blue. Madame Bruno, the woman at the bakery had said. He smiled to himself – he was in luck. He could not kill her

222

here, virtually under the eyes of the porter, but he would follow her, savoring the thought of what he would do to her before he killed her. He would pick the time and place and leave her in no doubt of who had the upper hand in this encounter.

She led him north, away from the Bièvre through several streets that were vaguely familiar, though he couldn't think why, finally stopping in front of an imposing building of the previous century, and entering it.

With a start, he recognized the place. It was a home for indigent old men. His grandfather's life had ended here. It had been twenty years and more since he had come here to sit at the old man's deathbed amidst the noises and smells of a ward full of old men. Duty had kept him at his post but he was seized now, as he had been then, by the desire to flee the place. Then the front door opened and one of the nursing sisters came out. To his surprise he heard not the brutal coughs of old men but the crying of babies.

The nun eyed him curiously. 'May I help you?'

He removed his broad-brimmed hat and spoke diffidently. 'My grandfather was a resident here. Is this still the Old Men's Home?'

She smiled. 'No – no longer. It was purchased by our Order and for some years has been the maternity hospital of Sainte-Marthe.'

'Ah. Thank you, Sister.'

She nodded and continued on her way.

A maternity hospital! Lisette had an infant she was boarding somewhere – could this be the place? It was an ideal setting for her to hide in – no man would think of looking for her here and would think twice before invading this ultra-female environment. It took another woman to point out the obvious. He felt a rush of gratitude toward the blonde woman. He would take special care to prolong their pleasure when he finally took her.

Now that he knew where Madame Bruno could be found, he decided he would take care of Lisette first, before she could go into hiding somewhere else. He stationed himself a little way down the street where he could keep watch on the front door. Obligingly, the blonde woman emerged a few minutes later, looking disappointed, and scurried back the way she had come. When she was safely out of sight, he knocked at the door of the maternity hospital and was admitted. The nun had no hesitation about admitting this polite, well-dressed man to the visitors' room where Lisette sat singing to her child.

'Hello, Lisette.'

He had come for her, as she knew he would. She had known men of his sort since her childhood. A person's guilt or innocence made little difference to them.

How had he found her? Why today, when she had had no visitors before this? He must have followed the blonde woman from the Gobelins. Damn her and her 'need' to know! Could she trade the woman's life for her own – did he know the woman was to be found at the Gobelins? It was worth a try. She must stay alive so that her daughter would live. The law forbade adoption of another's child, so she could not give her up to someone else to raise as their own. A foundling hospital, the only alternative, would be tantamount to a death sentence, and even if Marthe survived it, her life after it wouldn't be worth living.

She rose to face him, still grasping the child, wanting her to feel the imprint of her mother's arms until the last possible moment.

'I hear that you saw things you should not have, events in which other people are showing an interest, asking questions.' His tone was mild and conversational; one might have mistaken its low murmur for reassurance; but the blue eyes were brilliant, almost glittering, in their malice.

'I saw nothing,' she told him flatly, 'and I have said nothing to anyone, especially not to the police. I'm not a fool, Michel. You know that. The woman you followed here – *she's* the one you want – she's been working with them. I just want to stay here and forget the past and raise my child. Let me be, Michel.'

'Oh, I'll deal with her, all right – she's been asking for what I

224

have in mind. I just had to make sure you hadn't said anything about the Dutchman to her or anyone else.'

'I haven't,' she repeated. 'As I said before, I don't know anything *to* tell.'

'Good.' He smiled at her and saw the hope flicker in her eyes. He turned as if to depart and heard her slight sigh of relief. In one smooth movement, he pulled out his stiletto, turned again, plunging it into her side and withdrawing it. Her eyes opened wide in terror as she realized she'd been tricked. He gently removed Marthe from her arms as she crumpled to the ground and laid the bundle on one of the chairs. The baby had not made a sound; she was fast asleep. *I should kill you too*, he thought. *The bastard daughter of a whore – what chance do you have in this life?* A look of savage compassion crossed his face, but he did not take out his knife again.

Lisette gave a death-rattle and lay still.

He could hear the nun's voice as she ushered visitors into another room, but there was no one in the corridor. He walked rapidly to the door and let himself out into the street.

Chapter Twenty-two

After the humiliating conclusion of her interview with Lisette, Anne-Marie's only thought was to leave as quickly as possible. In her haste, she scarcely noticed the man in the wide-brimmed black hat who was conversing politely with Sister Berthe. One would have thought that Lisette's words had taken flight and pursued her like a flock of angry, pecking birds. She did not stop to draw breath until she was home with the door shut firmly against them.

She felt again like fat, awkward Mademoiselle Boulanger, object of her mother's scorn, her sister's condescension and the neighbors' pity, who could never do anything without having it pointed out how she put her foot in it. She flushed hot and cold as she recalled Lisette's accusations, reluctantly admitting to herself the truth of much the girl had said. She had rushed into the interview with all the eagerness and triumph of a hunting dog finding its quarry: no wonder the girl had reacted much as prey would have done – nervous, defensive, fighting back with all her resources.

I should have put myself in her place before confronting her – found a way to offer her protection, asked her cooperation instead of demanding it. It seems so obvious now. But I was so accustomed to exerting my will against those who tell me I should not or could not pursue this inquiry, that I pushed ahead regardless. And got the response I deserved.

When Niccolò came home for dinner, he was not as sympathetic as she had hoped. 'She is all alone in the world with a daughter to protect. She has witnessed a killing by a man who would not hesitate to kill again. She has been hiding at the maternity hospital for weeks and begun to feel safe. Then you come like something out of a nightmare and insist she put herself in danger again. Of course, she is going to say no. If you want her cooperation, you're going to have to find a way to allay her fears, provide protection and safety for her and the child.'

Anne-Marie sighed. 'Things she thought she had until I came barging in. I've gone about it all wrong,' she said despairingly.

'So, try again. You've been to the tavern, acted out her role there —' he gave a grimace of distaste — 'seen the sort of people she has had to consort with. That should give you some understanding of what she is going through.'

He kissed the top of her head and returned to his studio.

What if I had been in that tavern alone, without Paul to protect me? Being used by the men, unable to say no to them because that was my livelihood? She remembered, too, the attitude of the butcher next door. *What if this had not been one evening's masquerade but my way of life?* Anne-Marie shuddered, feeling the weight of its dreary violence. Lisette, young as she was, had already survived years of it. She had made her own way in the world, asking for no one's pity, least of all Anne-Marie's. She had faced Anne-Marie's demands from a position of strength, knowing her own truth — a truth that had little room for abstract notions of justice, or for putting herself in peril for Anne-Marie's ill-considered request.

I blundered; I was tactless; but it was a mistake, not a character flaw, Anne-Marie told the critical voices inside her head. *I can and will learn from my mistakes. I'll return tomorrow with kind words and try again.*

Mère Catherine, Mother Superior to the nuns who formed the nursing staff of the Hôpital de Sainte-Marthe, had been a nun for more than forty years, but she retained the upright bearing of her youth. She wore the white habit and black veil of the Order, her only ornament a large Cross of polished olive wood from the

Holy Land that echoed the green and brown tints of her magnificent hazel eyes. The daughter of a noble house, her breeding showed in the cultivated accents of her melodious voice. However politely she might frame a request, there was something in her way of saying it that left little doubt she expected to be obeyed. It was her inheritance that had made possible the purchase of this property for the Order twenty-one years before; her connections that brought well-to-do women to have their babies here; her shrewd administration of the funds that made the hospital prosper and allowed it to offer free services to those, like Lisette, who could not afford to pay; and her moral compass that insisted that women of Lisette's profession be given the same level of care as any other client. 'It is God's prerogative to sit in judgment,' she would tell others who disagreed on this point. '*You* do not need to.'

This morning she had been visited, for the second time in as many days, by Commissaire Ferrand and his man. Today he was there to make his report. Mère Catherine tried to take in what Ferrand was saying, a fantastical tale of spies in the war with Holland, hired assassins, silver buttons, and an interfering busybody from the Gobelins. It would seem to have all the plot elements of a Molière farce, had not the girl's death shown it was to be taken seriously. Lisette had been killed by someone responsible for other deaths, one of which she had witnessed. The nun shook her head in disbelief. Her own father had been an ambassador to the Italian states during the early reign of Louis XIII; she knew well the perils that diplomatic intrigues could bring about; but she had difficulty in connecting them to Lisette, poor child of the streets, who had found a haven here.

The interview took place in her office, a whitewashed, sparsely furnished room. A simple wooden table, papers and writing implements neatly arranged upon it, served as her desk. The large, equally plain bookcases held the hospital's meticulous records. She and her visitors sat in the rush-bottomed chairs used throughout the hospital. A *prie-dieu* was positioned against side wall, under the

Nativity scene that her predecessor Mère Marguerite had commissioned from Charles Le Brun twenty years before. The sole item of luxury in the room was the colorful carpet at her feet, a rare item indeed in a room as spare as this one.

Mère Catherine took pride in the hospital's safety record. The great leather-bound ledgers on the shelves behind her recorded the names of the mothers and children who had stayed here. It was true that death was not unknown at the maternity hospital – birth could be a brutal business for both mother and child. But, of the more than five thousand women and infants who had been patients, a mere two hundred and fifty had been lost, a success rate many a public hospital would envy. No one had died of the violence humans inflict on one another – until now.

Perhaps I have been too proud of my success; pride goeth before a fall, as the Bible tells us. I know that pride is one of my prevailing sins and that it deserves to be humbled. But I cannot believe that God would cause an innocent like Lisette to be killed for this purpose.

And now there was Lisette's orphaned Marthe to find a home for. They could care for her here while she was still an infant, but once she had grown beyond that she would need to be placed elsewhere. She would be a charity case unless they could find a sponsor for her. She sighed. Yet another thing to attend to on an ever-growing list.

She became aware that Commissaire Ferrand had finished speaking and was waiting for a reply. With an effort she brought her attention back to attend what he was saying. She was about to ask him to repeat his question when there was a discreet knock on the door.

'Enter!'

Sister Berthe came in. 'Reverend Mother, the woman who visited Lisette yesterday morning has returned, and she is,' her voice caught and steadied again, 'asking for her.'

The Mother Superior eyed Sister Berthe with concern. She had taken Lisette's death hard, not only because she was fond of the young woman but also for her role, as she saw it, in bringing it about. 'I let the man in,' she had sobbed. 'He was pleasant and courteous and claimed kinship with her. I was happy, thinking she would have a home at last, that real home she dreamed of. I led him to the room where she sat, before another knock on the outside door pulled me away.' No amount of gentle reassurance could persuade her that it was not her fault. Sister Berthe had spent the night keeping prayer vigil in the hospital chapel for Lisette's soul but had insisted upon returning to her usual duties this morning. She did not look at all well, her eyes swollen and red, her normally confident bearing drooping and listless.

Before Mère Catherine could reply, Ferrand and his man rose and positioned themselves behind the open door, where a visitor entering the room would not see them. Ferrand nodded solemnly to Mère Catherine and put his finger to his lips.

'Please show her in,' she said in her low, musical voice.

She looked searchingly at this woman whose visit had, knowingly or not, been the harbinger of death for Lisette. Sister Berthe had overheard Lisette's frightened voice raised in protest at something the woman had said. What had so frightened the girl? Was the woman an associate of the killer's, or merely a bystander who had the misfortune to be tangled up in this business? Mère Catherine could see no signs of evil in her, merely a neatly dressed, rather large person with a basket on her arm and a pleasant, puzzled look on her face.

'It is all right, Reverend Mother,' Ferrand said, stepping out from behind the door and causing the woman to turn in alarm and drop her basket. 'Madame Bruno is known to us. That is,' he added hastily, lest she put the wrong interpretation on his words, 'she has been assisting us in this matter. She would not have had any reason to harm Lisette.'

Ah – so this must be the busybody from the Gobelins.

'To harm Lisette?' The woman was puzzled. 'Of course not! I just wanted to—' Then, as the meaning of Ferrand's words sank in, she stared intently at him. 'She isn't – he didn't—' She could not form the words.

He answered her unspoken question. 'Yes, like the others.'

The woman turned white and swayed on her feet. Ferrand's man stepped forward quickly to help her to a chair. He took a small metal flask from his pocket and forced eau-de-vie between her lips. She coughed and sputtered as the strong liquor went down her throat, but the color returned to her cheeks and she was able to wave away the flask when he offered it again. He stoppered it and put it away.

The woman gave a final cough, wiped the tears from her eyes with the back of her hand, and turned to face Mère Catherine. 'I apologize, Reverend Mother. It was quite a shock. I saw her only yesterday . . .'

'What brought you to see her?'

Ferrand began to object. 'I already told—'

The nun gestured imperiously and he fell silent. 'I would like to hear in her own words how she became involved in this business.'

As she listened, she was impressed, despite herself, at this Madame Bruno's determination to get at the truth. It was that sort of dogged resolve on the part of the midwife that had brought more than one difficult birth to a successful conclusion.

'And what part did Lisette play in it?'

She repeated what the repulsive child of the slaughterhouse had told her.

'How did you persuade him to tell you about it?'

'I was masquerading as a prostitute myself that night.' The nun's eyebrows shot up. 'With a protector,' Madame Bruno added hastily, blushing as she realized the double meaning 'protector' could have. 'It had been impressed on me that it was no neighborhood for a respectable woman, and I'm not scrawny enough for a beggar.'

Under happier circumstances, Mère Catherine might have laughed.

'And this was — what? — a week ago? The man was killed in November, and Lisette came to us before Christmas, more than

231

three months ago. How did you ferret her out – track her down – run her to earth?' There was no levity at all in the nun's voice as she fired hunting similes at the woman.

'I asked Paul – that is, the man who came with me that night' – she was careful to leave Niccolò's involvement out of her telling – 'to ask around among the other prosti— the other women. One remembered that she boarded her baby here.'

'Sister Berthe heard raised voices. What did you argue about?'

'She refused to help me. She was afraid it would get her killed.' Tears welled in her eyes and ran down her face. Her voice grew harsh with self-condemnation. 'She was right.'

Ferrand leaned forward intently. 'Did she tell you anything that might be of use to us?'

'She asked whether Michel had sent me, and I asked her if that was the man with the blue eyes.' She explained to Mère Catherine, 'That's the man we have been seeking.'

Ferrand nodded.

'She was furious at my not knowing even his name, as if the mere mention of it on her part had caused her to reveal too much.'

'Sister Berthe described the man who killed Lisette as having light blue eyes.' Mère Catherine turned to the woman. 'He followed hard upon your heels. If you are not a confederate of his' – Madame Bruno shook her head vigorously – 'I can only conclude that he was following *you*, Madame.' She said it mildly, not reprovingly, but the accusation struck home. Madame Bruno started to shake all over.

'I thought you said you had him, after I told you about his room at Le Renard,' she protested to Ferrand.

'I sent two of my best men but the landlord denied all knowledge of him – said no one lived upstairs but himself. Of course, no customers at the tavern could recall ever seeing him, either.' He grimaced. 'Another time, he was seen in the neighborhood of the Abbey of Saint-Germain and our men tried to pursue him. But he slipped inside the Foire Saint-Germain' – the large Lenten fair held at the Abbey each year – 'and we lost him in the crowds.

He could easily have changed his appearance in there. But we will not give up until we have found him. When we leave here, we will escort Madame Bruno home and then go to Le Renard.'

'What makes you think you'll find him at home at this hour?' demanded Mère Catherine. 'He was out and about – here – yesterday.'

Ferrand shrugged. 'He does not work regular hours and is just as likely to be there as not. I cannot wait any longer. Madame Bruno's life is already in danger. What if he decides your Sister Berthe is a dangerous witness that needs to be eliminated?'

Mère Catherine was aghast. 'What dark cloud has descended upon us?'

He had no answer for that. The hospital had given shelter to Lisette, who wanted to turn her life around. Anne-Marie wanted the truth. Hendrik and his ill-fated conspirators wanted to bring about peace. The Duc de Languedoc wished to be a voice of moderation in an increasingly polarized court. A chain of good intentions had somehow led to tragic consequences. And he followed, mopping up, trying to bring justice to those in its wake.

After her visitors had gone, Mère Catherine sat in mourning for the loss of Lisette, a young mother and lay member of their community who had been snatched from them in such a brutal manner, leaving an orphan behind. Death had visited on the heels of this well-meaning woman whose attempts to achieve justice for one death had, it would seem, only precipitated another. She shook her head sorrowfully. As always in times of distress, she focused her gaze on the carpet at her feet. It was a family heirloom that had, in her youth, graced a table. She had always loved the deep jewel colors, the geometric intricacies of the central medallion, and the flowers that seemed to bud and bloom symmetrically but that, on closer examination, were each subtly different. It had been knotted in Isfahan, she had been told, a fabled city east of the Holy Land that her imagination had always painted in the bright colors of the carpet. When she inherited her parents' estate, she had given the bulk of it to the Order but insisted upon keeping this one childhood relic. It had brought her such comfort through the years, becoming a memorial carpet for departed souls – here in a blossom more faded than the rest, an elderly nun, there in a leaf curled protectively around a bud, a new mother and child. She looked for the flower that would be Lisette's memorial. The tulip on the far right whose petal was truncated by the border? No – Lisette's arm may have been incomplete on earth but in Heaven bodies were made whole. Mère Catherine chose a tulip in full bloom in the center for Lisette, appreciating its beauty even as the colors blurred through her tears.

She rose from her chair, crossed the room, and knelt on the *prie-dieu*. Clasping her hands in prayer, she looked up at the painting of the Nativity. That birth, too, foreshadowed a death. She bowed her head and prayed for Lisette's soul and her daughter's future.

Anne-Marie stumbled home in a daze with the two men at times holding her upright, oblivious to the curious looks and pointing fingers that would ordinarily have caused her acute embarrassment. Once inside the Gobelins compound, Ferrand's man went to the sculpture studio while the Commissaire helped Anne-Marie up the stairs. When a worried Niccolò appeared, a distraught Anne-Marie flung herself into his arms in the flood of the tears she had managed to keep at bay until now. He enfolded his arms about her and asked Ferrand quietly, 'What happened?'

'Lisette was killed yesterday morning in the same way as the others. We suspect the assassin followed your wife to the hospital. We are going out to Le Renard now to arrest him, but until he is safely in custody it is imperative that Madame Bruno stay within the Gobelins walls, preferably in these rooms.'

'But the Gobelins isn't a safe, enclosed place,' Niccolò objected. 'It is open to visitors all the time. Glacis could easily gain entry if he's dressed for the part.

'Would you like me to come with you? Could you use my help?'

'No!' Anne-Marie gave a cry of distress and tightened her arms about him.

'I don't think it will be necessary,' replied Ferrand drily. 'Besides, he does not know you and it would be safer not to draw his attention to you. I am having quite enough trouble protecting your wife.'

With that parting shot, he left them.

When Ferrand had gone, Niccolò held a sobbing Anne-Marie in his arms, making shushing sounds and stroking her hair. If she had been one of his small sisters or baby nieces and nephews, he would have picked her up and walked her back and forth across the floor as he had done so often at the farmhouse at home, singing a soft lullaby until the storm subsided and a sunny smile came out again. When Anne-Marie's tears had subsided into hiccups, he went to the cupboard and poured a cup of wine for her to drink.

Anne-Marie was grateful for his arms around her – the last time she had cried like this after returning from her evening with Paul, she had been alone, wondering if Niccolò would ever trust her again.

She took a sip of the wine but then shook her head. It was the second time that morning that someone had given her alcohol to calm her, make her feel better. She appreciated the gesture but did not wish to feel better. Her interference had brought about a young woman's death. Even though she personally had not plunged the knife, she felt she was to blame.

'You're not alone in this, you know,' Niccolò said in a low voice. 'I told you where to find her.'

She looked up at him. His face was a study in misery. Her heart turned over. That she should have brought him into this wretched business of Lisette was more than she could bear. Fresh tears welled up in her eyes as she reached up a hand to touch his cheek.

'Tell me what happened,' he said in a voice so loving and concerned she almost wept afresh. 'No more tears – please.' Now he sounded unnervingly like Ferrand in Mère Catherine's office.

'They told me she was killed in the room where I met with her. He appears to have come in immediately after I left. The Mother Superior suspected I was his accomplice, until Ferrand explained how I came to be involved. But it seems he was following me. Somehow, he must have found out who I am and where I live. And I led him to her.'

'And I,' Niccolò replied slowly, 'am the one who told you where to look.'

It was her turn to comfort him. 'Only because I asked it of you. You must not blame yourself!'

He shook his head dejectedly. With a heavy sigh, he stood up. 'I need to return to the studio. Monsieur Le Brun is anxious for me to finish this piece – it is to be part of a diplomatic gift and the ambassador arrives next week. Will you be all right now?'

She nodded and leaned forward to kiss him. 'Thank you.'

But she was not all right. Every word of warning she had received rose up to haunt her, every speech she had made about needing to know and about how her earlier inquiries had led to the rescue of Rachel and Mariët, rang foolishly in her ears. *If only I'd been content with that! Lisette had had no Pot-de-vin standing by to rescue her. I undertook dangerous work without concern for my personal safety, but it was she who paid the price.*

Should I carry on? Will it do more harm than good? Am I really capable of stopping the killer? He needs *to be stopped.* She winced at the word.

Chapter Twenty-three

Ferrand sent a runner to the Châtelet to fetch more men, including one of those who had visited Le Renard before. All wore stout leather vests and coats. They stopped a little distance from their destination for this man to describe the layout of the tavern and its surroundings. There were four doors, he told them, the front entrance, a side door that led round to the privies, a back door for deliveries, and next to it the trap door to the wine cave in the cellar. There was no door on the side facing the slaughter-house. Ferrand assigned each man to a post. The men nodded and departed silently to approach the tavern from different directions. Ferrand and his man continued along the riverbank.

It was a day of bright spring sunshine, but the light only served to illuminate the misery of the place and the dreary violence of its everyday activities. Butchers slashed knives across the throats of cattle; tanners carried off the fresh hides with their burdens of flies; laundresses pounded the men's bloody clothing upon the riverbank in water already fouled by waste of these industries. The washerwomen hated the dyers whose colors, separately brilliant but too often run together into a muddy brown, could stain a newly washed garment; the tanners, in turn, hated the laundresses for the soapy water that did no good to the rinsing of the freshly tanned hides. In a rare moment of quiet not filled by the bawling of terrified beasts, Ferrand could hear the women screaming abuse at someone who attempted to interfere with their work and his bellow of abuse in return. The combined smells of the river, slaughterhouses and tanneries was sickening even to Ferrand, who was by no means unused to Paris' squalid areas.

The tavern's sign with its painting of a red fox proclaimed not only the name of the place but also its character. This was not the clever fox of Aesop's fables and children's stories, inviting you inside with a smile, but the cunning predator of the farmyard, sizing up the customer as if he, too, were a tasty meal. Ferrand eyed the building with interest. The living quarters on the second story had, he was relieved to see, windows that were too small to jump out of. He raised inquiring eyebrows at his man stationed at the side door. The man gestured that the others were in place. Leaving one man to stand watch over the front door, Ferrand stepped inside.

Despite the sunshine, little light penetrated the filthy windows, which appeared to be cleaned on the outside by the rain and on the inside not at all. The sawdust on the floor, spread fresh every morning, already looked trampled and muddy. The gloom – and the silence that fell when Ferrand walked in – gave a sinister cast to even the most innocent of conversations. Only the trio of women at one table – washerwomen by the look of the raw, scabbed hands clutching their cups – continued to cackle at the tale told by one of them of the comeuppance someone's spouse had received at the hands of his lover's husband. The eyes of the other drinkers – including a cutpurse known to the Paris police, no doubt spending someone else's money – followed him warily as he approached the bar at the back of the room. One by one the men downed their drinks and left quietly. The landlord, pausing in his washing and drying of pottery cups, watched him stolidly, neither welcoming nor avoiding him.

'I am here to see Michel.'

'I told your other man, there is no one of that name here.'

'And I have it on good authority that he resides here,' Ferrand replied firmly. 'I wish to speak with him concerning two killings in Paris . . .'

The landlord shrugged. 'What happens in Paris is no concern of mine.' He resumed his work and now bent to reach under the bar, bringing out more cups for the midday trade.

'. . . and for the knifing of Hendrik Vlieger, Dutch resident of Paris, in this tavern the night of twenty-seventh November 1676.'

The man shrugged again.

Stung by the man's indifference, Ferrand added, more emphatically than was usual for him, 'Yesterday he killed a young woman who used to ply her trade out of this tavern, and who we believe was a witness to Monsieur Vlieger's death. Perhaps you will recall her – she was missing part of an arm.'

The landlord's head jerked up and he stared at Ferrand. 'Lisette is dead?' For once his stolid mask gave way and his face crumpled. To Ferrand's astonishment, two tears ran down his cheeks. The man's voice was ragged when he repeated, 'Lisette is dead?'

Ferrand nodded, his expression grim.

The landlord's look of woe was replaced by one of hate, but it was not directed at the police. 'You'll find Michel Glacis upstairs in the room on the right.'

'Glacis, eh? It certainly fits his cold heart.'

Ferrand drew his sword at the ready and ran quickly and lightly up the stairs. He rapped smartly on the locked door. 'Michel Glacis! Open up!'

Hearing someone stirring in the room, he knocked again. The bolt was drawn back and the door opened to reveal a hugely yawning woman whose sprawling bulk filled the doorway.

'Michel!' demanded Ferrand.

'Gone,' she replied with another yawn, 'as soon as René gave the alarm.'

'What alarm?'

She nodded towards the device on the wall, an iron ball on a chain that, when pulled from the floor below, knocked loudly on the wall. There was a fresh dent in the plaster next to it. 'Michel set it up. René pulls on a rope under the bar to move it. Then Michel goes out.' She pointed to a door in the wall. Ferrand opened it to find a narrow shaft just wide enough for a man, in which hung a thick rope, knotted with footholds. A chink of light at the bottom showed where an exit to the outside was located. He cursed – this was the one side of the building where he had not posted one of his men, as there had not appeared to be any egress. Knowing it to be useless, he climbed down the rope anyway and emerged into the light. As he had anticipated, no one was outside. He walked disgustedly to the front and informed his man there, but he left his other men where they were.

Ferrand and the man went up to Glacis's room. The woman had dressed quickly and was preparing to leave, hoping to avoid talking with them, but his assistant stood in the doorway while Ferrand sat her back down on the bed to try to question her. She was indignant that he thought she would assist the police.

'He's a good customer, and a regular. Whatever he may have done, he treats *me* all right.'

'Indeed. Is he the one who gave you those bruises?' Ferrand asked, pointing to fresh blue spots on her wrist and neck.

She shrugged. 'He likes it rough, but he pays well for his pleasures, not stingy like *some*,' she said pointedly, as though giving him her time for free were an extravagance she could not afford. Ferrand was forced to let her go after making sure she took nothing but the ten sous Glacis had paid her.

They were prepared to spend time making a thorough examination of the room, but it did not take long. It was surprisingly bare for a space in which someone had been living for several months. The cupboards held only a few eating utensils, the floor had been swept, the fireplace emptied of its ashes. There were no loose boards in the floor, no hollows in the walls or the rafters, no cubbyholes in the fireplace; and the mattress, emptied out onto the floor, proved to contain only straw occupied by vermin that attempted to wriggle their way out of the light before the men dealt with them as they would have liked to deal with Glacis. Not content with that, Ferrand cut down the warning device with an angry whack of his sword.

240

'He didn't grab everything to take when we arrived,' Ferrand said. 'It was moved out or disposed of already before we came. I wonder where he is living now. And whether he's there as himself or has found another disguise to take on.'

'We could try the Saint-Germain neighborhood,' replied the assistant. 'That's where he was last seen.'

Ferrand made a face at the thought of dealing with the Abbot, who shared the attitude of Le Renard's landlord toward the presence of police in his privileged area.

The landlord's room stood opposite Glacis's. On impulse, Ferrand tried the door. It was unlocked. What if the woman had deliberately misled them and Glacis was hiding in here? Ferrand swung it open in an abrupt move that would catch anyone hiding behind it. But no one was there. Unlike the other room, this one bore the clutter of daily life. There was a drawing pinned to the wall by the bed, the smiling face of a young woman. Ferrand went over to look at it more closely and realized with a shock that it was a portrait of Lisette. He had only seen her dead, but the drawing caught some of the vivacity she had had in life. She had been pretty, too, and one man, at least, had loved rather than used her. Ferrand felt a fresh wave of regret at her death, and anger that the man who had loved her had alerted her killer and allowed him to escape. He pulled the drawing off the wall and marched downstairs into the now-empty tavern to slam both portrait and warning device onto the bar.

'Proud of yourself, are you, helping Lisette's killer to escape?'

The landlord hastily lifted the paper off the bar before the damp could stain it and laid it reverently in a dry spot. 'He will be dealt with,' the man replied evenly.

'Ah. Going to inform Monsieur Le Marquis?' Ferrand sneered. 'He doesn't trust his operatives, so he has you looking after them for him?' The barman just looked back unblinking, his stolid face giving nothing away. 'Well, I just hope it is taken care of outside Paris, and before I have another body on my hands.'

Chapter Twenty-four

'Bless me, Father, for I have sinned.'

Anne-Marie, kneeling on the bare board that was the first part of a sinner's penance, spoke through the screen of the confessional to Père Ferré, the Gobelins priest who had officiated at Hendrik's burial four months before. Her body filled the small space, usually a source of embarrassment; but today it was a small thing in comparison to what troubled her. It was mid-morning on a weekday and the courtyard and buildings were busy with the residents creating beautiful objects for the King. Few people visited the Oratory at this time of day; Anne-Marie had chosen it to be sure of privacy. Ferrand and his man, Niccolò and Mère Catherine knew she had led Michel to Lisette but she did not want it common knowledge. Mère Catherine's voice saying, 'He seems to have been following *you*, Madame,' echoed in her head. Of course, God knew what she had done, and exacted His punishment in the writhing of her conscience, the dreams that haunted her sleep, and the dread and guilt that dogged her waking moments. She did not resent this but felt she richly deserved it, whatever Niccolò and Ferrand had said.

'Bless me, Father, for I have sinned. In seeking justice for one killing, I brought about another, a brave young woman with a child who is now an orphan.'

'That would indeed be a grievous sin. How did you cause this death? Did you wound her?'

'No.'

'Strangle her?'

'Of course not.'

'Point her out to another with malice, as Judas did to Our Lord?'

'Dear God, no!'

'Then in what way are you responsible?'

'She was in hiding. She had witnessed the killing of the man we found in the Bièvre, and she feared for her own life. I asked – others – to find out where she was, and I went to see her at the Hôpital Sainte-Marthe to try to persuade her to give evidence. I did not realize that the killer was following me' – she drew a ragged breath – 'but he was, and I led him to her. He entered the Hôpital after I left and stabbed her just as he did the others.'

Père Ferré shook his head. Hers was not the first case he had heard of good intentions resulting in bad consequences. 'Then the sin of the murder is his, not yours. Do not take on more guilt than is your share.' His speech was measured, logical, unemotional.

'But can't you see? He would not have found her to kill, had I not led him to her!' She was exasperated that she could not make him understand the gravity of her actions. 'Give me a stiff penance that I can perform in atonement.'

She heard him sigh in return.

'Do not be so harsh on yourself. There was no malicious intent in your seeking her out.' Wanting to lighten her burden, he added, 'You did well in finding the murdered man's wife and child.'

'Yes, and I rejoice that I did,' she replied warmly. 'They are thriving now.' She paused to gather her thoughts. 'But I did not stop there. I was filled with pride at my cleverness. I longed for new deeds, new conquests. I could not leave the work of finding the killer to the Commissaire whose job it was. I even involved my husband in my investigation. It was he and a friend who found where she was hiding, at my request.'

He repeated what he had said before and gave her a penance of prayer, fasting and alms, but she found it inadequate. She had always taken comfort in confession for the relatively minor sins she had hitherto committed, but she doubted any penance could atone for this one.

She spent the days following her confession in fervent prayer to God, to Christ, to her patron saints Anne and Mary that the soul of Lisette, who had died without extreme unction, would pass quickly through Purgatory and ultimately find the happiness that had eluded her in mortal form. As she prayed, she promised Lisette that she would do her utmost to see Michel Glacis brought to justice. It struck her that she had promised this to Hendrik: it was seeking for justice that had set in motion the events leading to Lisette's death. She shivered. Niccolò had asked her at Christmas, 'You've saved Hendrik's wife and child. Isn't that enough?' Flushed with the hubris of finding them, and of her successful defiance of all who had advised against it, she had pressed onward. She had succeeded – but it was Lisette who had paid the price. Her orphaned child, growing up without a mother, would continue to pay it. Anne-Marie mourned the little girl's loss.

Every word of warning she had received rose up to haunt her; every speech she had made about needing to know and about how her inquiries led to the rescue of Rachel and Mariët rang foolishly in her ears. If only she had been content with that! Lisette had been only a frightened young woman making her way as best she could in the world to take care of her daughter, with no Pot-de-vin standing by to rescue her.

Lisette and Glacis haunted her sleep. In one recurring dream, she would see them across a crowded room or market square. She would try to make her way through the throng to reach them and warn Lisette, only to find, when she got there, that they had moved on to her original starting place, always out of reach, Lisette always in peril. Sometimes the dream would end with Glacis strangling Lisette while the indifferent crowd ignored Anne-Marie's horrified pleas to intervene. Once Mère Catherine came into the dream, giving voice to Anne-Marie's conscience by accusing her of having caused this, while Anne-Marie's mother stood at the nun's side, shaking her head at how hopeless her daughter was.

Another time she dreamed that, exasperated at Lisette's refusal to go to the police, it was she who pulled out a long-bladed knife and killed the young woman. '*There*,' she had said, 'next time, maybe you will listen!'

Other nights, it was Glacis who entered her dreams, singling her out as the object of his lust, running his finger along the neckline of her blouse with a mocking smile. 'You want me, you know you do. I'll wear you out until you don't know whether you want me to continue or to stop. You'll beg for it. You won't be able to stop yourself.' She was making love to Niccolò in the dream, enjoying their warm intimacy, but when she glanced up, it was Glacis's face she saw. 'Where is Niccolò?' she screamed. 'What have you done with him?' Glacis came at her laughing, but instead of making love he was smothering her. She fought him off, clawing at him and gasping for air, only to wake up and find Niccolò holding her by the shoulders at arm's length so that her arms could not hit him, and looking at her in great distress.

After several nights, she began to dread falling asleep and lay tense and wide-eyed next to the peacefully slumbering Niccolò. Her days grew listless; she did not want to eat, only to sit before the fireplace to stare into the flames, the embers and finally the ashes. Niccolò's appearance at mealtimes took her by surprise, with nothing prepared. He made light of it the first two days but then grew worried when she just picked at the food he had prepared. 'Is my cooking that bad?' he joked. Anne-Marie burst into tears, sobbing out her apologies for not taking care of him as a wife should. Her moods continued to spiral downward as she brooded about Lisette's death, until she began to envision her own. Sometimes she was afraid of being killed; at other times she felt she would welcome it. At least it would help her atone for the other's death.

★

245

Doctor Lunague was spring cleaning his consulting room cupboards. The door was open to let in some of the warm outside air; it was at last a day mild enough to remain for long in that chilly room. Hearing footsteps enter, he turned with a smile of welcome that faded abruptly at the sight of Niccolò's troubled face.

'What is wrong? Are you hurt?'

'No – it is Anne-Marie. Since that young woman was killed, she – she is not herself. She has no appetite; she sits and stares all day; she has nightmares that someone is trying to kill her. I don't know what to do,' he said miserably, tears starting to his eyes. 'Nothing I say to her makes her feel better – brings her back to life. I am afraid for her.'

Dr Lunague took him by the arm, sat him down, and poured him a glass of red wine. A little color came back into Nic's cheeks.

'What you describe has the symptoms of Melancholia. The body is governed by the four humors – the Choleric, the Sanguine, the Phlegmatic, and the Melancholic,' he explained. 'Everyone has a dominant humor, but it is important to keep the four humors in balance. Anne-Marie, I have observed, is of the Sanguine temperament – calm, happy, steady – as are you. That is one of the reasons you are so well-matched. When faced with what she perceives as an injustice, it is her Choleric humor that is dominant – she is angry, indignant, a force of nature. To have the Melancholic humor dominant is indeed out of character for her.'

He crossed the room to pull a thick tome out of one of the cupboards. He found the page he wanted and scanned it quickly, punctuating his reading with thoughtful, 'Mm-hmm.' He looked up and said in a light, admiring voice, 'Melancholy is not altogether a bad thing, you know. It is often thought to be one of the attributes of the artist.'

'We are not talking about an artist,' Niccolò replied with an edge to his voice. 'We are speaking of Anne-Marie. How can we bring her humors back into balance?'

'My preferred treatment for balancing the humors is to prescribe certain foods best suited to encourage them. For instance, if we wanted to bring out her Choleric temperament, I would have her drink red wine and eat blood sausage and beef to feed the blood. To help Anne-Marie regain her normally Sanguine temperament, she should eat cheerful foods – eggs, with their bright yellow and white, milk and cheese and white wine.' He smiled. 'I often find that it is the patient's perception that he or she is doing something to bring about a cure that helps the body and mind to heal themselves. I will go to your rooms now and bring her back here for an omelet luncheon to start the treatment.' He hesitated and said with some diffidence, 'I wish I could ask you to join us, but Anne-Marie might be more forthcoming if she did not feel you were apt to be upset by what she said.'

Niccolò could see the sense in that. He nodded.

'Besides, I want to talk to her about death.'

Niccolò was startled. 'Surely that is the one thing she should not be talking about?'

'It is what is uppermost in her thoughts. The more others avoid the topic, the more alone she feels with her experience of it. You forget, perhaps, that I was an army surgeon for many years. I have more than a nodding acquaintance with violent death.'

After Niccolò had left, Dr Lunague fell silent, remembering his first battlefield experience during the Thirty Years' War. He had been unlucky enough to go through the final decade of that ghastly struggle which had laid waste to so much of northern and central Europe. Newly qualified, he had joined the army as an adventure and an excuse not to return to his village after medical school. His first battle had come all too soon. How unprepared he had been for the noise and the rapid pace of destruction and sickened by the carnage all around him! It had taken every effort of will to remain where he was, binding wounds, amputating limbs and cauterizing the stumps as men strained and screamed under his care. Some died; others thanked him later for saving their lives. But it seemed to him at the time that he could take little credit for it. He did what he knew how to do, what he had been taught, yet it appeared to make little difference as to whether one man lived and another died. He had been on duty from the first minutes of battle until far into the night, not finishing until the next morning's dawn was breaking, then collapsing to sleep for twelve hours, only to wake to the smell of blood and death and amputated limbs beginning to decay. Ten days later, he went through it all over again with another battle.

By summer's end he was indifferent to the noise, accustomed to the smell, and had come to terms with Death, who came for so many on the battlefield but left him alone. Sometimes he wondered if it was a cruel jest meant to drive home to him just how powerless he was. Looking up from his operating table, he thought he could perceive Death's grinning skeleton strolling, nonchalant, his scythe over his shoulder, gaily and arbitrarily harvesting men and giving the doctor a jaunty, mocking salute.

Oh yes, he and Death had been acquainted since the time he was Anne-Marie's age. But what could he say to help her?

'Madame Bruno will be joining us for lunch,' he told his housekeeper. 'I would like you to make one of your wonderful *omelettes au fromage* for us.'

He crossed the courtyard to the Brunos' building, mounted the stairs to their attic, and knocked.

The only reply was a loud meow. Their cat must be standing by the door.

He knocked again. 'Anne-Marie, it is Dr Lunague. I've come to see you. Please let me in.'

At last, he heard a shuffling sound, like an old person without the strength to lift her feet. The bolt was pulled back, and the occupant admitted him.

Niccolò was right to be worried. Had Dr Lunague not known it was Anne-Marie, he might have thought this another woman altogether. Her face was unusually pale, with deep circles under her eyes, her hair awry. The cut on her cheek, although mostly healed, was noticeable against her pale skin. Her not very clean clothes had been thrown on but not fastened. Overall, there was a flabby look to her, none of her usual bounce and energy. The front room was in a sorry state, with unwashed dishes and other detritus strewn about with no effort made to pick them up. It was unlike the house-proud young wife she normally was.

'Doctor, how nice!' She started to smile but her eyes grew wide and troubled. 'Is it Nic? Is he hurt?'

'No – he is well, but he told me you are not. I came to escort you to my house for luncheon.'

Reassured, her face dropped back into a lifeless mask. 'That is kind, but I am not up to going out.'

'All the more reason to come and take nourishment.' His voice was warm, persuasive. 'Come, put on clean clothes and arrange your hair. I'll wait for you.'

He was afraid she would put up further resistance, but she only nodded dully and shuffled wearily to the bedroom. He heard the lid of the wooden chest open and close and the rustle of clothes being taken off and put on. Then footsteps as she replaced her slippers with shoes and emerged from the room in a clean skirt and blouse properly fastened. She crossed to the mirror and combed her hair in a half-hearted way. 'I'll make the effort because you insist,' her bearing seemed to proclaim, 'but you'll see it's really no use.'

'Much better,' he enthused, ignoring the doubtful look she gave him, '*allons-y*.'

She blinked in the courtyard sunlight and shaded her eyes with her hand. He held her arm lightly to steady her on the cobblestones.

In the apartment over the surgery the table at which Anne-Marie had written her report was laid for a meal. Madame Martine, the housekeeper, having assembled the ingredients for an omelet, was encouraging the flames under the trivet and skillet. Doctor Lunague seated Anne-Marie and poured glasses of white wine. He raised his glass, 'To your health.' Then, more sharply, 'I mean that literally. Drink your wine.'

Obediently, she drained her glass. The wine brought a warm flush to her cheeks and she fanned her face with her napkin.

'That's better,' the doctor said. 'You have some color back in you.' She gave him a weak smile.

Madame Martine made a high, fluffy cheese omelet, temptingly browned at the edges, and brought the skillet to the table for the doctor to serve it. He thanked her and spoke to her in a quiet undertone. She nodded and left them.

Doctor Lunague put down a filled plate in front of Anne-Marie. She picked up her fork but put it down again without eating.

'I know that Lisette's death has upset you. When I was newly qualified and first became an army surgeon, each death was a personal affront.'

'Did you ever lead the killers to their victims?' Her harsh voice challenged him.

He grew silent and thoughtful. When he spoke, his voice was bleak. 'I stopped to assist a German soldier who was in great pain. He had dislocated his shoulder when his horse was shot out from under him and fell on its side, and his arm was tangled up in the reins. I put his shoulder right and was working his arm free of the leathers. "*Vielen Dank, vielen Dank*," he said to me, the German for *merci beaucoup*. I gestured to him to raise his arm and was about to undo the last tangle, when a bullet whistled past me to bury itself in his chest. His body slumped. I whirled around, frightened for my own life, to find a trio of French musketeers – marksmen with the guns of forty years ago – laughing and congratulating the one who had fired. "We heard voices in French and German and came to see if we could help you," said one. "He raised his hand," another told me. "We thought you were in danger," another sniggered. "Well, finish what you were doing," said the third, who had fired the shot, "I want to go through his pockets." He gestured with his gun to make it clear I would meet the same fate if I hesitated. I did as he asked.' The doctor fell silent and pushed away his plate as if repulsed by the food.

Anne-Marie, who had been listening intently, leaned forward and placed a comforting hand on his arm. He covered it

250

with his own for a moment and then raised his wineglass. 'Drink,' he said again.

She did as she was bid. Looking down at her barely touched food, she picked up her fork and began to eat with more appetite than she had in days.

'The soldier who shot your patient – was he disciplined for it?'

'I reported his action to his superior officer, but the man just shrugged. Among so many atrocities, what was one more? What did it matter if an enemy soldier died in battle or out of it? That was one less to worry about in the next battle! Perhaps *I* should be reported to *my* superior officer.' He snorted in disgust. 'It was an empty threat and we both knew it. Surgeons were in short supply as it was. I went back to work. Happily, I never saw any of those men again, or I might have forgotten my oath as a doctor and stooped to their level.'

'You wouldn't have!' she protested.

He gave her a rueful smile. 'I like to think not.'

They finished the rest of the omelet in silence. The doctor noted with approval that Anne-Marie's color and energy were reviving; her eyes were bright; her posture was both more alert and more relaxed. He brought out little cakes and poured minuscule glasses of Chartreuse. Her eyes lit up. 'You'll spoil me.'

'I wanted to lift you out of melancholy thoughts – it is not your natural humor – and restore you to yourself.'

'Can you restore Lisette as well?' The harsh, challenging tone was back in her voice. She slumped back in her chair and looked at the cakes with distaste.

'Only God can do that. I cannot help the dead; I can only do what I can for the living. And so can you. You cannot help Lisette. Making yourself ill will not bring her back to life. You have Niccolò to take care of. He has been so unhappy at your low spirits. He depends on you, Anne-Marie. When you are unwell or absent, it is as if a piece of himself were missing. You cannot let him down.'

She was listening intently but did not reply.

Gently, he said, 'Tell me about this young woman who affected you so deeply.'

Slowly, haltingly, Anne-Marie told him about the evidence of the butcher's son, her inquiries in the tavern, not knowing she was talking with the killer, the inqueries by Niccolò and Paul Vincent that had discovered where Lisette was staying; and finally, the short unhappy interview at the Hôpital Sainte-Marthe, at which Lisette had been in fear for her life. 'She was right.'

'And so are you, to want justice to be done. To face down those who would rather it was forgotten because it would be so much more convenient, so much less disturbing. You were right to find her and try to persuade her. It was the killer who was in the wrong – he and he alone.' He placed great emphasis on the final four words, looking intently into her eyes as he said them. 'You must believe this, Anne-Marie, so that you can carry on taking care of the living and questioning all those in authority and not living in fear that would have you turn back.' She dropped her eyes and smiled a little. 'You have the sort of courage one normally sees only on the battlefield. Do not let this business with Lisette rob you of that.'

She looked up in surprise and gratitude. Tears welled in her eyes and flowed unheeded down her cheeks. Tears that would not come when summoned earlier now would not stop.

Dr Lunague rose and went to the linen press to fetch a clean napkin. She buried her face in it. He continued to sit at the table as she cried it out, staring at the fire and feeling, all over again, his rage and sorrow at the wanton murder of the German soldier of so long ago. He could almost imagine that she was crying for this man's death. He had stayed in the room to let her know that she was not alone and did not have to face this alone, but he found her presence a surprising comfort. *I have carried this burden alone for too long,* he thought. He felt his own tears start to come as he turned to her and mouthed a silent *Vielen Dank.*

Chapter Twenty-five

The courtyard clock struck the hour and the doctor stirred. 'I am sorry to end our visit, but I promised to attend to one of the nuns at the Couvent des Cordelières at half past. I will escort you home first.'

Getting up from the table, she thanked him. He was pleased to note the warmth and energy in her voice.

'We want to restore you to your Sanguine self, my dear. Remember – eat foods cheerful in color and taste, to bring you happiness. Niccolò, too, will benefit from eating them.'

To Anne-Marie's surprise, Madame Martine had just finished cleaning the Brunos' two rooms when they returned. 'Everyone needs help sometimes,' was her gruff reply to Anne-Marie's voluble thanks.

When her visitors had left and Gâteau had emerged from her habitual hiding place when cleaning was in the offing, Anne-Marie walked around the rooms like someone newly awakened in a strange place. She had done this awful thing, yet people continued to show her such kindness!

With the reviving food and drink inside her, she could think clearly for the first time in days. Should she carry on? Would it do more harm than good? Was she really capable of stopping such an experienced killer? He *needs* to be stopped, she told herself, and winced at the words. She looked in the food cupboard and realized it was empty. Poor Niccolò! He hadn't had a proper dinner in days. Tonight, she would make something special. She would go out and buy—

The memory of Michel Glacis came back to her – out there, waiting, having marked her as his prey. She shivered. She could not go out alone; she would need to send Niccolò for supplies. She settled down to wait for him.

Robert Boulanger climbed the stairs to the rooms where his daughter and son-in-law lived. He was no longer so young as he had been, and the basket of bread on his arm weighed more heavily with each step. He paused at the top to get his breath back. He had stopped in Niccolò's studio first to make sure Anne-Marie was at home, and to admire the young man's latest creation, an elaborate support for a *pietra dura* tabletop. It was an object he had barely heard of six months ago, but now he nodded intelligently when Niccolò described it to him. It was only the second or third time he had come to the Gobelins, and he still felt intimidated by the place, though all he had met treated him kindly. Bread is a great leveler, he thought, rich or poor, court artist or sign painter, a carpenter of coffins or a woodcarver of elegance – all must eat, and all appreciate a good craftsman of bread.

He knocked on the door. To his surprise, Anne-Marie did not open it immediately but asked, in a cautious voice, 'Who is it?'

'It's Papa, Anne-Marie. Open up!'

She did so promptly, relieved him of the basket, and set it on the table before giving him a hug and a kiss. Gâteau leapt light-footed onto the table to investigate, sniffing delicately to see if perhaps a morsel of meat or fish, or even better, a stowaway mouse, was under the uninteresting bread. Disappointed, she jumped down again.

While Anne-Marie put the bread away, he glanced about the room. There were new silver candlesticks on the sideboard, replacing the pottery they had previously used; Niccolò must be doing well to afford those.

'What brings you to visit, Papa? Is everything well at home?'

'Yes, we are all well – but you have not visited two Wednesdays in a row, nor sent word. I was worried.'

She sighed. 'I'm sorry, I have not been myself these last two weeks – I lost track of the days. But I am better now.' She knew her father had noticed the wound on her cheek.

'Why? What happened?' He saw her hesitate, debating what to tell him, and drew his own conclusion. 'Has Niccolò mistreated you? I'll beat him to a pulp if he has!'

She burst into startled laughter. 'No, Papa, he has been kindness itself. Never think otherwise.'

'Then what is the matter? What is it that you don't want to tell me?'

'It's –' she took a deep breath and plunged on bravely, 'the man who killed Rachel's husband. He has killed someone else, the young woman who witnessed the crime, and it upset me.'

'But surely that has nothing to do with you!'

She flinched but faced him bravely. 'Yes, it does. I found out where she was hiding and, by accident, led him to her.'

'You led him to her? He was following you?' He stared at his daughter in open-mouthed amazement. 'And now you're hiding out. How did he come to know about you?'

'I – he – we – I met him in the course of my research.' She seemed reluctant to tell him more than that, and he decided not to press her. He was not sure what this 'research' would have entailed that would have brought her face-to-face with a killer. He could not even think what such a man would look like. His imagination supplied a shadowy cloaked figure with a broad-brimmed hat pulled over its eyes, rendering it faceless.

He struggled to find the words to say to her. Despite what she had told him, he could not quite believe she was in mortal danger. She was not a spy or riff-raff – neither so important nor so lowly as to warrant being murdered; she was a baker's daughter.

'Do the police know? What are they doing about it?'

'They are looking for him. They went to arrest him but he

255

eluded them. Oh, Papa, I should have followed your advice when you told me to leave well enough alone!'

He shook his head. 'That was before you found Rachel and Mariët. I was appalled when I learned what they had been through. You should see the little girl now, running around and laughing. She puts me in mind of you at that age.' He smiled with fond reminiscence. 'And they have given new life to Matthieu. He has the little one calling him Grandpère. It worries Marguerite lest he be tempted to leave his estate to her instead of to Toinette's boys, but they'll get their share of Boulangerie Robert,' he said complacently, adding after a moment's thought, 'as will you, of course.'

She smiled but did not reply. He felt sad that the bakery, his pride and joy, no longer played a central role in her life. She was becoming someone who was from his world but no longer of it. He cast about for a way to reconnect.

'Père Aimé was asking after you the other day. Would you like to talk with him?'

Père Simon, so well-loved that everyone called him Père Aimé, had been her childhood priest at St Nicolas-du-Chardonnet. He had baptized her and heard her first communion and watched her grow up. He had a welcoming smile for everyone, from wealthy parishioners like Charles Le Brun to the beggars and the diseased: they were all God's children in his eyes, thus all to be loved. Small and spare as a young man, his figure had thickened slightly with age – he was nearing eighty, and in the last year he had begun to use a stick when he walked, but lightly; he could still scurry fast enough, when he chose, to leave younger men panting in his wake.

'Oh, yes!' Her face lit up, then fell as she remembered the danger. 'But I am not sure that I should leave the Gobelins.'

'Niccolò and I will be with you. He would not dare attack when you are guarded by us,' he told her, puffing out his chest a little. 'Come now, and you can have dinner with us and spend the night, so you can return here in the daylight.'

*

256

They walked three abreast, with her father and Niccolò guarding her on either side. Although it felt good to be outside of the Gobelins, Anne-Marie found herself paying wary attention to the hands of every man she saw, looking for potential weapons. She knew Niccolò, too, was alert to the danger. Her father, with no idea of what to watch for, looked about with a belligerent expression that challenged all comers. Anne-Marie was dismayed to discover how weak she felt after two weeks indoors. Instead of striding boldly up the Montagne Sainte-Geneviève as she always had, she needed to walk slowly and stop twice to catch her breath. At the summit, they rested for several minutes at the church of Saint-Etienne-du-Mont before descending to the Rue Saint-Victor. When they had made it safely to St Nicolas, Anne-Marie went in search of Père Aimé while Robert Boulanger went down on his knees to give thanks. He did not want to even think about the dangers of getting them home again.

'May I speak with you, Père?'

'Of course, my child – or I should say, my grown-up Anne-Marie.' He smiled at her. 'Do you wish to make your confession?'

'I have already done so, and done my penance, but the matter I wish to speak of continues to trouble me. I would welcome your counsel.'

He led her to a small, rarely visited apse chapel, next to the one containing Madame Le Brun's tomb. To protect her privacy, he seated them so that her back was to the ambulatory, while he faced outward. As long as they spoke quietly, he told her, they would not be overheard.

She told him the story of what had happened since the finding of the dead man, hesitantly at first, as if expecting to hear from him some of the rebuffs she had encountered. He listened intently, enthralled. He had baptized her and watched her grow up in the shadow of her prettier sister. It was not his place to criticize her parents, but he had rejoiced when she found a young man who appreciated her true worth. Today, as she told him about her investigation, he felt proud of her. He knew Matthieu and had met Rachel and Mariët but had not known their history. He laughed out loud when Anne-Marie told him of her disguise for the visit to the tavern.

He grew serious again when she told him about the search for Lisette which had ended successfully and yet so badly. He approved of the penance Père Ferré had assigned her and pointed out that in going to Le Renard she put herself in danger, albeit with protection – she did not play it safe while leaving others in danger.

'I've been thinking, Père Aimé – what if Niccolò and I were to bring Lisette's child to live with us? That would help atone . . .' Her voice trailed off. She sounded as if she were trying to persuade herself of its rightness.

'A child is not an atonement, Anne-Marie. A child is someone to be loved. You should take her because you want her, not because she is a daily reminder of a painful event.' His voice was gentle but firm. He had the sad experience of too many families who raised their children as if they were a penance and had seen the bitterness such a decision could cause. Children were quick to sense when they were not truly wanted.

Anne-Marie's relief on hearing this told him his perception had been correct.

'Perhaps you could ask the Duc de Languedoc and his daughter to support the little girl, see that she is brought up well and given training? The Duc is well known for his generous alms.'

'A good idea, Père – I will ask them.'

They fell silent, comfortable together as the late afternoon shadows began to lengthen in the chapel.

Père Aimé cleared his throat. 'Your actions since the discovery of the dead man have given you opportunities to grow, and I am delighted to see you at last come into your own. Most of your actions have had happy results – but life isn't always like that. Sometimes our actions, although undertaken for good reasons, can have unintended bad results. It is painful when this happens, but you must learn to live with that. Make what amends you can and learn from your mistakes, but do not let them hold you back from all the good you have shown you can do.'

Her eyes were shining as she listened. Once again tears welled up and spilled out, but these were tears of joy.

The old priest blessed her and kissed the top of her head as he used to do when she was a girl. He waved a hand to summon Niccolò, who was waiting at a discreet distance. When the young man had joined them, he blessed them both.

'Take care of each other. You are both precious to me.'

That night, she slept in Niccolò's arms in her old bed, with no nightmares.

Her father bade them farewell the next morning. 'Just stay at the Gobelins until he's caught. You should be safe enough there.'

Anne-Marie smiled and nodded. But as they walked home, she thought of Willem and young Luc and their roles in the tragedy that had unfolded. The matter had already made its way into the Gobelins – woven into its fabric, so to speak. There was no place to hide out that could not be breached. She really needed to find a way to protect herself.

Chapter Twenty-six

'What you need,' Pot-de-vin told Anne-Marie, 'is armor.'

She and Niccolò were sitting with Pot-de-vin and Old Jean in the convent stables, two days after their return from the Boulangerie Robert. It was one of those warm spring mornings that give a taste of the summer to come. All around them, workers were preparing for planting. Tools and ploughs were sharpened, seed jars counted, harnesses cleaned and mended. The convent work horses looked over the doors of their stalls with interest, ears pricked, seeming to sense the work that was coming and looking forward to being outside.

The previous evening Anne-Marie had received a note from Mademoiselle de Toulouse inviting her to the Hôtel de Languedoc this afternoon. She thought of refusing, but it had been months since her last visit to the Place Royale, and she did not relish the thought of hiding out at the Gobelins – which offered only the illusion of safety in any case. Niccolò suggested they consult Paul Vincent – 'soldiers face blades and bullets every day' – about a means of protecting herself and went over to the convent stables to ask Old Jean when Paul was next expected. By fortunate coincidence, he had spent the previous night there.

Anne-Marie watched Niccolò and Paul greet each other. The last time they had met in this space, they had been adversaries; now they were allies who did not hesitate to ask advice of each other.

'We know how the man likes to kill,' Niccolò said, 'with the thrust of his stiletto between the ribs. Hendrik, Salomon and Lisette were all killed that way. It seems likely that he would attack Anne-Marie in the same manner. What is your advice?'

'To stop a knife like that, you'd need a buff coat' – he nodded at the stout leather garment he had worn during their visit to Le Renard, now hanging on a peg – 'or armor.'

Anne-Marie laughed, imagining herself in a full body suit like the illustrations of knights in old books.

'I could carve a vest for her,' Niccolò offered. He had fashioned the wooden supports in her stays. They held up her breasts better than the bundles of reeds she'd used before, and a lovely sexy time they'd had fitting it to her. Even in the worry of the current moment they shared a glance, remembering, smiling.

Pot-de-vin shook his head. 'Wood is heavy and uncomfortable to wear, especially as the weather grows warmer. She'll need something protective but lightweight and flexible.'

'She could have metal plates sewn into her stays, like a brigantine or a jack,' suggested Old Jean. Anne-Marie and Niccolò looked puzzled. 'Those were the coats that soldiers of my father's time used to wear, before buff coats became popular.'

'Let's ask Seigneur' – the nearest he could manage to Signor – 'da Milano, the Arsenal armorer what he would recommend,' Paul suggested. 'He might even have some metal plates ready to hand.'

Niccolò's face broke into a relieved smile. He glanced anxiously at Anne-Marie to see how she would take the suggestion. To his relief, she too was nodding and smiling.

She started to thank Pot-de-vin but he waved away her words.

'I only wish I had been able to do the same for Lisette,' he said in a tone of bitter regret. Anne-Marie leaned forward to place a comforting hand lightly on his arm. He nodded his thanks.

Thinking of her young life cut short, they fell silent. They could hear the young postulant singing as she milked her cow at the other end of the building. Anne-Marie thought enviously of her goodness and innocence. It had been only weeks since they had met, the evening Anne-Marie had light-heartedly gone off in her masquerade, secure in her belief of the rightness of what she was doing. Now, she had an innocent woman's blood on her hands.

Their plan of action decided upon, they departed promptly, as Paul needed to report to duty. Old Jean brought the stout staff with a hook that he used to fish items out of the Bièvre. Let someone try to attack them, he said, and he'd gaff a different sort of fish. Paul hailed an empty vintner's wagon that had finished its deliveries and was returning to the Seine. The driver was happy to earn a few sous by giving them a ride to the Quai des Vins on the Left Bank of the Seine.

The bridges were crowded, so Paul hired a boat to take them across the water to the Arsenal. Old Jean, out of habit, scanned the river for items worth retrieving, but Niccolò and Anne-Marie, who rarely took a boat ride within the city, were enchanted by the new perspective on so many familiar sights – the many boats that plied their trade on this stretch of the river, the Ile des Louviers in the middle of the Seine with its stacks of wood and barrels of gunpowder, and, as they neared it, the brooding presence of the Arsenal itself.

With two thousand men quartered there, Paul explained, it was a city within the city of Paris, importing vast quantities of food and wine, firewood and charcoal, leather and cloth and the raw material of munitions – iron, steel, bronze, brass, gunpowder (stored on the Ile des Louviers for safety) and flints – and exporting troops with their uniforms and arms – guns, swords, pikes, and the bayonets that had only recently come into use. The Quartermaster employed an office of clerks to keep track of it all.

Paul was very matter-of-fact but Anne-Marie, who enjoyed reading travelers' tales, could not help thinking of descriptions of the Traitors' Gate at the Tower of London. She gave an apprehensive shiver as they passed from the open sunlight of the middle of the river into the shadow of the Arsenal.

Once inside, however, she forgot her fears and looked about

her with great curiosity, eager to soak up this new experience. Paul Vincent plunged ahead, striding through the crowd greeting friends, entirely at home and at ease, but Anne-Marie and Niccolò paused to take in the scene.

At the bakery, most of the customers were women. The Gobelins was full of families, the men in their workshops and the women out and about getting water, going to buy food, carrying things to their husbands or fathers. But this was a world composed almost exclusively of men, all of whom seemed to be looking at her. She had never felt herself to be an object of particular attraction and was startled to find herself devoured hungrily by a hundred pairs of eyes both from the men out-of-doors and peering from the windows of the dormitories that stretched two and three storeys overhead. Instinctively she clung to Niccolò, who put a protective arm around her waist, signaling to all present that she was spoken for.

The moving crowd threw up great clouds of dust, and she sneezed, drawing a muttered chorus of blessings. Her nose twitched, identifying male sweat, wood smoke, wine, baking bread, the smell of horses. She could hear a sergeant bawling orders in one corner of the courtyard.

Paul turned his head to say something to them over his shoulder, then realized they were not behind him. He called to them to join him. They scurried to keep up, self-conscious at being strangers, not belonging. He led them through a series of courtyards to a trio of small buildings in the corner that held the workshops in metal – the farrier-blacksmith, the gunsmith and the armorer. Two horses were waiting outside the smithy, a matched pair clearly meant for the commanding officer's vehicle. As they approached, the armorer emerged from the workshop to hand the farrier the decorative medallions he had crafted for their harness. Paul hailed him.

'Seigneur da Milano, I've brought you a customer!'

Instinctively da Milano turned to Niccolò.

'No,' explained the latter, of habit reverting to Italian in conversing with a countryman – '*è la mia moglie* – it's my wife who needs it.'

The man's eyebrows rose in surprise, but he turned to Anne-Marie while Pot-de-vin explained what they had in mind. Da Milano was in his fifties, she estimated, with a fringe of white hair around a bald crown, and a flowing white mustache and goatee in the fashion of his youth. He had a twinkle in his eye and self-confidence in his bearing that reminded her of Charles Le Brun. They must be about the same age, she thought.

Pot-de-vin had finished. Signor da Milano was nodding and smiling. '*Certo, certo,*' he assured them. He glanced at Anne-Marie. 'Come indoors. I need you to remove your garment, and I'm certain la Signora would prefer not to do so in public.'

She blushed and nodded. He held the door open for them and they went inside.

Passing from the bright courtyard into the comparative gloom of the interior, the glowing coals in the forge and furnace automatically drew her eyes to their light. The room was well-ventilated with large windows at ground level to give the fire the air it needed and vents high above to let the smoke escape. The floor was of hard-packed earth. Stone walls held hooks for lanterns, tools, pieces of armor – back and breast plates, shoulder pieces, the leather straps that held them together – and other objects she could not identify. An ornate cuirass, a masterwork of the armorer's art, hung on one wall.

The noises of the busy courtyard were muted to a background hum. She could hear the crackle of the coals in the forge, the roar of the fire in the furnace, the pincers grabbing and positioning the hot plate, hammering on metal, and the hiss of the hot metal being quenched in a big barrel of water as two younger men – his sons, the resemblance was unmistakable – and a much younger apprentice worked a piece. The place smelled of burning wood, charcoal, hot metal, and male sweat – heat smells.

Pot-de-vin was explaining in further detail the kind of attack from which she would be most likely to need protection, feinting thrusts at her middle with an energy that caused her stomach to clench with fear even though his hands were empty. Da Milano approved Old Jean's idea of outfitting her bodice with metal plates (on the outside, so the cloth would be against her skin). He had a supply of them that he used to reinforce men's garments as well as to repair cuirasses and other larger pieces of armor, but thin and flexible enough that he could bend them to fit comfortably around her middle and overlap them slightly. He could sew them in now, in fact, but he would need to take the garment outside, where the light was better.

As he turned to indicate the curtained-off corner of the workshop where she could change her garments, his eyes alighted upon the man seated to one side, informally dressed in breeches and a shirt, without coat or wig, sketching so quietly that Anne-Marie had not even taken note of him. Even da Milano gave a start, as if he had forgotten he was there. 'Carlo, come here and let me introduce you to my visitors.'

As the man stepped into the light, he and Anne-Marie and Niccolò stared at each other in surprise. It was Charles Le Brun.

Le Brun was the first to find his voice. He smiled at his friend. 'I already know Old Jean and Monsieur and Madame Bruno. Monsieur Bruno works for me at the Gobelins. At least,' he amended with an eyebrow raised in mock-query, 'I *thought* he was working in his studio this morning.'

'I make good progress,' Niccolò assured him easily. 'I will finish on time.'

'I am happy to hear it,' was Le Brun's dry response. He turned to the soldier. 'We have not yet met. Charles Le Brun, painter to the King.'

'Paul Vincent, soldier to the King,' he replied, standing to attention, 'and protector to Madame.' He nodded at Anne-Marie.

Le Brun gave her a considering glance. 'I can see there is a story to be told. Perhaps, Madame Bruno, you will keep me company while Gabriele is working on your garment and explain to me *why* you need protection – and from what.'

Niccolò stepped forward to explain but Le Brun waved him to silence. 'Your wife is capable of speaking for herself, as I know only too well. I would prefer that you return to your studio to finish the support for the *pietra dura* table. I received an additional commission yesterday for which I have you in mind, so I want you to finish the table sooner rather than later.'

Niccolò hesitated, wanting to obey Le Brun but not wanting to leave Anne-Marie.

'Go on,' she urged him, 'I'll be safe here and it's not far to the Hôtel de Languedoc. I'll explain to Mademoiselle de Toulouse why you were not able to come.'

Signor da Milano stepped in to take control of the situation. '*È bene.* Madame, change your clothes behind the curtain in the corner. Monsieur Vincent, return to duty. Monsieur Bruno, get to your studio. Carlo, resume your drawing. I have work to do.' He turned and barked out a command to the young men at the forge, who had ceased work to goggle at the buxom blonde woman, a rare sight in this shop. They sprang into action, and again the crackle of the coals was punctuated by the hammering of metal.

Anne-Marie emerged from the makeshift dressing room with her shawl tied modestly over her shift and shyly handed her stays to the armorer. He indicated she should wait with Le Brun. She approached him apprehensively despite his seemingly genial expression and perched on the edge of her seat as if prepared to make an escape at a moment's notice. Le Brun merely smiled and handed her a glass of wine.

Nervous, she took a large mouthful before she realized that this was the sort of wine that would repay savoring rather than gulping.

'Good, isn't it? Gabriele's nephew sends it every year from the family vineyard.'

She took several more appreciative sips before she found the courage to ask, 'How do you know Monsieur da Milano?'

'I've known him ever since he came to Paris in 'forty-three.

His name is Gabriele Negroli. The Negroli have been armorers in Milan for six generations. He is the younger son – his older brother inherited their father's shop. His brother and nephews still work for the Dukes of Milan, but he was willing to take Mazarin's offer to set up his own studio in Paris with a royal appointment.' The Italian Cardinal Mazarin, born Giulio Mazarini, had been Louis XIV's chief minister from the time the boy king inherited the throne at age five until he reached his majority. A fervent patron of the arts, he had encouraged the best craftsmen of Europe to come to Paris. 'When he first arrived at the Arsenal, someone asked him his name, but he thought they were asking where he was from, so he replied, "*Sono da Milano*" – I am from Milan – and that is what he has been called ever since. When I was painting the battles of Alexander the Great, he not only helped me with the designs for the combatants' armor but also made a wonderful cuirass for my model to wear.' He led her to the piece she had noticed before. The center of the breastplate was beautifully crafted and engraved with a battle scene, while the rest was polished to a mirror-like brilliance. It would have been dazzling in the sunlight, making its wearer a godlike figure indeed.

'It was a labor of love on his part. There is so little call these days for such elaborate work. Truly, only a prince or a general of great wealth could afford it. There was no way I could pay him what it was worth, had he been willing to sell it. So, I made him a gift of a painting, a scene of Vulcan at his forge.

'Now,' Le Brun said, his expression becoming serious, even stern, 'tell me what you have been doing that requires so much protection. It isn't still the business of the murdered man, I hope. I told you that I did not want your activities to involve the Gobelins in this matter!'

'The Gobelins is already involved,' she responded tartly. 'One of your weavers was an associate of the dead man's. The silver button found in the man's hand was made in the silver workshops.'

He gaped at her in surprise. As her words sank in, dismay

crossed his face, and he sat back heavily. 'Tell me what you have found out.' His voice was no longer angry but weary with responsibility.

'Hendrik Vlieger, the dead man, was working for a group of Dutch spies seeking to end the war in the Netherlands. The weaver Willem was not a spy, but he was a friend of Hendrik. He had met the man who recruited Hendrik, a Dutch spy named Salomon.'

'Why didn't Willem identify his friend when all the workers viewed the body?'

'He was badly frightened, sick to his stomach afterward. He didn't know whether other members of their group would be targeted and didn't want to draw attention to his involvement – not only for fear for himself but also for what would become of his family if he were to be killed.'

'Why didn't Hendrik's widow tell me about him when I saw her after Christmas?'

'She didn't know he was at the Gobelins until we saw him by the well in the courtyard after your meeting. Niccolò spoke with him, and then Commissaire Ferrand interviewed him. He was able to tell them about Salomon – but when they found the man, he had been murdered in the same way as Hendrik.' She repeated what Niccolò had told her of the scene at La Bleue et la Blanche.

He sipped his wine thoughtfully as he digested this information.

'And the silver button – you said it was made in the Gobelins workshops?'

'Yes.' She told him the story of the apprentice Luc doing a favor for his brother. 'He thought they were for a masquerade ball or some other innocent purpose. He had no idea of the use to which they would be put.' She thought for a moment. 'I will anticipate your next question. He was not at the Gobelins the day the body was brought there; he was at his mother's funeral.'

Le Brun gave a flicker of a smile. 'Does he know for whom the brother was working?'

'No, Luc did not – and the brother has disappeared. But we – Commissaire Ferrand and I' – Le Brun raised his eyebrows at the pairing of their names but refrained from comment – 'know he commissioned the buttons for a man named Michel Glacis, who is suspected of several murders besides Hendrik's.'

'If the brother had knowledge that could threaten this' – he hesitated – 'Glacis? – no wonder he disappeared. Is Glacis why you are being fitted for armor?'

She nodded. 'His preferred method is a stiletto or knife between the ribs. It seemed prudent to get protection.'

'Do you know who he works for?'

'Mademoiselle de Toulouse – the Duc's daughter – overheard Louvois mention him when he was talking to someone in the gardens at Saint-Germain-en-Laye. It would seem he works for the Marquis.'

'Louvois,' he spat the name out with a grimace. 'If he finds out the Gobelins was involved, and makes it known, then I will look like an accessory to murder, condoning the activities of my workers, or at best a fool, unaware of what they have been up to under my very nose.'

'But it was his employee who committed the murders. Surely he could not blame you without having the same said of him?'

Le Brun thought over what she had said. The worry left his face. 'That's true,' he said softly. 'I don't know why I didn't think of that. Thank you, Madame Bruno.' Their eyes met in a look of mutual approval. 'And how did you come to the notice of Glacis?'

'In the course of my research, I – I asked some questions that were overheard.' She blushed more deeply than such an innocuous statement would seem to warrant and wouldn't meet Le Brun's gaze.

'Madame Bruno – Anne-Marie – if you have done something that will cause this man to pursue you into the Gobelins –'

This is it, she thought, *Niccolò and I are going to be kicked out for the safety of everyone else.*

'– then I must know the whole story so that we can keep you safe.'

She stared at him. 'I was afraid you were going to dismiss us,' she said with a nervous laugh.

'Three months ago, I would have. But you have found out things that, left unchecked, could seriously threaten the Manufactory. I am grateful and,' he hesitated as if making a reluctant admission, 'it seems I need you as well as your husband.'

She could not help grinning in relief.

'But now you can repay me by posing as Bellona, the goddess of war. I have in mind an allegory of the war in the Netherlands showing the enemies of France forging the weapons of war.' He took the cuirass down from the wall and strapped her into it. He demonstrated the position he wished her to take, looked at her critically, then stepped up to her and let her hair down, arranging it so it looked flowing and windblown. When she was standing to his satisfaction, he said, 'Now tell me – from the beginning – everything you have done, and what you found out.'

She began with the search for Rachel and Mariët, about finding another wooden cat toy similar to the one in the dead man's pocket, the old lady's information, the search on the Rue Saint-Honoré, and finding the mother and daughter just in time; about Niccolò's conversation with Willem, and the dead Salomon. Blushing, she told him also of her visit to Le Renard, the search for Lisette, the girl's murder, and her realization that her would-be customer at Le Renard was in fact the killer.

He grunted. 'How much of this does Commissaire Ferrand know?'

'All of it.'

'You told him, but not me?'

'You' – *did not wish to know of it*, she was about to say before she thought the better of it – 'you were at court or Valenciennes much of the time. He accepted my help.' *Eventually*, she added silently. She took a deep breath and said in a more conciliatory tone, 'Monsieur Le Brun, I apologize for going against your orders to

270

pursue this matter. Do not let it reflect badly on Niccolò – it was entirely my doing.'

'It is hardly more of a recommendation for him that he cannot control his wife,' he replied tartly.

'He has given me the courage to act as I do. I spent years in my father's bakery at the beck and call of my mother and the customers. Niccolò saved me from a lifetime of that.'

'One is always at someone's beck and call. I answer to Colbert and he to the King. Even the King must answer to God. Working in a bakery, you could at least be sure of eating. There are many in Paris who would envy you that.'

She grimaced. 'My father never tired of reminding me of that. But I have not stopped eating just because I left it.'

'So I see.'

She blushed.

'When this man has been caught, it seems we must find something to occupy your time and mind so you don't get into further trouble.' To her amazement, he was smiling.

Intent upon their conversation, they had not paid attention to the voices outside, but now they could hear good-natured bantering. Bringing a woman's undergarment out where soldiers could see it had let Gabriele in for a ribbing.

'Making sure no one gets at your wife, eh?'

'Your daughter is fighting off suitors, I see.'

'The camp followers are wearing armor too?'

'Going to make a chastity belt next?'

Laughing, he gave as good as he got: 'Maybe you'd like me to do this for your woman? I hear she's quite an armful!' Such statements were met with mock growls, followed by roars of laughter.

When he had finished sewing on the metal plates, he tested the garment by having one of the men give a hard thrust with his knife, both front and sideways, to make sure the plates were resistant to the point of the knife and that the blade could not slip

271

between them. Only then did he carry it inside and have Anne-Marie, who had finished posing in the cuirass, put it on. It fit quite snugly, but her blouse and skirt went over it easily. 'I feel like Joan of Arc,' she joked as she emerged into the courtyard, once again startled to find herself the object of scrutiny by so many men.

'How is it that you require armor, Madame?' one of them asked.

Pot-de-vin had cautioned her to be deliberately vague in explaining, 'You never know who knows who in such a large crowd – Glacis might have friends or acquaintances here.'

'A friend was stabbed,' she replied, thinking of Lisette with fresh regret. Her eyes filled and she wiped the tears away with the back of her hand.

The soldiers respected her grief and did not question her more closely, but they were quick to reassure her of the efficacy of steel. One told of how his cuirass saved him from a blow in battle; others followed with similar tales. New recruits who had not yet taken part in battle talked about their fathers and uncles. Listening to them, her perspective shifted: being attacked or stabbed or shot at seemed the most ordinary thing in the world, and the safe luxury environment of the Gobelins a distant unreality.

By now the hour for the midday meal was approaching. Immense kettles of soup were bubbling in the opposite corner of the courtyard; next to them makeshift tables were piled high with large round loaves of dark bread. The soldiers began to move toward the food. Anne-Marie's stomach growled. She hoped the courtyard noise would mask the sound, but Gabriele asked with a quick smile if she and Le Brun would like to join his family's meal. He was a permanent fixture at the Arsenal, while most soldiers came and went, so he and his family were housed nearby.

There, Le Brun showed her the painting he had made. It seemed to be a portrait of Gabriele at his forge, but he was wearing classical dress, and his three helpers – ! She stared at them and then at Le Brun.

'Why do they have only one eye in the center of their foreheads?'

'They are the Cyclops, helpers of Vulcan, Roman god of the forge. I've depicted Gabriele as Vulcan, and vice versa.'

She smiled and turned to the painting again, appreciating the glowing colors lit by the painted fire.

After the meal at Gabriele's, a happy noisy affair with his wife and daughters, sons and journeymen sons-in-law, and apprentices, Le Brun took Anne-Marie to the Place Royale in his carriage. As she was preparing to step down, he pressed coins into her hand. She tried to refuse but he insisted. 'Take a fiacre back to the Gobelins. Don't take any chances.'

'For once, Monsieur Le Brun, I will do what you say.' She tried to make light of her reply but could not prevent a catch in her voice.

He pressed her hand again. 'Take care of yourself.' He seemed about to say more but only smiled and nodded. She descended and shut the carriage door. 'Drive on,' he ordered. He did not look at her again, but she stood staring at the carriage until it turned a corner and disappeared from sight.

Chapter Twenty-seven

Suzanne gave a sigh of relief as her maid slid her favorite dressing gown, the one she kept at the Hôtel de Languedoc, over her shoulders. Wearing it, she could slip into another existence in the safety of home instead of the intrigues of the court. A fire had been lit in the grate, and the sweet odor of pine logs chased away the last of the mustiness of the room. It was her first visit home since Christmas. Carlo had greeted her with a profusion of deep happy barks and enthusiastic tail-wagging. He was again content-edly stretched out on the hearthrug in what he regarded as *his* room, soaking up the heat from the fireplace. 'I made do with the kitchen while you were away,' he seemed to imply, 'but now I too am in my proper place.'

She smiled at him as she stepped over to the harpsichord and opened the keyboard lid. Her right hand picked out a melody, but the tone was off. She would need to send for the tuner tomorrow and see if her music teacher could give her a lesson the day after. She shook her head in regret. Music was a source of much-needed solace, yet she had had so little time for it these past weeks.

Ever since her confrontation with Louvois, the court had felt an increasingly perilous place. The capitulation of St Omer and other fortified cities just days after the conquest of Valenciennes had consolidated Louvois's power. It seemed to Suzanne each time she saw him soaking up the congratulations of the court that he swelled up like a bullfrog with his sense of his own importance, until he threatened to burst. She imagined the seams of his coat and trousers coming apart, his silver buttons, silk ribbons and gold braid flying in all directions. It took an effort to not let her disgust show. She admired the way in which her father treated him as if he were neither more nor less than another member of the court. Louvois had not openly taken further steps to discredit her family, but he had dropped a word here, a word there, into the right ears and let the slander spread of its own accord. Suzanne felt acutely the courtiers' whispering behind fans, their empty, meaningless smiles, and the seeming compliments that did not quite hide nasty double meanings.

The Queen continued to be her ally but had no real power. Others were unwilling to speak on her family's behalf, for fear of bringing Louvois's enmity upon themselves. She had little in common with her Aunt Delalande and the rest of her mother's family. More than ever, she missed Geoffroi, far away in New France. She had written to him to warn him of the slander against their family, and of Louvois's complicity in it. New France was a military outpost as well as a settlement, and the Marquis's command and influence extended even there.

Nor did she have the comfort of Laure's company of late. The pink gown that her friend had hoped would attract the attention of the Comte de Chamilly had done so. Laure was wholly preoccupied with her budding courtship, and her happiness had wrought a remarkable transformation in her. True, she had expressed interest in Geoffroi, but he was in New France with no certain date of return, and the Comte was here and attentive. Suzanne was happy for her friend, but the Comte was a fervent supporter of Louvois. Already she felt a cooling-off of the long-standing friendship between them and wondered if de Chamilly had indicated a preference that his future wife find other friends more acceptable to his patron. She had tried to repair the rift by inviting Laure to come with her and her father to the Foire Saint-Germain tomorrow night, but after an initial acceptance, her friend had begged off. She would be visiting the fair with the Comte, and she did not suggest that they go together.

The Foire Saint-Germain was one of the highlights of the social season in Paris. This annual Lenten fair of luxury goods and delicious food and drink was held in the grounds of the Abbey of Saint-Germain in the six weeks preceding Easter. Many members of court had already visited it several times. When a woman appeared wearing a new jewel or lace frill or pair of gloves, one always inquired, 'Did you find it at the Foire Saint-Germain?' Suzanne had gone to the fair every year that she could remember. It was unthinkable to miss it; and with Good Friday just a few days' away, time was growing short. Her father felt the same. She wished Laure would come with her, for old times' sake.

She went to stand at the window. The promenade around the Place Royale garden was full of people enjoying the warmth and sunshine, many couples among them. She thought again of Laure's happiness. Anne-Marie and Niccolò had the same glow in each other's presence. Suzanne had had several suitors, but none that could measure up to her father and brother, the standards by which she judged all other men. The young men at court were too conventional, in the mold of her mother; none had that special spark she was seeking. And they appeared to be intimidated by her, whatever the size of the dowry she would bring. If only there could have been someone like Niccolò, with his creative spark and his easy virility. She blushed: it was unseemly to have such thoughts about a friend's husband.

She could afford to marry for love. There had been that young composer, Monsieur Charpentier, with whom she had worked for several weeks when she was preparing to perform one of his works for harpsichord at a private concert. By the end of which she was more than half in love with him. Part of his attraction was the thought of her mother's horror at the mere idea of marrying someone she regarded as little better than a servant. Suzanne longed to explain that they were equals in rehearsal; it was the music that was important, not their relative rank in society. But she held her tongue for fear her mother would put an end to her music lessons for fostering radical ideas. And then, at the concert,

276

he had gazed so raptly and devotedly at the soprano, Mademoiselle Emilie, that Suzanne's hopes died on the spot. This had been two years ago. It was so painful a memory that she could not bear to think of it often. At least it proved that she had a heart, whatever the young men at court might think.

She shook her head to clear it of melancholy thoughts. She would enjoy the Foire Saint-Germain tomorrow in her father's company. And today she would see Anne-Marie again and learn how her investigation had progressed since she had last had news of it during Niccolò's stay at Saint-Germain-en-Laye. It seemed much longer than a month ago. She smiled. Here, at least, were two allies in fighting Louvois's conspiracy. They could not be swayed by everyone else's opinion at court, because they were not *of* the court. When the next ship departed for New France, she would write to Geoffroi, telling him of this unlikely friendship that had sprung up between her and the Bruno couple. He, who daily rubbed shoulders with trappers and settlers, would be so proud that she too had made friends among those outside the aristocracy and the wealthy. He would enjoy meeting them when he returned.

Rose came to the door to tell her that Anne-Marie had arrived. The kitchen door must have been open as well, as the sound of Madame Dupont's voice floated upstairs. 'Mademoiselle is expecting you. I've made hot chocolate and *sablés*, her favorites.'

'I'll take them up,' they heard Anne-Marie offer.

Madame Dupont was scandalized. 'She'd never forgive me if I put a guest of hers to work doing something that's a servant's job!'

They heard Anne-Marie laugh. 'I'm not such a fine lady as all that!'

'It's not the way things are done in the Hôtel de Languedoc,' Madame Dupont said with finality. Suzanne could imagine her shaking her head to emphasize her words. She and Rose shared a smile before Suzanne assumed her lady-of-the-house expression and said, in her best imitation of her mother, 'You may tell our visitor I am receiving guests.'

Thus, when Marc brought up the heavy silver tray, Anne-Marie following in his wake, they found Mademoiselle de Toulouse seated in her armchair, the latest issue of the *Mercure Galant*, the court journal, in hand, acting out the role of the fine lady that her servants expected of her. It was only after Marc had served the chocolate and left that she rose to take Anne-Marie by both hands and greet her with a wide smile. She pulled her over to two chairs by the window so that they could sit in the sunshine. Looking more closely at Anne-Marie in the full light, she was struck by the change in her appearance. She looked haggard and weary, several years older.

'What happened to you?' she blurted out before she could stop herself. 'I'm sorry – that was tactless of me.'

'No, you are right.' Anne-Marie hesitated, unsure what to say next.

Suzanne poured two more cups of the hot chocolate. 'Here – drink this first.'

They sipped in companionable silence, helping themselves to *sablés* from the bowl. When Anne-Marie looked more relaxed, Suzanne tried again. 'What has happened?'

For the second time that day, Anne-Marie recounted her tale of the evening at Le Renard, the search for Lisette and its tragic aftermath. They had just come from the armorer, she said, trying to make light of the fact but pressing a hand to her midriff to reassure herself that the protection was indeed there.

Suzanne, listening to her tale of disguise and danger, found herself moved in ways she did not expect. To have actually met with the killer they sought, to be touched and desired by him – a repulsive thought but surprisingly – stimulating – as Anne-Marie, blushing, not meeting Suzanne's eyes, described his fingertips tracing the neckline of her blouse. She was surprised that her body could consent to such a thing while her mind deplored it. She admired Anne-Marie for her daring. To Suzanne and her friends, dressing as shop girls to attend the Foire Saint-Germain was as daringly lower-class as they would think of going, and then only because it was the fashion for everyone else they knew, in a setting that was known and safe. To have ventured into a tavern on the Bièvre, even with a soldier escort – it was like Geoffroi confronting the savages of Canada, except that the savages, as he described them, were not nearly so frightening.

Anne-Marie wept when she spoke of Lisette and her sad fate. Suzanne felt the same puzzlement she had when a princess's lap-dog died: acknowledging the woman's grief but unable to empathize. One knew women like Lisette existed, of course; one gave to the Church of the Madeleine for the nuns who sought to help them; one heard it whispered at court that so-and-so was no better than a common tart; occasionally, from the window of one's coach or chair, one saw them plying their trade; but the compassion she felt for them was perfunctory and dutiful and lasted only as long as it took to hand the alms to the Madeleines. She could not fully comprehend Anne-Marie's depth of feeling, the guilt that racked her. It saddened and dismayed Suzanne because it opened a gap between her and Anne-Marie at a time she felt lonely because of the loss of Laure's friendship. She cast about for a way to bridge that gap.

'Let me sponsor the child Marthe. That way she can be sure to be cared for. I'll pay for her to attend Saint Catherine's school, which I went to, and then learn a respectable trade.'

The delight on Anne-Marie's face was reward in itself. 'Are you sure? I did not mean to imply that you should . . .' Her voice trailed off, and Suzanne realized she had been hoping for this but afraid to ask.

'Nonsense,' she replied briskly. 'I will write to Mère Catherine tomorrow. I have the means and am happy to do it – for your sake. I hope it will make you feel better.' She reached out to lay her hand lightly on Anne-Marie's arm and was rewarded with a watery smile.

'Yes, it does. And,' she swallowed, looking embarrassed, and continued with a wobble in her voice, 'thank you for caring how I feel.' She cast about in her pockets for a handkerchief.

Suzanne pressed one of her own, soft and rose-scented, into her hand.

To give her friend time to recover, she began to tell her about overhearing Louvois and his associate in the stone arcade, their mentioning Glacis by name in the same breath as the conspiracy to place blame on her family. When she spoke of their mentioning the silver buttons, Anne-Marie realized she had not yet told Suzanne about Luc at the Gobelins and his brother. Suzanne and her father had not been at home when she had spoken with the servants about them. Here was proof positive that the buttons had not been made for the family.

'So now that Louvois is aware that you and your father know what he has been doing,' Suzanne nodded, 'will that cause him to put a stop to it?' Anne-Marie asked.

'It may stop him from doing things openly – for a while, at least – but it has not stopped him from whispering it about, accusing us by rumor and innuendo.'

'Can nothing be done to stop him?'

'The King needs his expertise in organizing the army in order to bring about a decisive victory in the Netherlands. That is a point of royal honor and national pride. Compared to that, my family's troubles are of little account, however noble a lineage we have,' Suzanne replied bitterly. 'Only the King can stop him, and he won't. All we can hope to do is stop his creatures, such as Glacis.'

Anne-Marie thought for a few moments. 'We know that Glacis ultimately works for Louvois – but does Glacis know this?'

Suzanne stared at her. 'What do you mean?'

'If Glacis were caught by Commissaire Ferrand and his men, could he supply evidence against Louvois? Could we use him against his master?'

Suzanne considered. 'Or, use Louvois's fear of Glacis to put a stop to both of them?'

They shared a brilliant smile at their mutual cleverness, until the reality of what they were plotting sank in. Suzanne reddened and dropped her eyes.

'That's the worst of it – we have begun to think and talk like Louvois. To win against him only to descend to his level – that would be the ultimate victory for him. I'm ashamed of myself.' She swallowed and looked bleakly ahead. 'And yet, there has to be something better than just waiting in dignified silence to be the next victim of Louvois's slander or Glacis's knife.'

Anne-Marie sighed. 'You're right, of course. But what can we do?'

The shadows were lengthening in the garden. Soon it would be time for Anne-Marie to go home, but Suzanne was reluctant to let her depart after re-establishing their connection.

'Have you been to the Foire Saint-Germain this year?' The question was out of her mouth before the thought behind it was consciously formed.

Anne-Marie shook her head.

'Neither have I. My father and I are going tomorrow night. Would you and Niccolò like to join us as our guests?'

'I would love to!' Anne-Marie's face lit up. 'But would it be safe – I mean – in such a crowd –' She pressed her hand to her side.

Suzanne frowned; she hadn't considered that. But she could not conceive of such a thing happening at the fair. Thieves and pickpockets, certainly; but murder? The assassin wouldn't dare try anything in such a crowd of the well-to-do. Despite the killing at the porcelain boutique, she associated him with places like Le Renard and the class of people who frequented it. It was unimaginable that someone so low-class, with such a dreadful occupation could seriously enter her world. 'We would all be together; you would not be on your own.'

'That is what frightens me. I brought the killer to Lisette. I could not bear it if I brought him to someone else – to you and your father.' There was real anguish in her voice.

'Lisette was a pr— a witness to a murder,' Suzanne amended hastily. 'I am the daughter of the Duc de Languedoc. I have never seen Glacis. I would not recognize or identify him. His orders come from someone who wishes to discredit our family. To kill one of us would only excite sympathy.'

Anne-Marie had no words with which to counter these arguments. She could only shake her head miserably. Suzanne came from a world in which fear for one's life was simply not a reality; it was something one only imagined from behind a thick protective pane of glass. At one time, Anne-Marie might have agreed with her; but the attack on Niccolò a year ago had demonstrated to her danger's omnipresence. She wished she could share Suzanne's certainty.

She did not realize she said this thought aloud until Suzanne replied, 'Come with us to the Foire Saint-Germain. Nothing will happen to us there. You'll see.' She looked steadily into Anne-Marie's eyes, willing her, by sheer force of personality, to consent.

Anne-Marie allowed herself to be convinced. 'I will speak with Niccolò about it. If he consents, we will come.'

To her disappointment, Niccolò too downplayed the risks. 'You have armor now. I will be at your side every moment. And I would not want to disappoint the Duc.' He smiled at her. 'You deserve an evening of pleasure after all you have been through. Write to Mademoiselle de Toulouse and tell her we would be happy to accept their invitation.'

Anne-Marie sighed. It seemed a hopeless task to make others understand the guilt she felt over Lisette and the foreboding she felt now. She wrote the note and sent it by messenger the next morning.

Chapter Twenty-eight

Michel Glacis checked his face in the shaving mirror to make sure his mustache and goatee were well-trimmed and that his black, broad-brimmed hat sat as it should on his brow. It was a pity the mirror was not large enough for him to be able to take in the effect of the full outfit – the sober black suit of good-quality cloth, the snowy linen shirt, the fine silk stockings and leather shoes. He had been quite surprised when he saw his full-length reflection at the tailor's shop. Although no stranger to changing his appearance, in these clothes he had felt something better – transformed – at least on the outside. Clean linen equaled clean living and moral rectitude, a mark of the new man he wanted to make himself out to be. He defied even the Paymaster to call him Mendiant. It startled and pleased him, even as he laughed at himself.

He was finished with working for Louvois. He was now Monsieur Gentil, 'un vrai gentilhomme,' and he had identity papers to prove it.

After his flight from Le Renard, he had made his way to the tailor, changed into his new clothes, and abandoned in a ditch the things in which he had last been seen as Glacis. (A beggar woman had pounced upon them, and he knew they would be in the hands of a *revendeuse* before nightfall.) He was now in permanent residence in Saint-Germain.

He turned from the mirror to look with equal satisfaction at his living quarters. While it contained the same basic furnishings as at Le Renard – bed, table, chair, armoire – they were of better

283

quality, newer and cleaner. And there were extras, such as the mirror and a woven mat on the floor. A window with a pattern of clear leaded glass faced the street.

He had got used to the smell of the slaughterhouse and the river while he lived at Le Renard. His olfactory memory was still surprised by how much better it smelled here. At Le Renard he kept his curtains drawn all the time, hiding out. Here, he had rough curtains he could close for privacy, but he chose to leave them open much of the time. Michel Glacis had had to hide, but Michel Gentil lived in the open.

Perhaps it would have made more sense to leave Paris, but the alien environment of the countryside held no appeal for him. He knew the city and, despite the police manhunt, was confident in his ability to blend in, in the guise of different characters; he could remain there undisturbed while he found something else to put his hand to. Paris was the city of the self-made man. Poor country boys had arrived here with less in their pockets than he had now, learned the ways of the city, invested their money, and ended up with fantastic fortunes. Why shouldn't he, a Parisian born and bred, do the same in a modest way? His eyes lingered lovingly for a moment on the secret compartment he had carved out of the wall for his hoard of coins. He was pleased to see that he had enough cash in hand to keep him going for a year or more, by when something else was sure to have turned up.

Glacis had frequented low taverns, but Gentil went to coffee houses, eavesdropping on investors and developers, becoming acquainted with them, making inquiries. He realized he would need to understand and sign contracts. Glacis had been virtually illiterate, but Gentil had hired a tutor to refresh his reading and writing skills. A copybook of writing exercises lay on the table next to practice sheets of his handwriting. He felt a spark of pride at how it had improved these last weeks. Sometimes their lessons took place in this room; other times they would walk to the Pont Neuf so that he could practice reading out loud one of the many public notices and news sheets posted on the bridge.

But underneath, he was still Michel Glacis. He had sewn a deep hidden pocket into his new coat to accommodate his stiletto and carried it at all times. It paid to be careful. Calculating how to use his new persona, he mocked himself for liking it and his new acquaintances for being taken in by it. When one of them, a collector, had enthused at length about purchasing from a picture dealer a painting that was a genuine Nicolas Poussin, not an imitation of his style by Sebastien Bourdon, Glacis, who had never heard of either artist, made the comments expected of him, all the while thinking, *You're no judge of what is genuine – you take* me *at face value!* It made him feel he could both belong and be superior to this class. And laugh at his own pleasure in his new skills – his reading and writing, for instance. He had stabs of real regret that his life could not have been different – he could have been an actor if he had had an opportunity in another direction – but he mocked himself for that, too, as a sign of weakness. The past could not be made over; it could only be avenged.

Dressed in his new clothes, he had passed Leclerc, the Paymaster, in the street and exchanged polite greetings with him without being recognized. He could so easily have gone up to him, now that a wide desk was no longer between them and no guard at the door, and paid him back, with interest, for every sneer and gibe, every reminder of the 'Le Mendiant' family name. He had fingered his knife; his hand had itched to do it; with an effort, he had forced himself to keep walking. Perhaps he would have his revenge one day, but not now.

And he would find Madame Bruno and see that she paid dearly for her deception. Perhaps, before he killed her, he would persuade her to make good on the temptations she had so fetchingly presented. The thought of the things he would do to her, the mingled pleasure and shame he would make her feel until she would not know whether to beg him to stop or to continue, roused him. After visiting the Foire Saint-Germain tonight, he would visit the brothel one of his new associates had recommended to him. Michel Gentil could consort with a better class of woman than

Michel Glacis was accustomed to, even if the sex was not as — robust – as he would have liked.

The Foire Saint-Germain was brimming with activity. Even at a distance, he could hear the loud hum of voices as if from a gigantic beehive. Outside, a steady stream of carriages stopped in the brightly lit forecourt to discharge passengers. Doormen admitted them while keeping away beggars and vagrants. Inside, three hundred and fifty – the Abbot had boasted of the number – brightly lit booths sold all manner of luxury goods as well as food and drink. Entering after dark was like going from night into daylight, with candlelight reflecting off the shining materials – gold, silver, jewels both genuine and paste, gold lettering stamped into the smooth leather bindings of books, silks and other fabrics shot with gold thread in brilliant, jewel-like colors. With Palm Sunday fast approaching, these final days of the fair took on a hectic gaiety. The scents of perfumes from the counters and the customers, of lavender and rose-petal sachets, succeeded, for the most part, in covering the smell of several thousand people packed closely together in a warm interior, though he knew from previous visits that this would be less successful as the night progressed.

Wares were temptingly displayed on counters by pretty shop-girls; men flirted as they made their purchases. Glacis did not buy until he came to a bookseller's stall. A volume of the *Fables* of La Fontaine lay open on the counter and he paused to read it, making out the sentences slowly and moving his lips to sound out unfamiliar words. He started when the bookseller spoke to him, embarrassed to be caught practicing what would have come easily to the others around him, but the man merely asked if he enjoyed what he was reading. He replied modestly that he was coming late to reading and was not sure what books he would like. The seller was only too happy to recommend several. He bought the La Fontaine and another volume, walking away with a lift of the heart. *I'm a person who buys books!* Even the cynical Glacis side of him could not dampen that pleasure.

He had visited the fair several times before to observe the

manners of the clientele, listening to the cadence and inflection of their voices and imitating them as he moved about and spoke with merchants and other customers. It amused him to observe the other role-players there. A group of young men, aspiring courtiers by the look of them, but perhaps only financiers' sons wearing all their finery at once, exclaimed over shoe buckles with jewels that might have been diamonds – or paste. A woman whom he remembered as a *grisette* in the Galerie du Palais was now wearing the most fashionable silks and walking arm-in-arm with a genuine marquis. Other young women of title and wealth wore the plain grey costume of the *grisette* and purchased accessories several times its worth.

'Good evening, Monsieur Gentil,' said a booming bass voice just out of his line of sight.

He whirled in fright, his hand going instinctively for his knife, but it was merely a new acquaintance, the financier Simon Courtin. He gaped at the man for a moment before he recovered his wits and bowed in reply.

'I apologize, I did not mean to startle you,' said Courtin. 'I merely wanted to say hello.'

They exchanged pleasantries about the fair for a few minutes, until Madame and Mademoiselle Courtin had finished making their purchases at a nearby vendor of hair ornaments made of tall egret feathers.

'Isn't it splendid?' asked Mademoiselle Courtin, including Michel in her quest for approval. 'I feel quite like an American Indian maiden in a feathered headdress. Do you think it will help recommend me to the Duc de Languedoc for his son?'

'Why should it do that, Solange?' teased her father.

'Oh, Papa, you know he is practically living with the native tribes in New France.'

'No, he isn't – I see him over there with his guests.'

'Not the Duc – Monsieur de Roussillon, the son, is in New France.'

'Since you are so eager to learn of his tastes, let us go over to him, and I shall introduce you.' He turned again to Michel. 'Good night, Monsieur Gentil.'

Michel nodded good night but continued to watch the group as they approached the Duc and Mademoiselle de Toulouse. The Duc acted with consummate courtesy. It was clear he knew very well why the man was presenting his daughter and asking so eagerly after his son. Now he in turn presented his daughter and her companions, a tall man with curly brown hair styled with a complete disregard for fashion and a blonde woman dressed as a *grisette*. Michel realized with a thrill of satisfaction that it was Anne-Marie Bruno.

Suzanne composed her face to look welcoming and tried not to let her distress show. She and Anne-Marie had taken leave of the men while the Duc introduced Niccolò to someone who might have a commission for him. Turning a corner to browse another aisle of shops, they had come across the Comte de Chamilly and Laure. Suzanne had not seen him to talk to since his return to court, but she responded politely to his inquiries and presented Anne-Marie.

'Buying new livery buttons, Mademoiselle de Toulouse? I understand they have turned up in the most unexpected places!' The Comte gave his words an amused drawl, but his eyes were sharp and inquisitive, intent on plumbing the depth of her discomfort. Clearly, he had wasted no time in aligning himself with Louvois.

Suzanne was stunned at so unexpected an attack by someone she scarcely knew. Her cheeks grew warm, but she gave him a look of icy dignity; she would not deign to reply. She looked to Laure to contradict him. She had told her the truth of the matter, the day they sat on the silver bench in the gallery at Saint-Germain-en-Laye. Surely Laure, to whom she and the Duc had shown nothing but kindness, would speak up in her family's defense. But her friend stayed mute, not wishing to jeopardize her budding romance by contradicting the Comte. She would not meet Suzanne's eye and seemed to be examining intently a display of lace cravats.

It was Anne-Marie who broke the silence. 'You are mistaken, Monsieur Le Comte. The Languedoc household was not involved. The button in the dead man's hand was a crude imitation.'

The Comte gave her a sharp look. 'Indeed. What else can you tell us about this?'

Suzanne squeezed Anne-Marie's arm in warning. Anything she told the Comte would make its way back to Louvois.

Anne-Marie smiled and shrugged. 'It was apparently a quarrel after a costume ball.' She put as much nonchalance into her tone as she could.

'How unfortunate,' replied the Comte. It was not clear which he found regrettable, the supposed quarrel or the exoneration of the Duc.

Suzanne was relieved to catch sight of Niccolò's brown curls a short distance away. 'So, you see, Monsieur le Comte, we have no need of new liveries.' She nodded at Laure. 'Good evening, Mademoiselle.' She was gratified to see her friend color deeply to the roots of her hair. Head high, she swept off arm in arm with Anne-Marie.

Laure had disappeared into the Comte and his concerns, his points of view, with a single-mindedness that frightened Suzanne. It was as though the Laure who had been her closest friend for so many years was no longer there. This gave rise to a new worry: she tried to remember if she had told her anything about Anne-Marie's investigation. If she had, Laure was certain to repeat it to the Comte. She did not want Anne-Marie to come to Louvois's attention.

When they reunited with Niccolò and the Duc, Niccolò was excited; the *marchand mercier* to whom the Duc had introduced him was interested in seeing examples of his work. It could lead to new commissions. Anne-Marie responded eagerly, in part to allow Suzanne time to recover.

The Duc asked in a low voice, 'What is wrong?'

She shook her head, too upset to speak. 'Later, when we're alone,' she told him.

The approach of the Courtin family came as a relief, allowing her to return to the ordinary social intercourse of the fair. She liked Solange Courtin right away; she was forthright in her actions and had opinions without political calculation – like Laure used to be. She found herself hoping she and Solange could be friends.

Madame Courtin repeated Solange's comment about the feathers. Solange blushed. 'You must think me very silly.'

Suzanne replied kindly, 'No, it is our artists who were mistaken, imagining the feathered crowns. Perhaps you would like to visit us at the Hôtel de Languedoc to see some of the drawings and artifacts my brother has sent us?'

As the Courtin family moved away, satisfied, the Duc raised an eyebrow at his daughter. 'You'll only encourage them.'

'I liked her,' Suzanne replies simply. 'And I need a new friend.'

She hadn't said anything to him about Laure, but he looked as if he understood. He patted her hand. 'I'm sorry, my dear.'

Through long habit, Michel Glacis kept his face still and calm, but his mind was seething. There was Madame Bruno, who had led him to Lisette. Who had raised his hopes that night at the tavern without having any intention of fulfilling them. Who turned out to be a baker's daughter and sculptor's wife, but who paid calls upon the Languedoc household and was now seen with them in society. Who now so obligingly appeared in an ideal setting for his purpose. The crowd at the Foire – the press of bodies, the noise, the distractions of the goods on display and the entertainment – would provide excellent cover for a quick thrust of his knife. It was a pity he would have to forgo the pleasures of her body, but an opportunity such as this was not to be missed.

After the encounter with the Courtin family, the Duc's group moved on, stopping here and there. Glacis followed at a safe distance. It struck him that he was wearing the same clothing as on that morning at the Hôpital. Had Madame Bruno caught a glimpse of him as she left? But he could see a dozen men here dressed in a similar fashion.

His chance finally came when they paused to listen to one of the performers, a tenor with a high, clear voice of power and sweetness that commanded a circle of silence unusual in the noisy hubbub of the fair. Even Michel noticed the quality of the singing; in other circumstances, he too would have stopped to listen and admire; but he had a job to do now. The Duc and Suzanne, Niccolò and Anne-Marie drew close, listening with rapturous attention. They were standing on the fringes of the group gathered around the tenor – perfect. The two women were standing side by side. He preferred facing his victims – he loved those moments of disbelief, then realization, then panic on their faces as his knife went in and they were completely in his power – but a nice sideways thrust should do it.

He drew closer until he was standing behind her to her left, just out of her range of vision. Her attention continued to be riveted on the singer. Glacis inched forward until he was close enough to smell the perfume she wore tonight – she had not worn any at Le Renard – and under it the remembered scent of her body. He was gripping the smooth steel handle of his stiletto but could feel again the soft warmth of her breasts as he ran his fingers along the plunging front of her blouse and the lust that had taken hold of him that night.

The tenor reached the ecstatic climax of his song. Time seemed suspended while he sustained a high note for longer than seemed humanly possible, then followed it with a liquid rush of notes without drawing a breath. The crowd let out theirs in a sigh of rapture.

In one smooth practiced movement, Glacis drew his knife and thrust it at Anne-Marie's side, prepared to feel the sexual release that killing often gave him. To his dismay, his knife skittered along metal, never finding an entry point into the flesh. Instead of the satisfaction of a job silently and efficiently carried out, there was the rasp of metal, the tearing of cloth, and his own snarl of frustration as he backed away, pocketed his knife, and melted into the crowd.

Chapter Twenty-nine

Anne-Marie fought to keep her balance after someone shoved her rudely in the side, but fell heavily against Suzanne, causing her to cry out. The tenor glared at them for spoiling the conclusion of his aria. Anne-Marie managed to stay upright, made apologies to Suzanne and the singer, and turned to confront whoever shoved her.

But the only one there was a woman wielding a painted fan. 'Madame – the clumsy oaf – he has ripped your dress!' She pointed with the folded fan.

Anne-Marie looked down. There was not only a rip in the dress but also a long scratch across the metal plates of her new armor. 'Did you see who did this?' she asked the woman.

'It was a man in a black suit and hat.' The woman turned to point him out but there were more than a dozen men similarly dressed in plain sight and probably hundreds more at the Fair. It would be impossible to identify Glacis until it was too late, Anne-Marie realized; there was nothing to prevent him from trying again.

She started to shake. A chair was brought for her, and a glass of eau-de-vie. Niccolò knelt and held the drink to her lips. She continued to shiver. Tenderly he chafed her hands, then held them, looking at her with concern as she at last grew calm. She stopped shuddering and gave him a wan smile.

'It worked!' he told her. 'The armor saved your life.' He gripped her hands hard, as if to pass his courage to her, and gave them a little shake. 'It saved your life!' he said again.

An official of the Fair, one of the lay personnel of the Abbey of Saint-Germain, came over to ask what had happened. Before Anne-Marie could answer, the Duc told him that someone had accidentally bumped into her and torn her dress.

'We don't want to create a panic,' he explained to Anne-Marie after the man had left. He gave her a long look, judging whether she was steady enough to stand. 'Come – we'll take you home with us. Then we can talk about what to do.'

It was nerve-racking to make their way through the crowded fair to the front court. Niccolò stayed close by her side, his arm protectively around her. It was a relief to climb into the Duc's carriage for the ride to the Place Royale.

They were not expected home for hours, but Marc and Rose had been talking in the kitchen, planning their wedding. Marc admitted them. Niccolò went with the Duc to his study, while Suzanne took Anne-Marie to her room, after requesting that Rose make a pot of hot chocolate and bring it to them. Suzanne's maid, not expecting her mistress to return so early, was still out for the evening. Anne-Marie took off the rented dress and the scratched stays and checked to make sure there were no scratches or other knife marks on her skin. Suzanne told her not to worry about the dress; her maid could repair it, or she would simply pay for it if it could not be repaired. There were more important things to think of now.

Rose brought up the hot chocolate, as well as several *sablés*. Suzanne and Anne-Marie were suddenly ravenous; they had had only a light supper, as they had planned to eat at the fair. Rose told them that Marc had taken to the study enough wine and bread and charcuterie for the four of them.

'Tell my father and Niccolò to start without us; we will be some time yet.'

After a half-hour, when Anne-Marie had finished her sewing and dressed again in her everyday clothes, they descended to join the men.

Because of the mild weather, there was no fire this evening;

the candles provided sufficient warmth. It was the first time the four had met in the Duc's study since that December evening when they had decided to pursue the investigation. It had seemed such a simple, noble thing to do. Anne-Marie sighed for her lost illusions.

After the women had eaten, the Duc took charge of the conversation, addressing Anne-Marie.

'Your husband and I have been talking about what would be the best course of action. We feel you should remain here at the Hôtel de Languedoc. Glacis will not come looking for you here – and if he did, Marc and the other manservants would protect you.'

Suzanne smiled warm approval. 'What a wonderful idea! Please stay!'

Anne-Marie was surprised by the invitation; she knew that the Duc and Suzanne rarely entertained overnight guests; there was a small spark of pride in her breast that she was accorded this honor. It was tempting, too, to reside for even a short time at one of the most fashionable addresses of Paris, surrounded by such furniture and fabrics, eating delicious food, waited on by servants – in short, to live like a duchess! She imagined herself in a fine dressing gown like the one Suzanne was wearing now, sipping hot chocolate and reading as much as she wanted in the middle of the day. But who would take care of Niccolò? That was her job.

'Would Niccolò stay here as well?'

'Certainly, if you wish it.'

He shook his head regretfully. 'I am sorry, but I cannot. It is too far to walk back and forth each day. I need to put in long hours at the studio. Monsieur Le Brun is most insistent that I finish the new commissions as quickly as possible.'

Anne-Marie imagined Niccolò returning to empty rooms at night, tired and hungry, and having to fend for himself. 'Then I would rather be with Niccolò. I have armor to protect me now. And Monsieur Le Brun has promised the Gobelins will safeguard me.'

'The armor protected you, but also the element of surprise,' the Duc pointed out. 'Glacis was not expecting it. Next time he will be. And you are still vulnerable in other areas — your chest, your throat, your back, your wrists.'

'The Gobelins is hardly a closed compound,' Niccolò reminded her. 'There is a watchman at the main gate but not at the back, where we cross the Bièvre. There are people constantly coming and going — making deliveries, visiting friends, showing the workshops to foreign visitors and dignitaries.'

'It is home, *our* home. I would rather be at home with you, Niccolò.' There was an edge to her voice. She did not like being told what to do, even if they had her best interests at heart. She had had enough of that from her parents. She was a married woman now and entitled to make her own decisions.

'If I stay here until Glacis is caught,' she continued, 'how long will that take? Weeks? Months? He has eluded capture for that long already despite the efforts of Commissaire Ferrand and his men.' A long stay at the Hôtel de Languedoc, which had seemed so tempting just a few minutes before, now stretched before her as bleak as imprisonment.

Her face must have reflected her misery, because Niccolò's face crumpled a little. 'We only want to keep you safe,' he said softly.

She smiled at him, then the other two. 'I appreciate that. I hope I do not sound ungrateful — or unaware of the dangers. But you will be returning to Saint-Germain-en-Laye after Easter. Just as your place is there, mine is at the Gobelins with Niccolò.'

The Duc opened his mouth to object but closed it and smiled slightly. 'You sound very like my Duchesse. Once she decided on a course of action, there was little anyone could do to dissuade her.' His eyes were shining with pride and fondness. Suzanne, whose feelings about her mother were so different and who had never heard her father talk with emotion about his dead wife, stared at him in amazement, Anne-Marie's dilemma forgotten for the moment.

'Niccolò?' Anne-Marie asked softly.

He turned to the Duc. 'It is not easy being married to someone with the will of a Duchesse.' His glance flicked to the two women, then back to the Duc. 'It seems I, too, must give in.'

The mantelpiece clock chimed twice; it was now two in the morning. The Duc was suddenly weary and could not summon further argument. 'I have dismissed the coach. Spend the night here. You may feel differently about going home in the morning.'

A yawning Marc showed them to one of the guest bedrooms.

Contentedly she lay in Niccolò's arms in the soft feather bed. '*Bonne nuit, ma Duchesse*,' he whispered in her ear just before she fell asleep.

Chapter Thirty

La Bobine, the bobbin, the tavern across from the Gobelins, was doing a brisk business. (The landlord had optimistically changed its name to La Tapisserie, the tapestry, when he took it over but reverted to the original name after everyone had nicknamed it Le Tapissoir, the urinal.) It was a warm Saturday evening, and the Gobelins' weavers and dyers, silversmiths and sculptors had received their pay for the week. Everyone was in good humor, particularly after the first glass of wine, celebrating the end of the work week before the solemnity of Sunday. Although the tavern was a strictly male preserve during the week, many had brought their wives on this celebratory evening. Willem's wife sat with her sisters who had also married artisans at the Gobelins.

'Where is Willem?' one asked. 'I don't see him with the other weavers.' She nodded at the group that congregated at two tables along the wall.

'He's over there by himself,' replied the wife, tipping her head toward the opposite end of the tavern. 'He's been out of sorts all week, but he won't tell me what's wrong.' Her sisters traded wary looks: they had had enough of Willem's grumbling over the years and had no desire to hear, from his wife, *her* complaints about *his* complaints. She shrugged. 'Well, if I don't know what it is, I can't help him with it.' Their faces eased and they moved on to other topics of conversation.

Only the blue-eyed stranger appeared to have any sympathy

for him. 'Poor fellow – he needs cheering up,' he said to the barman. 'What does he like to drink?' He purchased a bottle and carried it to the figure in the corner. The regulars exchanged amused winks and nudges. The stranger would soon learn what a bore Willem was.

Willem glowered at the genial crowd as he replayed in his mind his confrontation with Charles Le Brun several days before. He had been sitting at his loom, concentrating on an intricate area of the design that required deft manipulation of the bobbins and the *lisses*, with frequent checks against the painted cartoon. He had been fully absorbed in his work, almost happy for once, when a shadow fell across the loom. Someone was standing between it and the window, blocking the light. Willem, accustomed to this behavior from public visitors to the atelier who did not appreciate the importance of the natural light, asked him to move, without looking up. But the person stayed resolutely in place, forcing him to stop and glare at the clumsy oaf. It was Jean Jans, the master weaver of the atelier, who should have known better. Outlined as he was against the light, Willem could not see his face, but the stance of his body did not bode well.

'Monsieur Le Brun would like to see you in his office,' he said in a clipped voice.

The summons Willem had been dreading had arrived. His stomach twisted into a knot, but he tried to keep his voice steady and unworried as he played for time. 'Of course; just let me finish this tricky bit . . .'

'He said *now*.'

'Did he say what it was about?'

'No – but by the look on your face, you know. Maybe some of your nonstop whining finally reached his ears and he's as sick of it as the rest of us.' As Willem sat there, dreading the interview, the master weaver barked, 'Report to the office and get it over with! And come straight back afterward – I want to win this week.' The four *haute lisse* ateliers were in a friendly contest over which could be the most productive.

Reluctantly Willem began to move slowly past the other looms to the door. Their occupants, as preoccupied as he had been, did not look up.

'Quit dawdling and get going!' The master weaver's voice boomed through the space. Now everyone looked up to observe Willem leaving in disgrace. His nerve broke, and he all but ran from the room.

Le Brun's manservant was expecting Willem and showed him into the office. Le Brun was seated at his desk, the portraits of Louis XIV and Colbert behind him underlining the authority of his position. He neither offered Willem refreshment nor invited him to sit but fixed him with a stern gaze for several moments before he spoke.

'I was distressed to learn of your association with the Dutch spy ring.'

Willem flinched. How had Le Brun heard? Ferrand had not informed him – Le Brun had been away at court when Willem was questioned, and Ferrand had preferred to hold the threat of telling Le Brun over Willem's head as a guarantee of his future good behavior. And Willem *had* been good, working industriously at his loom and avoiding contact with any Dutchmen or Flemings outside his colleagues at the Gobelins. He had kept his promise to Ferrand – so why would the police have informed Le Brun?

Or had someone else done so? In that case, it must have been Niccolò Bruno or his wife. They were the only others who both knew of his association with Hendrik and had access to Le Brun. He scowled at the thought of them.

'Well, Willem?'

He started. He had almost forgotten Le Brun was there.

'I was hoping you would deny your involvement and show me my source was mistaken. But it appears to be true.' Le Brun leaned back, looking tired and disappointed. 'Still, before I pass judgment, I want to hear what you have to say for yourself.'

'Please,' Willem begged. 'I was never a spy. I knew Hendrik, the dead man. But I was never involved in the spying. I swear it!'

'Whether or not you were involved in it, you were aware of it – yes?'

Willem looked down and muttered something indistinct.

'I didn't hear you,' Le Brun replied. 'Was that a yes?'

'Yes.' His voice was low but the word was distinct.

'That is called tacit consent,' continued Le Brun implacably. 'You knew what was happening – a matter of treason against the Crown and the nation of France – and you did nothing to prevent it, nor informed the authorities.' He paused to let his words sink in.

'You saw what happened to Hendrik! I was afraid for my life!'

'Might I remind you that the Gobelins, for which you work, is one of the Royal Manufactures – that your livelihood depends on the King's generosity?' He gestured to the portrait behind him. 'Moreover, your treachery could cast doubt on the entire Manufactory, affecting not only your livelihood but also that of your colleagues, including your wife's family. It is a grave irresponsibility on your part! How do you think he' – he gestured at the portrait again – 'would react if I were to tell him of your treachery?'

'You wouldn't!' Willem gave the portrait an agonized look as though fearing it would come to life and condemn him then and there.

Le Brun tightened his verbal thumbscrews. 'Indeed, I could. As First Painter, I have the ear of the King.' He paused to let Willem sweat. 'But if I am satisfied you have learned your lesson and there will be no repeat of such activities, I am willing to be quiet about it – this time – for your wife's sake. I have known her and her family for many years and would not wish them to suffer disgrace.'

Willem almost swooned with relief.

'However, should I hear of *any* further transgressions of *any* kind on your part, I will not hesitate to give you up to the authorities. I cannot afford to have my loyalty called into question by being overly lenient to you. If need be, I will save my skin by giving up yours. That is, I think, a sentiment you can understand?'

Willem nodded miserably.

'I didn't hear your answer.'

'Yes! Yes, I understand!' Willem shouted.

'Splendid. I am delighted to know we shall have no further trouble from you.' He watched Willem sweat and writhe for another minute. 'Very well, you may go back to your loom.'

Willem slunk back upstairs to the atelier, past the inquisitive glances of the other weavers, and sat down at the loom. Reluctantly he pulled the *lisses* and picked up the bobbins, but his satisfaction in the work was gone for today.

'You look like you could do with some cheering up,' said a sympathetic but unfamiliar voice in his ear, interrupting his thoughts. He swung round, ready to tell the man to go to hell, but the stranger merely smiled and held up a bottle and two cups. Willem bit back the response he had been about to make and said with considerable truculence, 'Yeah, I could.' Recalling his manners, he smiled at the stranger. 'Sorry I was so short, there – I thought you were one of them' – he jerked his head at the Gobelins workers – 'come to rub it in.'

The stranger poured a generous measure from the bottle and said. 'It's a pity they don't appreciate you as much as they should.'

Willem cast a suspicious glance at him, suspecting the man was making fun of him, but the other's bland countenance held only kind concern. 'Tell me your troubles, friend.'

Willem drained the cup the stranger had put before him. He did not yet know whether to trust this man but he would make sure that he got his full share of the proffered bottle before it could be snatched away. He put down the cup and, slightly bleary-eyed, gave the stranger a skeptical look. 'What makes you so friendly? I don't know you.'

The other man leaned forward and said confidingly, 'I've heard you have a grudge at the Gobelins. I too have a score to settle there. I thought we could help each other out.'

Willem hesitated; he did not need any more trouble. Could this man have been sent by Le Brun as a test? 'And who might your quarrel be with?' he asked grudgingly.

'One of the women – she led me on and then went all virtuous and wouldn't come across.' He sniggered. 'She needs a lesson on keeping her promises.'

'A woman, eh?' Willem leered. 'Does she have a name? What does she look like?'

'She was reluctant to share her real name, but I fancy I would know her again if I saw her. Blonde, buxom' – his hands outlined a woman's generous figure – 'and dressed most revealingly.' There were a number of blonde women at the Gobelins but with his current preoccupation Willem's mind naturally gravitated toward one in particular.

'I may know such a one. Was she wearing . . .?' He described the outfit he had seen on Anne-Marie on the night of the visit to Le Renard.

'Yes, that's the one,' the stranger agreed. He leaned forward eagerly, appearing to hang on Willem's every word.

The weaver seemed to puff up with pride at knowing something the stranger did not. Had he been a bird, he would have preened his feathers. 'Her name is Anne-Marie Bruno.'

The stranger repeated it carefully, rolling it around his tongue as though tasting the other delights she would offer him.

Willem grinned broadly, delighted at the effect of his words, and threw caution to the winds. 'Then I am more than happy to help you. My quarrel is with her husband.'

'Indeed!' The stranger gave an amused smile and poured another generous measure into Willem's cup, nodding to encourage him to drink up. 'And what did Monsieur Bruno do to upset you so much?'

Willem was not so drunk that he could be tricked into incriminating himself. 'He carried tales,' he said briefly, 'to the wrong ears.'

'And got you into trouble for something you had hoped to get away with,' the stranger finished smoothly.

Willem was frightened by his perception, but the other only laughed. 'Don't we all? You wouldn't be human if you didn't,' he said easily. 'Relax – I'm not interested in what you've done – I only want your help in seeing that Madame Bruno gets what's coming to her – which I think will go a long way toward punishing Monsieur Bruno, *n'est-ce pas*?'

They grinned in complicity.

It was not merely by chance that Michel Glacis had found Willem at La Bobine, but the next step in a careful plan of action to make sure that Anne-Marie would be taken care of once and for all.

Glacis had come to the Gobelins the morning after the Foire Saint-Germain, arriving in time to see the couple return. They paid the fiacre driver and scuttled rapidly inside, casting nervous glances about them. Glacis kept his hat brim low, shading his eyes so that the intensity of his blue gaze would not draw their attention to him. He could not afford to be seen too often in this neighborhood; he would need someone to keep watch for him. He scanned the group of urchins that congregated near the gates of the Gobelins, ready to run errands and messages for the businesses of the area. He himself had done that as a boy to bring in a few sous for food. He had employed such boys in the past and found them reliable associates who knew how to keep their eyes and ears open and their mouths shut. He had never had to silence any of them. His practiced eye ran over the group but could not perceive any with the qualities he wanted. They were indolent, waiting for business to come to them, or engaged in scuffling with their fellow urchins. Then he felt a tug on his coat.

'Run an errand for you, Monsieur?' It was a thin boy in patched clothing, with brown hair and intelligent grey eyes. Here was the initiative Glacis was looking for.

He smiled at the lad. 'Not an errand – another sort of job.'

303

The boy took a step backward. 'I don't go with men, Monsieur.' He was poised to run should his words give offense.

Glacis, however, merely laughed. 'Neither do I.' He pointed at the Gobelins gates. 'Did you see the man and woman who got out of the fiacre?'

'Sure. Tall man with curly hair, blonde woman in a blue skirt. He's foreign. I ran an errand for her once. She gave me a piece of bread for it.' His stomach growled in remembrance.

Glacis smiled again and handed the boy two sous. 'Get yourself something to eat and then let's talk.'

Reassured, the boy accepted the coins. He went into a bakery and emerged with two large slices of bread. He offered one to Glacis, who shook his head. 'Keep them both.' The boy gave him a wholehearted grin in thanks and beckoned to a smaller boy, his brother by the look of him. He handed the second slice to the other boy and wasted no time in devouring his own.

'What do you want me to do for you, Monsieur?'

'That man and woman are Niccolò and Anne-Marie Bruno.' He watched the boy silently mouth the names to fix them in his memory. 'I have a particular interest in their welfare. I'd like you to keep your eyes open and let me know when they come and go each day. Can you tell time?'

The boy gave him a scornful glance. 'Of course I can! I always count the hours when the church bell rings them.'

Glacis nodded, satisfied. 'Good. I want to know their regular habits, to make sure they're kept safe. And I want you to keep your ears open, too, to find out if anyone has a complaint about them. I'll want to talk to that person.' His voice had a hint of menace in it. 'For this, I'll pay you five sous a day.'

'Ten,' countered the boy.

'Seven,' replied Glacis promptly.

'Eight.'

'Seven,' Glacis repeated firmly.

'Done.' The boy gave a parody of a military salute.

They arranged to meet at nightfall. For several days, the boy had nothing to report of the couple's movements; they were staying inside the compound, not venturing out.

If they were not going to come out, he would go in. He liked that idea – striking in the heart of what they felt was their safe place, revealing its – and their – vulnerability. Fortunately, reconnoitering the Gobelins, with its frequent tourists come to visit the tapestry workshops, would be easy to do. Rather than be seen in the suit he had worn at the Foire Saint-Germain, in which he might be recognized, he went to one of the tailors who outfitted visiting gentlemen with rented clothing, then visited a bookshop to purchase the Germain Brice guidebook to Paris recommended by the tailor. He was pleased to find he could understand many of the words in it and even read a few sentences.

His visit to the Manufactory had given him a good idea of the layout of the buildings, courtyards, and workshops, but he would need to find someone who could tell him where to find the Brunos' private quarters. He was mulling this over as he visited the weaving ateliers. There, he had recognized one of the members of Hendrik's group and knew he had found the right man to be an informant. His membership in that group was something he could use to persuade the man to cooperate, should he prove recalcitrant.

The following evening, the boy told him, 'One of the weavers was complaining about Monsieur and Madame Bruno, cursing them out loud.'

'Ah!' This was promising. Could it be Hendrik's old associate? 'Do you know his name?'

'Willem – a Fleming – he's gone in La Bobine every night this week and come out drunk. But last night was the first time I heard him talk about them,' he added hastily, lest Glacis suspect him of holding back information.

'Will he be at La Bobine again tonight?'

'Bound to be – the workers get paid today.'

'Good. I will come here when the clock strikes eight, and you can point him out to me. I'll pay you double.'

As he had suspected, this Willem was the weaver he had recognized. Willem had not recognized him, however, and had needed no threats to become a willing ally.

Willem's face gradually relaxed as the man's words sank in. 'What do you want me to do?'

'Just give me the information I ask for – I'll take care of the rest. Nothing more than that.' He brought a *louis d'or* out of an inner pocket and laid it on the table between them. 'I am willing to pay handsomely – providing it is all trustworthy, mind.' His eyes held a warning glint.

Willem licked his lips, his eyes focused on the coin's golden gleam that shed a radiance of its own on the dull surface of the scarred wooden table. 'What do you want to know?' He did not look at the stranger but addressed the coin instead.

'Tell me about the Gobelins. Where are the rooms occupied by the Brunos? Are they always on the premises during the day? Are there times they are likely to be away from the Manufacture?' Willem was only too happy to oblige. These were questions he could answer easily and readily. The stranger seemed pleased with his answers and pushed the coin over to him as the Gobelins clock struck midnight. Willem promptly put it in his pocket. Around them, drinkers were preparing to leave, and Willem's wife was signaling that they should too.

The stranger said in a rapid undertone, 'Let me think about how best to manage this. I will meet you in two days' time.' He named a tavern at some remove from La Bobine.

'But this is more convenient,' grumbled Willem. The genial effect of the liquor was beginning to wear off.

'I know,' replied the other with a flicker of impatience, 'but it might raise questions if we are seen together too often.' He slipped away as Willem's wife approached, before she could get a good look at him.

'Who was that?' she asked suspiciously, as Willem struggled to his feet.

'A new friend,' he replied, slurring his words. 'His name is –'
He tried to think. Had the man given him a name? He couldn't
recall.

'Huh.' She was under no illusions about the pleasure of her
husband's company. Anyone who would listen to his complaints
for that long must be someone of extraordinary patience – or
have an ulterior motive.

He was about to show her the *louis d'or* as proof of the stranger's
good will, when caution set in. She might demand to know what
he had promised for such a payment – or worse, take possession
of the coin so that he would never get any pleasure out of it. He
left it in his pocket.

She shook her head in exasperation. 'Come on, you – home.'

Michel Glacis strode rapidly away from La Bobine, shedding the
effect of Willem's company like a dog shaking off water. *Mon
Dieu*, that man was a bore! His grudge against the Brunos made
him useful, but three hours of his undiluted company was a stiff
price to pay. Still, if all went according to plan, he would not be
a nuisance much longer.

Glacis spent the following two days formulating in meticulous
detail what he would do to the elusive Madame Bruno. Three
times she had slipped through his grasp – at Le Renard, at the
marketplace where he recognized her blue cloak, and at the Foire
Saint-Germain. *His* grasp – a professional with years of experience! She was nobody – a baker's daughter, a woodcarver's wife,
a woman. He had bested far better opponents, other professionals
sent to kill him. He thought of how the Paymaster would roar
with laughter and heap ridicule upon him. Indeed, he was an
object of ridicule in his own eyes. For his own self-respect, he
must deal with her once and for all, striking at her in what she
perceived as her sanctuary. Only then could he depart, with his
head held high, from being Michel Glacis and wholeheartedly
focus his attention on becoming Michel Gentil.

And the woman was dangerous, more intelligent than she

looked, and as obsessive as he was. She had shown up at the tavern where the murder took place, far in advance of the police. She had found and interviewed Lisette, whom he had had to silence. Anne-Marie would need to be silenced in turn. He had learned the hard way that you don't leave loose ends and you don't show mercy.

But there was more to it than that. He had watched his grandfather and father be humiliated for being beggars and endured the Paymaster's taunts about his ancestry. While Madame Bruno, despite her humble origins, visited the Hôtel de Languedoc, went to the Foire Saint-Germain with the Duc and his daughter. Her husband worked for the First Painter to the King, who also moved in court circles. She was nobody, but her involvement in this case had raised her station in life – while he, Glacis, who had rid France of two dangerous spies, was treated like dirt by his masters. He felt a burning desire to bring her down to his level.

When his plan was ready, Glacis smiled. For once things would go his way and nothing – *nothing* – would get between him and his revenge.

The tavern Glacis had specified for his second meeting with Willem catered to a different clientele from the prosperous workers at the Gobelins; it had a smaller, meaner feel to it. No one spoke to Willem. The stranger hadn't shown up yet. It was a mistake to come too early – not only did it show an eagerness that the other might take advantage of, but it also meant paying for his own drink. He purchased the cup of wine and took it to a table by the wall where he could survey the room as he sat. He drained the cup quickly. The wine was coarse but potent, better than one would expect at a tavern like this. He had the landlord bring a large pitcher and another cup. He could happily anticipate, as he had a dozen times in the last two days, the unsuspected fate that would befall Niccolò and Anne-Marie. And all he, Willem, had to do was supply information about them! Information he was being paid for, no less! It was a heady feeling of power, to watch the action set in motion and for once not be the victim of it. Each time he caught sight of Niccolò crossing the courtyard or Anne-Marie at the well, he gloated at his knowledge.

He thought he had been careful not to let it show, but his wife noticed. 'What are you so pleased about all of a sudden?' she'd demanded the next day. He had mentioned Madame Bruno in his sleep, she told him. Then followed an argument that would have been laughable had his wife not been so upset. Had he been carrying on with her? He vigorously denied it. Lusting after her? He was appalled at the thought. It was his drinking companion last night who mentioned how much he . . .

A likely story indeed, she had sniffed. She was going to give Madame Bruno a piece of her mind, tempting other women's husbands. 'I suppose you're going to see *her*,' she had remarked as he prepared to leave tonight.

'Don't be ridiculous,' he had scoffed, and kissed the top of her head.

Then the stranger came in, and Willem waved him over.

Glacis eyed the weaver with disgust. Willem was well on the way to being drunk and waving at him with expansive gestures a blind man could have seen. But Glacis carefully ironed the annoyance out of his face as he approached the table and bared his teeth in what he hoped Willem would perceive as a friendly grin. The weaver smiled back, pushing forward a chair and a cup of wine.

'Well? What are you planning?' he asked eagerly and loudly. Several men at nearby tables turned inquisitive faces toward them.

'Keep your voice down,' Glacis hissed furiously. The weaver subsided. The drinkers shrugged and returned to their conversations.

'What are you going to do?' Willem asked with exaggerated softness, avid for details.

Glacis smiled at him. 'That's better,' he said, exuding warm approval.

Willem smiled in return, relaxing in his chair. 'What will you do?' he asked again in a voice barely above a whisper.

'Madame Bruno will belatedly discover the wisdom of following through on her promises. Monsieur Bruno will be deeply upset by his inability to prevent what is happening to his wife. I'll pay her a visit while the Gobelins residents are at the funeral.'

'Whose funeral?' Willem was bewildered. He could not think of anyone who had died recently at the Gobelins.

'Yours,' replied Glacis with a thrust of his knife.

Chapter Thirty-one

The day of Willem's funeral was sunny and mild. Going down to the well to fetch water, Niccolò thought he could detect the scent of the fruit trees blossoming in the Cordelières' garden. Usually it was Anne-Marie who went down for water in the mornings, but she had refused ever since the unpleasant scene at the well several days before, when Willem's wife marched up to her, hands on hips, arms akimbo, a furious expression on her face. 'You've been having an affair with my husband!'

Everyone turned to look at them.

'What? No! Of course not!' Anne-Marie was vehement in her denial.

'Then why is he talking in his sleep about you and your lovely charms?' the woman had shouted, giving the last words a particular venom. 'I tell you, he's *my* husband – keep your hands off him!'

Anne-Marie had stared at her in amazement. She burst into peals of laughter at the mere thought of lusting after Willem, laughter that went on and on, betraying the nervous pressure she had been under. Willem's wife had thought that Anne-Marie was laughing at *her*. Maddened beyond endurance, she had sprung forward to physically attack Anne-Marie. Only the quick reaction of the others prevented her from inflicting bodily harm.

The group of women glared at Anne-Marie, who would always be an outsider in the tightly knit community of weavers' families. Far from being the victim of an undeserved assault, she now found herself suspected of giving the other just cause. Someone fetched Niccolò from his studio to take her home.

Upstairs in their rooms, she burst into tears, sobbing to him that she didn't know how this rumor started. When her tears had dried, Niccolò said he would pay a visit to Willem and his wife to settle the matter.

'No!' she had insisted, clutching at his coat to keep him from going. 'That will only give the rumor substance. Let it die down of its own accord. I hope that, with nothing to support it, that will happen soon enough.'

Returning to their rooms with the bucket of water in hand, Niccolò wrinkled his nose. Anne-Marie had not taken their clothes and linens to the laundry boat on the Seine for more than three weeks. The room smelled sour, not fresh as it should in the spring air. Anne-Marie's fear seemed to contribute a smell of its own to the mix.

He cleaned the ashes from the fireplace, laid wood for a new fire and lit it so he could cook their breakfast. This was another domestic task he had taken over in recent days. He decided to cook the rest of the sausages he had bought for last night's dinner, hoping they would tempt Anne-Marie to eat. In this warm weather they were likely to spoil if not used quickly. He set the pan on the iron tripod and opened the bedroom door an inch so that the smell of cooking should draw Anne-Marie out. Within a few minutes, he heard the creak of the bedframe and the rustle of linens – she was getting up.

When she emerged, yawning, he greeted her with his customary enthusiastic, *'Buongiorno, Signora!'* But her answering smile was only a ghost of its usual self. His worried eyes followed her as she sat down at the table. Their home should have been a sanctuary for her, a place to feel safe. She had seemed happy enough at first, but the confrontation with Willem's wife, followed by the weaver's death, had shaken her badly. The fear was still there in her eyes, and her actions or, rather, the lack of them. Two weeks of hiding indoors and eating poorly had made her skin a pasty white; she made little effort to wash and dress; their rooms were as neglected as her person. He wished he knew how to break through this shell of fear to reach the buoyant, courageous Anne-Marie he knew was inside.

He brought the pan of sausages to the table and placed two on her plate. She thanked him but regarded the food with disinterest. He bit back the words telling her she must eat: he knew they would have no effect other than to annoy her. Instead he picked up a sausage he had purposely left uncooked and began to tease Gâteau. He would offer it, withdraw it, hold it close, hold it high to make the cat leap for it, all the while darting glances at Anne-Marie to see if these antics amused her as they usually would. Even a reproof about not playing with his food or giving it to the cat would have been welcome. But she merely gave him a surface smile that never reached her eyes. When Gâteau had finally hooked her claws into the sausage, he continued to tug on it gently until he allowed her to pull it out of his hands and retire to a corner of the room to eat her prize at her leisure. Then he attacked his own breakfast with a hearty appetite.

Finally, Anne-Marie spoke. 'What time is the funeral?'

'Ten o'clock. Are you sure you won't come with me? You have plenty of time to get ready.'

'No!' She shook her head and continued in a shaky voice. 'He was killed in the same way as Hendrik, the knife thrust in his side. Dr Lunague told us. At least this was one autopsy I didn't need to assist at.' She shuddered. 'And the setting was the same as Hendrik's murder, stabbed in a tavern where no one knew him, and the man he'd been seen with just walked out of there without anyone noticing when and where he had gone. Glacis wants me in the open, in the cemetery, so he can sneak up to me in the crowd. I'd never pay attention to the service; I'd be nervously looking around the whole time.

'And I doubt his widow will want me there,' she commented wryly, with a glimpse of her old humor. 'If I come, I'm a brazen

313

hussy flaunting myself, but if I stay away I'm admitting my guilt by being ashamed to show my face. It's better if I don't go.'

'I understand,' he replied. 'I would happily stay home with you but I must do what is expected of me as part of the Gobelins. I disliked the man, but to avoid the funeral would look as though I were carrying a grudge beyond the grave. I'll be back as soon as I can.'

After Niccolò had left, Anne-Marie shut and locked the door and turned tiredly to collapse into one of the armchairs. She stared unseeing at the embers in the fireplace as they burned down to white ash and went cold, while her thoughts went round and round well-worn paths. Her guilt over finding Lisette and leading the killer to her: she could never expiate for it, whatever the priest had said. 'You can't bring her back from the dead; you can only help bring her killer to justice.' Even the attack by Glacis at the Foire Saint-Germain did not help to ease her conscience.

And the threat continued, to her fright, from a killer who seemed able to change his appearance at will, so that she was never sure when he might be upon her, and who surely would not scruple to attack anyone she was with. It was not only herself that she put at risk. Then there was the discomfort of being imprisoned – first in her armored bodice and then in her home. It was all too much, she thought. Too much, too much, too much . . .

And now she was no fit wife to Niccolò, in bed or out of it. 'You've got Niccolò to look after – you've got to get through this for him,' Père Aimé had said. She looked down at her unwashed body in the dirty clothing, then raised her eyes to glance around the room she usually took such delight in keeping clean and spotless. Dirty dishes with the remains of breakfast, dust and crumbs all over, an old cobweb in one corner of the ceiling: poor Niccolò did his best, but it was her job, not his. She started to get up from the chair to deal with these things but collapsed back down again. Compared with Lisette's death and the other perils she had brought upon those she loved, what did these things matter? The Melancholic humor had her again in its grip and she didn't seem to know how to get out of it. Sometimes she could step back, recognize its presence in herself, and think, 'I should consult Dr Lunague for what to do to bring my humors back into balance.' But before she could do so, Melancholy would again come over her.

She was startled by someone knocking on the door with a force and rapidity that suggested urgency. 'Signora Bruno!' called the knocker. She recognized the high insistent tones of the mother of one of the Italian craftsmen. Was someone hurt? Did they need her help? Anne-Marie wished Niccolò were here. The old lady was difficult for her to understand because she spoke Italian so rapidly, and French with such a thick accent that it too sounded like Italian. But if she needed help, then Anne-Marie would do her best to provide it. She got up to answer the door.

Willem's funeral service took place in the Gobelins Oratory with Père Ferré conducting the service. The coffin was placed on a trestle in front of the altar. Sunlight streamed in the window. The weavers and their families, sitting in solidarity to bid farewell to one of their own, filled the front half of the space. Niccolò went up to the front row where the widow sat with her children and her sisters and offered his condolences. She graciously accepted them, seemingly unaware of the confrontations between him and her husband. It was clear she regarded him as the fellow victim of Anne-Marie's supposed flirtation with Willem. Niccolò took a seat in one of the rows behind the weavers and chatted with the man next to him.

'Hello, Anne-Marie.' Glacis smiled at her. She had started to smile in reply as one does to an acquaintance when the full realization of who he was sank in. She moved to shut the door, but he had got his foot in the doorway and easily pushed it open.

'I had the privilege of overhearing the elderly Signora at La

Bobine the other night,' he answered her unspoken question in a calm, amused voice, 'and the temptation to mimic her was irresistible. She is at the funeral, I expect. *Le tout Gobelins* appears to be there, except for you.' He shut the door behind him and locked it. He made no move to reach for her, just stood regarding her, waiting for her to react. It made her think of Gâteau catching a mouse, letting it go, waiting intently for its next move as an excuse to catch it again. It was in a cat's nature and appeared to be in Glacis' nature as well.

But I am not a mouse to be dangled, nor a rat in a trap, she thought with a return of her old spirit. *I can fight back.* For the first time in days she felt her old strength and resolve returning.

A weapon – she needed a weapon. She backed slowly toward the dresser, keeping the table between them, and felt in the drawer behind her for the carving knife and large two-tined fork she kept there. She brandished them defiantly in front of her.

Glacis chuckled. 'Do you think I'm as easily dispatched as a roast pig?'

He made a sudden lunge and feint at her, causing her to lash out wildly but to no avail. She retreated and he lunged again, a mocking smile on his face. He meant to wear her out, she realized, until he tired of the game and disarmed her. She must make a move he wouldn't expect.

She dropped the knife and fork, grabbed a chair and swung it wildly at him. He ducked but grunted in pain. She had hit him. She was filled with elation at getting some of her own back. She let go of the chair and ran to the fireplace for the poker.

Gâteau fled into the bedroom.

Anne-Marie picked up the poker, but he was behind her before she could raise it. He forced it out of her hand, pinning her arms behind her as he spun her around. 'Shh, shh,' he said gently as she struggled. 'If I were going to kill you, I'd have done so by now.' He smiled into her eyes. 'We have some unfinished business to take care of, from the evening of our first acquaintance.' He brought one hand to trace the neckline of her bodice with his fingers and back again. She spat at him but he ignored it. 'We were negotiating the price of a night together when we were so rudely interrupted by your soldier friend. If you remember, I promised you a strenuous romp in bed. I'm a man who likes to keep his promises and' – his voice took on a menacing edge – 'I expect women who offer themselves to keep theirs.'

He put his arm around her again and bent to kiss her. She moved her head this way and that so he was kissing her neck, her ears, her cheek, and finally her lips. She bit his lip, taking satisfaction in drawing blood, and tried to spit it into his face. But then he closed his mouth over hers, thrusting in his tongue, brooking no further evasion. She tried to draw back but he followed until she was bent far back, gagging on him. Only then did he withdraw and let her straighten, coughing and choking, gasping for breath.

Before she could fully recover he kissed her again, passionately, to arouse and seduce, moving her backward toward the bedroom as he did so.

Once inside, he pushed her back onto the bed and produced long scarves from his pocket. He tied her wrists to the bed frame and gagged her. He undressed her slowly, lovingly, caressing her, praising how desirable she was, occasionally kissing her gagged mouth, first one lip and then the other. Again, she thought of Gâteau playing with a mouse. He stood up and removed her skirt and petticoat, easily dodging her kicking legs. 'I'm leaving your legs free so that you can wrap them around me,' he told her. 'I know you will want to.'

She clamped them shut in response. He chuckled again. He undressed very deliberately, taking time to neatly fold his coat and shirt and lay them aside, drawing out her dread. As he dropped his lower garments, he turned to her. 'Look at how you've inspired me. Imagine how this is going to feel inside you.' He laughed out loud as her eyes widened in alarm at the size of him. She could only look on in horror as he approached the bed and started to climb into it.

★

Gâteau crouched under the bed, her ears alert to the noises above, her tail twitching, annoyed in every fiber of her being with this loud rude stranger. She emitted a low warning growl in her throat. Then the man let down his garments and she could see what looked like a fine fat sausage, even larger than the one Niccolò had given her this morning. She crept nearer the edge of the bed, stalking it as she would a rat. She watched fascinated as it seemed to rise of its own accord, leaving unprotected two fine fat dumplings hanging below it. Gâteau shifted her haunches to position her hind legs, paused, and sprang to claim her prizes.

The man screamed in panic, a loud satisfying noise that showed she had hit her target. His hand feebly tried to brush her off but that only made her cling all the more tightly with her sharp claws and bring her teeth into play. A deep rumbling purr started in her throat.

As the cat latched on to him, Glacis tried to do something about it, but his breeches were around his ankles and his coat with the stiletto was out of reach. He doubled over in pain, screaming, not realizing he was within the range of Anne-Marie's kicking feet. He felt her foot strike his head and staggered backwards, hitting the back of his head on something sharp on the wall. He slid to the floor and lay still.

Chapter Thirty-two

Anne-Marie lay panting and exhausted but triumphantly alive. She wondered if Glacis's screams would summon help. The others in their building might be out, but surely there was someone within earshot? Was *everyone* at the funeral? She must get up and out – quickly, before Glacis recovered consciousness. Pulling her wrists free of the tightly tied scarves was not possible, but with her right hand she managed to untie the other end of the scarf from the bed frame. It was then easy to untie both wrists and remove the gag.

She got out of bed. Glacis was lying on top of the clothes she had worn that morning – and she could not anyway bear the thought of putting them on again – so she quickly grabbed other garments, dressing without noticing what they were. She must get out into the open, to the safety of other people, before he regained consciousness. She would go to Le Brun's house and have him send for the police.

Afraid of what Glacis would do when he recovered consciousness, she called to Gâteau. For once the cat came voluntarily when summoned and submitted to being picked up and carried, nestling her head against the underside of Anne-Marie's jaw, purring, her claws pressing gently through the fabric of the shift. Anne-Marie carried her down the stairs and into the courtyard just as everyone was returning from the oratory.

She looked around for Niccolò. There – he was standing with his back to her, talking with Monsieur Le Brun. Le Brun was staring at her in astonishment. 'Madame Bruno! What has happened? Are you all right?'

Niccolò spun around, happy to hear that Anne-Marie had at last emerged from their rooms. But his smile died as he took in her disheveled appearance, the bruises on her face and arms, the exhaustion evident in every inch of her. He rushed forward to support her before she collapsed.

She looked at him with fright in her eyes, as if a stranger were staring out from Anne-Marie's familiar face. 'Get Ferrand,' she rasped in a voice he scarcely recognized. 'Glacis. In our rooms.'

She started to shake, then, and burst into tears. Sobbing against his chest – he could not persuade her to let go of the cat – she was again the Anne-Marie he knew, needing comfort he understood how to give. He felt concerned but also relieved.

'Take her to my house,' Le Brun told him. 'I will ask Dr Lunague to see to her.'

As Niccolò led Anne-Marie away, he could hear Le Brun giving orders to two stout men to guard the Brunos' door and another two to stand below the bedroom window, should Glacis attempt to leave before Ferrand and his men could arrive.

Le Brun's manservant showed them into the office where they had first met Ferrand. It was only a few minutes before the doctor came, but by then Anne-Marie was shaking so hard she could not stop. 'Shock,' said Lunague promptly, and rang for wine and cakes. Niccolò had to hold the glass to her lips.

Gradually, as the wine warmed and calmed her, and the sweet food comforted her, Anne-Marie was able to stop shivering. She took several deep breaths and gave Niccolò and the doctor a shaky smile. She reassured Monsieur Le Brun, when he came in, that she felt much better. He disappeared again and must have spoken to his wife, as Madame Le Brun came in soon after, full of motherly concern. She invited Anne-Marie to come to her dressing room, where the doctor could examine her. Gently Niccolò took the cat from her.

Anne-Marie had to steel herself to endure his examination. She could not bear the thought of yet another man not Niccolò touching her. He was gentle with her, however. He found bruising on her wrists and her mouth, he told her, but no broken bones, and she was not even badly scratched. 'You have been very brave,' he said. When he had gone, the maid brought in warm water, soap and towels, and Anne-Marie was finally able to wash away the residue of Glacis's attack. After she had dressed again, Madame Le Brun brought her a soft shawl; although the day was warm, Anne-Marie was glad to wrap herself in it.

Ferrand, coming into Le Brun's office with his sergeant to make their report, found Anne-Marie clean, dressed, and calm, with a cat purring in her lap. Much as she had exasperated him in the past, today he was able to greet her with a smile.

'Michel Glacis is dead, Madame. You have nothing further to fear from him.'

He watched her give a sigh of relief that ended in a shaky breath that was almost a sob. Her husband took her hand and held it firmly and reassuringly in his. Her other hand went to her empty wineglass. The manservant darted forward to refill it.

'I am sorry to need to ask this, but – tell me what happened, Madame.'

'I think Willem was killed not to lure me out to the funeral but to make sure everyone else was away so I would be alone, with no one within earshot,' she began. She recounted the main actions of Glacis's attack, and he did not press for details. She looked straight at Ferrand the whole time she was speaking, and did not glance at Niccolò, but Ferrand could see the pain of what she had been through reflected in the set of his mouth, his angry eyes and flushed cheeks. He had let go of her hand to clench and unclench his own.

Just as well Glacis is already dead, Ferrand thought. Aloud he

321

said, 'You say he tied your hands to the bed – then how did you manage to put those long deep scratches on his privates?'

'Oh, that wasn't me – that was Gâteau!' She indicated the cat, who was purring proudly on her knees, looking contented and innocent. 'She leapt up from under the bed to attack him and he doubled over. That's how I was able to kick him in the head.'

Ferrand stared in astonishment at the cat, who looked back and blinked. He tried to keep his professional composure, but his lips twitched. The small smile he permitted himself could not be contained and bubbled up into a deep roar of laughter. The others joined in. Even Anne-Marie could see the humor in it.

Gâteau alone did not share in the mirth. She yawned, nonchalant in her victory, and stretched her paws in front of her as if to show off her claws. The men regarded them with healthy respect and kept their distance.

When Ferrand could speak again with the gravity the situation demanded, he told them he would make arrangements for Glacis's body to be removed. 'It will be properly disposed of,' he said with grim satisfaction, picturing in his mind's eye the hospital's anatomy theater.

'The bedroom will need to be thoroughly cleaned,' he continued. 'When he died, his body released' – he hesitated – 'matter.'

'I will have one of the stable boys take care of that,' Le Brun said. 'They are used to it. And one of my housemaids will do the cleaning – if that is all right, Madame Bruno?' He turned to Anne-Marie. 'Or in light of what happened, would you prefer to move elsewhere?'

She shook her head. 'It is our home. Once all trace of his presence is removed, I will feel safe there.'

'Then my job here is done.' Ferrand and the sergeant rose to take their leave. He addressed Anne-Marie once more. 'I do not need to tell you, Madame, what a lucky escape you have had. I am grateful for the assistance you have given the police by ridding the world of Michel Glacis, but I hope that reflecting on this experience will cause you to think twice about undertaking another such endeavor.' He bowed to the assembled company and left.

Anne-Marie was glad of the quiet of the next several days. It gave her the time she needed to come to terms with what had happened. She still felt guilty over leading Glacis to Lisette; but she had atoned for it by having been placed in danger herself. She had not escaped unscathed.

Far worse was the realization that she had killed a man. However much she had done it in self-defense, however much he had deserved it, she hated the thought of causing the death of another. It had always been Glacis who killed; she felt keenly the shame of coming down to his level. Père Aimé had given her absolution for her deed, and she had gladly done the penance he prescribed. The Church had forgiven her, but it would take some time for her to forgive herself.

Several days after Glacis's appearance at the Gobelins, Charles Le Brun was summoned to Saint-Germain-en-Laye. The King had decided to celebrate the victories in the Netherlands with a fête at Versailles – a night of music, dance, and fireworks – that was to take place in three months' time. The sculptors of the Gobelins were to help with the preparations. Le Brun assured Louis of his full cooperation, all the while mentally reassigning commissions at the Gobelins to accommodate this new demand.

While there, Le Brun requested a private meeting with the Duc de Languedoc and Mademoiselle de Toulouse in order to inform them of the outcome of the enquiry into the silver button. Anne-Marie had wanted to write to tell them, but Le Brun had counseled that, with Louvois involved, it was safer not to put things in writing. The meeting took place in their apartment in the Old Château. (Le Brun cast a critical eye over the décor; a few well-placed items from the Gobelins would help to bring it into current fashion.) The Duc and his daughter were horrified at hearing about the attack on Anne-Marie and laughed heartily in relief at the story of her rescue by the cat.

The Duc took several thoughtful sips of wine. 'Perhaps you could find employment for Anne-Marie during the preparations for the fête. They will need all the help they can get – and fully occupied, she is less likely to run risks.'

Le Brun was relieved. He had been wondering how to keep Anne-Marie out of trouble. He thanked the Duc and said that he would speak that day with the office of the Menus Plaisirs, the organizers of court celebrations.

Anne-Marie was delighted to learn she would be sewing costumes and that she and Niccolò would spend several weeks at Versailles, helping to prepare the palace and gardens for the fête. Not even Le Brun's frown as he cautioned her to limit her focus to her assigned tasks could dampen her spirits. She had heard of the magnificence of the King's fireworks and longed to see them. She would do nothing to jeopardize that chance. Should she be unfortunate enough to encounter another corpse in future, she would definitely leave the investigation to someone else.

Historical Afterword

The Gobelins Tapestry Manufactory was founded in 1662 and has been in continuous operation to this day; you can visit it to see tapestries being made and view exhibitions. When possible, I have used the names of actual personnel at the Manufactory: Charles Le Brun (1619-1690), its founding director, and his wife Suzanne; Jean Jans, the head of one of the tapestry ateliers; Claude de Villiers, head of the silver studio; Dominique Lunague, doctor (although I have him working there three years earlier than his actual arrival, and his backstory is entirely my own creation); Père Ferré, Catholic priest; Jean-Baptiste Tuby, sculptor; Saint-André, painter. Other historic characters who appear in the novel are Louis XIV and Queen Marie-Thérèse, Jean-Baptiste Colbert, the Marquis de Louvois, Gabriel Nicolas de la Reynie, André-Charles Boulle, and the composers d'Anglebert, Marc-Antoine Charpentier and Marin Marais. Pot-de-vin is also a historic character; his name turns up in the King's account books as one of the soldiers who helps to dig out the Lac des Suisses at Versailles. All other characters are fictional and bear no intended resemblance to anyone living or dead.

The circumstances of France's 1672–1678 war in the Netherlands are as I have described them – an early victory followed by a long stalemate that was broken in 1677 with the siege and capture of Valenciennes and other fortified cities. However, the spies and agents in the novel are fictional.

Whenever possible, I have placed characters in actual historical settings. The Hôtel de Languedoc is fictional, but the Place Royale (renamed the Place des Vosges during the French Revolution) still exists. The Hôpital Sainte-Marthe is set in the sixteenth-century Hôtel Scipion, which still exists, and which has served as an old men's home and then a maternity hospital. The Arsenal has disappeared, but the Church of St-Nicolas-du-Chardonnet, which contains Le Brun's mother's tomb as well as the tombs of Le Brun and his wife, is still an active church. The Couvent Sainte-Catherine also existed (it has now disappeared) but was in fact a monastery; I have changed it into a nunnery with a school for girls for the purpose of the novel.

The Bièvre flowed above ground until the early twentieth century, when it was so polluted that it was enclosed to flow underground. There has been some discussion recently about bringing it above ground again. You can find a walking tour of the route of the Bièvre on the internet.

I also enjoy using actual works of art when I can. The cabinet on which Niccolò Bruno is working at the opening of the novel is based on one at the J. Paul Getty Museum, Los Angeles. The tapestry of the *Triumphal Chariot* which Willem is weaving and the tapestry of *December: Château de Monceaux* that Saint-André is working on are also based on works at the J. Paul Getty Museum. The silver table on which Claude de Villiers is working is fictional but representative of the massive silver furniture made for the royal residences. The bird's head bowl sent to the Duc de Languedoc is based on a similar bowl at The Nelson-Atkins Museum of Art, Kansas City. The panel of Saint Peter that I have Niccolò carve for Saint-Nicolas-du-Chardonnet is based on a relief carving of Saint Peter of a later date in the church. The cabinets described in Boulle's workshop are typical of his work.

Suggestions for further reading

Nonfiction:

Wolf Burchard, *The Sovereign Artist: Charles Le Brun and the Image of Louis XIV* (London: Paul Holbertson, 2016)

Joan DeJean, *How Paris became PARIS: The Invention of the Modern City* (New York: Bloomsbury, 2014)

Florian Knothe, *The Manufacture des Meubles de la Couronne at the Gobelins under Louis XIV* (Turnhout, Belgium: Brepolis Publishers, 2017)

Fiction:

Judith Rock's series of four novels set in Paris in the 1680s, featuring her amateur sleuth, Charles du Luc:

The Rhetoric of Death (New York: Berkley Books, 2010)

The Eloquence of Blood (New York: Berkley Books, 2011)

A Plague of Lies (New York: Berkley Books, 2012)

The Whispering of Bones (New York: Berkley Books, 2013)

Susanne Dunlop, *Emilie's Voice* (New York: Simon and Schuster, 2005)

Acknowledgements

Many people helped and encouraged me in the research and writing of *A Fine Tapestry of Murder*. I particularly want to thank Gillian Wilson and Charissa Bremer-David, who unstintingly shared their knowledge of French decorative arts with me when I worked at the J. Paul Getty Museum. The Sisters in Crime Border Crimes Chapter, Kansas/Missouri, cheered me on with their advice and encouragement. Nancy Pickard, Linda Rodriguez and Sally Goldenbaum showed me how to structure a mystery novel. Writing residencies at Ragdale, Lake Forest, Illinois, and The Writers' Colony at Dairy Hollow, Eureka Springs, Arkansas, gave me time and space to concentrate on the book in its early stages. I also benefited from attending the 2014 mystery writers' conference at Book Passage, Corte Madeira, California. Members of my writing group, Joyce Ann Davis, Diann Markley, Valerie Bonham Moon, and Peg Nichols read an earlier draft of this book and provided much valuable feedback, as did Jennifer Montagu, Judith Rock, and Mary Sebastian. Thanks also go to Katrin Lloyd and my eagle-eyed editor jay Dixon at Accent Press. A further debt of gratitude goes to the many friends who listened and encouraged me while I puzzled out plot points and character motivations.

This book is dedicated in loving memory of my parents, Gladys and Harold Friedman, who both enjoyed a good whodunit and inspired me to write one.